The Venetian Masquerade

Philip Gwynne Jones

CONSTABLE

Constable

First published in Great Britain in 2019 by Robinson

Copyright © Philip Gwynne Jones, 2019

1 3 5 7 9 10 8 6 4 2

The moral right of the author has been asserted.

A CIP catalogue record for this book is available from the British Library

ISBN: 978-1-47212-973-4

Typeset in Adobe Garamond by Initial Typesetting Services, Edinburgh
Printed and bound in Great Britain by Clays Ltd, Elcograf S.p.A.

Papers used by Constable are from well-managed forests and
other responsible sources

Constable
An imprint of
Little, Brown Book Group
Carmelite House
50 Victoria Embankment
London EC4Y 0DZ

An Hachette UK Company
www.hachette.co.uk

www.littlebrown.co.uk

Philip Gwynne Jones was born in South Wales in 1966, and lived and worked throughout Europe before settling in Scotland in the 1990s. He first came to Italy in 1994, when he spent some time working for the European Space Agency in Frascati. Philip now lives permanently in Venice, where he works as a teacher, writer and translator. He is the author of the Nathan Sutherland series, which is set in contemporary Venice and which has been translated into several languages, including Italian and German.

PRAISE FOR *THE VENETIAN GAME*
BY PHILIP GWYNNE JONES

'He puts not one foot wrong with his topography and knowledge'
– Jeff Cotton, *Fictional Cities*

'A crime book for people with sophisticated tastes: Venice, opera, renaissance art, good food and wine . . . I enjoyed all that and more'
– *The Crime Warp*

'The Venetian setting is vividly described and Gwynne Jones's good, fluent writing makes for easy reading'
– Jessica Mann, *Literary Review*

'Gorgeous escapism with stacks of atmosphere and double-cross'
– Sue Price, *Saga* magazine

'A civilized, knowledgeable, charming antidote to the darker reaches of the genre, full of entertaining descriptions of the city . . . Lovely. Makes you want to book a flight to Venice straight away'
– N J Cooper, Bookoxygen.com

Also by Philip Gwynne Jones

The Venetian Game

Vengeance in Venice

To Venice with Love: A Midlife Adventure

For Mum and Dad, with love.

It took me many years to find la strada giusta.
Thank you for your patience.

La commedia è finita!

(The drama is finished!)

Final line of Ruggero Leoncavallo's *I Pagliacci*

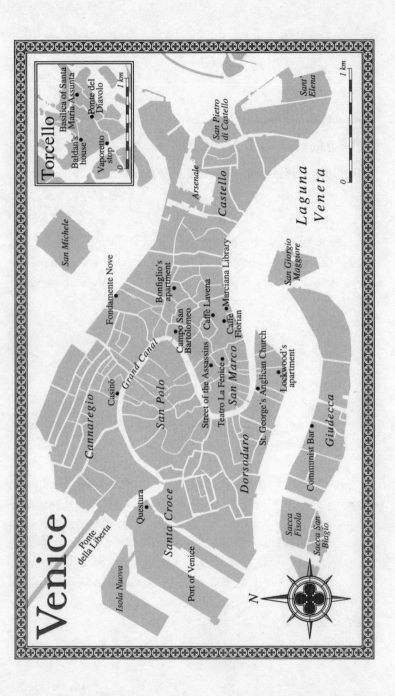

Venice

Torcello
- Basilica of Santa Maria Assunta
- Baldan's house
- Ponte del Diavolo
- Vaporetto stop

San Michele

Fondamente Nove

Cannaregio

Casinò

Grand Canal

San Polo

Campo San Bartolomeo

Bonfiglio's apartment

Caffè Lavena

Marciana Library

Caffè Florian

San Marco

Arsenale

Castello

San Pietro di Castello

Sant' Elena

Street of the Assassins

Teatro La Fenice

St. George's Anglican Church

Lockwood's apartment

San Giorgio Maggiore

Laguna Veneta

Dorsoduro

Giudecca

Communist Bar

Questura

Santa Croce

Ponte della Libertà

Port of Venice

Sacca Fisola

Sacca San Biagio

Isola Nuova

N

1 km

0

1 km

Chapter 1

Napoleon Bonaparte elbowed me out of the way as he strode along the Calle Caotorta. Hand thrust into his greatcoat, he scattered pedestrians to his left and right with the same insouciance with which he had once disposed of the most powerful armies in Europe. Only his bicorne hat, slightly askew and with a label jutting out from beneath the brim, indicated that this was a rather more modern 'Attila to the Venetians'.

I raised my hand in protest and made to call out but the Little Corporal was soon lost in the fog. Federica placed her hand on my arm.

'Don't make a scene, *tesoro*.'

'Gah!' I threw my hands in the air. 'Bloody tourist.'

'You were a tourist yourself once, *caro mio*. And not so long ago either.'

'I know, I know. But I never went around pushing local people out of their way as they went about their business. I swear it's people like that who are causing more damage to this city than the original bloody Napoleon and— I'm ranting again, aren't I?'

She nodded.

'Sorry.'

'It's your birthday, Nathan – try and have a nice time.'

'I am having a nice time, I promise. I'll have a nicer time once I have a spritz inside me.'

She took my arm in hers, and patted my hand. Then she jabbed me in the ribs.

'Ow!'

She didn't break her stride. 'This is my treat, remember? Do try and be grateful.'

I stopped, and gave my ribcage an exploratory rub. Then I smiled. 'I am. Really. And I am excited. But *Carnevale* just makes me a bit . . .' I ran out of words and settled for a grumpy little rumble that Gramsci would have been proud of.

Fog was lying thick upon the city, and Napoleon had long since disappeared into the mist by the time we emerged into Campo San Fantin. 'Spritz?' I suggested.

She looked up at me, quizzically. 'Really? I thought you'd be wanting to head straight in. To make the most of the experience.'

'I would. But it has to be said, you get rather sad little measures inside. It's fine to be there and people watch. But all the people you're watching are doing the same thing. Looking at a sad little glass of prosecco and wishing they'd gone to a proper bar for a proper drink.'

She laughed. 'And I thought it was all about the music.' She steered me into the Bar al Teatro. As we opened the door, the heat and light hit us, as if we were moving from black and white into Technicolor. Napoleon had beaten us to the bar, and stood flushed of face with a small glass of red wine in one hand. The rest of the space was packed out with impossibly pretty young women in domino masks, and brooding *ragazzi* in cloaks and tricorne hats.

I stared at the mass of young people that separated us from our next drink.

'I hate *Carnevale*,' I said.

'Well, don't.'

'It's just it's this horrible, artificial . . .'

'. . . and tacky appropriation by tourists of a traditional Venetian event . . .'

'Exactly! And another thing is . . .'

'Or,' she squeezed my hand, 'is it just nice people coming to Venice, dressing up and having a nice time?'

'Oh.' I looked down at her. She raised her eyebrows. 'Am I being grumpy again?' She nodded. 'It's only because I care.'

'I know you do, Nathan. I see it all the time. You care more than the Venetians.'

'It's just that – I don't really mind, you know, but the city just gets so damn busy.' I checked my watch. 'We've only got twenty minutes and we're not even going to get to the bar—'

'—in time.' She finished my sentence for me. '*Spritz al bitter*?' I nodded. Somehow she'd managed to steer us through the crowds.

Napoleon finished his glass of wine and stared across the bar at me. Then he nodded, and gave a half-smile, as if to indicate that we should let bygones be bygones, before thrusting his right hand inside his greatcoat and striding forth in search of new worlds to conquer. Or maybe Josephine.

Fede and I clinked glasses. She kissed me on the cheek. 'Happy birthday, *tesoro*.'

'Thank you, *cara*. I'm a lucky man, you know?'

'I do know.'

'I mean, it's not as if it's a significant birthday.'

'Significant?'

'Doesn't have a five or a zero in it.'

She laughed, and kissed me again. 'Well then. Happy insignificant birthday, darling.'

'Do you know, if I'd been born just twenty-four hours later, I'd have shared a birthday with Tony Iommi?'

'Who?'

'Tony Iommi. Guitarist with Black Sabbath. Less than the standard complement of fingers. You know?'

She shook her head. 'You were out with Dario last night, weren't you?'

I smiled. 'Is it so obvious?'

'So – given it's not Tony of Black Sabbath – who do you share your birthday with?'

I shook my head. 'Ah, I was hoping for Roger Waters. Actually, no, I think Dario was hoping for Roger Waters. I'd have been fine with Bach. Wagner. Monteverdi even. Anyway, I had my new intelligent phone and we looked it up and—'

'And?'

'Yoko Ono.'

Fede fell silent for a moment. Then, 'Seriously?'

'Seriously, yes.'

'But that's brilliant!'

'Really?'

'Of course it is. Much cooler than someone from Black Sabbath.'

I must have looked cross, but then she smiled and placed a

finger on my lips and shushed me. Then I smiled too, and we clinked glasses again.

'So tell me about tonight.'

'I've told you about it.'

'Tell me again. I wasn't listening the first time. All I know is that it's important to you.'

I placed my spritz on the counter. 'Monteverdi. Four hundred and fifty years. *L'incoronazione di Poppea*. Lockwood. Baldan.' I looked to my left and then to my right. There was just enough room to pick her up and spin her around, before I kissed her full on the lips. 'Best birthday present ever,' I said.

'I'm glad. Even if you're making a scene. But tell me more.'

'It starts here. All of it. Oh yes, sure, people had written things that you might define as *opera lirica* before. Hell, Monteverdi had done it himself. But there's something different about *Poppea*. There's a drama to it. A real, proper sense of drama. And, of course . . .' I paused.

'Of course?'

'The bad guys win. I kind of like that.' I paused to drain my spritz and set it down on the counter. Then I checked my watch. 'We should go.'

Fede grabbed my wrist and turned it over to look at the time. 'We've got plenty of time.' Then she looked at my face and smiled. 'But you'll get into a state if we don't leave immediately, won't you?'

I nodded, and smiled apologetically.

'Okay, let's go. I do want this to be perfect for you, you know?'

We elbowed our way out of the bar, as gently as we could, and out into the *campo*. The cold hit us, but only for a moment, as we stepped out the few yards towards La Fenice. We made our way up the steps, and I smiled as I reached for the tickets within my coat pocket. Lockwood. Baldan. *Poppea*. And then my eye fell upon the strip of paper plastered across the poster for the night's performance. I stopped in my tracks.

Fede gripped my arm. 'What's the matter?'

'I don't believe it. I don't believe it.' I raised my hands in front of my face and rested them against the poster. Then I gently thudded my head against them. 'No, actually, I do believe it. Because this just happens every bloody time.'

'What do you mean?'

'She's cancelled.' I drew myself upright, and took a deep breath. I was, genuinely, trying not to cry. 'Every time. Every time I've tried to see her. Every time she's cancelled. I'm sick of it.'

Fede rested her hand on the small of my back. 'Oh, I'm sorry, *caro*. I'm so sorry. It'll still be good, won't it?'

I nodded. 'Oh, it will be. Might even be better. I'd just like to see her, you know. Just once. Isotta Baldan. She's kind of a legend.'

'I'm sorry.' Fede steered me through security, where our tickets were scanned, and up the stairs to our box. 'It'll still be good,' she repeated.

I sat down and looked around me. It was a better seat than I'd had in years. I usually found myself standing, or hidden behind a pillar or, on one memorable occasion, sharing a box with a sociopathic murderer.

'Arcangelo Moro?' Federica was following my thoughts.

I stiffened, and then my shoulders dropped and I laughed. 'Yes.'

'In his grave three years now.'

'I know. Still, I should be grateful to him in a way.' I squeezed her arm and smiled at her. 'That was the scariest opera I've ever been to. But he had the best seats. Definitely the best seats.'

'Best I could do, *caro*. I'm sorry, I don't have the same resources as a corrupt art thief.'

'It's fine.' My voice was distracted as I stared at the ceiling. 'It's absolutely brilliant.'

'So.' Fede paused. 'We don't have your favourite singer tonight.'

I shook my head. 'She's not my favourite singer. Not at all. It's just – well, she's Venetian so this would have been a big deal for her. Monteverdi in his anniversary year. You know?'

'I understand. But she's young, isn't she. There'll still be plenty of time.'

'I'm not sure. They say her voice is going.'

'They?'

'The music press.'

'And what do you think?'

'What do I think?' I must have sounded surprised.

'Yes, what do you think?'

I was aware of a certain note of challenge in her voice. 'I think it's a shame I'll never see her at her best. Even if her voice isn't what it was. She's a good actress. And . . .'

Fede didn't say a word, but just nodded as if I should continue.

'. . . and . . . well, she's very pretty.'

'Pretty?' Fede raised an eyebrow.

I gave up trying to pretend. 'Beautiful.' I said.

'Beautiful but unreliable. It would never have worked, Nathan.' I opened my mouth to protest, but she shushed me. 'That's a joke, you know? So tell me about Mr Lockwood?'

'Lockwood. Thomas Joshua Lockwood, to be precise. I've got any number of recordings by him. A few with Isotta Baldan for that matter. There's nobody who knows Monteverdi better.'

'There we go then. At least he's here.'

'Probably cancel, given my luck,' I grumbled.

'Stop that.'

I sat down, and rested my elbows on the padded balustrade. I looked up at the pinky-blue ceiling, and then around at the other boxes, which were already filling up. And then I felt the tension draining from my shoulders. It was beautiful, chocolate-box, fake, imperfect. I didn't care. Isotta Baldan or no Isotta Baldan. This was *Poppea*, on the 450th anniversary of the birth of Claudio Monteverdi, conducted by Thomas Joshua Lockwood. I grinned, and leaned out into the auditorium in order to get a better look. Then I turned back to Fede.

'He used to be a monster you know? I saw him once, back in the UK. In Cardiff, St David's Hall. We were both much younger then, of course. Difference is, I'd come down from Aberystwyth on the bus and he'd probably been driven in or flown in, I don't know. Anyway, he was conducting *The Magic Flute* for Welsh National Opera. And it was the best thing I'd ever seen, and I don't even like Mozart all that much. It was one of those evenings when I kept checking my watch, just to reassure myself there was still plenty of time left to go. So I hung around the stage door afterwards. I didn't have anything for him to sign. Not really. No CDs or anything. I suppose I had my programme, but it wasn't about getting a signature. I just wanted to say thank you. And then . . .'

'And then?'

'He just pushed me aside. I don't think he was even trying to be rude. He just didn't acknowledge that I was there. As if the little people didn't count. Pushed his way past, and into his car.'

'Not a nice man, then?'

I shook my head. 'Not in those days. There were terrible stories about him. About how you had to stand in line to hate him. He was powerful enough to make careers and break them. I think there are a number of ex-wives. And then—'

'Then?'

'He seems to have changed. Apparently he's positively cuddly now. I don't know why. Like I said, I haven't kept up with the music press. Shh, here he comes.'

The orchestra – on stage, rather than in the pit – had finished tuning up, and Thomas Joshua Lockwood walked on. He'd aged since I last saw him. His hair had thinned, and his features had softened. Previously he'd looked stern and ascetic, whereas now he had the look of a friendly and well-fed owl. He wore a dark green crushed velvet jacket with ruffled shirt cuffs that gave him the aspect of a superannuated gentleman spy.

The musicians struck up the prelude and I realised how the staging was going to work. Instead of dividing musicians and singers between pit and stage, they were to share the same space. Perhaps it was a statement on the indivisibility of music and word in the lyric theatre. Or perhaps it was just a bit cheaper. It didn't matter.

Fortune, Virtue and Love made their way to the front of the stage as they argued over who had most influence in human affairs. I liked to think it was Love. I'd be prepared to make a case for Fortune. I certainly hoped it wasn't Virtue.

The three goddesses left the stage and made way for Ottone, lamenting his hopeless love for the perfidious Poppea. Well-enough sung and acted, but not so much so that I felt the need to check out the artist in the programme. What I really wanted was to see Poppea so I could compare her with Baldan. Shockingly, I felt my mind wandering away from the stage.

I took a look around the auditorium. Packed out, of course. I looked down at those in the stalls, and felt a little envious of their perfect view. However good a box might be, the view of the stage – from the sides at least – was invariably a little compromised as you needed to turn your neck for a proper view. An evening of Wagner, therefore, risked a seriously cricked neck.

I tried to drag my attention back to the stage, but there was something about the audience that didn't seem quite right. I couldn't put my finger on it, as my eyes darted around, and then it hit me. There was no one in the box directly opposite. I took another look around. There were no other vacant seats that I could see, and so the empty box stood out like a missing tooth. Four seats with a perfectly good and uninterrupted view. I thought about how many times I'd attempted to save money by booking seats with a restricted view, and how many times I'd ended up with my nose six inches from a pillar. Then I thought of how much money Fede must have spent on the tickets, and felt guilty for not paying attention. I took her hand and gave it a squeeze, as I dragged my attention back to the stage.

Nero was sung by a countertenor blessed with a beautiful voice and – equally importantly – a splendidly sleazy and sweaty aspect. Perhaps not physically convincing enough for his younger, sexier Poppea, but he had the charisma to pull it off. I took a quick look at my programme, my eyes straining now that the lights had been lowered, trying to make out the name of the singer playing the prospective *imperatrice* of Rome. Sartorelli. Maria Giulia Sartorelli. Very pretty. Lovely voice. Good actress. Excellent in almost every respect, and, yet, she was no Isotta Baldan. I tried to suppress a sigh. It didn't matter, I told myself. Well, okay, it did. Just a bit. But I wasn't going to tell Federica about it. It had been a lovely surprise when she'd told me where we were going, and I wasn't about to spoil it. Nevertheless I felt my attention wandering, yet again.

The box opposite was briefly illuminated by a shaft of light from the corridor. Some late arrivals. Two people, one of whom was wearing a hat and dressed in a long coat, or cloak. Strangely, they chose not to sit in the front row, but behind where the view would necessarily be restricted. Presumably they were expecting friends. Very noble of them not to grab the best seats for themselves, I thought.

On stage, Seneca and Nero were at daggers drawn, a scenario fated to end badly for the elderly sage. I shook my head, angrily. I was wasting the evening. Federica touched my cheek, and looked at me quizzically. I smiled back at her. I was determined to enjoy the evening, if only for her sake.

We reached the end of the first act. And if the evening thus far had not been quite as perfect as I might have hoped, it had been nonetheless splendid. The lights in the auditorium did not come up, as expected, but remained dimmed. We sat in semi-darkness as the singers, the musicians and, finally, Lockwood left the stage.

There was a smattering of applause, but Lockwood turned to the audience and held his hands up in a placatory gesture, shushing them. I wasn't sure, but I thought he might have given a little smile. The old Lockwood would have reacted in fury to anything as barbarous as applause spoiling his little *coup de théâtre*. The new one did nothing more than gently wave his hands, as if he were an elderly primary school teacher admonishing a favourite but over-excited class.

He gave a little bow – there was no disguising the smile this time – and turned to leave the stage. Then he stopped and stared out once more at the audience. No, more than that. He was staring at the box opposite ours. Then he shook his head, wiped his hand across his forehead, and walked off-stage.

I fumbled in my jacket for my opera glasses. Chunky and heavy, I'd bought them on holiday in Russia, years ago, where I'd assumed their weight meant they were strictly reserved for Soviet military use. I always brought them and never used them. I fiddled with the focus as I stared across at the box opposite.

The figure in the coat, or cloak, and hat was at the rear of the box, but on his feet, with his right arm raised. He held something in his hand – an envelope, perhaps, or a book – which he waved slowly from side to side. I twirled the dial, straining to see, and gave a start. There was something terrible about the face, something grotesque.

'What's the matter, Nathan?'

'Nothing.' I fiddled again with the dial, but the figure had gone. There was nothing to be seen except a rectangle of light, where the door to the corridor was open. I looked back to the stage, but Lockwood was nowhere to be seen.

Chapter 2

'Are you all right, *caro*? You look as though you've seen a ghost.'

I shook my head. 'I don't know. Did you see Lockwood, though? Did you see where he was looking?'

'Just looking out at the audience. I was thinking how happy he looked. Not at all like you described him, all terribly serious.'

'Yes, but after that?'

'He just turned and walked off the stage.'

'You didn't see him pause? You didn't see him staring at that box opposite?'

She shrugged. 'Yes, but only for a second or two. I assumed he'd recognised someone.' She looked over at the box. 'Anyway, there's no one there.'

'Not now. But there was for a moment. In the shadows at the back. He was waving something above his head.' I repeated the motion myself, but Fede reached up and gently pulled my hand down into her lap. Some of the people in the stalls, I noticed, were looking up at me.

'I've got the idea, Nathan. You don't need to demonstrate it.'

'Sorry. But there was something else. His face – or her face. There was something awful about it. It was—' I stopped.

'Go on.'

'I don't know. I saw it for just a second, maybe less. He was in shadow, and had a hat on as well. But there was something about the eyes, something malignant.'

We sat in silence for a few seconds. Then she spoke. 'You need a drink, *tesoro*.'

'I think I do.'

'How long have we got?'

I checked my watch. 'Another twenty-five minutes.'

'Come on then. Back to *Teatro*.'

I grabbed my coat and we left our box, ready to fight our way back through the crowds . . .

'Negroni?'

I shook my head. 'Spritz, I think.'

'Are you sure? You look like you need something stronger.'

'I'd rather have one at the Brazilians, later. Besides, I'd like to remain awake for the second half if at all possible.'

'Oh. So you are having a good time then?'

I smiled. 'Of course I am.'

'I wasn't sure, you know. What with you seeing your own personal Phantom of the Opera.'

'Phantom of the Opera. I like that. It's a great title for a book.' I chewed on the olive from my spritz, as I dropped the cocktail stick into a bin. 'Seriously, though. There was something there.'

'Not even somebody, but *something*.' She sighed. 'Let's have a look at those glasses of yours.' I reached into my jacket, and passed them over. She weighed them in her hand. 'These things weigh as much as a housebrick. Why do you still use them?'

'I just kind of like the style. They're Soviet army issue, you know?'

'There was a need for the Red Army to be kitted out with opera glasses?'

'So the man in the shop told me. It's possible. They're a very cultured people.'

She put them to her eyes, and adjusted the focus to the left and then to the right. 'I can't see a thing through these.'

I dropped my olive stone into the bin. 'Neither can I. Not really.'

She sighed. 'So apart from that, Mr Sutherland, how are you enjoying the show?'

'Oh, very much. I mean, she's very good. Poppea, I mean – Sartorelli. Probably better than Baldan herself. It's just—'

'Just that she's not a legend?'

'That's it. She might be a better singer, but she's not Isotta Baldan. Does that sound a bit pathetic?'

'It does a bit.' Then she smiled. 'But I do understand.' She looked at her watch, and then drained her spritz. 'Come on, we need to get back.'

Lockwood looked tense and drawn as he returned for the second act, but, as soon as he raised his baton, he was transformed. I don't know what it was, but there was something more compelling about the second act. Sartorelli appeared more engaged, Lockwood more driven as the drama worked itself towards its merciless, cynical conclusion.

'Fantastic. Just fantastic.'

Fede smiled. 'You're happy?'

'No. More than that. Best birthday ever.' She smiled one of her smiles that could have lit up the whole auditorium. 'Mind you, I'm not sure happy is the right word.'

'Horrible people get away with horrible things?'

'Exactly.'

'So why do you spend your time listening to this stuff?'

I shrugged. 'Because if I wasn't, I'd just be listening to Jethro Tull all the time. Oh, hang on, they're coming on again.'

We politely applauded as Lockwood and his cast took another curtain call. And then another. 'How many?' whispered Fede.

'I'm told Pavarotti once took one hundred and sixty-five in Berlin.'

'You're joking!'

'Not at all.'

'How many left?'

'One hundred and sixty-one, I think. But we probably won't get that far. It was very good, but not *that* good.'

Lockwood smiled, and nodded at the audience. He turned to his orchestra, picking them out section by section and motioning soloists to their feet to receive their own individual applause. He turned to face the audience again, and grabbed Sartorelli's hand, raising it to his lips.

And then he stopped.

Even at a distance I could see that he was grabbing Sartorelli's hand so tightly that she was wincing with pain. The other hand went to his face, shielding his eyes as if to see better beyond the glare of the stage lights.

He swayed on his feet for a moment as Sartorelli wrenched her hand from his and threw an arm around his shoulder. Then she started to scream, a perfect high C that cut through the applause of the crowd. *My God*, I thought, *he's having a heart attack*. Then Lockwood recovered himself and I noticed that she was not looking at him, but at the box opposite ours. The occupants were no longer hiding in shadows at the back. One of them was slumped forward in his seat, his arms dangling down over the side of the box, whilst his cheek rested on the soft pink padding of the balustrade as if blissfully asleep. Of the other, there was no sign.

The screaming continued, the high C warbling and raucous now. I raised myself to my feet, and craned my head out of the box. Still unable to make anything out, I reached for my opera glasses and fiddled with the focus until the image, imperfect as it was, swam into view.

His face was obscured by long greyish-blond hair. Asleep? Impossible, given the noise. A heart attack? Then I noticed darker streaks in his hair, and a spreading red stain on his shirt.

I put the glasses down. Sartorelli had ceased to scream, but the refrain had been taken up by other members of the audience. Fede clutched my arm, and looked at me.

'Well,' I said, 'it *had* been the best birthday ever . . .'

Chapter 3

'Stabbed,' said Dario. He closed his *Gazzettino* with a rustle, and delicately tossed it back on to the shelf with the other communal newspapers.

'So it seems.'

'Otherwise, though, it was good?'

'Oh, great up until then. I know the *prima donna* cancelled, but it was still fantastic. I mean, really fantastic. It was just the place to be, you know. Monteverdi's 450th anniversary. *Poppea* at La Fenice. Lockwood conducting.'

'Man in the box opposite being horribly murdered.'

'Well, yes. But apart from that.'

'Wouldn't have happened at a Pink Floyd gig.'

'To be fair, Dario, it's not a regular occurrence at the opera either. They don't put a disclaimer on the tickets or anything.'

He laughed, and then checked his watch. 'Okay *vecio*, thanks for lunch but I've got to go. What are you doing next week?'

'Federica's going to Florence for a couple of nights. There's some sort of conference on new restoration technologies. She's presenting a paper on,' I struggled to remember, 'gilding techniques during the Venetian renaissance. At least I think that's what it is.'

He nodded, impressed. 'She's very clever, isn't she?'

'She is.'

'Do you ever wonder what she's doing with you?'

'All the time. Anyway, Gramsci and I are going to be a couple of bachelor boys for a few nights.'

'We should do something. The three of us. I'll give you a call.'

'Great. You're in Venice this afternoon, right? I'll be in all afternoon, drop by the Brazilians if you've got time.'

'I'll try. Going to be busy though.' I raised my eyebrows, but he shook his head. He pulled out his wallet and put some money down on the counter.

'It's supposed to be my turn,' I protested, but he shook his head.

'Come on, Nat, let's walk.' He'd seemed distracted and ill at ease over lunch, and looked troubled. We left Bacarando, and I turned up my collar against the chill of the fog as we made our way into Campo San Bartolomeo. Dario paused, and leaned against the railing at the base of the statue of Carlo Goldoni.

I nodded in the direction of Campo San Salvador. 'I'm going that way.'

He gently inclined his head towards the *sotoportego* that led deeper into the *sestiere* of Castello. 'I'm going that way. Calle del Cafetier.'

'Nice.' I wasn't sure what he was getting at, or why he was feeling the need to hang around just after we'd left the bar. I felt the need for my usual post-spritz cigarette, but Dario, I knew, would have none of it.

'Go ahead, Nat.' He must have seen my fingers twitching near my pocket.

'Seriously?'

He nodded. That was a bad sign. I reached into my coat and pulled out a packet of MS.

'What's going on, Dario?'

'I'm going to Calle del Cafetier, *vecio*.'

'And?'

'That doesn't mean anything to you?' I shook my head. Around us, crowds of laughing tourists, bemasked and becloaked, made their way to and from the Rialto Bridge. 'Calle del Cafetier. You know where the Boscolo bakery is? Or was.'

I nodded. 'Yes, of course, the one that's being sold off—' I stopped.

'That's the one,' Dario said.

'Oh hell.'

'Exactly.'

The Boscolo bakery had been in the news a lot in the past few weeks. It was still run by the same two brothers who had established it over forty years ago. Their landlord had died, and so the property had passed to his son. Any protection and all contracts they previously had were now void. And he wanted them out, so that he could sell the building.

'So what's it going to be?' I said.

Dario shrugged. 'Hotel. Or tourist apartments. One of the two.'

'And,' I paused for moment, 'it's your company that's dealing with it?'

'We're handling the sale, yes.'

I lit a second cigarette from the stub of my first. Dario didn't say a word. Bad signs were piling up. 'I'm sorry,' I said.

He sighed, his face down, staring at his shoes. 'It's a dirty job at times, my friend.' I tried to interrupt, but he shushed me. 'No no. It's a dirty, nasty job at times. You know, when I was a kid I used to go to the Boscolo Brothers and buy bread after school before taking it home to *Mamma*. And now – now I'm the guy who's working for the *agenzia* who's selling off the place they've lived and worked in for the last forty years. And for what? To turn it into another hotel? Because, God knows, this city needs another one of those.' He linked his arm in mine and gently, but firmly, steered me through the crowds towards the window of the *farmacia* that faced out towards Goldoni's statue. He tapped on the glass and pointed at a red LED display in the centre of the window. I knew what he was going to say. For nearly ten years now, the Farmacia Morelli had displayed the current population level in its window, inexorably moving downwards, as a silent admonishment to the city council.

'Fifty-four thousand, nine hundred and fifty-three. Fewer than fifty-five thousand Venetians left. How many were here when you moved here, *vecio?*'

'Not sure. More than sixty thousand though.'

'Exactly. So we've lost nearly ten per cent of the population in, what, less than ten years?' I nodded. He turned and leant the back of his head against the pane. 'And I'm part of the bastard problem. My company is making money out of selling a useful business that's going to become a useless business. *I'm* making money out of it.' He chuckled, hollowly and mirthlessly. '"Selling Venice by the Pound", you know, that's a pretty good title for an album.'

I'd never seen him like this before. I put my hand on his

arm. 'Dario, stop this. This isn't your fault. If your company wasn't doing it—'

'Somebody else would. I know, buddy, I know. They'd be queuing up. Queuing up to hammer the nails into the coffin.' He blew his nose.

'This may be a stupid question but – would a cigarette help?'

He wiped his eyes, but then he laughed. 'Yes, it's a stupid question and no, it wouldn't. And don't think you're always going to get away with smoking just because old Dario decides to go off on an emotional trip, eh?' Then he looked serious again. 'It's just that – I know I left for Mestre years ago but I wondered if I'd ever come back. And I always hoped that Emily would be able to. And now I wonder if there'll be any city for her to come back to by the time she's grown up.'

I ground my cigarette underfoot. A third, I knew, would make me feel sick. 'Come on, Dario. You guys survived how many plagues? You survived Napoleon. You even survived Pink Floyd and the "Night of Wonders". You'll survive. You always do.'

He shook his head. 'Not this time, Nat. Not this time. This time it's—'

Something caught my eye. The red LED screen had plinked for a moment and the number had changed. I punched his arm. 'Dario, look!'

'What?'

'The screen! It said fifty-four thousand, nine hundred and fifty-three before, right?'

'It did?'

'It did! And now it's fifty-four thousand, nine hundred and fifty-four.'

'You mean?'

'It's gone up by one. We live – I live – in a city with a population explosion.'

'Fantastic!' He picked me up and kissed me on both cheeks. 'You always bring me luck, Nathan, you know that.' He put me down, and I wheezed for breath. 'Now, I could stand here and watch this screen all afternoon. Maybe we'll see some new people arrive. But I've really got to get to work now. I'll see you soon, okay? *Ciao, vecio.*'

He turned, and strode off, disappearing under the *soto-portego*. I looked upwards towards the statue of Goldoni. The great playwright, splendidly bewigged under a tricorne hat, was striding forth without a care in the world in the direction of Campo San Salvador. I smiled up at him and made my way in the same direction.

Chapter 4

A warm light shone from inside the Magical Brazilians. The fog lay thickly on the Street of the Assassins, and I thought it might be nice to stop for a *caffè corretto*. Two tourists were sitting outside, bundled up against the cold and drinking hot chocolate with mittened hands. The sight of them made me smile. It was mad, of course, the temperature near freezing, yet just a little bit lovely at the same time. I could make time for a coffee with a shot of grappa. I saw Eduardo inside, working away behind the bar. I placed my hand upon the door, and then stopped.

Someone was staring at me from the end of the *calle*. Dressed in a knee-length coat, with a fedora atop his head, the fog preventing me from making out his face.

The figure stepped forward, and gave a gentle doff of his hat. 'Hello, Nathan.'

'Vanni?' A smile spread across my face. 'What are you doing here?'

'Oh, I was just passing by and thought it might be nice to have a chat.'

'Vanni, you never pass by San Marco. What's going on?'

'Well, it's far too cold for a spritz at Bar F30 – I'm sure you'll agree?'

I nodded. 'There are other places.'

'There are. I didn't want to call you into the *Questura*. I thought it would be better to be discreet.'

'Am I in trouble?'

'Oh, Nathan.' The fog, and his splendid moustaches, couldn't conceal his smile. 'When are you ever in trouble, *caro mio*?'

'You'd better come up.' I unlocked the main door and led him upstairs. Gramsci *miaowed* his disapproval. I'd been five minutes too long, evidently, and had brought home an uninvited guest. 'Come in, Vanni. Can I get you a coffee?'

'That would be very nice, thank you, Nathan.' He bent down, and reached his hand out. . .

'Don't!'

He snatched his fingers back.

'He's not very good with strangers. Sorry.'

'I can see.' He sucked at his fingers.

'He's getting better. Really. Come into the office.'

I dragged my chair round to the same side of the desk as Vanni, who nodded approvingly at my modestly expensive coffee machine. He placed his hat upon the desk. Gramsci leapt up, claws extended, and I whisked it away just in time. The label on the band caught my eye. 'Borsalino.' I whistled. 'A genuine Borsalino. You're going up in the world, Vanni.'

He grinned. 'From my wife. A fiftieth birthday present.'

'Some present. But you should have let me know.' He waved my protests away. 'I'll hang it up out of reach.' I went back into the hall and placed it on top of the coat rack. 'So, when was it – your birthday I mean?'

'Well, Barbara treated me to the hat last week. But my actual birthday,' he smiled, 'is today.'

'Tony Iommi!'

'I'm sorry?'

'Doesn't matter. Anyway, it's the day after mine. We should have done something together.'

'Next time.' He smiled. 'So, did you do anything nice for your birthday, Nathan?'

'Federica took me to the opera.'

He smiled. 'So I heard.'

I inserted a capsule into the coffee machine with a satisfying 'clunk', then pressed the start button. 'Did you, now?'

He smiled. 'Well, we have the details of everyone who was there, of course.'

'Of course.' I withdrew his cup, put it on a saucer, and slid it across the desk to him. 'Sugar?'

He shook his head, and patted his stomach. 'Barbara thinks I need to lose a bit of weight.'

'Trust me, Vanni, I hope I look that good at fifty.' I put another capsule into a machine, and made myself a cup. Then I shook a sachet of sugar into it, and went to sit next to him. 'So what's this all about then?'

'Well, you were at the opera last night.'

'This you know.'

'And you were in the box opposite the man who was murdered.'

'Yes. I told your people that. Although you could have worked that out for yourself. La Fenice has records, I imagine.'

He nodded. 'So you would have had as good a view as anyone. What did you see?'

I shrugged. 'Not that much, to be honest. I remember that something was bugging me during the first act. There seemed to be a bit of coming and going from that box. The door opening, light flooding in. It was distracting, you know, when I was trying to concentrate.'

He nodded, again. 'Anything else?'

I stirred my coffee. 'Yes. There was something about one of them. Something grotesque. I thought he was just wearing a hat at first, but his face – I couldn't make it out, but there was something wrong.'

'Like this?' He reached into his jacket and pulled out an envelope from which he withdrew a photograph. A mask, lying on a red plush velvet chair. A wide-brimmed hat atop a grey-ish-green face, a beak protruding from under two great black, expressionless eye sockets. I picked it up and stared at it. Then I placed it back down on the desk and looked up at Vanni.

The plague doctor.

The Black Death struck Venice for the final time in the great Italian plague of 1630, carried by Venetian troops returning from the Thirty Years' War. Within twelve months it had killed nearly a third of the population, and the Most Serene Republic was never fully to recover as either an economic or political power. As the contagion brought the city to its knees, the plague doctors would move from house to house, not so much for curative or even palliative purposes, but simply to record the extent and boundaries of the infection.

They dressed in the equivalent of a modern biohazard suit. A waxed overcoat stretched to the ankles, whilst the doctor himself stared out through glass lenses in a grotesque bird-like mask, the beak stuffed with herbs to keep out the stink of corrupted flesh. If you were dying, one of the last things you would see would be the image of 'Doctor Beak' staring down at you through those expressionless glass lenses. For reasons I'd never quite fathomed, it was one of the most popular choices of costume during *Carnevale*.

'The plague doctor,' I said.

He smiled. 'Doctor Beak, himself. Very popular at this time of year.'

I nodded. 'Makes sense. I couldn't make out his face. Just the fact that he was wearing a hat, and there was something grotesque about his features. He wasn't wearing this, then? The dead man, I mean.'

Vanni shook his head. 'No. We found it in the box. Just lying on the chair.'

'Oh hell.' I knew what was coming next. 'A carnival-goer then? He was a Brit, wasn't he?' A British citizen, with all the associated red tape and bureaucracy to struggle with in repatriating the body. Not to mention the hassle of dealing with the inevitable press attention.

'No.' He shook his head again. 'We thought that as well. But he's not British. Fact is, he's not any sort of *straniero*. He is – or was – Venetian.'

'Really?'

'We've checked his papers. His name was Matteo Zambon.' He paused. 'Does that name mean anything to you, Nathan?'

I shook my head. 'Never heard of him. Sorry.'

'Are you sure? *Professor* Matteo Zambon. Used to work at the *conservatorio*.'

I thought for a moment. 'No, really. I've never heard of him.'

'Hmm. Okay. It's just that he seems to have heard of you.'

'What do you mean?'

Vanni said nothing, but reached into the envelope again and took out another photograph, this time of a business card. I took a closer look. Cheap-looking card, with a slightly tacky Union Jack motif. At the bottom of the card were the words 'Professional Translation Services' and, emblazoned across the central horizontal stripe of the flag, the name 'Nathan Sutherland'.

Chapter 5

'Where was this?'

'In his wallet. Amongst other things. You sure you haven't heard of him?'

I shook my head. 'Absolutely certain. Well, almost. Zambon's not an uncommon surname. I probably have done some work for someone of that name, but I don't remember a Matteo.'

'You have records, of course?' I gave a weak smile. 'For tax purposes?'

'Oh yes. Of course. Of course. But I'd be lying if I said they were in good order, especially if the client was several years ago.'

'Okay. But if you can't remember him, how you can be sure it was several years ago?'

I opened the top drawer in my desk and took out a small cardboard box. I opened it, and took out a business card. 'I changed the design on my business cards over two years ago. I thought perhaps all the Union Jack stuff was a little bit tacky. So it's possible *signor* Zambon is a client from several years ago but, if he ever was, I really don't remember him.'

Vanni drummed his fingers on the table. 'Pity.'

I rubbed my face. 'I'm trying to think. He worked at the *conservatorio* you say?' He nodded. 'Okay, I've done some musical stuff in the past. There's a guy on Giudecca, a composer, who I did some work for a few years ago. I was trying to help him out. Some cowboy had set up his website for him and translated *Messa in re minore* as "Mass for a small king".' We both laughed. 'His name isn't Zambon. He probably knew him though. He might have passed on my card.'

I heard a scrabbling sound from the hall. 'Oh hell.' I rushed out just in time to snatch Vanni's Borsalino out of the reach of Gramsci, who was frantically trying to claw his way up the wall to reach it. I went back into the office, and placed it on top of the filing cabinet. Gramsci leapt up after it, and I whisked it away with a sigh. I proffered it to Vanni. 'Look, I'm sorry, but it might be easier if you just—'

'Wore it?'

I nodded. 'Yes. Sorry.'

'No problem.'

'You see, this is why I never wear hats.'

He placed it on top of his head, and adjusted it. It really was very fine indeed.

'I think we're nearly finished anyway. Could I just ask you to have another look through your records? Just in case.'

'Sure. If you think it'll help.'

'You never know.'

'Okay, I'll check. But I think I'd remember someone from the *conservatorio*. That sounds more interesting than the usual sort of work I get. And he might not even have been an actual client. I could just have given him a business card on the off-chance. You know how it is.'

'I do. But have a look anyway. Maybe call this man on Giudecca. And let me know.'

'I will.' Vanni got to his feet, and smiled. 'So, er, is there anything else you can tell me about it?'

'Oh no. Of course not.'

'All you have to go on is an old business card of mine?'

'Not quite all. The unfortunate *signor* Zambon had booked the whole box at the opera. But according to La Fenice, only one ticket was used. It might be useful to talk to the others, if we can find them.'

'Only one? I definitely saw two of them. Is there nothing on CCTV?'

He sighed. 'Oh, you'd think so, wouldn't you? They have cameras downstairs and in the auditorium. In the corridors, no. Or at least, none that were working.'

'What about staff? Or the firemen, there always seem to be plenty of them around.'

'We thought of that. They patrol according to a particular schedule and pattern. Whoever did this must have known that. I didn't tell you any of this, of course.'

I tapped my nose. 'Not a word, Vanni.' I heard the rattle of keys in the door. 'Fede?'

'*Ciao, tesoro.*' Gramsci mewled a greeting. 'Hello, unfriendly cat.' She came through into the office, unbuttoning her black trenchcoat. She smiled at Vanni.

He beamed. '*Mia cara dottoressa.* Lovely to see you again.' He got to his feet and bent to kiss her hand. Then he saw the expression on her face, changed his mind, and turned it into a handshake.

'Likewise. Nice hat, by the way.' She took off her coat, and unwound her scarf. 'It must be over a year now. I keep telling Nathan you must come round for dinner.' She kissed me on the cheek, her lips still freezing cold.

'No no no. You must come round to ours. I don't think you've met my wife.'

'I don't think so, no.'

There was a moment of silence as Vanni nodded and beamed some more. 'Well, I must be going. Do think about what I said, Nathan. And give me a call, any time.'

'I will, Vanni. See you soon, eh?'

'An old business card? And he thinks it might be a clue?'

'Possibly. At any rate he asked me to have a think. There's this guy on Giudecca I did some work for a few years ago. Another musician. I'll give him a call tomorrow.'

'Not now?'

'Not now, *cara mia*. We're going downstairs for a Negroni at the Brazilians, and then I'll cook something fantastic to eat.'

'Oh good. How fantastic?'

'Very fantastic.'

'Exciting. Any clues?'

'No. Because I haven't thought of it yet.' I went through to the kitchen and opened the fridge. 'Pancetta. Radicchio. Looks like pancetta and radicchio risotto then.'

'Lovely.'

I took a tub of stock out of the freezer and placed it in the sink. 'One Negroni should give it time to start defrosting. Okay, let's go.' I pulled on my coat.

'Is that really all Vanni has to go on? An old business card of yours?'

We made our way downstairs, and out through the front door. 'Not quite. There was one more thing. It seems they found a plague doctor mask in the box.'

'So narrowing the list of suspects down to about twenty thousand then.'

I smiled. 'Indeed.'

As if to prove my point, a group of masked revellers walked past us; a group of young women in cheap domino masks bought from a tat stall, and, a few paces behind them, the taller, more imposing figure of a plague doctor.

'There you go,' I whispered, 'Maybe he should be helping police with their enquiries.'

The figure stopped and turned, although I was sure he couldn't have heard me. I stared into his expressionless eyes, and then he turned again and made his way along the Street of the Assassins, following the giggles from the group of girls who were now disappearing into the fog. I stared after him.

Fede dug me in the ribs. 'Come on, *caro*. Our drinks will be going cold.'

I smiled, and linked my arm in hers, as we made our way into the Magical Brazilians.

Chapter 6

'*Ciao, Gian. Ci sentiamo.*'

I put the phone down, and smiled at Federica, who was stretched out on the sofa reading that morning's *La Nuova*.

'You seem happy. Good news then?'

'Absolutely. Gianandrea's got a couple of new recordings coming out. He wants me to translate the liner notes.'

'That's nice. What about the business card?'

I shook my head. 'No. He did know the guy, though. He used to work at the *conservatorio*, as Vanni said. He taught Renaissance and Baroque singing for over twenty years.'

'Oh right.' She nodded at the paper. 'That's what it says here.'

'Ah, there's a proper obituary then?'

'Yes. Take a look.' She folded the newspaper and tossed it through the air to me. I stretched out my arm for it, only to have Gramsci snatch it away at the last second. He squirrelled it away under the table, and sat down on it.

I sighed. 'I don't suppose you could just tell me the salient points?'

'There weren't many of them. Just a brief biog and lots of tributes from ex-students, old *compagni* and the like.'

'*Compagni*?' My ears pricked up.

'Yes. He was a long-standing member of the Communist Party.'

'Do you remember any names?' I was on my feet now.

'Not really. I didn't think I was going to have to memorise it.'

'Sergio Cardazzo? Lorenzo Bonzio?'

She shook her head. 'I can't be sure. Does it matter?'

'Sergio. Lorenzo. My old buddies from the communist bar on Giudecca. If he was a party member they probably knew him. More than that, they both had my old business card. Just for keeping in touch, you know, at the end of the Moro business.'

'Oh right. Are you going to phone them?'

'Better than that.' I kissed her forehead, and made my way to the top of the stairs. 'I'll go over there and see them at the bar.'

'Will they be there?'

'They'll be there. I think they live there.'

'Why don't you check the paper again?' A sound came from under the table. We looked as one, to see Gramsci scrabbling away on top of his copy of *La Nuova,* and shredding it into pieces. 'Okay. Maybe not.'

I pulled my coat on. 'I'll see you later, okay?'

'Don't think I'm clearing that up!'

'I'll do it later. *Ciao, cara.*'

I needed a better winter coat, I reflected, as I made my way up through Campo Santo Stefano and over the Accademia Bridge, fighting my way against the hordes of masked tourists. Every year, I forgot how cold the city could get in the winter months. In four months' time, I'd be complaining about the inadequate air conditioning in the apartment, and Federica would be pressing me to join her in the mountains for the summer. But, for the moment, Venice was damp and semi-visible under a blanket of fog.

I made my way along the Rio Terà Foscarini, on my way to the *vaporetto* stops on the Zattere. The Worst Busker in the World was not there for me to flick a coin to. It struck me that I hadn't seen him for some time. I hoped he was all right. He'd been a bit of a fixture throughout all my years in Venice, and had made a surprising amount of money from me, considering he knew, at best, half a tune. Perhaps he'd been able to retire?

I hopped on the next boat to Palanca. Even though it was only one stop, I went inside to take advantage of the warmth of the cabin. The windows were fogged, and I wiped mine clear with my sleeve. A slate-grey lagoon under a slate-grey sky. I ran my hands through my damp hair. I hadn't been to see the *compagni* for how many months? We'd stayed in touch after the Moro affair, but the weekly games of *scopa* had gradually become monthly ones. And then bi-monthly. And then a couple of times a year. Last summer. It had been last summer.

A fine sleet was now blowing its way across the lagoon, and the cold wind bit into my face. I paused for a moment outside the communist bar. The Warhol-style paintings of Antonio Gramsci, Karl Marx, Enrico Berlinguer *et al* in the window were the same as they ever were, but a trail of red flashing Christmas lights wound their way around them, in order to add a touch of communist carnival atmosphere.

The bar, as it ever was, was empty of customers other than Sergio and Lorenzo and an elderly barman with a drooping white moustache. There was silence for a moment. Sergio looked up at me, then back at his playing cards, and then placed them down on the table and stood up.

'Investigator Nathan.' It had been his pet name for me since the Moro case.

'Sergio.' I smiled. 'Lorenzo.'

Sergio didn't smile back. Lorenzo looked embarrassed, and turned quickly to his hand of cards.

'We've not seen you here in a while, *Eccellenza*.'

'I'm sorry. Things have been busy.'

'Too busy for the *compagni* now, perhaps? Too important for a couple of old comrades playing cards in their old bar?'

I held up my hands. 'It's not like that Sergio, it's just—'

He interrupted me. 'Or maybe it's just you got tired of getting your arse kicked sideways at *scopa* every week?' There was another moment of silence, and then he grinned and threw his arms wide.

I bent down to hug him. Sergio was short and powerfully built, but I couldn't help noticing that he'd lost some weight. Lorenzo, always taller and more ascetic-looking, had not risen from his chair but just nodded and smiled at me. I looked from one to the other and felt a moment of pain. Of guilt. I hadn't seen them in over six months, and they'd both visibly aged. One day, perhaps, I'd turn up for a game of *scopa* only to find there was no longer any game going on. I'd make more effort, I promised myself.

'Sit down, *investigatore*, and have a drink.'

'Spritz?' I asked.

Sergio sighed. Lorenzo smiled. 'Sergio still holds that a spritz is an effete drink of the *borghese.*' He wagged his finger. 'I keep telling him it's just a drink. Not a weapon of the revolution.'

Sergio shook his head, and held three fingers up to the barman. 'One jug of red, three glasses.'

I dragged a seat up to the table. 'He's new here?' I nodded towards the barman.

Sergio nodded. 'Lorenzo's dad.'

I looked from Lorenzo to the barman and back again. Lorenzo, most likely, would never see his seventies again. 'You're kidding?'

'Of course I'm kidding. But he's the only guy here older than we are. So we call him Lorenzo's dad.'

'Has he been here long?'

'Six months. But we think he'll stay. He's a proper party man. Not like the young kids we usually get.'

The old fellow tottered over, a jug of red wine in one hand and three tumblers in the other. I reached for the jug in order to give him a hand, but he shook his head and waved away my offer of help, which set the wine sloshing alarmingly. The tumblers rattled as he set them down. Sergio gave him a pat on the back. '*Grazie,* Marco.' He filled us up. '*Cin cin.*' We clinked glasses.

Sergio swept up the cards on the table and shuffled them. 'So, are we going to play?' He paused. 'Or is there another reason for Investigator Nathan to be here?' They both looked at me.

I rested my elbows on the table, and held my glass of wine in both hands. 'Yes, you're right. There is.'

'You're investigating?' smiled Lorenzo.

'Not exactly. Well, not at all really. It's just my friend Vanni – you know, the cop? – well, he had a question for me.'

'About the murder at La Fenice?' Lorenzo was still smiling. 'You what?'

'The murder at La Fenice. The one that's been in all the papers. Even *Il Manifesto*.'

'That's right. But I don't—'

Lorenzo cut me off. 'You want to know about Matteo Zambon, is that right?'

'That's right.' They were both smiling now. 'You utter bastards. Why didn't you say something? Or just ring me?'

'We don't trust cops, my friend,' said Sergio. 'Even someone like Vanni. And besides,' he took off his glasses and polished them on his sleeve, in order to avoid looking at me, 'we thought this way there was more chance of you coming over here again.'

'Ah, hell,' I said. 'Now I feel bad.'

'Well, so you should,' grumped Sergio, prior to refilling the glasses. He raised his in salute. 'So, *compagno*, what do you want to know about Matteo Zambon?'

Chapter 7

'I take it you know him – knew him – then?' I said.

'I wouldn't presume to say we knew him, exactly,' said Lorenzo. 'We knew of him, certainly.'

Sergio harrumphed.

'He was a party man, though, wasn't he? He never dropped by here for a game of cards, or to talk about the struggle?'

Sergio harrumphed again, and swirled his wine. His opinion of the late *signor* Zambon, it seemed, was not a high one. I turned to Lorenzo and raised my eyebrows, quizzically. He seemed the more likely to give me sentences.

'He was. He used to. But then there was a bit of unpleasantness.' I turned to Sergio in anticipation of another harrumph, but none was forthcoming and he restricted himself to a brusque shake of the head. He muttered a single word, 'Splitter.'

I nodded. 'Ah. I think I understand.'

'I think you do. Back in 1991 – the Great Schism, Sergio calls it,' Lorenzo chuckled, ' – Matteo was one of those who joined the PDS. You know the PDS?'

'*Partito Democratico della Sinistra*. The successor to the old Communist Party?'

There was a terrible silence. Sergio said nothing, but was turning an unhealthy shade of purple. Lorenzo patted his arm and gave an embarrassed little cough. 'Erm, well one of them, perhaps. Sergio and I stayed with the old party. Matteo and many others – the majority—'

'*Giuda Iscariota*', muttered Sergio.

'Well it's true, Sergio, we might not like it but it's true. Matteo and the others were the majority. We stayed with the PRC – the Refounded Communists – well, apart from those who founded the CU – the Unitarian Communists – but most went off with the PDS.'

I was starting to lose track of the acronyms. 'And the PDS then became the PD – the *Partito Democratico*?'

'Oh no. First there was the DS – *Democratici della Sinistra*. And *then* there was the PD.'

'Okay. So the PCI split into the PRC and the CU on one side and the PDS who became the DS who then became the PD on the other. Have I got this right?'

Lorenzo smiled. 'More or less. Of course we haven't mentioned the PdUP or the DP yet, let alone SEL.'

'Oh. Should we?'

'Well, they do all contribute to this rather fascinating period in Italian pre- and post-communist history and—'

Sergio gently, but firmly, placed his hand over his comrade's mouth. 'No,' he said. 'No, we shouldn't.'

'Okay. Thank you. Really. So I'm guessing you haven't had much to do with Matteo Zambon over the past – how many years?'

'I haven't spoken to him since February 3rd 1991.'

'Right. A quarter of a century then. Blimey, you guys know how to hold a grudge, don't you?'

Sergio shrugged. 'Some things are important. So, Zambon hadn't set foot in this bar since February 2nd 1991—'

'Not February 3rd?'

'That was a Sunday. We didn't open on Sundays in those days.'

'Right.'

'Anyway, it's been just over a quarter of century – as you said – since he came in here. And then two weeks ago, he just marched in here, cool as you like, ordered an Aperol spritz. I tell you, *investigatore*, Marco there had to haul me off him.'

I looked over to the bar. Marco was slumped in a chair, his face covered by a copy of *Il Manifesto*, and gently snoring. He didn't look like the hauling-off type.

'So what did he want?'

Lorenzo gave a gentle cough. 'He wanted to talk to us. To me specifically.'

'After twenty-five years he decided to let bygones be bygones?'

'Not exactly. He thought I could help him.'

'But you hadn't spoken in—'

'Nine thousand four hundred and ninety-seven days,' said Sergio.

There was silence around the table. 'Sergio takes this sort of thing very seriously,' said Lorenzo.

'Evidently.'

'He didn't want to speak to Sergio. He wanted to speak to me. I'd stayed in touch with him.' Sergio glowered. 'Don't look at me like that, *compagno*,' Lorenzo snapped, 'we'd worked together in the past. Sometimes real life gets in the way of ideological purity.' He turned back to me. 'He taught at the *conservatorio,* you know. I taught a few classes there myself. Semiotics of opera libretti.'

'My goodness.'

He smiled and drew himself up a little straighter. 'It's a niche, but an important one. Anyway, as I said, we'd had to keep in touch over the years for professional reasons. And he wanted me to recommend a translator to him. Naturally I thought of you. I gave him your business card and told him to get in touch.'

'Thanks. Didn't lead to anything, unfortunately, but thanks anyway. What did he need doing?'

'I don't know.'

'Oh.'

'He just said he was working on some old manuscripts at the Marciana Library. Do you know it?'

I shook my head. 'I know it, of course. But I've never been there.'

'No reason why you should, perhaps. Now Matteo spoke good English. But he said these manuscripts were beyond him. He needed a proper translator. And more than that, he said he needed someone he could depend on to be absolutely discreet. And so, as I said, I thought of you.'

'I'm flattered. So. Do you know what he wanted me to be discreet about?'

'No idea, I'm afraid. He never got in touch?' I shook my head. 'A pity. I wonder if we'll ever find out. But what a wonderfully operatic ending.'

'Oh yes. It certainly was.'

'And think of the assassin. How desperate would you have to be to kill someone in the open like that, knowing that you could be seen by over a thousand people?'

'It's one hell of a risk, certainly.'

'Nevertheless, someone took that risk. So,' Lorenzo drummed his hands on the table, 'now you know as much as we do. So what are we going to do?'

'We?'

He smiled. 'Like last time.'

I shook my head. 'Lorenzo, last time we *did* anything together a good man was killed. I'm just going to pass this information on to Vanni and let the *Questura* deal with it.'

'Oh. What a shame.'

'Maybe. But best for all concerned. I've got into far too much trouble in the past. I'm going to let this one go.' Then I paused. There was something bothering me. 'But why would he come here? He could just get a list of translators from the internet or from the *Pagine Gialle*. Why come to a bar he's not been in for over twenty-five years and risk getting punched into the bargain?'

Lorenzo sighed. 'There'd been some disappointments in his career, Nathan. He'd had to retire early. He'd fallen out with a number of people.' I raised my eyebrows.

'Money,' Sergio muttered.

'Money, yes. Anyway, for a number of reasons it seemed I was one of the few people he hadn't fallen out with. He thought he could trust me.'

'You're saying you were going to set me up with a potential client with a dodgy credit record? Well, thanks for that.'

'Oh, we'd have sorted it out. Wouldn't we. Sergio?'

Sergio was staring at the table. 'Money,' he said. 'The root of all evil.'

'That's a misquotation, Sergio, and you know it. It's *the love of money is the root of all evil.*'

'Same thing.' He dabbed at his eyes, and then looked at his watch. 'I've got to be going, *compagni.*' He patted me on the shoulder. 'Don't stay away too long next time, *investigatore.*' He reached into his coat.

'I'll get these, Sergio,' I said.

He patted me on the arm again. 'No you won't.' He laid a few notes on the bar. 'Give these to Marco as soon as he wakes up. See you tomorrow, Lorenzo.' He gave us a half-wave, then turned up the collar of his coat and walked out into the wind and sleet, holding his hat on with one hand.

'Is he all right, Lorenzo? I've never seen him like that before.'

'He's all right. It's just strange for him, that's all. You know what I was saying about money?' I nodded. 'Sergio's been paying Zambon's rent for the past year.'

'I thought they hadn't spoken for twenty-five years.'

'They hadn't.'

'And so . . . ?' I left the question hanging.

'He'd heard Zambon had money problems. Big problems. He didn't want to see him out on the streets. Some things are bigger than the Party.' He paused, and smiled. 'Even to Sergio.'

I looked out of the window, but Sergio was long gone. 'I see.' I pulled my coat on. 'Okay, thanks, Lorenzo. I'll be in touch.'

'I thought you said you weren't going to get involved.'

'Oh, I'm not. Not at all. I'm going to go home and telephone Vanni, and then forget all about this.' I paused. 'But I
might just stop by the Marciana Library on the way.'

Lorenzo grinned.

Chapter 8

I took the next boat to San Zaccaria, and made my way to Piazzetta San Marco. I walked between the two great granite columns that marked the entrance to the most elegant drawing room in Europe. They had once been the only legal gambling space in the city, and, less happily, a place of public execution. Saint Theodore stood on top of one column, on an unconvincing crocodile. On the other roared the Lion of Venice, the symbol of St Mark, who had replaced the unfortunate Theodore as patron of the city. Theodore had been particularly venerated in the Eastern Church, and a new up-and-coming Western power like the Most Serene Republic needed a patron saint rather more to their tastes. And why bother with an obscure little eastern saint like Theo, when you could have a fully fledged Evangelist? Even if they did have to steal his remains from Alexandria.

Theodore still remained on his column and unconvincing crocodile, half forgotten to the extent that nobody seemed to be in complete agreement as to precisely which Saint Theodore he had actually been any more.

To my right stood the Doge's Palace, and, to my left, the elegant arcades that served as the façade of Jacopo Sansovino's

Biblioteca Marciana, described by no less an authority than Andrea Palladio as the finest building since Antiquity. A building so wonderful that I had never, ever been inside it.

The entrance lay between a sandwich shop and the Gran Caffè Chioggia. A few tourists, masked, braved the temperature and sat outside, listening to a hardy pianist in black tie playing 'We Have All the Time in the World'. Others sat inside, in the warm wood-panelled rooms, drinking coffees and hot chocolates and peering out through the fogged windows. I smiled as I remembered my first visit. I was still married, then, and not long in Venice. Jean and I had sat down outside, consulted the menu and then literally bounced out of our seats as we read the price for a single gin and tonic. We fled before a waiter could accost us, wondering if the menu had actually been priced in *lire* instead of euros.

I walked past the four heroic statues that guarded the entrance to the library, and through the double doors that led to the reading rooms.

'I'd like to become a member, please,' I said to the young man behind the desk.

'Of course, *signore*. Are you resident in Venice?'

'I am.' I passed over my ID card and he flicked it open. He tapped away at a keyboard.

'You're a translator?' I nodded. '*Laureato*? PhD?'

'*Laureato*.'

'Thank you. Institution?'

'University of Aberystwyth.'

He paused. 'Could you spell that?'

'I could. Is it important?'

'*Be*', not really. I could just leave it blank.'

'I think that might be easiest.'

'Okay. We just need a photo.' He adjusted a small camera clipped to the top of the monitor. 'Big smile.' I wasn't sure if he was joking. A few seconds passed and then, as if by magic, a laminated card appeared. He handed it over to me. 'Do you know how to find your way around?'

I hadn't been inside a library since my student days. 'No,' I admitted.

He made a sad face. 'Okay.' He gestured through the glass-panelled wall behind him. 'That's the reading room. All books there are free for you to browse. Catalogues, PCs, microfiche are at the end of the hall. If you want a book brought to you, fill out one of these.' He indicated a white form. 'These are for modern books, post-1850.'

'Not all that modern then.'

He gave a half-smile. 'Modern to us. For older or rare manuscripts, you fill out the yellow form. All clear?'

'Absolutely.' Probably. 'You've been very helpful. There is just one other thing. A colleague of mine was working here recently. I wonder if you could tell me which books he was looking at.'

'Why?' He frowned.

'I'm his translator. I need to know what he was working on.'

He shrugged. 'Sure, I can look it up. It might be quicker if you just phoned him.'

'That would be difficult. He died two days ago.'

'Oh. I'm sorry.' A question was left hanging in the air.

'I'd just like to know what he was looking at. So I can finish his work.' I decided to chance a little joke. 'Probably going to find it difficult to get paid, of course.' There was an awkward silence. Wrong decision, Nathan.

He turned the monitor on the desk to face him, and tapped away at the keyboard. 'Name?' he asked.

'Sutherland. Nathan Sutherland.'

'Your friend's, sir.'

'Ah. Sorry. Matteo Zambon.'

He looked up from the monitor. 'Zambon? The one who was killed at the opera?' My new acquaintance obviously kept up to date with the *cronaca nera* in the newspapers.

'That's him.'

'I'm sorry,' he repeated. 'Did you know him well?'

'Not at all. It was just business.' That, at least, was basically true.

He tapped away again. 'How far back would you like me to search?'

'Erm,' I hadn't really thought about this, 'just the past month please.'

'Let's have a look.' He tapped away. 'One work from the restricted section. If you want to look at it, you need to complete a request form, and one of my colleagues will bring it to you. You fill out a yellow form for this one, not a white one, okay?'

'Could you let me know what it is?'

He turned the monitor around so that it was half facing me. 'I'm sorry, my English is not so good, perhaps it's better if you read it yourself?'

'Thank you.' I craned my head. *The Diaries of Thomas Rowlanson, secretary to Sir Isaac Wake, ambassador to The Most Serene Republic of Venice by appointment of King Charles.* The names meant nothing to me. With the exception of King Charles.

'Would you like someone to bring this to you?'

'Yes. Thank you.' I scribbled my name and the reference number on the yellow form he passed to me. Then I made my way over to the entrance to the reading room, and laid my hand upon the door.

'I'm sorry sir, one moment please.' I turned around. He pointed at my shoulder bag. 'Everything you take into the library must be in a transparent bag. Security, you understand? Everything else must be left in a locker.'

'Of course.'

He passed me a key. 'I need a *documento* as well. Passport, driving licence, ID. You get it back when you leave. Otherwise people forget about the key when they go home.'

'I see.' I handed over my ID. I slid my bag into the locker, and then rolled up my coat and placed it on top. I nodded at the librarian. 'Foolproof, eh?'

He smiled back at me. 'Absolutely foolproof, sir.'

I closed the locker, dropped the key into my jacket pocket and made my way into the reading room.

Chapter 9

The interior of the library was a sort of reverse TARDIS, in that it appeared to be smaller on the inside, an effect caused by dividing the space into a central reading room with smaller spaces for photocopying and catalogue research around the outside. Glass doors at one end opened to a stone staircase leading up to the rare manuscripts section. Access to this area was restricted by a sign reading 'Access Restricted'.

The glass-panelled roof gave the impression that the room was both outside yet inside at the same time. The greyness of the sky and the stonework cast the upper galleries in semi-darkness, in contrast to the reading room itself where the lamps on each woodworm-ridden table suffused everything in a warm amber glow. At the end of the great hall stood a marble monument to Francesco Petrarch, the great poet crowned with laurel wreaths and clutching a book to his bosom with both hands.

Every table was occupied by serious-looking young people, students – I assumed – from one of the city's two universities. I looked around, conscious of being the only person in the room who didn't know what he was doing. There only seemed to be two remaining seats. Students, evidently, were not what they had been in my day. Then again, if the library at my old university had been like this, I might have spent more time there as well.

I sat myself between two young women, one of them working away on a laptop next to a pile of books on the mosaics of the basilica of San Marco. The girl to my right texted away on her *cellulare*, whilst holding open a plain brown volume, its pages heavily foxed with age. I tried to make out the subject matter, but the smallness of the typeface made it impossible. She caught me staring, and I smiled and looked away. She turned back with a faintly discernible tut of annoyance.

A short crack broke the silence, and everyone on the tables around us looked up. The young man diagonally opposite was cracking his knuckles. He had the look of a younger, more handsome Karl Marx and, indeed, was reading what appeared to be a graphic novel on the life of Che Guevara. He leaned over and whispered something into the ear of the girl to my right. They both gave a hushed laugh, and looked at me. I smiled again, and pretended to be looking for something in my jacket pocket. I was suddenly very aware of needing something to read, and looked around.

The nearest shelves were labelled '*Relazioni Ambasciatori*'. I made my way over and chose a volume at random, and sat back down again. I smiled at them both. *See, I'm doing proper research too.* I turned to the front page. The book dated from the late nineteenth century, part of a series reprinting the letters and reports from members of Venice's diplomatic service, from those far-off days when the Republic had had need of a diplomatic service. I flicked through the first section, the memoirs of Lodovico Falier, ambassador at the court of Henry

VIII from 1528 to 1531. Henry, it seemed, was already up to all sorts of tricks with Rome, and desperately trying to get shot of Catherine of Aragon, but Lodovico had been recalled to Venice just before things got really interesting.

There was a gentle cough from behind. I turned to see one of the archivists looking down at me, and holding a small, leather-bound volume. 'Your book, *signore*.' He checked the yellow slip. 'Rowlanson, Thomas?'

I nodded. 'Thank you.' I replaced the memoirs of Lodovico Falier on the shelf, and turned to the reminiscences of Thomas Rowlanson.

My predecessor in Venice had had an uneventful time of things. Or perhaps he'd simply been too good at his job. Too diplomatic, one might say. Henry Wotton, the first ambassador to the Republic, seemed to have had a fine, adventurous time of it, buying up Titians and Tintorettos, talking theology with Paolo Sarpi and, on one occasion, rescuing Thomas Coryat by gondola from a fight with an irate rabbi who had taken a dim view of Coryat's attempt to convert him. Rowlanson, by contrast, as Secretary Resident to Sir Isaac Wake, had had a quieter time. Or maybe it was only Sir Isaac that got invited to the best parties, as Rowlanson's diaries seemed to be little more than records of appointments that his master had kept.

And yet, there was something naively touching about them. He may not have had the most interesting life, but he'd been a regular guy going about his regular job as best he could. It just happened to be in Venice. In a way, I was the nearest thing he had to a successor. Perhaps he'd thought his words – records of catering arrangements, the best restaurants, the cheapest market stalls to use and which Venetian diplomats spoke the best English – could serve as a 'how to do it' guide for those who came after. Sitting in the warm, amber glow of the Marciana Library almost four hundred years after my predecessor vanished from history, I found myself wishing him well.

The diary was a slim piece of work, but Rowlanson's crabbed hand and the language – early modern English – made it slow going. No wonder Zambon had felt the need for a proper translator. Nevertheless, I was struggling to see what he could possibly have found of interest in the rather bookish memoirs of a long-dead English diplomat.

I checked my watch. Time was getting on, and there was no way I was going to finish it today. I looked at how much of the book remained. Several days' work, at least, and I wasn't sure if it was worth my while. The book wasn't made for flicking through at high speed, and the yellowing pages crackled as I turned them.

Then something caught my eye.

16ᵗʰ April, 1630. It was a delight to celebrate the recent marriage of sig'ra. Giustiniana, at the most lovely palace of Mozzenigo at which was performed the work of the excellent sig. Claudio Monteverdi, The Rape of Proserpina. *Never has this beautiful space seemed quite so lovely as this night. Sig. Monteverdi spoke with me that same evening. He expressed sadness that his friend, my master, Sir Isaac could not be with us, and that he will pray for his safe return to us soon, if that be God's will. Following which he kissed me, wished Sir Isaac godspeed, and pressed into my hands the music of*

Proserpina as a gift to my master upon his return to the Republic.

Well now.

Palazzo Mozzenigo. Perhaps Rowlanson meant the Palazzo Mocenigo. But which one? *The Rape of Proserpina*? I shook my head. The name meant nothing to me. How much did I know about Monteverdi? More to the point, how much had I forgotten about Monteverdi? *Orfeo. Ulisse. Poppea.* I'd never heard of *The Rape of Proserpina*.

Whatever. It wasn't something that needed to concern me now. Or at all. I checked my watch again. I still had a little time before I needed to think about heading back. I'd pick up some *frittelle* for Federica and me on the way home, and then perhaps we'd head down to the Brazilians for a Negroni whilst I thought about what to cook for tea.

What little natural light remained was fading now. I switched on one of the table lamps. Rowlanson's handwriting was still difficult to read. Glasses. Had I reached the age at which I needed reading glasses? I bent my head further over the book. I was aware of a gentle scraping sound from the position opposite me, and then a delicate waft of perfume. A shadow passed over the surface of the book, and a hand – slender, bejewelled, with nails painted in tiger stripes – reached over to touch it. I looked up in irritation, and then jumped back in my chair with surprise, scraping it across the floor to the obvious annoyance of the others around the table.

There was no mistaking the face. I'd seen it so many times. That long, dark hair and pale, pale skin. So lovely. I'd seen it on the music pages, and the cover of celebrity gossip journals. But never, sadly, on stage.

Isotta Baldan smiled a million-euro smile at me. 'I was wondering,' she said, 'if you've nearly finished with that book?'

Chapter 10

Be calm, Nathan, I told myself. Be cool. Don't babble.

'Gosh.' I had never, ever used the word 'gosh' in my life before. 'My goodness me. Oh, my goodness me.'

I was, in all probability, babbling.

She continued to beam at me, and if a few euros were knocked off the smile, I didn't notice. 'Mr Sutherland?'

'Nathan Sutherland. Yes. That's me.'

'I'm—'

'Oh, I know who you are.' I could feel my cheeks flushing. 'I definitely know who you are. But how on earth do you know my name?'

'The archivist told me. When I was looking for that book.'

'Oh, I see.' I wasn't sure if that was quite in order, but Isotta Baldan, I was quickly learning, was someone it might be difficult to say no to.

We were no longer taking care to speak *sotto voce* and a few people at adjacent desks shushed us. We looked around, and saw the archivist appear as if from nowhere. His manners were far too exquisite to suggest that he would become involved in something as vulgar as a row. The slightly pained expression on his face was more than enough to tell us that our behaviour was just a little bit disappointing to him.

Baldan pouted, ever so slightly. 'Perhaps I should go. I can always come back tomorrow.'

'Oh, are you quite sure?' Babbling, I feared, was about to recommence. I took a deep breath, as quietly as I could. 'That is, I think I'm finished with this for the day.' I pushed it gently towards her. 'You're most welcome to it. Please.'

She shook her head. 'No. I think we're disturbing people.' The young man with the Karl Marx beard looked over at her and shook his head. He grinned. The young woman opposite him scowled, and he hurriedly wiped the smile from his face and attempted to look serious.

Baldan took the book from my hands, her fingers ever so gently brushing mine. 'Come on,' she whispered, 'we should go.'

'We?'

For the first time, she looked slightly annoyed. 'Yes, of course. I think we should talk.' She got to her feet, and made her way to the exit from the reading room without waiting to see if I was following. I scraped my chair back, and looked around for the archivist. I made a scrawling motion with my finger in the air, as if I were calling for the bill in a restaurant. He nodded, went back to his desk, and brought me the yellow form to sign, indicating that I had returned everything. I looked over to the exit. Baldan was poised on the threshold, looking back at me. I held her gaze as I scrawled something unintelligible on the yellow form, and slid it across to the archivist without looking at him. Then, doing my very best not to scurry, I made my way to the door.

Young Karl Marx caught my eye and winked at me, to the disgust of his girlfriend, who humphed and stalked off to the stacks.

Baldan was waiting for me. I fumbled with my locker key, dragged out my coat and struggled into it. I pulled out my bag and slung it over my shoulder.

She was wearing a black cotton jacket over a polo neck, with knee-length boots over designer jeans. She was tall, nearly as tall as me, and Junoesque but in a good way. Oh yes. Most definitely in a good way. She looked at me, expectantly.

'Erm, don't you have a coat?' I asked. 'It's going to be chilly out there.'

'Your coat, *signora.*' A young man emerged from a back office, and helped her into an ankle-length black fur coat. A real fur coat. Live in Venice long enough, and you soon get to recognise the difference. He passed her a matching headband, which she slipped on to her head, running her fingers through her hair and flicking it this way and that until she was happy with the results.

'Are you ready, Mr Sutherland?' she said.

'Yes. Absolutely.' We made our way to the door.

'The key, sir,' said the librarian.

'Oh, sorry.' I reached into my jacket, fished out the locker key, and passed it over. 'Thanks for everything, *buona serata.*'

He let me get as far as the door before he called after me again. 'Your document, sir.' I turned around, to see him waving my ID card at me.

'Ah. Yes.' Not quite as foolproof as all that then. He stretched across the desk to pass it to me. I think he might have smiled, but I couldn't be sure. Then I turned to follow

Baldan, who was holding the door open for me and continuing to smile that effortless million-euro smile.

The pianist was still playing outside the Gran Caffè Chioggia. I noticed that he was wearing fingerless gloves, but I found it hard to believe that he had any sensation left in his hands. There was something about the melody that caught my attention. Minor key, plaintive. I knew it from somewhere but couldn't quite place it. I became aware that Baldan was speaking to me.

I looked over at her. She raised her eyebrows, ever so slightly, and looked annoyed. 'I'm sorry,' I said. 'I was miles away.'

'I could tell. I was asking if you'd like to go for coffee.'

'That would be lovely. Thank you. I'm sorry, I was just listening to the pianist. There's something about that melody. I'm sure I know it but I just can't put my finger on it.' I laughed. 'I'm sure that never happens to you.'

Her face softened, and she smiled. 'You'd be surprised. Coffee, then. But not here. Too many distractions, perhaps?'

I smiled back. 'Too many distractions. Okay, anywhere in mind? Florian, Quadri?'

I was only joking, but she seemed to take my suggestions seriously. Then she shook her head. 'No. Not today. Come with me.' To my surprise she linked her arm in mine, and led me through the arcade, where sparkly silver lights hung in curtains, and into the *piazza* proper.

The square was full of masked visitors all taking a late afternoon *passeggiata*, the purpose of which, it seemed, was simply to be seen and photographed by other tourists in fancy dress.

Baldan sighed. A long, silvery sigh. 'I love *Carnevale*.'

'Really?' I was unable to keep the surprise out of my voice.

'Yes, of course.' She looked askance at me. 'Don't you?'

I shrugged. 'I've got to be honest. I just don't get it.' I gestured with my free hand at the masked throng. 'I mean, I just don't understand what it's all about. It just all seems so made up, so artificial.'

'Well, of course it is. That's what's so wonderful about it. It's masquerade. All these people. When they go home, what are they? Bank managers, accountants, housewives?'

'Translators?' I added.

'Oh, I don't know. I think perhaps some of them are a little bit too serious, Mr Sutherland. But maybe even them, sometimes. And now everyone else is here, in Piazza San Marco, and they're princes and princesses and kings and demons.' A little boy, dressed in a Spider-Man costume, ran across our path and tripped. Isotta caught him before he could fall, and set him on his feet again. 'And superheroes.' She followed him with her eyes, as he ran off in search of his mamma. '*Che carino.*'

'You make it sound like the theatre.'

'Because that's exactly what it is. All this is a stage. The greatest set in the world.' We were now halfway across the *piazza*, directly in front of the basilica, where a line of *passerelle*, temporary walkways, had been placed in the expectation of *acqua alta*. 'Do you know,' she continued, 'I could just jump up on one of those, right now, and start singing and nobody would think it strange at all. I wonder if they'd even notice.'

'Oh, I rather think they would.'

'Well maybe. But it wouldn't seem strange, would it? It

would just be one of those things that people do during *Carnevale*. All part of the theatre. All part of the opera.'

I don't know where I found the courage, but I stopped in my tracks and gently held her back. 'Go on then.'

'What?'

'Go on then. Get up on one of the *passerelle* and start singing.'

Her hand went to her mouth. She looked left, and then right, and then laughed. She looked at me and the faint lines at the corners of her blue eyes crinkled. 'Not this time. Maybe next time.'

We continued our way across the square, threading through the crowds and the kiosks selling cheap masks and tricorne hats. Nothing that had been made within a thousand miles of Venice. Above us, pigeons and gulls circled in the hope or expectation that someone would throw them something to eat. A young man in a shabby grey fleece and woollen hat thrust himself in front of us, and tried to push a red rose into my hand. 'For the lady.'

I tried to wave him away, but he continued trying to pass the drooping flower to me. I knew exactly how this worked. If I touched it, he'd take it as a sale and create a scene until I gave him some money. I held my hand, palm outwards, in front of him, and shook my head. 'Not interested,' I said.

He nodded, and tucked the rose away in a bag full of similarly sad-looking blooms, oblivious to a few withered petals that fluttered to the ground. He moved the flowers aside and pointed inside at what they were covering. Small transparent plastic bags of grain. Bird seed.

'You want feed the birds? Ten euro?'

'No, I don't.'

'You're in Venice.'

'It's against the law.'

He shook his head. 'Is traditional.'

Before I could say anything further, Baldan had unlinked her arm from mine and pushed him, with both hands in the middle of his chest, sending him staggering back. Flowers dropped from his bag and, just as he regained his balance, she was on him again and sent him reeling backwards. This time he dropped his bag and roses and bags of seeds spilled across the ground. Before he could bend to pick them up, she had grabbed him by his jacket and hissed in his face. 'Get out my city, you piece of shit. You want me to call the cops? You want them to check your *documenti*? You want them to check your *permesso*? You want them to send you home? Back to your shit country?' She kicked his bag across the paving, scattering its contents. He scrambled after it, picked it up, and ran off.

I looked around. People were pointing and laughing. Two cops at the base of the Torre dell'Orologio were looking over in our direction. One of them put his hand on the other's shoulder, and said something. They looked over at us and both laughed.

Baldan put her hands to her face, and breathed deeply. She wiped her eyes. Then she took a silver comb from her bag, put her hands to her hair and, as before, teased it this way and that until she was satisfied. Then she linked her arm in mine, again, and continued across the square. 'I'm sorry,' she said, 'but that sort of thing really pisses me off.' There was something discordant about hearing her swear with that lovely voice.

She led me into the Caffè Lavena, which I knew as the one place in the piazza where you could get a drink *al banco* without the aid of a second mortgage. Baldan stood at the bar, and a *barista* snapped to attention. She turned to me. 'And now I need something stronger than coffee. What would you like?'

I paused as I ran through the combinations in my head. A prosecco wouldn't hit the spot at this hour, but a Negroni seemed a bit too serious. Besides, I didn't want to have to explain to Federica that I'd spent the afternoon drinking cocktails with a glamorous internationally famous soprano. 'A *spritz al bitter*,' I said.

'*Spritz al Campari, spritz al Cynar per favore.*' An artichoke-based cocktail. I had tried one, but only once. She noticed my look and smiled. 'It's better for the voice than Campari,' she said.

'Really?'

'It's what I tell myself.'

Her hands, I noticed, were shaking. 'Would you like to sit down?' I looked around, but all the seats were taken. 'Although we would have to sit outside.'

She shook her head. 'Too expensive. Even for me. First there's waiter service charge. Then there's another for listening to the musicians. Did you know Wagner used to drink here?'

'I did. And, you know, I wouldn't pay the service charge even if it was the man himself behind the piano, tinkling out the Wesendonck Lieder.'

She laughed, and briefly touched my arm. 'Do you like Wagner?'

'I do. I love him. Horrible man, but I still love him.'

'Me too. It would be nice to be able to sing Wagner, but my voice.' She put her fingertips to her throat.

'Not quite right?'

'No. My mother would have loved to have had a Wagnerian daughter, but I always knew I never had that sort of voice.'

'Your mother? Ah, hence your name?'

'*Esatto*.' She sipped at her artichoke-based spritz.

'And so, *signora* Baldan, can I ask you why you needed to look at that book?'

She looked left and then right, and then whispered to me in a mock-conspiratorial tone. 'It's supposed to be a secret.'

'I can keep secrets.'

'You can?'

'I'm the honorary consul, you know.'

'My goodness. So you're a diplomat?'

'Not a diplomat. But very diplomatic.'

'Well then.' Again, she looked left and right, and smiled. 'It's about Monteverdi. You know Monteverdi?'

'Not personally. I like his music very much.'

'And what do you know of his music?'

I took a deep breath. 'The Madrigals. The Vespers. The operas. I don't pretend to know much about the man himself. Born in Mantua, wasn't he?'

She shook her head. 'Cremona. He made his name in Mantua.'

'Okay. Then he came to Venice, and became the *maestro di cappella* at St Mark's.'

'Replacing Giulio Cesare Martinengo. Who wasn't very good, poor man. Monteverdi sorted everything out, *grazie al cielo*. Now, about those operas?'

'*Orfeo. Ulisse. Poppea.*'

'And?'

'And – some others. Lost for ever, unfortunately.'

'Almost certainly.' She paused. 'Tell me about Matteo Zambon.'

I set my drink down on the counter. 'The man who was murdered at La Fenice?'

'The same. You were working for him, no?'

'No. He had my card, that's all. I think he wanted some translation work.'

'He never telephoned you? Never emailed?'

'No.'

'And that book he wanted you to translate? The one you were looking at just now?'

'A diary written by a humble little English *apparatchik* nearly four hundred years ago. My predecessor if you like.'

She smiled. 'Tell me about it.'

'He went to some splendid parties. He cooked a lot of fish. In many ways he was a man after my own heart. But you seem to want me to tell you lots of things, *signora* Baldan.'

She touched my arm, and laughed. 'I must seem terribly bossy. But I'm going to ask you one last thing. And then that's it, I promise. Did he ever meet Claudio Monteverdi?'

'He did. At the premiere of . . .' I scratched my head, trying to remember, 'an opera I'd never heard of.'

'*Le nozze d'Enea?*'

'No, that's not it.'

'*Proserpina rapita?*'

'That's the one. Mr Rowlanson had seen it at a wedding banquet. More than that, his master had been given the score by Monteverdi himself. As I said, it isn't one I know.'

Her expression changed, and she looked both angry and disappointed. 'Most people haven't. It's been lost for centuries.' The dazzling smile returned. 'Proserpine is ravaged by the god Pluto. A symbolic rape to celebrate a wedding feast.'

'I suppose they were different times.'

'Not different enough, I sometimes think. But how lucky Mr Rowlanson was. How many people have heard *Poppea*? Hundreds of thousands, millions. And how many ever heard *Proserpina*? A few hundred, a few thousand at most. How lucky he was.'

'He seemed to have enjoyed it.'

'And yet, of course, he didn't know quite what a privilege it was. Well now, Mr Sutherland. We must have a good talk, a proper talk about Monteverdi. And Matteo Zambon. But not here.'

'I'd be delighted. My office is just ten minutes away.'

She shook her head. 'No. Not now. I'll call you.' I took out my wallet and offered her a business card. 'Nathan Sutherland.' She pronounced it the Italian way with a short 'a' in the first syllable.

'*Nay*than,' I corrected her. And then, for the second time that afternoon, I gathered all my courage together. 'Do you know, you broke my heart two nights ago?'

'I did? Oh poor Mr Sutherland, what did I do?'

'You didn't do anything. That's what broke my heart.' I paused. 'I was at the opera.'

Her hands flew to her face. 'Oh, I'm sorry. I'm so sorry.

But I really couldn't sing. I had a terrible fever and my voice was in pieces.'

'It's okay.'

'No it isn't. It isn't at all. I'll make it up to you, I promise.'

'Oh, don't worry. Really. The other soprano, *signora* Sartorelli, was—' I stopped.

She tilted her head to the side. 'Was?'

'She was – quite good.' We both laughed. I checked my watch. It was really time to be going home.

'You have to go?'

'Yes. I need to throw balls for my cat. And then I need to cook dinner for my partner.'

'In that order?'

'Oh yes. Terrible things will happen otherwise.'

'Well, I have to go too. I don't have a cat, but I also have to cook dinner for my partner.'

I buttoned up my coat. 'Well, I have to say it's been a lovely afternoon.' And then a memory flashed into my mind. I clapped my hands in front of my face. 'Of course. *Eye in the Sky*!'

'I'm sorry?'

'"*Eye in the Sky*". By the Alan Parsons Project. That's what the pianist was playing outside the café.'

'What on earth is the Alan Parsons Project?'

'Erm, they were an English progressive rock band. You probably don't know them. Maybe you know the song.' I sang a little bit from the chorus.

She put her hands to her face and laughed her silvery laugh. 'You are funny. But you really shouldn't sing.'

'Oh. Not at all?'

'No. Not at all. Never.' Then she leaned over and kissed me on the cheek. 'But you are funny. Before we came in I was feeling stressed. And now I am not so stressed. Goodbye, Mr Sutherland.'

'Call me Nathan. Please.'

'Nathan, then. And you must call me Isotta. Let's keep in touch.'

We stepped out into the cold evening air. I watched her make her way back across the *piazza*, until she was lost in the fog. Then I turned, and headed off in the direction of the Street of the Assassins, and home.

I thought of Federica, sitting at home writing her paper and entertaining an unfriendly cat. This afternoon was going to take a bit of explaining.

Chapter 11

'You look happy,' said Fede. She was still sitting on the sofa where I'd left her that morning, typing away, a half-eaten sandwich on the table.

'I am. Oh, I am,' I said, hanging my coat up and kicking a foam ball across the floor for Gramsci to chase.

'Tell me all about it then.'

'Spritz first?'

'Of course.'

I went out to the kitchen in order to fix the drinks. Gramsci padded along behind me in the hope of food, and mewled until it arrived. The recipe for a good basic spritz was a simple one. Pour white wine for three seconds. Pour Campari for three seconds. Two ice cubes. Top up whatever space remained with sparkling water. There was also the *spritz royale*, which involved replacing white wine with prosecco. I'd improved on it even further by substituting prosecco for the water as well. Spritz Nathan. I took the tumblers through.

'*Cin cin.*' We clinked glasses, and I told her of my meeting with Sergio and Lorenzo, and my visit to the Marciana Library.

'And then?' said Fede.

'And then? I don't understand.'

Fede stared over the rims of her glasses at me. 'Nathan, nobody looks that happy after a meeting with some elderly Marxists and an afternoon in the library.'

'Oh, and *then.*' I blushed. 'Well, I sort of met a celebrity.'

'A celebrity?'

'A real, proper celebrity.' I paused. 'Isotta Baldan.'

'My goodness. Well, I assumed it wasn't Francesco da Mosto. I don't think he'd have made you blush quite so much.'

'I'm not blushing,' I said, blushing.

'Of course not, *cara*. It's probably the spritz.' She drew her legs up under her. 'Go on then. Tell me about your date.'

'It was *not* a date—' And then I stopped, as I could see she was smiling. 'Well, she seemed, you know, normal.'

'Normal?'

'Yes. And, well, nice.'

'Nice?'

'Yes. That's the surprising thing. She's never featured in any top ten lists of nice sopranos. Or people. They say the only reason nobody calls her *Draculetta* is because the name was already taken.'

'Nice and normal then. Well I suppose everybody's a bit easier-going when they're not at work. Is she pretty in real life?'

'Oh, I can't say I really noticed.' Fede reached for one of Gramsci's balls, throwing it at me and pinging it off my nose. 'Ow. Well, yes, she is. Very pretty. Very pretty indeed. Beautiful, you'd have to say.'

'I think I've got the idea, *caro*. So what did she want?'

'Apart from my body?'

'Apart from that.'

'She wanted to talk about Matteo Zambon.' Fede raised an eyebrow. 'The translation work he wanted was in early modern English. Hard to decipher. Even harder if you're not a native speaker. And then she wanted to talk about Claudio Monteverdi and a missing opera I'd never heard of before.'

She nodded. 'Right.' She paused again. 'Matteo Zambon, who was murdered two nights ago.'

'The same.'

'So, what are you going to do?'

'Exactly what I should have done with the Moro case. And the Paul Considine case. I'm going to go to Vanni and tell him everything I know.'

'Everything?'

'Absolutely bloody everything. Somebody might have got himself killed over this already; I'm not going to risk it happening to someone else. Not again. This time I'm going to be sensible.'

She leaned her head on my shoulder. 'Well done, *tesoro*.' She looked down at the remains of her disappointing sandwich. 'Now, I've hardly eaten all day. If you cook me a nice dinner I promise to forget all about your date with the glamorous soprano.'

I grinned. '*Pasta alla Norma*? They're supermarket aubergines, not Italian, but still . . .'

'Suitably operatic, *caro mio*. Suitably operatic.'

Chapter 12

Vanni looked tired, stressed and red-eyed. I knew it must have been something serious as he insisted on meeting at the *Questura* itself instead of at Bar F30.

'Vanni, you look shattered. You look like you've slept in your clothes.'

'Why thank you, Mr Sutherland, but you didn't have to come all this way just to tell me that.'

'I thought you'd like to know about my business card and how Zambon got hold of it.' He nodded, wearily, and I ran him through my little adventure of the previous day.

He scribbled a few notes on a pad, then tore the front page off, brought it up close to his face and reread it. 'That's it?'

'That's it.'

He scrunched the page into a ball, and threw it at the door, from where it bounced into a waste-paper basket.

'Do I take it,' I said, 'that you were hoping for something more?'

He rubbed his eyes, leaned back in his chair and yawned. Then he patted a thick cardboard file on his desk. 'These,' he said, 'are the details of everyone who Zambon owed money to.'

I picked it up, and weighed it in my hands. Substantial. 'Wow,' I said.

'There are a lot of people with a motive. More than is helpful.' Then a thought struck him. 'One of the communists, you say, was paying his rent?'

'Sergio, yes.'

'Surname?'

'Cardazzo.' Then I realised what he was doing. 'Hang on, Vanni, Sergio won't have had anything to do with this.'

'I'm sure he didn't, Nathan, but his name's going on the list anyway.'

'No, this isn't fair. You can't do this.'

'Yes I can.' He licked his pencil, scribbled away on a piece of paper, and filed it away.

I glared at him. 'That's not on, Vanni. I'm here to help, remember?'

'I know. And I'm sorry.'

'So what about Isotta Baldan. And Monteverdi?'

'What about them?'

'You don't think they're connected?'

He sighed. 'It's not impossible. But there are so many people with a motive. People who also have the advantage of still being alive. I think we're going to check them out first before we start looking at Ms Baldan.'

'Okay. So you think I should just let it go?'

'I don't understand.'

'The whole translation thing. It's not as if I'm likely to get paid, after all.'

'No, no.' He paused, tapping his pencil on the table. 'No. I think you should do it. Just in case. It'll be something that I don't need to look into.'

'No problem. You never know, it might be interesting. Maybe we'll even find something?' Then a thought struck me, and I smiled. 'Hey. Does this mean I'm working undercover?'

Vanni stopped tapping his pencil and glared at me. 'No.'

'Oh. Don't I get a badge?'

'You do not get a badge.'

'Or a gun?'

'And you most certainly do not get a gun.'

'No badge, no gun. I have to say police work isn't what I was expecting.'

Vanni breathed out heavily, and opened his mouth to speak. Then he saw the expression on my face and shut it again.

'Vanni, you're knackered. Come on. Let's at least go for a coffee on the corner, eh?' I checked my watch. 'I'll buy you breakfast.'

He nodded, and forced a smile on to his face. 'Thanks Nathan. Let's do that.'

Vanni drank a double espresso, and emptied two sachets of sugar into it. I made him eat a brioche, in the hope that the sugar rush would at least keep him going for the next couple of hours. Then I made my way home via the Rialto market, where I picked up two *passarini* – Venetian flounder – for dinner.

Federica was out, having some research to do at the Querini Stampalia. I checked the fridge, to make sure I had everything for that evening. *Passarini* in a breadcrumb and parmesan crust, with radicchio in an orange and walnut dressing. I liked Saturdays. They gave me time to properly mess around in the kitchen.

I'd recently stepped my number of weekly surgeries up from two to three sessions a week. There was a reason for that. Brexit was proving very good for business. Every week worried expats would make an appointment, and sit in front of me hoping that I'd tell them that everything was going to be all right. Which I did. I did not, of course, know this for sure. Nobody did. In spite of all my reassurances, I knew full well that nobody really knew what was going on.

It also brought me a steady stream of clients wanting documents to be translated as they set out on the two-year process of acquiring Italian citizenship. I both appreciated and hated the extra work, profiting as I was from other people's fears. In an attempt to justify it, I told myself that if I didn't do it someone else would, and at least I would do a professional job.

But Saturdays, as they should be, were a day off. I went through my record collection. There was really only one choice. *Poppea*, of course, Thomas Joshua Lockwood's recording from 2012, with Isotta Baldan in the title role. I was sure by now that I was never going to see her live on stage, and so this was the next best thing. That was okay. After all, there probably weren't that many people who could say they'd had a spritz with her.

I slid the CD into the player, then stretched out on the sofa and closed my eyes. I heard the scrabbling of claws against fabric. I opened them again. Gramsci was perched on the back of the sofa looking down at me. I knew where this was heading. He'd lurk there in the hope that I'd fall asleep, in order to jump down on top of me, with hilarious consequences. I stretched up a hand and tried to lift him down. He miaowed furiously, his claws sunk in to the fabric.

I gave up. Let him do his worst. I closed my eyes, and listened to Virtue, Fortune and Love arguing amongst themselves, as I had done at La Fenice three nights previously. Federica wouldn't be back until early evening. I'd listen to the first act, then go down to the Brazilians for a spritz and sandwich lunch. Then back up to listen to the rest of *Poppea*, and there'd probably even be time for a snooze before I had to start on cooking dinner. I realised I hadn't bought anything for Sunday. No matter. There was probably something in the fridge that I could improvise with. And there was always pizza for emergencies.

The entryphone buzzed just as I was dropping off. I yawned and got to my feet.

'Hello?' I always answered in English just in case it turned out to be somebody with an emergency problem for the honorary consul.

'Mr Sutherland? My name is Lockwood. Can I come up?'

'Mr Lockwood.' I raised an eyebrow. 'Of course.' I buzzed him up.

I looked across to the sofa where Gramsci was curled up on my seat. 'Well now, puss. We've got an important guest. So best behaviour, eh?' I wondered if I should switch the music off, and settled for turning the volume down.

I held the door open for Lockwood as he made his way up the stairs. He was wearing a *tabarro*, the Venetian one-piece cloak, and an astrakhan hat. It would have been a most elegant look were it not for the fact that his glasses were fogged

up, giving him a slightly comic appearance. He also, I could
not help but notice, had a large Alsatian on a lead.

'Mr Sutherland?'

'That's me. I'm delighted to meet you, sir. And, er?' I
indicated the dog.

He smiled. 'Call me Thomas, please. And this is Karajan.
Do you mind if I bring him in? It's a foul day out there.'

'Is he good with cats?'

'Oh he loves them.' He suddenly recognised the back-
ground music, and nodded and smiled at me. 'One of mine.'

'I really was listening to it. I promise I didn't just put it on
to impress you.' We both laughed. 'Can I take your cloak?'

'Thank you.' He unwound his *tabarro* and handed it to
me. I felt the weight of it as I hung it up. Good material.
Expensive. He passed me his hat. A Borsalino, like Vanni's. I
popped it on top of the coat stand.

Gramsci padded in and looked us all up and down. He
made his way over to the coat stand, and stared at Lockwood's
tabarro, hanging just within reach. He crouched down, his
muscles rippling, preparing himself for a jump.

Karajan gave a long, low, rumbling growl.

Gramsci froze, as if noticing the large dog for the first
time. His eyes flicked one way and the other, sizing him up,
calculating his chances. Then he stretched himself to his full
height and hissed.

Karajan continued to growl as Gramsci, slowly and
deliberately, padded backwards until he reached the bottom
of the bookcase. He turned, just for a moment, to sit back
on his haunches and size up the distance. Then, with one
leap, he was on top, setting it rocking. I hurried over to

steady it with my hand. Gramsci looked down on us, hissed balefully, and then lay down, turning his back on us in contempt.

'Right. Well, come through to the office, please. And perhaps you might like to bring Karajan too. Can I get you a coffee?'

'That'd be nice.' I slipped a capsule into the machine and it hummed away. He nodded approvingly. 'Marvellous things, aren't they? I'd love one myself but Isotta simply won't have one in the house. Says they're *una bestemmia,* a blasphemy against proper coffee, and only a Moka will do.'

'Isotta?' I kept my face straight. I hadn't known.

'Yes. You've met her, of course.'

'Just yesterday.'

'You made quite an impression on her.'

'I'm flattered.' Then a thought struck me. 'Oh dear. I hope it wasn't the singing.'

Lockwood chuckled. 'No no. Although she did tell me about it.' He sipped at his coffee and gave a contented little sigh. I found it hard to reconcile the amiable figure in front of me with the one who had pushed past me brusquely outside a concert hall in Cardiff over twenty years ago. But then, I thought, two decades could change a man.

'I hope it's not consular business, Mr Lockwood – Thomas. I mean, I hope you've not been robbed or lost your passport or anything similar?'

'Nothing like that. No, this is more of a social call. I was wondering – we were wondering – if you might like to come for dinner tomorrow?'

'My goodness. Well I have to say I wasn't expecting that.

But I'd be delighted. We'd be delighted. That is, if I can bring my partner?'

'Of course you must. I'm not much of a cook I'm afraid, but Isotta really is a little marvel. She did ask me to check if there's anything you don't eat.'

'We eat anything and everything. Apart from oysters. Oysters might actually kill me.'

He chuckled again. 'Well, we wouldn't want that. It's, I suppose, a sort of housewarming party. Wouldn't do to kill one of the guests, would it? Might cast a bit of a shadow over things. No oysters it is, then.'

'That's kind of you. Everything else is non-lethal. A house-warming, you said?'

'That's right.' I could tell he was waiting for me to ask him where. It would, of course, be somewhere on the Grand Canal.

'*Canal Grande*?' I smiled.

He looked taken aback, and a little displeased. 'Good heavens, no. No, I need somewhere much quieter.' He paused, for emphasis. 'Torcello.'

'Seriously?'

'Seriously.' He was smiling again now. 'We have a small property there, and I received official residency here just a couple of days ago. The idea is to live there full-time once it's been fixed up a bit, and a few other things sorted out.'

'Well congratulations, but why Torcello? Isn't it a bit remote? I mean, it's the very end of the line.'

'And that will suit us just fine. Time and space to write and compose. And as for the touring, well, much of the time one's living out of a suitcase anyway. I need somewhere to call home and Torcello suits me just as well as London ever would.'

I wondered if the loneliest island in the Venetian lagoon, an island that until two days ago had an official population of twelve, would be quite the place for Isotta Baldan but that, of course, was something to keep to myself. 'Well, thank you very much, Thomas, we'd be honoured,' I said. 'What time would you like us to come?'

'Oh, come mid-afternoon. The weather's supposed to be fine and we can have a proper stroll around. It'll be good to get away from all the hurly-burly in town. And do please stay over, we have a couple of spare rooms and I'm assured they're quite liveable now.'

'Are you sure?'

'Absolutely sure. Otherwise you'll have to catch a night boat home and you won't get back until the small hours. No, I won't hear of it. We'd be delighted if you could stay.'

'Well, likewise. Thank you very much, *maestro*.' He waved his finger in mock admonishment, but I could tell he was secretly pleased by the use of the honorific.

He took out his card and passed it to me. 'Please telephone me when you arrive and I'll come out and meet you. Torcello's not all that big, as you know, and there aren't that many buildings still standing, but it's still possible to get lost. I've managed it myself a few times.'

'I'll do that.' I looked at the card. 'Two addresses?'

'We have a place just off the Zattere. Just until everything is shipshape on Torcello.'

I assumed our conversation was over, and got to my feet but he showed no sign of getting up. I felt embarrassed and immediately tried to change the movement into something other than a hint that he should leave. I clicked my fingers. 'Sorry. Just excuse me one moment.' I went into the living room and returned with the *Poppea* recording. 'I wonder if you might sign this for me.'

He smiled. 'I'd be delighted.' He jiggled the insert out of the jewel case, and reached for the pen on my desk. His hand paused. 'May I?'

'Of course.'

He took it and wrote his name across the cover. His writing was taut, controlled, elegant. Like his conducting. He re-inserted the cover, taking care not to snag or rumple the edges, and passed it back to me. 'Bring it along tomorrow. I'll get Isotta to sign it as well.'

'Thanks.' I nodded towards the living room. 'I've got more you know. Recordings.'

'Bring them along as well.' He paused. 'How many? I have made rather a lot.'

'A lot.'

He chuckled. 'Okay, well maybe not all of them.' He got to his feet. 'We'll see you both tomorrow.'

'Should I bring anything?'

'Only yourselves.' He got to his feet and we shook hands. We walked to the stairs, where both he and Karajan paused to look up at the top of the bookcase. 'Perhaps not your lovely cat though, if that's not a problem?'

'No problem. He's not a good traveller.' I shook my head at the memories. 'Are you, Grams?'

Gramsci continued his silent protest. I would, I knew, pay for this later.

Lockwood threw his *tabarro* around himself and adjusted his hat. Then he turned and smiled at me. 'By the way. I should just say one thing. Do be ready to do some work.'

'I'm sorry? Oh, is it one of those parties where we all help to redecorate and then end up drinking champagne and eating fish and chips from the paper?'

'Nothing like that. Nothing like that at all.' He smiled once again, and clapped me on the shoulder. 'We're going on a treasure hunt, Mr Sutherland.'

Chapter 13

'So how about that, then?' I said. 'Don't say I never take you anywhere.'

'Okay then, you never *used* to take me anywhere.'

'Hmm. Okay. Harsh but possibly fair.'

'I mean, when you said I needed to pack for tomorrow night, I thought perhaps we were going to the mountains. And then when you said we were going to Torcello, I thought what a lucky girl I must be if my lovely boyfriend is taking me to the Locanda Cipriani.'

'Sorry, *cara*, not this year. Maybe next birthday. Erm, when is your birthday again?'

'Next month.'

'Okay. Well, maybe the birthday after next. But still, it's a personal invitation from one of the most renowned conductors of his generation and his glamorous partner.'

'Yes. I was thinking about that. Pass me that CD, would you?' I passed the *Poppea* recording over to her. She dug her nails under the booklet in order to drag it out and I could see the edges starting to catch.

'Careful!'

'I'm being careful. There we are.' She flicked through it and stopped when she came to a black and white photograph of Baldan. 'She really is quite beautiful, isn't she?' I opened my mouth to speak. 'You don't have to answer that.' She turned to another page, and a picture of Lockwood. Slightly heavy features, with thick-rimmed glasses and a shock of curly white hair. She turned back to the photograph of Baldan, and then back to the one of Lockwood.

I could tell what she was thinking. 'That recording was made back in 2012. He looks a fair bit older now.'

'Mmm. I wonder what's going on there?'

'Well, he's a brilliant man. You know what they say. Smart is sexy.'

'No one's that smart.'

'Oh, what a cynic the lovely Federica Ravagnan is. Baldan's probably got more money than he has. After all, Thomas Joshua Lockwood never gets asked to advertise expensive watches.'

'What's this treasure hunt all about then?'

'Isotta mentioned a missing work by Monteverdi. I think they're trying to find it.'

'Seriously?'

I shrugged. 'It's possible. Or at least it's not impossible. It could be lying on a shelf in an archive, unlabelled and over-looked. Somewhere in Venice, or Mantua or Cremona. Just waiting to be discovered. The trouble is it would take almost infinite patience and time.' I got to my feet. 'Right, I've got flounders to fillet.'

She nodded in the direction of the kitchen. 'Spritz first?'

A mewl came from behind the sofa. 'Only if you entertain Gramsci.' She was about to protest but I waved my hand. 'You know the deal.'

'Hmmphh.'

I fixed two spritzes, and took one through to Federica, who was throwing foam balls for an indifferent Gramsci.

'How long do I have to keep doing this?'

'Until he gets bored.'

'He's bored now.'

'No he isn't.' She stopped throwing and retrieving. Ten seconds passed. Gramsci started mewling and scratching at the sofa. 'You see?'

'But he wasn't doing anything.'

'Yes he was. He was watching you throwing things and having to bend down to pick them up. In his malevolent little mind that constitutes playing.'

I went back to the kitchen before she could protest further. Then I took my two sharpest knives and turned to the two large, plump *passarini* in the fridge. They always looked so beautiful on the fishmonger's slab, and then you filleted them and realised they flattered to deceive in terms of how much edible fish there actually was. No matter. Breadcrumbs and parmesan had been invented in order to bulk out disappointing cuts of meat and fillets of fish. I put them on to fry in some olive oil and butter, whilst I shredded a head of radicchio, threw in some chopped walnuts and tossed it all with some olive oil and freshly squeezed orange.

Fede came through and poured herself a glass of wine. She looked at the fish frying away, and put her arms around me. 'Lovely.'

'I hope so. They're a bit small.'

'That's why people don't eat them so much these days. It doesn't matter. I wonder what we'll get tomorrow?'

'Anything except oysters. Isotta's a little marvel, apparently.'

She frowned. 'A *little marvel?*'

'I think Lockwood's a bit old-fashioned.'

'Evidently. So, do you think he's really found something?'

'Searching every archive in the north of Italy. And beyond.' I shook my head. 'Impossible. But if he had . . .'

'Do you think we'd get a credit?'

'*Proserpina Rapita*. The Sutherland–Ravagnan edition. I like that.'

'Perhaps so. Or the Ravagnan–Sutherland edition. I like that more.'

Chapter 14

It's no great distance from Venice's *centro storico* to Torcello.
At least, not as the crow flies. The problem is, the crows
aren't getting you there. ACTV are. At this time of year
there was no direct service in the afternoon, which meant
the only route was to get a boat from Fondamente Nove to
Burano, and then change to cross the short stretch of lagoon
to Torcello. A slightly frustrating journey which went some
way to explaining why – until the arrival of Lockwood and
Baldan – the population of the island had been in decline for
approximately one thousand years.

We trudged up to Fondamente Nove, both of us wrapped
up against the cold and the damp of the thick fog that was
descending on the city. The masked revellers in Piazza San
Marco would hardly be able to make each other out. Come
the summer months the boat to Burano would be full to
bursting with tourists making their way out to the prettiest
island in the lagoon. Even on weekdays, schoolchildren – with
no *scuola superiore* to go to on their home island – would add
to the numbers. But on a cold and foggy Sunday afternoon,
the numbers were more manageable. We even managed to get

a seat together. Federica dozed over the paper, until I gave her a gentle prod as we approached Burano.

It had been years since I'd been out there. Four years, almost to the day. Jean had taken me out there for dinner on my birthday, in the last year of our marriage. I'd eaten the best sardines of my life at Il Gatto Nero, as we chatted to a friendly waiter who'd learned his English in Leith. And then we got the boat home together and hardly spoke. Not because we were angry, but simply because we were running out of things to say to each other.

Fede rubbed the sleep from her eyes as we alighted and made our way along the *fondamenta* to the stop for the boat to Torcello. A fine grey mist hung over the lagoon, but even that wasn't enough to detract from the brightly coloured houses along the way.

We waited perhaps ten minutes until the *vaporetto* arrived to take us the short distance to Torcello, where a few of us disembarked, the other passengers waiting for the boat to turn around and make its way back to the *centro storico*.

Two nuns chatted to each other as they made their way to the canal path that ran through the centre of the island. A venerable priest stood trying and failing to light his pipe, until I offered him a lighter and he nodded in gratitude. The other passenger was an elderly man in an ankle-length coat, looking around as if unsure exactly where to go. Strange, given that on Torcello there was only one direction in which to go. Undoubtedly a tourist, I thought to myself, given the inadvisability of wearing a long coat in the season for *acqua alta*.

Federica yawned and patted my arm. 'Are you going to call your friend then?'

I nodded, and took out my phone. Fede had decided that it was finally time for me to enter the twenty-first century, and so had bought me a cheap smartphone for Christmas. I missed my faithful old Nokia, but had to admit I was finding it convenient.

'Call Lockwood,' I said.

Federica nudged me. 'Don't do that,' she said.

I didn't have time to reply before Lockwood spoke. 'Mr Sutherland?'

'Nathan, please.'

'You've just arrived?'

'We're at the *vaporetto* stop. Do you want to give us directions?'

'No need. Why don't you meet us at the basilica? Impossible to get lost then.'

He was right. There was only one proper route across Torcello, the one that followed the path of the canal and led to all that remained of the centre of a town that had once held twenty thousand people.

'Great. See you there,' I hung up. 'Don't do what?' I said to Federica.

'Don't do that "call Lockwood" thing.'

'But it's part of what the phone does. I thought you wanted me to get up to date with all this stuff?'

'Yes, but that sort of thing is just for young people. If you're over thirty you look like a mad person.'

'Oh. All right. Let's go.'

'Do you mind if I tag along?' The speaker was the man in the long coat. He laid his hand on my arm. 'I couldn't help over-hearing. You're here to meet Tom Lockwood, I understand.'

'That's right.'

'Splendid. So am I.' He had a mellifluous, light-baritone voice which made me think he was probably a good singer. 'I'm afraid I really don't know the way so I'd be ever so grateful if you could chum me.'

I smiled at him. 'Well, if you're heading for the basilica it's pretty much impossible to get lost. But, yes, of course we'll chum you.' He had, I noticed, a slight limp and walked with a stick, so Federica and I slowed our pace. The elderly priest, by contrast, stepped it out surprisingly quickly and was soon lost from sight.

We made our way along the canal path. Torcello never became as choked with visitors as the *centro storico*, but in the height of summer there would be a line of boats along the canal with people picnicking and enjoying the sunshine away from the clamour of the city centre. Today, there were a bare half-dozen *motoscafi* gently rocking in the swell, the lapping of waves being the only sound apart from that of our footsteps.

'Not like the centre of town, is it?' said our new companion. 'Every last canal there seems to be lined with boats. I wonder how difficult it is to get a mooring?'

'The last I heard, the going rate for a bribe to get on the waiting list was about a thousand euros, depending on the degree of urgency,' I said.

He chuckled. 'I think you're teasing me, Mr Sutherland.'

I wondered how he knew my name, but let it pass. 'I am. But only a bit. It might be more like fifteen hundred now, Mr—'

'Maitland.' He didn't offer a first name.

'Pleased to meet you. This is *dottoressa* Federica Ravagnan.'

'Pleased to meet you.' He touched the brim of his hat, and Federica smiled at him. 'It's so quiet here,' he continued. 'Makes one want to whisper the whole time. There's not even any birdsong.'

'I think that's because Hemingway shot them all,' said Fede.

Torcello had a regular busker, of modest and non-distressing quality, who plied his trade in the spring and summer. However, realising that earnings would be thin in the cold winter months, he had taken his trade elsewhere. The restaurants alongside the canal remained open, more in hope, perhaps, than expectation. I pointed one of them out to Maitland. 'Best fried fish in the city.'

He smiled, politely, then pointed to a low stone bridge just ahead of us. 'Rather a strange-looking one. No parapets.'

'That's the *ponte del diavolo*,' said Federica. 'Probably named after a family with the surname Diavoli. Or at least that's one explanation.'

'The other being?'

'That it is what it is. The Devil's Bridge.' She lowered her voice to add drama. 'A young woman, they say, made a pact with a witch. Her lover was a young man in the Austrian army, killed in action. The witch said she would make a deal with Satan to bring him back to life, but the price would be the souls of seven Christian children who would be brought to him at midnight on Christmas Eve.'

'My goodness. This does sound rather grim. I hope there was a happy ending.'

'Of a sort. A young man heard the witch bargaining with the Devil. He was, of course, appalled at what he heard so he followed her home and killed her before she could start procuring children. But the Devil never knew that. So, every Christmas Eve he sits and waits for the witch to arrive, in the form of a great black cat.'

Maitland gave a mock shudder. 'Marvellous. Although I'd expected something rather grander from something called the Devil's Bridge.'

We made our way onwards until we reached what had once been the centre of town. The decline of Venice was as nothing compared to this remote island that had once been richer and more powerful than La Serenissima itself. One day the plague had arrived. And then it returned. And returned once more. And as the swamp area around the island increased and the number of malarial mosquitos grew, the population wearily made their way to the other islands, stripping Torcello of any building material that might prove useful.

The island now lay in the area known as the Dead Lagoon. It would be incorrect, however, to describe it as a ghost town. There were always visitors in the daytime so, even here, there was need for a kiosk selling drinks and refreshments, and the stray cats that inhabited a ramshackle sanctuary made out of cardboard boxes always looked well fed.

A melancholy air hung over the place, especially on a cold grey day. Maybe it was the absurdity of an island where the population was almost reduced to single figures – and where humans were outnumbered by felines – boasting a cathedral, a parish church and associated priest, and a civic museum. Perhaps it was also the fact that the island served as a silent, mournful *memento mori* to Venice itself. Remember that you too must die.

'What's that?' Maitland twitched his thumb in the direction of something that resembled a great stone armchair.

'That, Mr Maitland, is the Throne of Attila,' said Federica.

He looked it up and down, but I could tell he wasn't impressed. Or, perhaps, he was just making a show of being unimpressed. 'Bit like the Devil's Bridge, eh? I'd have expected something a bit more from Attila the Hun.'

Federica shrugged. 'Well, it probably wasn't his. Attila never made it this far. It's more likely to be the bishop's chair. Or perhaps where magistrates were inaugurated. No one knows for sure.'

A fine drizzle was falling now. Outside the church of Santa Fosca, the elderly priest was, again, trying to light his pipe. He looked at me, and smiled hopefully.

'One moment.' I gave Fede a quick pat on the arm and hurried over to him. I took out my lighter. 'Here you are. *padre.*'

He puffed away, shielding the bowl of the pipe from the light rain as best he could, until it was lit. 'Thank you.'

'No problem.'

'I'm always forgetting them, you know. Lighters, matches, all that sort of thing. I'm not supposed to smoke inside any more. So they tell me.' He checked his watch. 'Five minutes until Vespers.'

I looked around. I saw no sign of a steady stream of parishioners making their way to Mass. He caught my expression and smiled again. 'Just me, Sister Assunta and Sister Magdalena.' The two nuns from the boat. 'Not bad for a wet Sunday in February.'

'It isn't?'

'Oh no. Sometimes I've said Mass to an empty church.'

'I'm sorry.'

'Don't be. You're welcome to join us, you know?'

'Ah. Well, I would, but I'm with my friends and we're supposed to be meeting someone and—'

'I'm teasing, *signore*.'

'Oh. Oh, I see. But we really are meeting people. Perhaps you've heard of them. An English conductor and a Venetian singer. She's quite famous.'

'Isotta Baldan.' He gave a gentle, rumbly smoker's cough sending up a plume of blue smoke.

'You know her?'

'*La Baldan*. I know her. I baptised her.'

'You *baptised* her?'

He nodded. 'I think it was the last baptism I did here. Which would make it the last one on Torcello. I think that was the last time she ever came to church.' He shook his head, and chuckled. 'She lived here as a child, you know?'

'I think she might be moving back. Perhaps she'll become a regular here?'

'And increase the congregation by 50 per cent. Perhaps. We can dream.'

'Nathan?' It was Federica, calling to me. I looked over to them, and then ran my hand through my hair. It was starting to properly rain now.

'Sorry!' I called back. I turned to my new friend. 'I'm sorry, *padre*, but I think I need to go.'

He nodded, and smiled. 'Remember me to Isotta. Tell her Don Andrea was asking after her.' I gave him a wave, then ran over to Federica and Maitland.

'Thinking about converting?'

'Not exactly. Just felt a bit sorry for him. It must be a thankless job on a day like this.' I looked up at the slate-grey sky. 'Come on, let's get under cover. Before the heavens properly open.'

There was usually a manned cash desk for visitors to the basilica, but whoever was in charge had given up and gone home for the day. Only about thirty minutes of daylight remained, and anyone arriving now would not really be seeing the interior at its best.

We made our way inside, where the atmosphere immediately felt warmer and damper, perhaps a result of the electric lamplight reflecting off the great, golden mosaics. Our breath steamed in the damp air. Federica did a couple of little jumps, trying to get some warmth back into her feet, as Maitland ran his hands through his thinning hair, and looked around, awestruck. There was no attempt now at a studied insouciance. Fede smiled, partly in satisfaction that Maitland had nothing disparaging to say, but more, I thought, from the sheer pleasure of seeing someone experiencing the Basilica for the first time.

A church had stood on this site since the seventh century, and been hurriedly remodelled in anticipation of the end of the world in the year 1000. The apocalypse had yet to arrive, but the entire west wall, given over to a mosaic of the Last Judgement, gave a flavour of what it might be like.

At the top of the wall, Christ sat in judgement as the souls of the departed were weighed. Those that were found wanting were prodded downwards into a river of fire by a group of sorrowful-looking angels, to where an infant Antichrist, sitting on Satan's knee, ushered the damned into hell, with the merest ghost of a smile upon his lips. A hell of fire, disembodied limbs and grinning worm-eaten skulls.

For over one thousand years, this had been the last thing seen by the faithful making their way out of church. A warning. Think on this and be afraid.

The Doomsday Mosaic.

Chapter 15

Maitland shook his head in wonder. Despite the horrors being depicted, a broad smile broke across his face. Federica walked up to him and gently put her hand on his shoulder.

'First time?' she said. He nodded. 'Lucky you.'

'It's quite something, isn't it? I mean, I think I've been to almost every church in Venice but this – this is something special.'

'The Greeks made it, some say. We'll probably never know. Not for certain. But for me, this is the equal of anything in San Marco. Although we're looking the wrong way.'

'I don't understand.'

'We're looking the wrong way. Turn around.' She gently steered him through one hundred and eighty degrees. 'The Doomsday Mosaic is all very fine. But the real masterpiece is over there.' She gestured towards the great, golden dome of the apse, at the base of which were mosaics of the apostles. Above them, isolated in the middle of that glorious, shining hemisphere, was the attenuated figure of the Virgin, holding the Christ child.

'The Virgin *Theotokos*. The *Dei Genetrix*. The God-bearer.'

A tall, thin young woman, alone except for her child.

Staring out at the viewer with a look of barely controllable pain. If the Doomsday Mosaic was all violence and action, this was all silence and stillness. The effect, in its own way, was just as powerful.

Maitland clasped his hands together. 'It's so beautiful. So, so beautiful,' he whispered.

'It is, isn't it?' The voice came from behind the rood screen that separated us from the chancel. I gave a little start, but I recognised the voice. 'I heard you come in. I didn't like to interrupt. It's a special thing, after all, to see it for the first time. Don't you agree, Nathan?'

'Isotta?' We walked down the main aisle and under the rood screen. The area behind the altar was built up of brick steps in a semi-circular pattern that resembled an amphitheatre. Baldan was seated halfway up, her arms resting on the steps next to her. The pose gave her a regal appearance, accentuated by her long dark-blue fur coat, trimmed with white. Almost as resplendent as the Queen of Heaven above her.

'Hello, Nathan.' She waited for a few moments, as if giving us all time to appreciate the effort she'd put in, before rising and making her way, carefully, down the stone steps. She kissed me on both cheeks and then turned to Fede.

'Federica Ravagnan.'

'*Piacere.*' She kissed her. Then she turned to Maitland, and frowned, just ever so slightly. 'I didn't know we were expecting three of you?'

'My name's Maitland. Christopher Maitland. I'm a friend of Tom's.'

'Tom? Oh, *Thomas.*' She paused. 'I'm so sorry, but he must have forgotten to mention you.'

'Well, he certainly is a friend of mine. And he's here at my request.' Lockwood's voice came booming out from the front of the church, and we turned to see him, standing at the base of the Doomsday Mosaic. He made his way forward, grinning with pleasure, and threw his arms wide.

'Christopher. My dear fellow.'

'Tom. How wonderful to see you again.'

The two men hugged each other. 'I'm so sorry, darling,' said Lockwood, turning to Baldan. 'I should have said something. It's supposed to be a surprise. Only Christopher here is going to be of absolutely invaluable help on our little treasure hunt.'

'Treasure hunt? You're being more mysterious than usual, Tom.'

'I am, aren't I?' Lockwood clapped him on the back. 'You'll find out though, soon enough. Well, come on everybody, let's get going. I know this is all rather lovely but it'll still be here in the morning and there's lots to talk about.' He linked his arm with Isotta's, and steered her down the aisle towards the exit.

Her face was expressionless. 'Oh, I know what you're thinking, darling, but we've got plenty of space and I've made up a bed for Christopher so you don't need to worry about that.'

'And dinner?' Her voice was flat, controlled.

'Ah. Well, I confess I hadn't thought about that. But I'm sure you'll manage admirably.' He turned to look back at us. 'She's a marvel in the kitchen you know. An absolute little marvel.' Baldan refused to look at us, and turned to make her way back down the aisle, her heels clacking on the mosaicked floor. Lockwood, still clutching her arm, had to step it out to keep up with her, as did Maitland.

Federica leaned in to me and whispered in my ear. 'This could be a long night.' I nodded. The same thought had occurred to me.

Lockwood paused to untie Karajan, whose lead was fastened to a fence. Maitland bent over and made to scratch him behind the ears. Karajan growled, and Maitland thought better of it.

We made our way back along the path, the bells of Santa Fosca ringing to summon a faithful flock that would never arrive. It had almost stopped raining now, little more than a fine, damp air that clung to our faces. Lockwood explained the story of the Devil's Bridge to Maitland, who nodded and clapped his friend on the shoulder as if he were hearing the story for the first time.

Just after the bridge, we turned right and started to make our way along a path that led through open fields. Federica stopped, and took my arm. She pulled me around, and I followed her gaze. A great, black cat was sitting at the base of the bridge. It stared at us for a moment before scurrying across it and into the trees.

'He's turned up early this year,' she said.

The trail led for perhaps half a kilometre along a narrow but paved road that cut its way through marshland. The air was chilly, and the fog growing thicker. I was grateful that Lockwood had not chosen to invite us in the height of summer, when the fields would be swarming with mosquitoes.

We passed through a rusty iron gate. The path now was

no longer paved, but muddy underfoot, and lined by a few scrubby trees, and led to a two-storey house of dark stone, silhouetted against the grey sky.

Maitland, Lockwood and Baldan stood outside the front door as Isotta fumbled in her bag for a key. Then she opened the door, pushed it open and paused on the threshold. She smiled one of her glittering smiles.

'Welcome to my home,' she said.

'And leave something of the happiness you bring,' I whispered to Federica.

'What's that?' she asked.

'It's from *Dracula*.'

She giggled and dug me in the ribs, but Isotta did not appear to have noticed. We made our way inside – the door-knocker, I could not help but notice, was in the shape of a skeletal hand – and I closed the door behind us, grateful to be out of the cold and the damp.

The ground floor was one great, open space dominated by an enormous dining table, with a kitchen area against the rear wall. To our right, two swords were crossed above an ornate fireplace, the mantelpiece supported by two slightly camp-looking loinclothed figures, with a bas-relief of two horn-playing angels on the overmantel. The effect was somewhat diminished by the four-bar electric fire that sat in the grate but even on Torcello real fires had long since been outlawed. To our left, a stone staircase led to an upper gallery.

I gave a low whistle of appreciation although, as my breath steamed in the air, I was struck by the thought that it must be an absolute bugger to keep warm. Isotta smiled at me, as if she knew what I was thinking. 'It does take a little time to warm up at this time of year.' She reached into her bag and pulled out a Thermos. 'But I've come prepared. I think some hot chocolate will help.'

'She really does think of everything,' Lockwood chuckled.

Isotta reached into a cupboard above the oven and took down five mugs. Then she stood on tiptoe to peer further inside, and frowned. 'Almost everything. I thought we had some brandy. It will have to be grappa.'

'Even better,' I said.

Isotta poured out five mugs of hot chocolate and topped them up from a bottle that, from what I could see, did not contain the sort of grappa one bought at Spar or Conad. Federica held up her hand just in time. 'Not for me,' she said.

'You don't like it?'

'Hot chocolate, yes. Grappa, no. It's the work of the devil.'

'I understand.' Isotta smiled. 'And perhaps we've seen quite enough of his work today already.'

'Immortal souls and all that,' chuckled Lockwood, who appeared to be overflowing with good humour. I found it hard to reconcile the cuddly, jovial and well-padded figure before me with the ascetic figure of legend, who'd struck terror into the hearts of half the musicians in Europe, and not a few of the audiences.

'I'm prepared to risk it,' I said, and we laughed as we clinked mugs. The heat was starting to bring some feeling back into my hands. I took a sip and felt the warmth flooding back into me, and the gentle buzz of the alcohol in my brain.

The door rattled, for an instant. Isotta smiled again. 'It's the wind across the lagoon. Everything is so flat here. And nothing in this house quite fits properly. Not any more. It is all, you might say, a work in progress.'

We finished our hot chocolate. 'Christopher, you're down here tonight,' said Lockwood. 'You've got the smallest room, I'm afraid, but it should be quite comfortable enough.'

'I'm sure it will be, Tom. And then we must have a proper talk.'

'After dinner, old chum. After dinner.'

'Federica, Nathan. If you'd like to follow me, I'll show you to your room,' said Isotta. 'Do be careful on the stairs, they are treacherous.' I could see what she meant. There was no bannister. She led us to the upstairs gallery and along the landing, from which we could look down into the great hall below. Lockwood and Maitland were still chatting animatedly. Isotta gave a little sigh.

'Darling?'

'Yes, my love?' He looked up.

'Do take Mr Maitland's bag into his room, please. And show him where everything is.'

'Of course. Of course.' He patted Maitland on the back. 'Come on, old chap, let's get everything cleared away, eh?'

Isotta shook her head, and muttered under her breath. Then she looked back at us and the smile returned as if it could be turned on at will. 'Come. Please.'

Federica reached over and touched her shoulder. 'I'm sorry. Just one moment.' She was staring at a picture on the wall. 'Is that what I think it is?'

The entrance to the Grand Canal. A view I'd seen a thousand times, both in real life and in art. Gondolas and *traghetti* working the area outside the Church of the Salute. I looked at the tiny figures on the *fondamenta*, and on board the boats. Surely not? Only one Venetian artist had ever painted such perfectly characterised little miniatures.

'Giovanni Antonio Canal.' Isotta put her arm around Federica's shoulders. 'Canaletto.'

'It's original, isn't it?' said Fede.

Isotta nodded. 'Of course. It was the most precious thing my family owned. Even more than this house.'

I gave a long, low whistle. 'Impressive.'

'If you stand further back you'll get a better view of it.'

I stood back, and placed my hand upon the balustrade. It moved, a little more than I'd have liked. I blanched, and moved away from it. 'Some other time,' I said.

She saw the expression on my face, and smiled again. 'We must get it moved,' she said, 'or perhaps it's easier to fix the railing. Dear Thomas isn't very practical, though.'

She moved along the corridor without glancing back at us. I gave the balustrade another experimental shake and shuddered when it trembled under my hand.

Isotta led us into a small bedroom dominated by a four-poster bed that would take some dedicated choreography for us to make our way around without getting in each other's way. A plain wooden chest lay at the end of the bed, with a single wardrobe painted in a floral pattern tucked away in a corner. A small table supported a plain bedside lamp and a photograph in a frame. There was nothing special about it, but somehow it caught my eye. I picked it up. Just a faded Polaroid in a nondescript frame. A strikingly beautiful woman with bright red hair and a simple domino mask, smiling, in front of the Basilica of San Marco. I looked from the photograph to Isotta and back again.

She nodded. 'My mother.'

'I can see the resemblance.'

'I never had such lovely hair, though. That always made me sad. This was taken during *Carnevale* in 1987. I would have been ten years old. In those days it was still for the Venetians. Just about. Mother would tell me how people would meet in the *piazza*, masked and costumed, and eat and drink and sing the old songs. And now . . . *pffft*.' She sounded sad, rather than angry. 'She died, I think, just two years after this photograph was taken. I was still very young.'

'I'm sorry.'

She shrugged, but traced her fingers over her mother's face. 'I should put this back in my room though. I found it only the other day. When we were unpacking.'

'Isotta,' Fede's voice was hesitant. 'You said something about the painting. About how it was the most precious thing your family had owned. Even more than the house.' Isotta nodded. 'Can I ask what happened?'

'Of course. We lost the house after *Mamma* died. My father took it badly. We moved away. Out to the Lido. I was never happy there. When you grow up somewhere without traffic, it's hard to change.'

'Your father?' Fede left the question hanging.

'We don't speak any more. I don't even know if he's alive.'

'I'm sorry.'

'Don't be.' Her voice was sharp, and her body tensed. Then her hand went to her forehead, and she rubbed the bridge of her nose. She closed her eyes for a few seconds, and when she opened them again the tension had dropped from her. 'Dinner will be in an hour. Or I should say, an hour or so. Is that enough time?'

'It depends. Should we change?'

'My goodness, no.'

'In that case, we're ready now.'

'Very good then. One hour. Can you stir polenta, Nathan?'

'Oh, I'm a master at it.'

'In that case, can I ask you to come down in twenty minutes?'

'You can indeed.' I gave a little bow.

'Good.' She turned to Federica. 'It's going to be a special evening. The first evening cooking for friends, back in my own home. You understand that? In my own home.' She took Federica's hand. 'We're going to be great friends, I know. All of us.' And then, with another dazzling smile, she was gone.

We waited for her footsteps to recede. Then Fede sat on the end of the bed, swinging her legs. We waited a little more, until we could hear Isotta's tread on the stone staircase. Fede flopped backwards on to the bed, her arms spread wide.

'So. What do you think?' I said.

'I think they're a bit of an odd couple.'

'Well maybe. But perhaps people say the same thing about us?'

'Oh, they do.'

'They do?' I sat down at the head of the bed, and stared down at her.

'Yes. Don't worry. I always stick up for you.' She smiled up at me.

'What else?'

'I also think that she seems *quite* nice, that I wouldn't want to get on the wrong side of her, and that poor Mr Lockwood is going to be in lots of trouble for having invited his friend without telling her.'

'That is kind of annoying, though. If she'd planned a meal for four and now there's an extra mouth to feed.'

She shook her head, her hair spreading out upon the covers. 'More to it than that. I don't think she's spoken to him directly since they met. Oh, and one more thing . . .'

'Yes, *dottoressa?*'

'Torcello is expensive. Seriously expensive. Even by the standards of Venice. So I wonder just who's responsible for buying back the family home?'

'You're a terrible cynic.'

'Don't tell me you hadn't thought the same.'

'I had thought the same.'

'And anything else?'

I leaned over so my elbow was resting on the bed, and my face was a few inches from hers. 'I'm thinking this place must be a bugger to keep clean.'

'Mm-hmm. Anything else?'

A gust of wind rattled the shutters. 'And I'm also thinking it's going to be very difficult to keep warm tonight.'

'Oh *caro*, you'll be spending all evening stirring polenta. I don't think you need to worry about that.'

'Stirring polenta? Oh.'

My face fell, but then she smiled up at me again.

Chapter 16

Maitland and Lockwood clinked glasses and chatted as I stirred polenta. Fede had been right. Standing over a hot stove and stirring continuously had warmed me up more than I needed.

'How are you doing, Nathan?' asked Isotta.

'Well enough,' I lied, switching from my right hand and a clockwise motion to my left hand and an anticlockwise one, a strategy that Federica's Uncle Giacomo had once told me would irrevocably impair the flavour and ruin the dish. But then Uncle Giacomo had strong opinions on many things and, more importantly, was not here.

'There is, I believe, such a thing as instant polenta?' I suggested.

Isotta shook her head. 'It's not the same. Trust me. Keep stirring.' She looked over towards the table. 'I think we need to rescue lovely Federica.' I followed her gaze. Fede was, indeed, looking a little glassy-eyed.

'Fede? Can you give me a hand over here?' I called.

She gave an apologetic little smile to Maitland and Lockwood, who appeared not to notice, and came over to join us at the hob. 'Thank you,' she whispered.

'Everything okay?' I kept my voice low.

'Up to a point. They're discussing life at Cambridge. Student "pranks", I think they call them.' She dropped her voice even further. 'Don't you people ever grow out of this stuff?'

I shrugged. 'Some people, no.'

'You hardly ever talk about your student days.'

'I went somewhere less glamorous. We just try to forget.'

'Federica, darling,' Isotta, ever so gently, interrupted us. 'We have a little problem.' She waved a skewer at her. There were, unmistakably, a number of small, dead birds impaled on it. *Spiedo di Quaglie*. Quails, wrapped in pancetta, separated by a slice of *ciabatta*, stuck together on a spit and ready to be roasted. Isotta moved closer to Fede. 'There were supposed to be four of us. So two birds each. And now we are five. So what are we going to do?'

Fede turned and took a quick look around. 'Easy,' she said.

'Easy?'

'For sure.' She took a closer look at the contents of my pan.

'Easy? How?'

'Five of us. Three men. Two women. Eight birds. Logically they get two birds each, and we get one.'

'I see.' Isotta seemed a little disappointed.

'Except, of course, that this is bullshit. Firstly, you're doing all the work. Secondly,' she looked at my pan again, 'the main course is *polenta pastizada*. So you're thinking, I'm a singer, I need the protein for my voice?'

Isotta nodded.

'So,' Fede continued, 'You get two. Thomas,' she looked over her shoulder, 'okay, he looks quite well fed but he's our host. He gets two. Mr Maitland I know nothing about. Possibly he looks like he needs a good meal. He's also the unexpected guest.'

'The uninvited guest,' muttered Isotta.

'The thirteenth at the table. Whatever. He has to have two as well. Which leaves me and Nathan with one each. I say I'm on a diet. Nathan,' she patted my tummy, 'does the same.'

'Why thank you, *cara,* what a brilliant idea,' I said.

She kissed my cheek. 'Not at all, *tesoro.*' Then she looked down at the pan I was stirring, and grabbed my hand. 'Not anticlockwise. You'll ruin the flavour.'

I pulled the last tiny bone of the quail from between my teeth and crunched on the crispy, salty little strip of pancetta around the outside. I looked wistfully at Maitland and Lockwood who still had one plump little bird each remaining.

'So tell me, Thomas, how did you and Mr Maitland—'

Maitland sucked the flesh from the bones of a tiny quail leg and waved a hand. 'Christopher, please.'

'How did you and Christopher meet?'

'We were at Cambridge together. At Magdalen. I was an organ scholar. Christopher was doing something terribly clever, I forget exactly what,' said Lockwood in a way that suggested he hadn't forgotten at all.

'History, and mediaeval Italian,' said Maitland.

'That was it. And then one day – we must both have been around twenty – he conducted me in the Monteverdi Vespers.' He smiled at Federica. '*Vespro della Beata Vergine,*' he said. Fede stiffened, ever so slightly, at the implication that she might not have understood the English title, and I grabbed her hand underneath the table. 'I had, I think, quite a nice light tenor voice at that time. But there was something a bit different about Christopher. There was always something a bit special about him. Always *il miglior fabbro*.'

Maitland chuckled, and reached across the table to pat Lockwood's hand. 'But we ended up in the same place, old friend. We took different routes but we both got there in the end.'

Isotta had discreetly gathered up our plates, and returned from the kitchen with a great stone slab in her arms, bearing a steaming mountain of polenta, golden with melted cheese and topped with chunks of veal and *sopressa* and mushroom. She placed it in the middle of the table, and passed round five heavy ceramic bowls, each embossed with the lion of St Mark. The lion's paw rested upon a book bearing the legend *Pax tibi Marce, evangelista meus*. Peace be with you Mark, my Evangelist. The open book signified a time of peace. I hoped it was a good omen.

Isotta thrust a great wooden serving spoon into the middle of the dish, and we helped ourselves as if we were pulling Excalibur from the stone. I took a steaming, molten forkful and gasped with the heat, at the same time as the sheer meaty, cheesy savouriness of it all made me want to laugh with utter delight. I took a long draught of wine to cool down my burning tongue. The wine was red *vino sfuso* served in rustic brown ceramic cups. Cheap red wine to accompany a veritable feast. Isotta Baldan was, after all, very much a true Venetian.

She took a rather more delicate sip of her wine than I had, and placed her cup gently upon the table. She placed her knife and fork upon her plate, then folded her hands together. She stared at Maitland with those blue, blue eyes. 'So, Christopher. You say you and Thomas ended up in the same place?'

Maitland dabbed his lips with his napkin, and smiled. 'Well, yes. It seems we did.'

'Thomas is conducting the three Monteverdi operas with the orchestra of La Fenice.'

'I know.' Maitland nodded. 'It's marvellous. Absolutely marvellous.'

Isotta paused, for just a couple of seconds, and then her words slid in like a knife. 'And so what brings you to Venice, Christopher?'

'Me? Oh, I'm here with my choir.'

'Oh, how lovely.' She paused, again. 'Where from?'

'Saint Wddyn's'

Silence, again. Every pause weighted for maximum effect. It was, I supposed, what made her such a great performer. I decided to give him a hand. 'Saint Wddyn. Slightly obscure Welsh saint. Well, I say slightly, I mean very. But it's a highly regarded public school. On the border near Shrewsbury, isn't that right?'

Maitland nodded, and looked at me with gratitude. 'That's right.'

'A school choir,' Isotta purred. 'How lovely. How charming.' Again she paused. 'And so, tell me, Christopher, where are the children singing?'

'Well, they're not exactly children, *signora* Baldan—'

'Isotta, please.'

'Isotta. They're sixth-formers.' Isotta looked blank. 'The older students. We're performing at St George's.'

Isotta clapped her hands together. 'Oh, but that's marvellous. That's one of my favourite churches in the city. You must tell me when it is; we'll definitely come, won't we, darling?' She turned to Lockwood.

'Well of course we will, my love, of course we will.'

'But really,' she turned back to Maitland, 'what a lovely place for a concert. It's one of my favourite places to go in the summer. To get away from the crowds. To just sit there and look at those great works by Tintoretto.'

'Tintoretto?' Maitland had been smiling with pleasure, but now his expression clouded. 'Oh, I'm sorry, Isotta, but I don't think you understand. I don't mean San Giorgio Maggiore. I mean St George's. The Anglican church.'

Isotta shook her head. 'I'm so sorry. The Anglican church. I keep forgetting that there is an Anglican church. Remind me where it is?'

'Between the Accademia and the Guggenheim. Campo San Vio.'

'Oh, there. Of course. I forget that that's actually a church. It was a warehouse once, wasn't it?'

'It belonged to the Salviati family, I believe.' I turned to Maitland, who had flushed ever so slightly. 'The highly mosaicked building on the Grand Canal. That was theirs.'

Maitland nodded. 'I do know it.'

'They made their fortune in glass. Their warehouse was sold to the Anglican Church at the end of the nineteenth century. It really doesn't look like a warehouse these days.'

Isotta put her head to one side, as if unconvinced. 'You sound like you're a regular there, Nathan?'

Federica nearly choked on her wine. '*Magari!* You should

hear him complaining when he has to go along for the carol service.'

'I like the carol service. Really. But I only go along for that, and Easter. Oh, and Remembrance Sunday. I really do have to be there for that. Anyway, the Tall Priest keeps asking me when I'll become a regular but—' I shook my head.

'There's a fine tradition of Anglican choral music, of course,' said Lockwood. 'It's unique. Nothing like it in the Italian Church. Remind me again, what are you performing, Christopher?'

'Stanford. The Magnificat and Nunc Dimittis. And the three motets.'

'Oh, I love those,' I said. 'They're so pretty.'

Maitland smiled at me, and hummed a little of *Beati Quorum Via*, his right hand drawing little patterns in the air. 'A little difficult without any female voices but we're blessed with a couple of game young countertenors.'

Isotta frowned. 'Stamford?'

'*Stan*ford. Charles Villiers Stanford.'

'I'm sorry, I don't know him.'

'Irish composer. But ferociously English in many ways,' I said.

'Anyway, they're lovely pieces, darling,' said Lockwood. 'We really must go. Even you might learn something.'

'Of course,' she smiled. 'If we can fit it in with rehearsals at La Fenice.' She pushed back her chair and got to her feet. 'Federica darling, can you help me clear the table?' Fede cast me a dark glance, but got to her feet.

Isotta returned with a platter full of S-shaped biscuits and a bottle of Vin Santo. 'I didn't really have much time for dessert. I hope these are okay.'

'*Essi Buranèi,*' I said, taking care with the Venetian name. 'Did you make these yourself?'

She laughed. 'Oh, no. I love to cook, but life, I think, is too short to bake biscuits.'

I dipped one in my glass of Vin Santo, just to soften it slightly. The Venetian equivalent of dunking a digestive in a cup of tea. I nibbled away at it. 'They're still very good,' I said.

'Well, they were bought with my own fair hands.' Isotta giggled, and tossed her head coquettishly. Again, I squeezed Federica's hand under the table. We munched away in near-silence for a few minutes as I tried to think of how I could drive the conversation away from English music and the merits of St George's as a performance space in comparison to La Fenice.

When we had finished the biscuits, Lockwood removed the platter and swept his area of the table clean with the arm of his jacket. Then he refilled everyone's glasses. He raised his in the air. 'A toast, I think. To new friends and old. To breathing new life into this house. To my lovely Isotta.' We clinked glasses, stretching across the table in order to do so. 'And now, I think, I can tell you the real reason we're all here.'

Maitland chuckled. 'Dear Tom, you always were one for the big dramatic gesture. Are you going to say that one of us is a murderer? Or is one of us going to leap to their feet, clutch their throat and keel over?'

'Even better than that, Christopher. Even better. It's all about our treasure hunt.'

Chapter 17

'I'll just be a few minutes.' Lockwood pushed his chair back from the table and made his way upstairs.

Maitland lightly drummed his fingers on the table. 'Well now. I wonder what all this is about. Anyone know?'

I looked across the table at Isotta. She put a finger to her lips and shushed me before I could say anything.

Lockwood scurried back down the stairs, and lost his footing. My heart leapt to my throat, but he regained his balance and bustled over to the table. He was carrying a beaten-up leather document holder. He placed it on the table and undid the clasp. Then he took out a sheaf of papers, wrapped in tissue paper, and lifted out the top sheet, stained brown and foxed with age. He placed it on the table in front of Maitland, who reached into his jacket for a pair of glasses. He cast his eyes over it, nodded, and then turned to Lockwood, who was beaming across the table at him.

'You recognise this?'

'Of course,' Maitland nodded, 'The frontispiece to the libretto of *Proserpina Rapita*.'

'*Proserpina Rapita*. The great lost opera by Claudio Monteverdi.' Lockwood rolled the words around his tongue.

'Interesting.' Maitland removed his glasses, and laid them on the table.

'Interesting. Is that all you can say?'

'Where did you get this?'

'I'll tell you in a moment. But have you nothing else to say?'

'Do you have the rest?'

Lockwood rested his hand gently on the pile of papers. 'All of it. Every page. The complete text by Giulio Strozzi.'

Maitland picked up his glasses again, polished them on his sleeve, and then pored over the manuscript again, as if there were something he had missed. He shook his head.

'Look again, Christopher.'

Maitland took another look, and then his face cleared. 'Oh, I see it now. How interesting. It's not signed by Strozzi. Or rather it is, but he's using that pseudonym he sometimes used. Luigi Zorzisto.'

'Exactly. Anything more?'

Maitland moved his hand down the page to the bottom. Then he stopped, and touched the page, almost reverently. Lockwood grinned at him in delight.

'Monteverdi's signature?'

'Monteverdi's signature. What we have here is a complete copy of the libretto of *Proserpina Rapita*, co-signed by Monteverdi himself and Strozzi using his *nom de plume*.'

'My goodness. Well, that's delightful, Thomas. Absolutely delightful.' Maitland, I could tell, was striving to be polite.

Lockwood seemed disappointed. He had, quite obviously, been expecting something more. 'Is that all?'

Maitland shrugged, and forced a smile on to his face. 'As I

said, it's delightful. Full of interest for the scholar. But,' and
here he paused for a moment, 'it is just the libretto, isn't it?'

'What do you mean, "just the libretto"?'

'Tom, lovely as this is, there's no actual music here. It's just
the text. Just the plot. Copies of which have been known to
exist for years. My goodness, you know that as well as I do.
The Marciana have the original. There's a copy in Munich, I
believe. There are probably others if one could be bothered
to search.'

'It's signed by Monteverdi himself. And, for some reason,
Strozzi uses his pseudonym.'

'Well now, that does, I grant you, make it interesting. But
it is, at the end of the day, just the text.' He laughed. 'I'm
sorry, but for a moment there you had me thinking you'd
found the whole thing.'

Lockwood did nothing but smile.

'What are you saying, Tom?'

Lockwood looked over at Isotta, who beamed back at him.
She grabbed his hand, leaned over and kissed it, patted it, as
if to give him courage. He reached once more into the document
holder, and took out another sheaf of papers, equally
antique-looking.

'What about these?' he said.

Maitland cast his eyes over them. '*Come dolce hoggi l'auretta.*
Song for three voices. The only known surviving fragment.'
He looked up at Lockwood. 'Tom, you know this.' Concern
was starting to creep into his voice.

Lockwood's expression didn't change. 'Have you seen this
edition before, Christopher?'

Maitland shook his head. 'No.'

'Are you sure? Quite sure?'

'Thomas, I am absolutely sure. I have seen every extant edition of *Come dolce hoggi l'auretta*. Every one. And this is not one of them. So you've found another edition. Congratulations. And with the libretto as well, there's plenty here to interest the scholar. But—'

'But nothing, Mr Maitland.' Isotta's voice was ice. 'Show him, darling. Stop playing with him.'

Lockwood reached into the leather folder for a third time. This time, he took out two sheets of yellowed paper. He moved to place them on the table, and then paused. 'Look at these, Christopher. Look at these and be honest, be absolutely honest with me. What are they?'

Maitland was looking tired now, as if the game was starting to bore him, but he rubbed the bridge of his nose and replaced his spectacles. He said nothing for five minutes, his face moving birdlike from one sheet to the other. Lockwood beamed like a proud father, whilst Isotta's face bore a look of absolute triumph.

Maitland removed his glasses, and placed them on the table. He rubbed his face. Suddenly, he looked about ten years older.

'My God,' was all he said.

Lockwood put an arm around his shoulders. 'What do you see, Christopher?'

'*Quanto nel chiaro mondo*. It's the final dance.'

'And?'

'And it was lost. Lost for ever. Except—'

'Yes?'

'Except this is it.'

'You're sure? Absolutely sure?' Lockwood's voice was urgent.

'It's not Monteverdi's hand. Whoever transcribed it also wrote out *Come dolce.* But the music, the music is like a fingerprint. His voice started to crack. 'My God, Tom, you've done it. You've found a missing fragment by Monteverdi.' He leapt to his feet and threw his arms around Lockwood's neck. 'But this is marvellous. My dear fellow, this is marvellous.'

Lockwood hugged him in return. 'Tell him the rest, darling,' said Isotta, swirling the remains of her wine.

'Christopher, it's not just this fragment. There's more to it than that. So much more to it. We've found it all. The whole damn thing. We've found the complete score of *Proserpina Rapita.*'

Chapter 18

Maitland appeared unable to speak.

'You have got to be kidding,' I said.

Isotta smiled, and Lockwood shook his head. 'I am – we are – deadly serious.' His voice dropped to a whisper as he leaned over the table, staring at each of us in turn. 'Libretto and score. Strozzi's text. Monteverdi's music. All of it.'

'Tom.' It was Maitland, having recovered his voice. 'I simply must see it. The whole thing. Have you told anyone? There'll need to be a press release. They'll be queuing up to perform it. And—' He sat down again and dabbed at his eyes. 'Oh my goodness me, just look at me. I don't know what to say. But this is marvellous, extraordinary. Oh, but when can I see the whole thing?'

There was a brief moment of silence.

'Soon, I hope,' said Lockwood.

'But you do have it? You said you had it.'

'As good as,' said Isotta.

'As good as?' said Federica, who had been silent up to this point, and was also the only one not to have moved from her chair.

'Exactly.'

'So tell us more. How on earth did you find it?'

'Matteo Zambon?' I said. She nodded. Maitland looked confused, and I turned to him. 'Matteo Zambon. Ex-professor of music at Benedetto Marcello *Conservatorio*. A man who's forgotten more about Claudio Monteverdi than most people ever knew.'

Maitland shook his head in irritation. 'I know who he is. We met a few times.'

I turned back to Isotta. 'So what did you do? Employ him to go through every archive in Cremona, Mantua and Venice?

'Nothing so complicated,' said Lockwood. 'As a matter of fact, he made contact with Isotta. He said he had a complete score – or to be absolutely precise, he said he had the means of acquiring a complete score – and was willing to sell it. For what was actually a more than reasonable price. Poor *signor* Zambon was rather in need of money, and it wasn't too difficult to bargain him down. A modest amount of money for something almost without price.'

'Except that,' Federica paused, 'you don't have it.'

Lockwood flushed red for a moment, but then sighed and shook his head. 'Not the whole thing. No. Only this small extract.'

'And Zambon is now dead. Murdered at La Fenice four nights ago.'

Maitland ran his hands through his thinning hair. 'I'm having trouble keeping up with all this. Murdered? Tom, what have you got yourself involved with?'

'Zambon owed an awful lot of people an awful lot of money, it seems,' said Lockwood. 'He was a gambling man, so I'm told.'

'He had a number of enemies,' said Isotta. 'Or, at least, people he was in debt to. And one of them, it seems, decided to call in that debt on Wednesday night.'

There was a brief silence, and then Federica spoke. 'No,' was all she said.

'I don't understand, Ms Ravagnan,' said Lockwood, with more than a hint of irritation in his voice.

'What I said. No. It makes no sense.'

'Tell us more, *cara dottoressa,*' said Isotta, ever so sweetly, and lingering over Federica's honorific.

Fede shrugged, and swirled her wine in her glass. She gently inhaled the bouquet, and took a delicate sip. I knew exactly what she was doing and loved her for it. Just making everybody wait, so that all the attention was on her. Out-playing Isotta at her own game. 'A man with a string of gambling debts built up over years suddenly starts coming into money courtesy of Mr Lockwood, am I right?'

'Well, yes,' said Lockwood.

'A proper sum of money? Tell me what *a modest amount* means.'

'Well, it depends what you mean by—' Isotta flashed her eyes at him. 'A considerable sum of money, would be more accurate.'

'And so one of his creditors decides to kill him – or have him killed – just as he starts to accumulate the means of paying them back. More than that, to have him killed in one of the most public places in Venice and, coincidentally, just after he's arranged to sell a manuscript that might, actually, be priceless.' She sipped at her wine again. 'No. Too many coincidences. Way too many coincidences. Zambon was killed precisely because he had the score of *Proserpina Rapita*.'

'Nobody else knew about it.' Isotta's voice was glacial.

'But somebody found out. And they were prepared to kill because of it. To kill in a public place, in front of more than one thousand witnesses.' She sipped again at her wine. 'To kill someone who has discovered a lost opera score, in an opera house. It's quite a statement. And – although I'll admit I don't have any direct experience of this – not the sort of thing one would do over a grubby little gambling debt.'

Isotta and Lockwood both raised their voices, as Maitland flapped his hands in an attempt to calm them down. 'This may be so, but surely the important thing – the most important thing – is where is the manuscript now?'

The question hung in the air.

'We don't know,' admitted Lockwood.

'Not yet,' said Isotta, practically spitting out the word *yet*.

'But this is unbearable. To be so close.'

'This is where Mr Sutherland comes in,' said Isotta, forcing a smile back on to her face.

'Me? I don't understand.'

'We know Zambon was using you as a translator.'

'I never met him. We'd never even spoken.'

'We know you were at the opera the night he was killed. And we know you are a diplomat, of sorts.'

'Of sorts? Well, it's stretching the definition to breaking point. Where are you going with this?'

'Zambon's records. All his research. All his notes. His computer. The police will have them all. And somewhere, there, is the clue we need.'

Lockwood gave a little cough. 'And so, Mr Sutherland, we thought you might be able to help us. If the police have found anything. You might be able to find out.'

'I'm sorry, but that's impossible. They would no more speak to me than you.'

'But you are the honorary consul? You have contacts with the police? Surely if you explain Zambon was a colleague they'll be willing to help.'

'I do have contacts, yes. But this is a live police investigation. I simply can't interfere with that. I'm sorry.'

'But Mr Sutherland – Nathan – you do understand what's at stake here?'

I nodded. 'I do. Believe me, I do. But I can't get actively involved. I don't have that sort of relationship with them. And it's not as if there's a British subject involved.'

'I'm involved.' Lockwood was red-faced now, and jabbing a thumb into his chest. For one awful moment I thought the words 'Do you know who I am?' were about to be invoked, but then Isotta threw up her hands.

'We do understand, Nathan.' Lockwood opened his mouth. 'Hush, darling. We must just be patient a little longer.' Again, he opened his mouth to speak and, again, she shushed him. 'Just a little longer,' she repeated. She reached for the Vin Santo, and refreshed our glasses. 'Come now. Let's all calm down. Let's just enjoy the rest of the evening.'

We sat in silence for a few minutes. Then, when I judged that it was safe to do so, I spoke. 'Isotta, Thomas. There is a way around this. We know what Zambon was looking at in the Marciana Library. We go back to first principles, and retrace his steps. Believe me, I want to find a lost Monteverdi opera just as much as you do.' I caught the expression on Lockwood's face. 'Almost as much as you do,' I corrected. 'I'll help. I promise.'

Isotta smiled; this time, I thought, with real warmth 'Thank you, Nathan. You're quite correct. We just need to retrace his steps.'

Lockwood closed his eyes, and nodded in agreement. 'I'll recompense you for your time, of course.'

I nodded.

Maitland jumped in. 'I'll help, Thomas. I'll do anything I can.' He chuckled. 'And obviously you don't need to worry about paying me.' I glared at him, but then he caught my eye and I changed it into the best smile that I could manage.

Isotta raised a glass. 'Thank you, Nathan. Thank you, Mr Maitland. A toast, then, to our great adventure.'

'If you think that's wise,' said Fede.

'What do you mean, *dottoressa*?'

Fede shrugged. 'As I said, *mia cara* Isotta. I think somebody was prepared to kill for this. So yes, let's all go on an adventure, by all means. If you think it's wise.'

Chapter 19

'I'm very proud of you, you know?' I said.

Federica put down her book and pulled her glasses down the bridge of her nose, the better to look at me. 'You are?'

'Oh yes. I always am, of course. But especially so tonight.'

She reached behind her to tug the pillow upright. 'Well, thank you. But why?'

'Well, I think you were very brave. Isotta's a bit scary. At least, I find her a bit scary.'

'Just scary?'

'Just scary.'

'Oh good. She's very talented, isn't she? As an actress I mean. Or as a director.'

'How do you mean?'

'Well, the way it was set up.' The wind rattled the windows, and she pulled the bedsheets closer around her. 'Gathering everyone to the lonely country house, before the great secret is unveiled. Quite a *coup de théâtre*.' She patted her book. 'Dame Agatha would have approved.'

'She would indeed.' I glanced down at the cover. A gloved hand, driving a knife through the ace of spades. *Cards on the Table*. Federica had taken to reading in English, thinking the practice would do her good. I had hoped she'd take to speaking English like a 1930s sleuth but, sadly, it was yet to happen.

The windows rattled again, and then I heard a noise from downstairs. A door slamming. And then slamming again.

'I hope no one's having a row,' I said.

'Hmm. The atmosphere was a little frosty at times, wasn't it? But I can't hear any voices. And somehow I don't think Isotta Baldan is one for the silent treatment.'

'Me neither. More shouting and smashing of crockery, you mean?'

'Exactly. Something altogether more operatic.'

The door continued to bang. I sighed, and swung my legs out of bed.

'Where are you going?'

'I think the front door's blown open. Bloody thing's going to keep me awake all night.'

'Don't be silly, let them deal with it.' The lights flickered for a moment, and we looked at each other. 'Mr Maitland's downstairs, isn't he? He'll get up in a moment and sort it out.'

'Maybe he's a heavy sleeper.' I struggled into my trousers and pulled a T-shirt on. The lights flickered once more, and then everything went dark. 'Oh hell. Now what's all this about?'

'It's the wind, *caro*. Don't get in a state. They'll be back on in a minute.'

The door continued to bang. 'You're probably right. But I am going to sort that door out. Maitland's obviously capable of sleeping through anything.'

'Let's hope that's all it is.'

'You mean—?' The light from her mobile phone clicked

on, and I could see her tapping the cover of her paperback. I chuckled. 'Oh, I see!' I reached in my pocket for my phone, and switched its light on. It wasn't much of a beam but it would be enough. 'I'll be back in two minutes.'

She got out of bed. 'Wait for me.'

'What? No, don't be silly.'

She pulled her jeans on, and reached for her shirt. 'I'll come with you.'

'No you won't. This is far too Dame Agatha.'

'To hell with Dame Agatha. I don't trust you not to fall and break your neck.' She finished buttoning her shirt. 'Come on, let's go.'

We made our way along the landing, guided by the light from our phones, and then downstairs. The door had indeed blown open, and banged rhythmically in the wind. I made my way across the front room, faster than I should in the darkness, and had almost reached it when I slipped on something underfoot. I would have fallen, but Federica was there to steady me.

'Sorry,' I whispered.

'I said you'd break your neck.'

I shone the beam from the phone down at the floor. Leaves, dusted with snow, had been blown inside and were swirling in the wind. 'Hell, it's snowing. What if the path gets blocked?'

Federica stuck her head out of the door. 'It's not much. Probably be gone by the morning. The forecast said there might be a bit. Why do you think I brought my boots?'

I looked down at my trainers. 'Maybe I should have thought of that. I've got a surgery in the morning. What if we can't get back?'

'Then the country will just have to muddle along in your absence, *caro*. And I've got a train to Florence to catch, remember?' Her breath steamed in the air. 'My God, it's cold. Come on, let's go back to bed.'

I nodded, and closed the door. It shut with a satisfyingly solid clunk. 'It's a good lock. It shouldn't have blown open.'

'Someone didn't close it properly, Mr Holmes.' She hopped from one foot to another in an attempt to get some warmth back into her. 'Come on. Bed. Now.'

'Okay. What about the light?'

There was a click, a hum of electricity, and then the room was flooded with light.

'Is that better?' The voice came from behind us. I turned to see Maitland, in his dressing gown, standing at the entrance to the cupboard under the staircase. 'Something must have blown. Took me a while to find the fusebox. Then I just pressed everything until the lights came on. I understand it happens quite a lot with the electricity in Italian houses.'

'It does,' said Federica. 'Never make a cup of tea and vacuum at the same time.' She smiled at him. 'You've not been vacuuming at this hour I hope?'

'My goodness me, no.' The wind rattled the front door again. 'It sounds like there's a bit of a storm brewing. Probably something to do with that.'

'Almost certainly.' Fede smiled again. We stood in silence for a few moments. 'Well, goodnight, Mr Maitland.'

'Goodnight. Sleep well.'

'I'm sure we will,' I said, and we made our way upstairs to bed.

Chapter 20

The snow, as Federica had predicted, was almost gone by the morning, washed away by heavy rain. Maitland said he'd make his way back to the *centro storico* later, once he'd been up the *campanile* and taken a look around the museum. He had no rehearsals scheduled until that afternoon. Choristers, he explained, like all students, were never one hundred per cent first thing on a Monday morning.

We trudged our way through the slush and the mud, until we reached the main path. My feet were icy by the time the *vaporetto* arrived, and I squelched my way through the near-empty cabin and took a seat at the back. The window was fogged with condensation, and I cleared it with my sleeve so at least I could tell where we were. Then I stared down at my sodden trainers, swept the rain from my hair and thought bleak thoughts about cold, wet Venetian streets. Gramsci would be wondering which chair was the comfiest and which radiator the warmest. I'd left him sufficient kitty biscuits to last until midday but there was no guaranteeing he wouldn't have already scoffed the lot, in order to give himself something to really get angry about by the time I got home.

Fede broke in on my thoughts. 'You could always buy a proper pair of boots, you know?'

'I've got a proper pair of boots. It's just that—'

'—remembering to wear them is the difficult part?' I nodded. Rain was still pattering against the window. 'And there are these things called umbrellas, as well?'

'I don't like umbrellas. You know that. You have to carry them everywhere. They don't work in narrow streets. And then you end up losing them.'

'Okay. You're right.' She looked down at her boots, patted her umbrella, and smiled at me. 'It's going to be a long walk back home from Fondamente Nove in this weather.' She smiled at me, and I scowled back. 'Come on, Mr Grumpy, you'll be home soon enough, and your nice cat will be pleased to see you.'

'He's not a nice cat, and the only time he's pleased to see me is when he thinks he's in imminent danger of starvation. If he had opposable thumbs he wouldn't need me at all.'

'Come on now. There'll be warm socks and hot coffee as well.' She smiled, and leaned her head on my shoulder, wincing just ever so slightly as icy water dropped from my hair on to her cheek. 'Anyway – and more importantly – what do you think about Mr Maitland?'

'In general, or anything in particular?'

'About last night.'

'I thought it might be. Do you think he did it? Unlocked the door, switched the lights off?'

'I did wonder. Isotta was rude to him. About his choir, about his career. And then we started talking about *Proserpina Rapita*. About someone being prepared to kill for it. Then we all went off to bed, in a lonely house in the middle of a storm. Yes, I did wonder if he'd done it. Just hoping to scare her. Except—'

'Except?'

'It's silly. More than that, it's childish. Whatever else he may be, he's not childish.'

I nodded. 'So the alternative is that the door really wasn't closed properly, and the storm caused a fuse to trip. That's the nice alternative. The other one is that someone else made their way in, switched off the power, and left leaving the door open. Just as a sign. Just to show that they could. And that thought is more than a little scary . . .'

Crap Vendors, as I called them, made their living selling, well, crap. In many ways, fluorescent plastic darts and splatty plastic balls had become as much of a souvenir of Venice as a piece of imitation Murano glass. Cheap selfie sticks were continuing to sell well, following their recent introduction into the collection. Love locks had declined in popularity: residents, taking no delight in seeing them affixed to historic bridges, frequently took the law into their own hands by removing the padlocks with boltcutters. The more enterprising ones then sold the locks on as scrap metal. Rose sellers tended to be a nocturnal species, whilst bird seed selling was an altogether more covert activity. Bag sellers needed to be physically fit, the job of fleeing from police whilst carrying a heavy sack of contraband being a demanding one.

Yet, in the rain, Crap Vendors transformed themselves into Useful Vendors, selling disposable umbrellas for five euros. The umbrellas, it had to be said, were not actually advertised as being disposable. They might charitably be described as reconditioned. Reconditioned in the sense of being rolled up and slid inside a plastic sleeve. Still, you got what you paid for: a small umbrella, likely as not missing a few essential parts, that would get you home just about dry. Someone like myself, who scorned the use of proper umbrellas, was always cheered by the sight of a Crap Vendor changing into a Useful Vendor on a rainy day.

Federica had documents to print and copy, as well as slides to produce, for the conference in Florence, and headed off to the copy shop in Campo San Luca. I made my way back to the Street of the Assassins, went upstairs, and dropped the now-useless umbrella into the bin. Gramsci flopped over on to his back, and waved his paws in the air in his best approximation of what a nice cat is supposed to do, but was unable to keep up the pretence for long and snatched at my fingers when I reached down to tickle his tummy. I knew this could only mean one thing, and made my way into the kitchen where I reached down his box of kitty biscuits and refilled his inevitably empty bowl.

'I need to put you on a diet, Fat Cat,' I said, as happy little crunching sounds came from around my ankles. I knew I almost certainly wouldn't. The thought of a fitter, slimmer, more active Gramsci didn't really bear thinking about.

I went through to the office, fired up the computer and switched the coffee machine on. Then I took two sets of papers from the filing cabinet and arranged them on my desk. The first was a basic step-by-step guide to obtaining Italian citizenship. One day, I thought, I might start on the process myself but the very thought of starting out on a journey that was likely to take two years or more made me feel tired. The other was a 'Brexit and how it affects you' guide, although, in all honesty, I could just have replaced it with a sign saying 'Nobody knows. Try not to panic.' Nevertheless, people found it reassuring. At least, I hoped they did.

Rain continued to patter on the windows. I took a look outside. There was no sign of the skies clearing. Unlikely, I thought, that anybody would be turning up this morning. It was a day for tourists to stay indoors, to huddle in icy churches or to warm themselves in galleries

The entryphone rang. I sighed and stole another glance out of the window. Two figures, both wearing waterproof jackets, both carrying backpacks. Stolen passport or stolen bank card? One of the two. I buzzed them in, hung their coats up to drip dry, and offered them coffee.

They couldn't have been more than twenty-five years old. She was blonde and pink-faced from the cold. He looked a couple of years younger, with a shaggy mop of hair and beard. Possibly still students? They both looked upset. Then again, the downside of my job was that most visitors did.

'I'm sorry,' I said, 'you've picked a foul couple of days to come and visit.' They nodded. 'So tell me all about it. What can I do for you?'

The young woman reached into her bag and took out her purse. She rummaged inside it, took out a receipt, and slid it across the desk to me. I saw the name of the restaurant at the top of it, and immediately knew what this was going to be about. One of the most well-known restaurants in the city. Well known for all the wrong reasons.

'Oh hell,' I said, and immediately wished I hadn't as they

both looked at me with a mixture of surprise and suspicion. Then I saw the figure at the bottom of the receipt and there was no holding the words back. 'Oh, bloody hell.'

'You know about this?' The young man's voice was strained.

I nodded. 'I do. Tell me what happened.'

It was becoming a depressingly familiar story. One of the tackier restaurants in the area near Piazza San Marco had been making a killing from tourists in recent months. A friendly doorman, capable of identifying tourists at one hundred metres, would usher you inside to where an equally friendly waiter would usher you to a table and sit you down with a nice glass of prosecco. Yes, yes, there is a tourist menu (laminated, with photographs of all the dishes, and translated imperfectly into five languages) but today we have some wonderful fresh fish. Yes, there is house wine, but could I recommend something to go well with seafood? Perhaps some mixed antipasti to start, typically Venetian? For dessert, perhaps tiramisu, made in our kitchen? Coffee? Limoncello?

Yes sir, it is a lot of money but you see the fish is priced per hundred grammes. And it was a special bottle of wine. The limoncello is home-made. And this? This is the *coperto*, for bread. Everyone charges it, sir.

I was getting heartily sick of dealing with this. I took another look at the bill. There wasn't much change from six hundred euros. Six hundred euros for a crappy meal in one of the crappiest restaurants in town.

The young man ran through his story, which matched the narrative in my head in almost every detail. I tapped on the receipt with my pen in the hope that it might bring me some inspiration. Something I could actually do.

'What happened? After you received the bill.'

He shrugged. 'We said there must be a mistake. Then we said we weren't going to pay. Then he started shouting and—' He trailed off.

'He said he was going to call the police?'

He nodded. 'So we paid up.'

I continued to tap with my pen. I wondered what I could say. I could advise them never to eat in places with laminated illustrated menus, or where they tried to drag you in off the street. It was a bit late for that now. I could ask if they'd at least checked Tripadvisor or googled the name of the restaurant. Then I remembered that the place in question had got round that by removing the sign above the door.

'I am really, really sorry that this has happened,' I said.

'But can you do anything?' his companion asked.

I sighed, and laid down my pen. 'I could try writing to the mayor,' I said.

'Will that do anything?'

I'd tried this a couple of times now. The last time he had at least replied to me. He'd told me the tourists in question were a couple of miserable cheapskates who should learn a bit of *Veneziano* if they didn't want to get ripped off in future. I figured that was not what they wanted to hear.

'Probably not. But I will try. I'm sorry.'

'You're sorry? We're sorry. Sorry we ever came here.' Her voice was breaking now, and she shook her head in anger. 'We got engaged just a week ago. This was supposed to be special. Three days in Venice, during Carnival; it's rained nearly all the time and now this. How can they do this? How do they get away with this?' She shook her head again, as if trying to shake out the bad stuff.

I decided to be honest. 'It's because they know they have an infinite supply of tourists. It doesn't matter how many bad reviews they get. Bad publicity doesn't make the slightest bit of difference. They can afford to give somebody an absolutely miserable experience and charge them through the nose for it. They know you're never, ever going to come back. But there'll be thousands of others queuing up.'

'You're damn right we're never going to come back.' Her partner put his hand on her arm, but she shook it off. She was crying now. 'They should be grateful we're here. Everyone tells us Venice needs tourists. And they treat us like this.'

'I'm sor—'

'Don't say you're sorry!' We let her cry for a while, and I pushed a box of tissues across the table to her, as delicately as I could manage. She snatched one out and blew her nose. She took a couple of deep breaths and then swatted the box away with her hand, sending it flying.

We sat in silence for a moment, and then I turned to her companion. 'Look,' I said, 'can I ask how much longer you're in town for?'

'Until tomorrow,' he said.

'All right. Well I know this isn't going to make up for what's happened, but I know a number of good restaurants in town. I could recommend somewhere, book it for you if you like. So you can go somewhere nice on your last evening. I can probably get them to knock a few euros off as well.'

Immediately, I knew I'd said the wrong thing. 'Knock a few euros off?' He was angry now as well. 'What is this, someone comes along with a complaint and you send them off to your mate's place? What do you do, split the difference?'

'It's not like that at all. I'm just trying to help.' I slid a pen and paper across the desk to him. 'Look, just leave your name and address. Just so I can contact you, if there's any joy from the mayor.'

'Don't bother. Just don't bother. We've wasted our time here.' He got to his feet. His partner, after grabbing the receipt back from me and stuffing it inside her bag, did the same. Then she changed her mind, fished it out again, and threw it at me. It bounced off my chest, off the table, and dropped perfectly into the waste-paper basket.

She repeated his words. 'We've wasted our time here. Just like we've wasted our time and money in this shitty city.'

They didn't wait for me to see them out, and the sound of the door slamming reverberated around the flat.

I folded my arms on the desk, and laid my head in them, enjoying the silence. Then something landed on the desk with a soft thud. I raised my head. Gramsci was staring at me with his big, amber eyes.

'You're thinking, "that could have gone better", aren't you?' He miaowed. I leaned back in the chair and looked down at the waste-paper basket. Only half full. I shook my finger at him. 'Fortunately, I have a solution.' I reached for the pile of Brexit Survival Guides and took a sheet from the top. I scrunched it into a ball, and dropped it into the basket. 'I have a solution,' I repeated. 'Something that is going to make me feel a whole lot better.' I took another sheet, and repeated the operation. Then another. Then another. And another, until I'd exhausted the pile and the basket was brimming with paper.

Gramsci watched in silence as I positioned the basket in the middle of the room. Then I backed away as far as I could, took a few deep breaths, and ran at it. I kicked it with all my might, sending paper flying in every direction, as the basket spun through the air and came to rest upside down against the rear wall. Gramsci gave a little yowl of delight, and scurried over to jump on top of it.

I sat back down behind my desk, and the two of us stared at each other in silence. I was sick of this. Sick of having to stand up for the city all the time. Sick of having to say that things weren't so bad when they so manifestly were.

There was a rattle of keys in the lock, and Federica came in. She looked at the two of us, and at the floor that was now carpeted with scrunched-up paper balls.

'Oh, that's nice,' she said. 'Have you invented a new game?'

I scowled.

'Let me guess? Brexit?'

I shook my head. 'Worse?'

'The restaurant? *That* restaurant?'

I nodded.

'Oh dear.' She moved behind me and put her arms around my shoulders. 'Did this make you feel better?'

'Yes.'

'Is picking up all those balls of paper going to make you feel better?'

'Yes.'

'Really?'

'No.'

She reached into her coat and took out a paper bag, which she shook at me. 'Would *frittelle* help?'

Against my will, I smiled. 'Yes. They most certainly would.'

'I queued for fifteen minutes at Tonolo.'

'Well that helps even more. The fact they're from Tonolo, I mean. Not the fact you had to queue.'

She shrugged. 'Queuing is part of the experience there. Especially at this time of year.'

I rubbed my hands. 'Right then. Coffee and *frittelle*. Can you imagine a more nutritious lunch? What did you get?'

'*Veneziane.*'

I smiled, made my way through to the kitchen and filled the Moka. 'I think I've finally come to the conclusion that they're the best.' And they were. If there was one thing I truly, unequivocally enjoyed about Carnival, it was the presence in the shops of *fritole* or *frittelle*. Venetian-style doughnuts, sometimes filled with chocolate, *zabaglione* or cream. In a move guaranteed to offend the purists, some shops had recently taken to filling them with Nutella. I preferred them in the original style, simply studded with raisins and dried fruit, and dusted with sugar. In that way, I thought, they probably counted as one of your five-a-day.

I brought out two cups of coffee and two plates, and we sat around the desk to eat.

'Are we calling this lunch?' Fede asked.

'We probably ought to. I think there's sufficient calories in here to keep us going. Possibly for the next couple of weeks.' I licked the sugar from my fingers. 'I must update the spreadsheet.'

'Spreadsheet?'

'My spreadsheet of *frittelle*.'

'You keep a spreadsheet of *frittelle*?'

'Of course. It's important to keep track of the best ones. Otherwise we might not remember next year. In some ways I think it's my life's work.'

She shook her head. 'You're mad. So is there anywhere we haven't tried?'

'Everyone seems to rave about Rosa Salva in Mestre.'

'They do. It's a bit of a long way to go, though.'

'I know.' I paused for a moment, and then added as casually as I could. 'You're back on Wednesday, aren't you?'

'That's right.'

'So you won't be working on Thursday?' She nodded. 'And so?' I left the question hanging.

'And so I could go all the way to Mestre just to buy you *frittelle*, is that it?'

'No, no. Not just for me. You could get one for yourself as well.'

'Why, thank you. I'll be sure to get there before the doors open.'

'Oh, that's ever so kind. Thank you.' I brushed the sugar from my lips. 'Am I clear?'

She looked at me for a moment, and then kissed me. 'You are now.'

I hoicked Gramsci off the upturned waste-paper basket, and started gathering up the balls of paper. 'So what do you think? Should I write to the mayor again?'

'You could. What do you think he'll do?'

'I think he'll tell me to *vaffa* again.'

'So what's the point?'

'Well, I think it will annoy him. That's enough, surely?'

'It certainly is.' She checked her watch. 'Right, I need to pack, and then I need to head off.'

'What time do you get back?'

'Early afternoon. They won't pay for us to use the *Frecciarossa*. So it's a bit of a long journey.'

'Okay. No surgery on Wednesday, so I can waste time in the kitchen and make you a nice dinner.'

She smiled. 'That'd be nice. Now I must pack.' She looked at the floor, still strewn with rolled-up balls of paper. 'You can pick these all up in the meantime, can't you?'

Chapter 21

It took perhaps five minutes to refill the waste-paper basket, and not much longer for Federica to pack. Gramsci miaowed as she set her wheelie bag down by the door.

'That's right, unfriendly cat, you have Nathan to yourself for two whole days.' She went through into the kitchen, and I heard her opening the fridge. 'There's not much food in here, you know? Are you going to be all right for two days?'

'I did manage to survive before you came along, you know. Admittedly as a hollow-eyed wreck of a man.' I paused. 'What do you mean by "not much food"?'

'There's some cheese. Some lasagne sheets. I'm sure I've seen a bag of walnuts somewhere.'

'Okay. I can see a cheese and walnut *lasagne* coming up.'

'You can't.'

'No?'

'No. That's one of my favourites.'

'Okay. Well then, I'll cook it for you when you get back and I'll just live on *cicheti* for the next couple of days. Deal?'

'Deal.' She came back from the kitchen and smiled down at me on the sofa. 'So what are you doing for the rest of the day? Are you heading to the Marciana again?'

'I don't think so.'

'No?' She seemed disappointed.

'Maybe tomorrow. I might give Mr Maitland a call. I thought it would be useful if the two of us could spend some proper time there. Beside, I've got a better plan for this afternoon.' I went to the CD rack, and took down a copy of the *Vespro della Beata Vergine*. 'Jordi Savall's recording.' I slid the disc into the player, and the opening versicle rang out, *Deus in adjutorium meum intende*. Then I lay back down on the sofa, put my hands behind my head and closed my eyes as the *Gloria Patri* rang out.

I felt a tapping on my forehead. I opened my eyes again. Fede was looking down at me. 'This is it? This is your plan?'

I sighed, reached for the remote control, and stopped the music. 'This is my plan.'

'Lying on the sofa and having a little sleep?'

I wagged my finger at her. 'No, no. The whole mystery begins and ends with Monteverdi, doesn't it? So I need to get into his head.' I pressed the play button again. 'I saw him once you know. Jordi Savall. It was at the Edinburgh Festival, *Orfeo*. He strode through the audience whilst dressed as Monteverdi. He had the whole get-up on, right down to the beard. So that got me thinking – if we're solving a Monteverdi mystery, we've got to start thinking like him. Which means starting with the *Vespers*.' I closed my eyes again.

'You're serious, aren't you?'

I opened one eye. 'Oh, absolutely.'

'So, when I get back on Wednesday you'll have worked everything out?'

'Probably. I might even have the beard.'

'You are not allowed to have the beard. Come on, *carissimo*, I need to go. Doesn't your lovely girlfriend deserve a kiss goodbye?'

'She most certainly does.' I leapt to my feet. 'And a hug as well?'

'Oh, if there's one going.'

'It's going to be strange, you know? You being away.'

She hugged me. 'It's only two days. If I have time I'll try and find something strange and Florentine for you to cook.'

I gave her a hug and a kiss. 'Brilliant. Love you.'

'Love you too.' I lay back down on the sofa, and closed my eyes. I heard her keys rattle in the door. 'Nathan?'

I opened one eye. 'Yes, *carissima*?'

'You won't just spend the entire time sleeping?'

'Not at all.' I closed my eye. 'This is research.'

I awoke on the sofa several hours later, having dozed off – by my reckoning – sometime during *Pulchra es*. It had been, in many ways, a pleasant afternoon, but there was no getting away from the fact that I had singularly failed to get into the mind of Claudio Monteverdi.

Gramsci hopped up on to the arm of the sofa and perched in between my feet.

'Well now, puss. Let's imagine you've got a copy – the only copy – of a lost opera by Claudio Giovanni Antonio Monteverdi. Now, what would you do? Would you give it to the world for free? Meaning that your name would be remembered and honoured down through the generations.'

Gramsci remained silent.

'Or would you sell it privately to a man who, in all like-lihood, would give his very soul to possess it? Meaning you would be a very rich cat indeed. You could probably have a Versace scratching post to not scratch.'

He showed no sign of responding, so I continued. 'Or – and I think we're now approaching the crux of the matter – would you just prefer to sit on it, and tear it into a thousand pieces?'

He yowled, and jumped off the arm of the chair on to my chest, where he poddled away.

'Ah-hah, I think we've got it.' I pushed him off. 'Okay, I guess it's feeding time. Maybe for both of us.'

I went into the kitchen and refilled his bowl. I checked the time. Late afternoon still. I could, I supposed, go to the shops and get something to cook. Or I could just head off to Da Fiore, have some *cicheti* and call them dinner. And then the two of us could just have an evening on the sofa watching an old horror movie.

That's what I'd do. I had my coat on and was ready to sneak out whilst Gramsci was distracted by food, when my phone rang.

'Dario?'

'*Ciao*, Nathan. Are you doing anything tonight?'

'Gramsci and I are going to watch *The Abominable Dr Phibes*. And then, if we're not too tired, we might even watch *Dr Phibes Rises Again*. Do you want to come over?'

'My English isn't good enough, you know that.'

'I'll put the subtitles on.'

'No, I've got a better idea. Why don't you come round for dinner?'

'Dinner? Not just a beer at Toni's but actual dinner? Are you sure?'

'Absolutely. I told Valentina you were on your own for a couple of days and she said she was worried about you regressing to a feral state. So yes, definitely, come round.'

'Brilliant. Thanks ever so much. What should I bring?'

'Nothing. Don't worry about that. If you can get here about seven you can say *ciao* to Emily before she goes to bed.'

'Aww. Lovely. I'll see you then.'

'Great. Oh yeah, one more thing. You remember the guy who was murdered at the Opera the other night. Matteo what's-his-name?'

'Zambon. Matteo Zambon.'

'You'll never believe this, but Vally was reading the *Gazzettino* and saw his photo and said "oh yes, I used to work with him".'

'Seriously?'

'Small world, isn't it?'

'Too right it is. Okay, Dario, I'll see you at seven.' I hung up.

I checked my watch. I really should get Valentina some flowers, but that wasn't going to be possible now. I could, at least, pick up a decent bottle of something from Dai the Wine as I made my way to Piazzale Roma. And something for Emily? Difficult at this time of day. I looked down at Gramsci's basket. A small stuffed fluffy rabbit, unplayed with from the day it first came out of the packet. I picked it up and brushed it with my hand. Almost like new. The very thing. I put my coat on and stashed it away in my pocket, as Gramsci stared at me in disbelief.

Chapter 22

Dario, Valentina and Emily lived on the outskirts of Mestre, a thirty-minute journey by tram. It was nearly seven o'clock by the time I arrived.

Dario buzzed me in, and I swithered as to whether I should take the stairs for the sake of a bit of exercise. Then I remembered that this was one of those apartment blocks which always went on for one more floor than it should. I took the lift.

Valentina opened the door to me, Emily in her arms, and smiled.

'Hello, Nathan.'

'Hi, Valentina.' I leaned in to give her a peck on the cheek which she returned as best she could. 'Hello, Emily.' I gave her a little wave.

Emily gave me a hard stare.

I thought I'd try again. 'Hello, Emily,' I repeated, this time in the high-pitched cartoony voice that I reserved exclusively for dealing with small children.

Emily stared at me uncomprehendingly for a second, before turning and burying her face in her mother's arm.

Valentina laughed. 'I'm sorry, Nathan, she's a bit shy. Come on, Emily, say hello to Uncle Nathan.'

Emily turned her head towards me. I could see her cheeks flushing and her eyes filling up. I reached into my pocket in desperation, pulled out Gramsci's rabbit and waved it at her, nodding the head up and down. 'Hello, Emily, say hello to . . . to Mister Floppy.'

A smile broke out across her little face. 'Mister Floppy!' She held her hands out towards me, and I pressed the recently christened Mister Floppy into her hands. She pulled it to her, and cuddled it furiously.

Valentina patted my shoulder with her free hand. 'Well done!'

I wiped my brow. 'Did I get away with it?'

'You did. She was thinking about crying for a second there. Now say goodnight to Nathan, Emily.'

'G'night, Nathan.' She held a hand out towards me, and I gave her my finger to squeeze, just briefly, before she returned to the rabbit.

'G'night, Emily.'

'I'll get her put down. Just take your coat off and go through, Nathan.'

'*Ciao, vecio.*' Dario was standing in the doorway to the living room, a bottle of beer in his hand. 'Can I get you one of these?'

'That'd be nice. I think I've earned one.' He cracked the top on a Peroni, and passed it to me. We clinked bottles. I grinned at him. 'I did it! I made conversation with a small child and neither of us burst into tears!'

Dario laughed. 'See, I knew you could do it.'

'I don't know what I'm doing, though. They can sense that.'

'Don't be silly. You talk to your cat, don't you?'

'Yes. About art and politics and progressive rock.'

He shook his head. 'There are times when I don't know if you're being serious or not. Anyway, we'll have you babysitting for us next.'

'You're joking!'

'No I'm not. Serious.'

'Wow.' I felt scared yet just a little bit pleased at the same time. 'I feel very grown-up. Thanks, man.' I heard Valentina returning. 'Just one thing – Emily's not allergic to cat hair is she?'

He frowned. 'Not that we know. Why?'

'Oh, no reason.'

I wiped the remains of the *ragù* from my plate with the last piece of bread.

'Marvellous. Thank you, Valentina.'

'A pleasure.'

'Really, that was a brilliant *ragù*.'

'Half pork, half duck. My mother always said that made the difference. Tin of tomatoes, red wine, and simmer it away for as long as you want.' She paused. 'Federica's back on Wednesday, you said?'

'That's right.'

'There's some left. You could take it home and have it as a ready meal?'

'Hmmm. It's a pleasant thought. But I'll be fine, really. You should have it.'

'No problem. I'm sorry, I hope you don't think I was making you out to be a bit—' she paused again.

'Pathetic?' suggested Dario.

Valentina flipped him across the back of the head with her napkin. 'I certainly did not mean pathetic. Now just for that you can do the washing-up.'

Dario made a mock grumpy face, gathered our plates together, and went through to the kitchen. The two of us sat in silence for a few moments.

'Dario said you were at the opera the other night. The night of the murder.' I nodded. 'Horrible. Poor man.'

'You knew him, I understand,' I said.

She shook her head. 'Not well. I worked in admin there, you know. Up until Emily arrived.'

'What sort of man was he?'

'Nice. Polite.' She sighed. 'Had his problems.'

'The gambling?'

She nodded. 'I didn't know him well, as I said. But there were people at the *conservatorio* – people who'd been there years – who did. He'd been a good man, a great man, once, they said. And then he started gambling. Then he started being absent. Days at first. Then longer.'

I took a drink. 'Sounds like my dad.'

There was silence for a moment. 'Oh. I didn't know. I'm sorry.'

'It's okay. Well, no, it's not okay.' I smiled at her. 'But you know what I mean.' I paused. 'He still held down a job, though?'

'Hah! You know how difficult it is to get rid of people in academia? He only had a few years until retirement so the administration just thought,' she shrugged, 'what's the point, you know?'

'Did he ever sell stuff?'

'There were rumours. He had quite a collection of manuscripts, they say. And sold them piece by piece. In *nero*, you know. Cash only.' She folded her hands together, and rested her chin on them. 'You seem to want to know a lot about this, Nathan?'

I smiled. 'I'm sorry. It's a long story, but it might just be that he'd discovered something wonderful. Something that might actually be priceless.'

Her face darkened. 'Nathan, don't get involved in this. He knew some very bad people.'

'I'm not getting involved. It's just – well, he had a business card of mine. He was going to ask me to do a bit of work for him. A treasure hunt, if you like. It's a bit of fun, really.'

'A bit of fun?' She dropped her voice to a whisper, and leaned across the table. 'You think about Federica. And then you think about *him*.' She jabbed her finger in the direction of the kitchen. 'Because you know if you get into trouble again, you can always call Dario and Dario will come running. Well, not this time.' She sat back, her face flushed.

'I'm sorry.'

We sat in silence, listening to Dario humming tunelessly in the kitchen.

'You know,' I said, 'it would be kind of brilliant if Dario came in here and saw us both having a nice time together. And I've had a lovely evening, and you've been so kind. I am grateful. Really. And I'm sorry.'

Her face softened. 'Me too.' She reached across the table

to squeeze my hand. 'Thank you for the present. Emily loves Mister – what's his name?'

'Floppy. Mister Floppy.'

We both laughed and listened to a heartfelt but imperfect rendition of 'Shine On You Crazy Diamond' coming from the kitchen.

Valentina smiled. 'That's Emily's favourite, you know? Sometimes the only way to get her to sleep is to have Daddy sing Pink Floyd to her.'

Dario chose that moment to come back into the room and saw us laughing together, and his face broke into the broadest of smiles.

Chapter 23

A fine rain was falling as I waited for the tram back to Venice. It would be quiet, as always. A few late-night travellers, perhaps a group of noisy youths or a drunk or two if I happened to be unlucky.

'Serravalle . . . Oberdan . . . Volturno . . . Bissuola . . .' The bored-sounding automated voice counted down the stops towards the centre of Mestre. I sent a text to Federica and looked out of the window, watching the suburbs slide past. I closed my eyes and gave a contented sigh. It had been a good evening. I'd had a spiky relationship with Valentina for years, but we seemed to have moved on. I opened my eyes again, and flinched. The view was now distorted by a reflection in the glass. A masked face, with black lenses for eyes. Staring at me. I turned, and looked around the carriage.

There, a few rows from me, sat the figure of the plague doctor.

I hadn't seen him getting on. Heading off to a late-night party in Venice, presumably.

My phone plinged. Federica texting me back. I looked at the message, smiled, and texted back ; 'you too'. There was probably an emoji for this sort of thing, but they were beyond me at the moment. I put the phone back in my pocket, and looked up again.

He'd moved. He was now just one row of seats away. I shook my head. I must have been mistaken.

The tram pulled in to the central Mestre stop and a group of young people got on. Girls in cheap domino masks. Italians. Ah, so that was it. They were probably all going to the same party together.

They sat at the other end of the carriage. Damn. So much for that theory. I stared out of the window, using the reflection to keep an eye on my travelling companion the whole time.

'Manuzio . . . Cattaneo . . . San Marco . . .' The tram pulled in to Sansovino, where the girls got off. I cursed under my breath. I'd been hoping they were going all the way to Venice. I got to my feet and made my way further down the carriage, as if I was getting off at the next stop. I took a look around. An elderly couple were sitting at the far end, near the driver's cabin, and I took the seat next to them. I looked down the length of the tram. Doctor Beak had not moved.

'Molmenti . . . Boerio . . . Forte Marghera . . . San Giuliano . . .' The couple got to their feet, and smiled and nodded to me as they made their way to the door. I looked out as the doors hissed open. There was nobody else on the platform. Nobody was going to get on. For a moment, I considered getting off. I didn't know San Giuliano at all, but buses probably stopped here. Or I could wait for the next tram. Was there even another tram at this hour? The doors closed, and the moment was gone.

Just one more stop and we'd be in Piazzale Roma, and people would be around. I shook my head. Stop being so bloody silly, Nathan. It's just some guy – or girl – going to a late-night party. I looked over my shoulder to the driver's cabin. Locked, of course.

The tram pulled on to the Ponte della Libertà, and I could see the lights of the petrochemical works of Porto Marghera starting to recede into the distance, with the reassuring sight of the lagoon on either side. Five minutes now, and we'd be there.

The Doctor got to his feet, and turned to face me. Standing in the centre of the carriage, he reached into his coat, and pulled out a pair of black leather gloves. Slowly, deliberately, he pulled them on, and then held his hands up in front of him, turning them this way and that, as if to admire them. The masked, black-gloved figure of a thousand Italian *gialli*.

I risked a glance through the window. Two minutes, at least, until we reached Piazzale Roma.

Doctor Beak took a step towards me.

I got to my feet. I considered hammering on the door of the driver's cabin. Would he even hear me?

The Doctor took another step.

I looked around in desperation, and then an idea struck me. I stepped to the side of the carriage, and curled my fingers around the emergency handle.

He stopped. I glared into the black lenses of his mask. 'You take one more step, just one more, and I'll pull the handle. The tram will screech to a halt. And then people will come. Nod if you understand.'

He made as if to step towards me and I tensed, ready to yank down on the handle. Then he stopped and nodded, slowly, as I continued to hold his gaze.

Our stand-off continued as the tram pulled into the terminus. Then the doors hissed open, and people swarmed into the carriage. Late-night partygoers heading back to the mainland. Six Napoleons pushed past me. Three hours ago I'd have been annoyed. Now I felt as if I should shake their hands.

I half walked, half ran to the *fondamenta*, and jumped on to a mercifully crowded night boat. Doctor Beak was nowhere to be seen. I slumped back in my seat, feeling my muscles relax and the stress draining out of me. Well played, Nathan. I checked my watch. Late now. Too late to settle down with Gramsci and watch films. Perhaps it was for the best. I was no longer in the mood for a late-night horror.

Chapter 24

'You look tired, Nathan,' said Maitland.

I yawned, and nodded. My second cup of coffee of the day hadn't helped any more than the first. 'I didn't sleep well.'

'Sorry to hear that.' I reached for my wallet, but he stopped me. 'No, my treat, I think.' He pushed a note across the counter and smiled. 'Keep the change, please.'

We left the Caffè Lavena and walked out into an already busy Piazza San Marco. He looked around the square, and shook his head. 'It's so long since I've been here. It's changed so much. Is it always like this?'

'Not always. There are still times when you can almost have the place to yourself. Early mornings, late at night.'

'There's still a magic to it then?'

I smiled. 'There is. Sometimes.'

He patted my arm. 'Anyway, thank you for coming out. I thought it would be nice if we could go through some of these mysterious documents together.'

'No problem. You'll have to join, of course. They don't let you take guests in.'

'I'd be delighted. I think it might be rather charming to have a membership card for the Marciana Library.'

'You've got documentation – passport, driving licence? Something like that?'

'I do. Are they very strict?'

'They are. By the way – the school where you work?'

'St Wddyn's.'

'Yes. Perhaps best not to mention that. I think it might confuse them.'

We took a break after a couple of hours reading, and went outside to be able to talk properly. I made the most of the opportunity to have a cigarette.

'So what do you think?' I said.

Maitland shrugged. 'Well, it's a beginning. But all it's really told us is that there was once a copy of *Proserpina* in circulation. It's not of any help in itself in verifying if Mr Zambon did or did not have a copy.'

'If he did have a copy, why would he be needing to research all this stuff anyway?'

'Provenance, I suppose. To demonstrate he actually was the legitimate owner. But mainly I suspect he'd just be interested to know how it survived. Musicologists love this sort of thing.'

'Okay. So we need to track its passage over the years, as best we can. Back to Rowlanson, then?'

Maitland gave a thin smile. I couldn't muster much enthusiasm for the task either. Rowlanson had settled into a pattern of describing his shopping, eating and domestic habits in more detail than was strictly necessary. And there was another volume to follow.

'I was just thinking,' he said, 'that it might be useful to

look at Wake's correspondence. To cut out the middle-man, so to speak.'

'Yes, that makes sense. Good idea. Is it likely to be here though?'

'Almost certainly not. Unless I'm very much mistaken, I believe the British Library has it. And there is rather a lot.'

I sighed, and stubbed out my cigarette. 'So, back to Mr Rowlanson's laundry lists then?'

'It appears so.' He looked at his watch. 'Now I've got a rehearsal with the boys this afternoon. What do you say to two hours' more work and then we call it a day? After lunch, of course.'

'I'd say that makes the prospect very nearly bearable.'

We made our way back inside, and again went through the rigmarole of handing over identification and folding away our coats within the lockers.

I put my hand on the door into the reading room, but Maitland stopped me.

'I was just thinking,' he said, 'about the second volume. Why don't you finish the existing one, and I'll move on to volume two. It'll speed things up a bit.'

'Are you sure? Isn't there more chance of us missing something?'

'Well, there could be. But then we can come back later in the week and swap over. Just to double-check.'

'Right. Oh good.'

'Good man.' He patted my arm and we made our way inside.

Was it just my imagination, or did Petrarch's gaze really change to one of mild disappointment as I yawned and checked my watch? Twenty minutes to go. Rowlanson's accounts of the best places for the unwary traveller to buy food may have indicated that he had been a man after my own heart, but were also serving to make me hungry.

Where to go for lunch? I didn't really know anywhere for a cheap bite to eat near Piazza San Marco. I supposed if Maitland was willing, we could go to the Brazilians, which would just leave him with a fifteen-minute walk to St George's.

I felt a hand on my shoulder, and started. Maitland stared down at me. I couldn't read his expression, but I bent over the book again as if to indicate that I was hard at work and not merely daydreaming. Even at my age, there was something about the schoolmasterly air that he carried that was enough to drag me back to secondary school.

'Nathan,' he kept his voice low. 'I think you should come and see this.'

I followed him to where the book lay, closed, on his desk. He pulled out a chair for me. 'Now I've been working my way through the second volume. Very much as per the first. Not entirely without interest, but nothing to help us either. But there was something not quite right about the book itself. Loose pages, I thought, or imperfectly bound.' He opened it up, and looked across at me. 'And then I turned the page and, well, this is what I found.'

He turned the page. Instead of the dry, heavily foxed pages of Rowlanson's diaries, the following sheet was a page of A4 printer paper that had been interleaved into the book.

The images on the sheet were clearly visible. The brass sign that read 'N. Sutherland. British Honorary Consul' from the outside of the house. A photograph of myself standing at the bar of the Brazilians, taken through the window. Federica, just closing the main door, the keys still in her hand.

'Son of a bitch,' I murmured.

Maitland closed his eyes, ever so gently, as if reprimanding me for using bad language.

'Should we step outside again?' he suggested.

'Son of a bitch!' I repeated.

Maitland watched patiently as I stalked up and down, chain-smoking furiously.

'Is this helping, Nathan?'

I tugged the remains of my cigarette from my mouth, ground it underfoot and reached for the packet. Maitland grabbed my hand, but I shook it off.

'Look Nathan, I accept this is probably all rather upsetting—'

'Upsetting? I've got a stalker. More than that, it seems Federica has as well.' I yanked a cigarette from the packet and clicked at the lighter again and again, as the breeze prevented it from catching.

Maitland raised his hand to his mouth, and gave a gentle cough. 'If I might just make a suggestion?'

'Oh, please do.' I flicked the lighter again, with similar results. 'Suggest away.'

'Well, I can either stand here and watch you fail to smoke cigarettes – which, incidentally, is a disgusting habit – or . . .'

'Or?'

'Or we go back inside and find out who left those images in the book.'

'And just how do we do that?'

He looked at me as if I were simple-minded. 'My dear fellow, as was demonstrated to me only this morning, in order to take a book out from that period, it is necessary to sign and leave one's name.'

I paused for a moment, and then grinned. I felt the urge to give him a hug but remembered in time that Christopher Maitland was an Englishman of a certain age, and, as such, probably unused to being hugged by casual acquaintances. 'You're a genius,' I restricted myself to saying.

'Why, thank you.'

We made our way back inside, removed our coats, and entered the reading room. I stood and tried to restrain myself from tapping my foot with impatience as the librarian dealt with another request.

I recognised him as the young man who'd issued my library card four days previously. That, I hoped, would make things easier.

'*Signore?*' He gave me a brief nod of recognition.

'*Ciao*. You remember the other day? I asked you which books Matteo Zambon had been reading. Now,' I'd scribbled down the title and reference number of the second volume of Rowlanson's memoirs, 'could you perhaps tell me who the last person was to take this volume out?' He hesitated for a moment, and then tapped away at the keyboard in front of him.

'The last person to request this book, sir, was Matteo Zambon.' He frowned. 'No, wait. That can't be right.'

'What do you mean?'

'The book was requested by *signor* Zambon yesterday.'

'What? That's not possible. Zambon died nearly a week ago.'

'I know that, *signore*. There must be a problem with our records. It's just that—'

'That?'

'It was definitely his card that was used, *signore*. There is a five digit number on the *tessera*. There is no possibility of a mistake.'

'There must be. Whoever took him the book must have transposed the number from the line above.'

'No, *signore*. The book has not otherwise been referenced since 1997. There is no mistake here.'

I nodded. 'Okay. Thank you.' He gave me an embarrassed half-smile. We both knew what must have happened.

I went back to the *sala lettura* where Maitland was waiting for me, in front of the copy of Rowlanson's second volume of memoirs. He raised an eyebrow.

I shook my head. 'I think we need lunch.'

'Not just yet. Take a look at this.' He spun the book through one hundred and eighty degrees so that it was facing me. He looked over his left shoulder and then his right to reassure himself that no one was looking, and then laid his hands on each side of the book in order to flatten it just a little bit more. 'You see.'

I bent over it, but could see nothing. 'I'm sorry?'

He sighed in exasperation. 'For heaven's sake.' Then he twitched his glasses off his nose and passed them over to me. I gave him an awkward little smile and put them on, sliding them down my nose so as to see as best I could. Then I took them off again, and moved them nearer the book, and then nearer to my face as if playing the trombone. Maitland sighed again. 'Oh, Mr Sutherland.' Again, he checked over his left shoulder and then over his right. He pushed down with more force on the book, pressing it flatter. 'Now look. Carefully. What do you see?'

'Nothing. I'm sorry.'

'Exactly. Nothing. Now why?'

I moved his spectacles nearer to the book, as I leaned back in the chair to move my head further away. And then I noticed it.

'There's a page that has been cut,' I said. 'Possibly more than one. I can't quite see.'

'At least two. Like you, I can't be certain. But cut very cleanly, as close to the edge of the page as possible. So that no one would notice.'

'Wow. So what do we do? Should we tell someone?'

He shook his head. 'I think not. Not yet, anyway.'

'And the extra page? The one with the photographs on.'

'I'd suggest leaving it there. At least for now.' He raised his hand, and nodded to one of the assistants who passed him a form to countersign the book as having been returned.

'And now?' I said.

He held out his hand to me, and I passed him his spectacles. 'Now, Mr Sutherland, is very much time for lunch.'

Chapter 25

Maitland refused a second spritz, as he had refused the first. He needed to keep a clear head, he said.

'How do you think he did it?' he asked.

I took a bite from the unexciting tuna and egg *tramezzino* on my plate. I'd found a Chinese bar near the piazza for lunch. It wasn't great, but it had seemed the most likely to offer us lunch for a non-ridiculous amount of money.

'Strange as it may seem, removing the pages from the book might have been the easiest. You'd have to be careful. Just pick the right moment, when no one is looking. One quick cut, as near to the spine as possible.'

'What would he do with the pages? Conceal them on the shelves?'

I shook my head. 'Too risky. Who knows when they might be discovered? No, I think he just waited until he could scrunch them up and stick them in a pocket.'

'The photos, then?'

'That would be easy. Anything you bring in has to be in a clear plastic envelope. It's unlikely that anybody would think of checking the contents. And even if they did, so what? It's just a sheet with three photographs on.' I munched on half of the olive from my spritz, and grimaced. 'Hmm. Not good. Really not good.' I dropped the rest into a bin.

'I still don't understand how he got in by using Zambon's name.'

'I wondered that myself. But I've got an idea. Show me your library card.' He opened his wallet and passed it to me. I took mine out as well. 'Look at them – the photographs, I mean.' Taken with a cheap webcam, both were overexposed as a result of the electric light in the library. The images were recognisable as Christopher Maitland and Nathan Sutherland, but only just. 'If he had Zambon's card and looked even vaguely like him, would the staff really stop to think about it? Or would they just think, hey, it's an old photograph and the guy's got a different haircut?'

'And the documentation? The ID you have to leave?'

'Bank card. Credit card. Anything that doesn't have a photograph on it.'

'It all sounds incredibly risky to me, Nathan. After all, there was a possibility that somebody at the library might actually have known Zambon.'

'Exactly. It was one hell of a risk. But he was desperate enough to take it. That's one thing that worries me.'

'And the other?'

'If he had Zambon's library card and – let's say – bank card, the odds are that he took them off his body at La Fenice.' I drained my spritz, and crunched the remains of the ice cube. 'So basically my girlfriend and I are being stalked by a man who is very likely a murderer, and one willing to go to some pretty desperate lengths.' I wished I had another spritz, but knew that way madness lay. 'Still, you've got to laugh, haven't you?'

'I'm never quite sure when you're being serious, Nathan.'

'I'm being ever so serious.' I reached for my wallet. 'I'll get these.'

'Are you sure?'

'Yes. Still being serious.'

'That's very kind. Thank you. He glanced at his watch. 'And I should be going.'

'Okay. Have a good one. I'll drop by later, as I said.'

'Do that. We can have another chat afterwards.'

'How many of you are there? In the choir, I mean.'

'Thirty choristers. We have a couple of countertenors, as I said,' he shook his head, 'but not enough. Perils of teaching at a boys' school.'

'And you're looking after all of them?'

'Good God, no! At my age that would kill me. No, we've got parents, volunteers, that sort of thing. As long as I look after them during rehearsals I can avoid most of the shepherding about.'

'That's nice. Gives you a bit of a chance to see the city.' I paused, and looked at him. How old was he? Mid-seventies, perhaps? I weighed the words in my head. 'Did you do anything nice yesterday? After the rehearsal?'

He shook his head. 'Too tired. I had an early dinner at the hotel, and then an early night. How about you?'

'Oh, I just had dinner with some old friends. In Mestre. Nice and easy to reach by tram.'

He didn't react. It was he who'd decided to start on the second volume. Who'd found the photographs, who'd noticed the missing pages. I looked at him again. Impossible. Surely?

Chapter 26

Isotta had been deliberately rude about the Anglican church in Campo San Vio a few nights previously, but she was right about one thing. Many Venetians didn't know it even existed, and even fewer had ever been inside. It typically opened just once a week, for Mass on Sunday mornings, serving the small expat community and tourists. Thousands of visitors passed by every day, paying little attention to what was, after all, just another crumbling building in a city full of crumbling buildings. It had once been the property of the Salviati family, serving as a warehouse for the Venezia-Murano Glass and Mosaic Company, until the Anglican Church acquired it in the late nineteenth century.

I could hear the sound of an organ playing inside, and the sound of a boys' choir singing, enthusiastically, if imperfectly, Stanford's *Justorum Animae*.

Two tourists sat eating pizza, oblivious to the cold, on the steps beneath the plaque that commemorated the Great War. I thought about remonstrating with them, but what would be the point? I could go around every *campo* in Venice and find people doing the same. I ran my fingers lightly over the inscriptions on the bronze doors, recording those lonely places where British servicemen now lay buried, and tested their weight. Locked. No visitors wanted during rehearsals. I walked around the corner into the *calle*, and knocked on the battered side door.

There was no answer. I knocked again. It was possible, I thought, that no one could hear me. Then I heard a bolt scraping, and smiled.

The Tall Priest dragged the door open, the warped wood scraping across the concrete floor; his angular frame hunched over in the cramped entrance, looking somewhat ridiculous. He swore, impressively and creatively, as the door groaned and squeaked. With a great deal of effort, he dragged it open, and stood upright to look at me.

'Good God! Nathan Sutherland. We're honoured. We weren't expecting you until November.'

He stepped aside to let me in, and then banged away at the door, pulling the latch one way and then another until it slid home. 'Blasted thing is completely bastardly buggered,' he swore.

Father Michael Rayner. Six foot four in his stockinged feet. Thin as a twig, grey of hair, bushy of moustache. No fan of progessive rock. An occasional, but creative and onomatopoeic, swearer. Three years the unpaid *cappellano* of St George's, a church that seemed just that little bit too small to contain him.

'Should you really be speaking like that in a House of God, *padre*?' I said.

'He'll forgive me. He's big on that. Now what can I do for you? Don't tell me you've decided to come over to our side?'

'I'm afraid not.'

'Pity.' He gave a wicked smile. 'I won't give up, you know?'

'No?'

'Certainly not. Part of the job description. So come on, tell me.'

I gestured towards the vestry door. 'I'd like a quick chat with Mr Maitland.'

'Oh, right.' He checked his watch. 'I think they're just about done with rehearsals for the day.' A boy soprano keened a line as best he could, and Rayner did his best to suppress a wince. 'God knows, I hope so.'

'Not so good?'

'I'm sure they're doing their best. Sit down, eh?' He motioned to a chair. 'Best sit here for a bit until they finish. Mr Maitland seems to be a bit of a perfectionist. He got terribly cross with me yesterday for reorganising the hymnbooks in a way he felt to be excessively noisy.'

I sat down on a black folding chair that was far too small for me. The vestry was cramped and also had to serve as a small kitchen. On one side hung vestments of various shapes, colours and, presumably, significance. On the other, an incongruously large fridge freezer sat next to a tiny two-ring electric hob. Perhaps they'd deliberately chosen small furniture to maximise what remained of the space?

'Can I get you a coffee, Nathan?' said Rayner, towering over me like Gandalf over Frodo.

'That'd be nice, thanks,' I replied, resting my chin on my knees.

Rayner filled a small kettle with water, and plugged it in. Immediately, the vestry lights went out.

'Son of a—

'It's all right, *Padre*, don't worry.'

'It's not all right. Bloody building is collapsing around me and every week something else goes wrong.' He shook his head. 'Don't know how much longer I can bloody stand it.' Then he scowled. 'And don't call me *padre*, you know I've told you not to.'

'I'm sorry. I just don't know what else I should call you.'

'I keep telling you. Michael is fine. Father Michael on work days. Mike if you want a punch in the face. Now, what's this all about?'

I paused. 'Erm, well, I really just need a bit of a chat with Mr Maitland.'

'Right. Would this be anything to do with, shall we say, a rather important piece of music that's gone missing?'

'Oh God, he's told you about that. We were supposed to be keeping it to ourselves.'

'"Thomas Joshua Lockwood and the case of the missing Monteverdi manuscript". I'm sorry, I didn't know it was supposed to be a secret. The trouble with secrets, of course, is that they're no fun unless you tell someone. Oh, and don't take His Name in vain. Only I get to do that.'

'Sorry. It seems unfair though. You get to have a good swear and I don't.'

'Perk of the job, as I said.' A particularly piercing passage of Stanford assailed our ears and he grimaced some more. 'Look, I don't really feel the need for a cup of coffee. And I don't think my life will be any the less for not hearing the entirety of the rehearsal. Shall we just go to the pub? Maitland can join us there.'

'Sure. Pubs are good.'

'I'll get the lights back on first.' He flicked a switch in the fusebox next to the door and the electricity kerchinged into life. 'Then I've just got a few things to sort out in the office upstairs. Maitland would like to use our printer and the wifi doesn't seem to be working. Are you any good with that sort of thing?'

'Afraid not.'

'Okay. I'll switch it off and back on again. If that doesn't work, I'm giving up. Wasted too much time on it already.'

I nodded. We made our way into the church itself, and Rayner did his best to contort his frame around the low, narrow staircase that led up to the organ loft and small office. I took a seat in the rearmost pew. There was a thump from the staircase, and a brief outburst of swearing, and I smiled.

St George's was by no means the church I knew best in the city. For that matter it wasn't even the church called St George's that I knew best in the city. There was no great art to be seen and yet, in its own quiet way, it was full of interest. The tombstone of Joseph Smith, 'Consul Smith' himself and Canaletto's patron, was set into the north wall, having long since been moved from his original resting place on the Lido. I supposed that, in a way, the venerable Smith was also one of my predecessors. His legacy had been a collection that formed the basis of the Royal Collection of Drawings. I wasn't sure I had anything that approximated a legacy as yet. Perhaps it would be my spreadsheet of *frittelle*?

The choir were struggling manfully through *Beati Quorum Via*, which dragged my attention back to the front of the church where they were rehearsing in the sanctuary area, underneath the altarpiece where St George and St Jerome stood either side of Christ. At least, he was St George these days. Legend had it that he had originally been St Liberalis of Treviso, another military saint. A nineteenth-century repainting of his flag, reversing the colours, had turned him into George. The reredos shone bright and gold against the peeling plasterwork of the sanctuary. Federica had been involved in the regilding work, some years before we even met.

I shifted in my seat. In a city full of churches with uncomfortable pews, St George's managed to stand out. Then there was a clattering of feet on wooden steps, and Father Rayner emerged from behind a curtain at the back of the church.

He made a 'drinky-drink' movement with his hand, to which Maitland responded with a smile and gentle nod of his head.

'Right, that's everything put to bed. Let's go.'

'Is it working?'

'Of course not. I'll move it downstairs later. The signal's better.'

'Where on earth are you going to put it?' I asked, looking around the tiny space of the vestry.

'On top of the hob.'

'Isn't that rather dangerous?'

He shrugged. 'I wouldn't think so. It hasn't worked in years.' He gave the door a pull, and it juddered open, the wood scraping against the floor.

'Where are we going, by the way?' I asked as we stepped out into the *calle*.

'Church Pub.'

'Church Pub?'

'You'll see.' He twisted his key one way and then another in an attempt to get the side door to lock. 'Bloody church-warden should bloody do something about this,' he cursed.

'Squirt of WD40 should do the trick?' I offered.

'Oh yes. I'd never have thought of that. Be a good chap and come round in the morning, would you?' There was, finally, a satisfying but unconvincing click from the lock as the latch slid into place. 'The thing that worries me is that nothing short of a tank is going to get through the bronze doors at the front. So one day I'm going to find the lock on the side door is buggered and that'll be that. Four hundred years of Anglican history in Venice will be at an end. Come on. Pub.'

He led me along the *calle*, past one of those fast-food coun-ters that always seemed to be serving disappointing-looking slices of pizza to soon-to-be-disappointed tourists, to the bar on the corner.

'Do I take it it's too cold to sit outside?'

I looked at two tourists, perched on bar stools next to a table supported by a beer barrel. Their faces were bitten with cold. I shook my head, and Rayner led me inside.

'Spritz?' I nodded. 'Bitter?' I nodded again.

The bar was crowded, but being a priest in Venice did give you a certain amount of visibility. Being a tall one, even more so. He held up two fingers and the barman, big, baldy and beardy, smiled in return.

'*Ciao, padre.*'

'*Ciao,* Alessandro.'

'Oh, so he gets to call you *padre,*' I muttered.

'It's a perk of his job.'

I took a look around me. I'd never been in there before, and instantly regretted the fact. A dark, cosy little gem of a pub. A chalk board listed a range of beers beyond the usual Peroni, together with a number of variations on the humble spritz. Rayner caught my eye and smiled. 'You should try one of his Negronis. Alessandro's not just the owner, you know. He's an absolute artist. He adds five drops of Angostura bitters. With a pipette.'

I whistled. 'I think I need to try that. Although I worry about being unfaithful to Eduardo.'

'Eduardo?'

'My barman.'

'Ah. I understand. Well, Paul teaches us that God won't tempt you beyond what you can bear. And if you are tempted, he will provide a way for you to endure it.'

'Which is?'

'I find giving in helps.' Alessandro arrived with our drinks. 'Your health, Nathan.' We clinked glasses. 'Oh, try the sandwiches. I hardly need to cook these days. The porchetta and radicchio might be the best in Venice.'

'I will, thanks. That's just saved me having to cook dinner. So what's this place really called?' I asked. Rayner sipped at his drink, and pointed wordlessly at a sign above the bar. 'Corner Pub?' He nodded. 'A pub, on a corner. It's not just a clever name then? So why do you call it Church Pub?'

'It's a pub near the church. After church, we go to the pub. *Ergo*, Church Pub.'

'Fantastic.'

'You know when the church is open, Nathan.'

'Ah, but now I know when the pub is open as well.'

There was a gust of freezing air from outside, as Maitland

limped through the door, plonked himself heavily onto the stool next to us, and sighed.

'A tough day, Mr Maitland?' said Rayner.

'I think you can safely say that. I'm getting too old for all this. It's like herding cats. Thirty teenage boys away from home for the first time in a country seemingly exclusively populated by attractive young women. You can practically hear the hormones raging.'

'Would a drink help?'

'Very much so. What do you recommend?'

'The usual.' Rayner held a finger up to Alessandro, who smiled and got to work.

Maitland looked at the two of us. 'Anyway, I hope I'm not interrupting a private conversation?'

'Dear Mr Maitland, I am trying to save Mr Sutherland's wretched soul. But that can wait until another time.'

I turned to Maitland. 'So,' I said, 'have you seen Lockwood since Torcello?'

He shook his head. 'I'm afraid not. He does seem to be incredibly busy. Hardly surprising, I suppose.'

'Okay, but one of us will need to speak to him. Sooner rather than later. Just to tell him that there could be some very, very bad people mixed up in this. And to tell him to be careful.'

Maitland sipped at his drink. 'Well, good luck with that. Tom won't let this die easily.' Again, he paused. 'With respect, neither of you really know him. I do. I've known him for nearly a half-century. Don't be fooled by the cuddly old man image. There's a will of absolute iron there. Do you know, when he was a young man, he used to conduct with his eyes closed? It was an affectation, of course. He knew Herbert von Karajan used to do the same. But it was just to demonstrate his absolute mastery of his material. He once told me that he could make a singer on stage look at him by force of will.'

I shook my head. 'That's mad.'

'Oh it's nonsense, of course. But I think he genuinely believed it. Tom's problem is that when he wants something badly, he thinks he can actually will it into being.'

'I can see that.' I swirled the ice cubes in my drink, and looked over at the bar. What I really wanted was a Negroni with Angostura bitters. Eduardo need never know. I dragged my mind back to the matter at hand. 'Can I ask you what you think of Isotta?'

He gave a twisted little smile. 'Well, she doesn't seem to like me very much.'

'To be fair, Tom should have mentioned there'd be a fifth person at dinner.'

He chuckled. 'True. True. But there's something of the smiling assassin about her, don't you think?'

'I think that sums her up. She's very attractive, though.'

'Is she? I hadn't noticed.'

Rayner raised an eyebrow but said nothing.

'She rather reminds me of his first two wives,' said Maitland. 'He does seem to have an eye for younger, fiery sopranos.'

Rayner smiled, and shook his head. 'Too much information. I think I'll leave the two of you to it. But do let me know what happens. I'll see you tomorrow, Christopher. I'll see you in November, Nathan.' He got to his feet, and patted me on the shoulder. 'I was joking when I talked about giving in to temptation, you realise?'

I gave him a wave as he struggled to manoeuvre himself through the door, and then turned back to Maitland. 'Okay. You know about this sort of thing and I don't. If you found a lost work by a great composer, what would you do?'

He shrugged. 'I don't know. Present it to the world, I suppose. However one goes about doing that sort of thing.'

'You wouldn't keep it for yourself?'

'No. Of course not, what would be the point? It's not like having a rare book or a painting. I can imagine one wanting to own an original score. To having something you could look at, and touch, knowing it was written by the sacred hand of Joe Haydn or someone.'

'So an autograph score by – I don't know, Bach, Haydn, Wagner – how much would that go for?'

Maitland chortled away and almost choked on his spritz. 'Wagner's a bad example.'

'Just for psychopaths?'

'Exactly. But seriously, just as an illustration, an autograph score for Mahler's Second Symphony was sold about a year ago for well over a million dollars.'

'Wow.'

'But here's the thing. Everyone who cares about it knows what it sounds like. Everybody who cares about it has a recording. It only has worth if you're so obsessed with Mahler you actually want to own something that was his. It's a slightly more highbrow version of those weirdos who'll pay silly money for Maria Callas's underwear. If it was a lost work, what could you possibly do with it?'

'Assuming you could read music, you could still listen to it. In your head, at least.'

He shook his head. 'What would be the point? If you had

a copy of *Proserpina*, surely you'd want to hear it performed. You'd want to *see* it performed.' He opened his mouth to speak further, and then paused. 'I'm not sure if I should tell you this, Nathan. It's breaking a confidence.'

I made a little 'zip' motion across my mouth, and immediately felt silly. 'I won't say a word. I promise.'

'I was quite close to Tom's second wife. I don't know if you know anything about her?'

I shook my head.

'They weren't married for long. She once told me that he was one of the most boring people she'd ever met.'

'I don't understand that. I mean, he's brilliant.'

'He is. But he's also obsessive. For Tom, there really isn't very much beyond music. So this, to him, must be an absolute torture. To be so very close to something like this, and to see the possibility of it slipping from his grasp. The crowning achievement of a lifetime in music. It must be a torment.'

'Poor guy.' The words sounded weak, but I really couldn't think of what else to say.

We drank in silence for a while.

'So, are you going to go to the police?' Maitland asked. 'To tell them what happened today?'

'Probably not. I'm not sure what could be done.'

He nodded. 'I was just thinking about what we might do next. There are people I know at the Fondazione Monteverdi in Cremona. They'll know, if anyone does, about any fragments that might have been sold at auction, for example.'

'Is that likely to take a long time?'

'The Fondazione appears to be the work of one elderly gentleman. He is, however, a good friend. That will help.'

'Excellent. You mentioned Wake's correspondence?'

'Again, there are people I know at the British Library and the National Archives. That might take some time – as I said, there is rather a lot of it – but we just need to join the dots up.'

'You are going to be careful about this, aren't you, Christopher?'

He gave a little chuckle. 'My dear fellow, it seems as if it's you they're interested in, not me.'

'Thanks. I hadn't forgotten that.'

'I'm sorry. A bad joke. And I will be careful. But you know, the other evening at dinner – when Isotta spoke about Tom's glittering career, and La Fenice? And made rather an obvious comparison with my little school choir?' He set his drink down, and stared directly into my eyes. 'Well I may only be a teacher in a minor public school but I, Mr Sutherland, am going to find this manuscript. If it exists.'

Chapter 27

Maitland had no plans for the evening. I should, I suppose, have invited him round for dinner, or at least suggested we go out to eat together, but I wasn't in the mood for company and invented an excuse about an urgent translation that needed to be done. I had a porchetta and radicchio sandwich, conceded that it might genuinely be the best in Venice, and made my way home. I just wanted to be in front of the television with a glass of wine and an old movie playing. More than anything I wanted Federica home, safe and sound.

I texted her to say I'd meet her off the train the next day. She said there was no need, but I told her I felt like making a big romantic gesture and was going to do it anyway and, if she was very lucky, there might even be flowers involved.

I wasn't in a horror mood, so I put an old Marx Brothers movie on. *Duck Soup*. I lay on the sofa and chuckled away, all the while wishing I'd bought another sandwich. Gramsci grumped around, occasionally miaowing for attention or doing his best to position himself directly in my line of sight. Despite his name, he'd never been much of a Marxist.

The great thing about old films – apart from the fact that the world always looked better in black and white – is that they have a sensible running time. *Duck Soup* clocks in at little more than an hour. I checked the time, and the level of wine left in the bottle. Nearly ten o'clock, and a couple of glasses. I could watch *Monkey Business* as well and still be in bed at a sensible hour. Inevitably, the phone chose that moment in which to ring.

'*Pronto?*'

'Nathan, *caro mio*.'

'Isotta?'

'Of course. How are you, Nathan?'

'I'm not sure. Federica's away. It all feels a bit strange.'

'Of course.' There was a brief pause. 'I thought it would be nice if we could take a coffee together.'

'Thank you. I'd be delighted. Tomorrow morning is going to be rather busy but perhaps—'

She cut me off. 'I thought perhaps now. Tonight.'

'Tonight?' I sat bolt upright on the sofa.

'Tonight. I know it's late but I've been rehearsing with Thomas. And I do need to speak with you. Please, Nathan . . .' Her voice tailed off.

'Okay. Of course. Where should we meet? If you're at La Fenice, there's a place I know in Campo Santo Stefano.'

'No. Piazza San Marco. At Florian's.'

'My goodness.'

'You know it, of course?'

'Well, yes.' Naturally, I had never, ever taken a coffee there. 'What time?'

'Eleven-thirty.'

'They'll still be open?'

'It's Carnival. And they'll stay open for me. *A dopo*, Nathan.'

'*A dopo.*' I hung up.

Gramsci and I stared silently at each other across the sofa.

'Don't look at me like that, all right?'

Gramsci, of course, said nothing.

'It's a coffee, that's all.'

He continued to stare at me.

'Yes, of course I'm going to tell Federica.'

He hopped off the sofa, and slunk away. I stretched out again, and closed my eyes. What the hell was this all about? I could, should, call Fede, but it was getting late now. She had an early train in the morning. And, besides, it would be difficult to explain on the phone. Better to talk about it, properly, tomorrow.

I watched *Monkey Business* but my head wasn't in the right place. I turned the television off, went to the door, and pulled my coat on.

Gramsci sat in the middle of the floor, looking at me.

'I'll be back before you know it, Grams, okay?'

I had closed and locked the door before I heard a pathetic little *meep* from inside. I cursed, unlocked and opened the door again. He hadn't moved. I waved a finger at him. 'Not a word, okay? Do you understand? Not a word?' I slammed the door, and made my way downstairs and into the street.

Chapter 28

I had never been inside *Caffè Florian*. You could, I knew, just take a coffee *al banco* – standing at the bar – for three euros. That was a lot of money for a coffee but, hey, you were at Florian's. I'd never made use of it, however. There seemed little point. If I wanted a coffee, there were other places to go that were nearer and, more importantly, cheaper. If I was ever going to go there, I told myself, I would only go for the full experience, sitting inside in the *Sala Orientale* drinking coffee from the most delicate china, listening to the musicians, and imagining myself to be Marcel Proust.

I wondered how much a Negroni would cost there, and how many lawnmower manuals I would need to translate in order to afford one. I shook my head. There probably weren't enough lawnmowers in the world.

It was a cold night, and I pulled my coat around me. Even during Carnival, there were few people in the piazza at this hour. The musicians outside the café seemed to be packing up, but a warm golden light shone from inside.

I stood in the arcade of the *Procuratie Nuove,* and lit a cigarette, my hands shaking a little, and not just from the cold. There was something just a little bit thrilling about this.

I didn't like to ask myself why. I checked my watch. Eleven twenty-five. A smoke, I thought, would calm me down before I went in.

'You're early.' The voice was Isotta's. 'Have you been waiting long?'

'I've just got here.' I stretched my arm out and gestured at the *piazza*. 'I thought it would be too cold to sit outside. And I'm not usually in this part of town. It's just so lovely to have the chance to stand here, to smoke a cigarette, and take it all in. And to think.'

'And what are you thinking about, Nathan?'

'That, right now, my cat is very cross with me.'

She laughed her silvery little laugh again. 'You're making fun of me.' She wasn't glammed-up tonight, no fur coat or headband, just a simple black leather jacket. Simple, but probably expensive, I thought. Even in the semi-darkness, I could tell that she wasn't wearing make-up. It made her look younger, somehow, and took away the slightly hard edge from the loveliness of her face.

She reached into her jacket and took out a silver cigarette case. On some people it might have been seen as an affectation, but on her it made perfect sense. I could no more imagine her carrying around a packet emblazoned with health warnings and gruesome images than I could imagine her spitting in the street.

'Could you . . . ?' She left the question hanging in the air. I reached for my lighter. Proper smokers, those who go to the trouble of buying cigarette cases, do not forget to take a lighter with them when they go out. It was part of the performance, I knew, but nevertheless my hands shook as I attempted to light her cigarette, and the flame blew out.

'Are you cold, Nathan?'

'Yes,' I lied.

She cupped her hands around mine, the better to shield the flame from the breeze and, for a moment, our faces almost touched. Then she moved away and breathed out, ever so slowly, the smoke curling in the night air.

'*Che gelida manina*,' she said, and we both smiled at the joke.

We stood in silence and smoked and looked out at the *piazza*. Then she dropped her cigarette to the tiled floor of the arcade, and ground it underfoot.

'Come, Nathan, we have much to talk about.' She linked her arm in mine, and together we walked into the most elegant coffee bar in the city.

There were few customers by now, and the head waiter approached us with an apologetic expression on his face, his hands spread as if to indicate that the café would be closing shortly. Then he recognised the face of my companion and his expression changed.

'*Signora* Baldan, it's always a pleasure to see you.'

She nodded and smiled. 'Likewise, Giorgio. Is there anyone in the *Sala Orientale*?' He took a look over his shoulder and shook his head. 'Wonderful, we'll take a coffee there. Giorgio, if anyone else should come in could you direct them somewhere else please? We need a little privacy.'

'Of course, *signora* Baldan.'

We walked through and took our seats. I'd seen photographs of it before, of course, but nothing had quite prepared me for the actuality. Paintings of women in states of modest undress lined the walls, and were reflected in gold-framed mirrors, whilst the ceiling, geometrically patterned in gold, added to an almost kaleidoscopic effect. The seats were covered in red plush. The overall effect was just ever so slightly erotic.

'It's better here. Not so easy to be seen from the street. I don't want any prying eyes.' She looked downcast for a moment, and I noticed a scratch above her right eye that the darkness without had prevented me from seeing. I was about to ask her about it, when Giorgio reappeared and she immediately turned on a smile that bounced off every mirror in the room.

'*Caffè corretto*, please Giorgio.' He nodded his head, a centimetre at most. 'Mr Sutherland, what would you like?' Mr Sutherland this time, then. Of course, it was necessary to use a certain formality in front of staff.

'The same for me, please.'

Again, that almost imperceptible nod. He gently stroked his pencil moustache. '*Corretto con grappa?*'

'Thank you,' I said.

Isotta nodded. 'With the *Nonino Pirus*.'

I tried not to gulp. I'd vaguely heard of *Pirus*, and knew that it came in at about fifty euros a bottle. I had a half a bottle of supermarket grappa in the fridge at home, and even that, I thought, was a step up from the stuff drunk by the men who slept in shop doorways. And Isotta was planning to pour a shot of *Nonino Pirus* into a cup of coffee and add sugar to it. I tried to recall exactly how much money was in my wallet, and fervently hoped this was going to be her treat.

Giorgio returned with a silver tray, removed two almost transparent porcelain cups, and placed them on the table. Then, with due reverence, he removed the cork from the bottle of grappa, sniffed it delicately and, placing one hand behind his back, topped up the two cups of coffee. He gave a stiff, almost military bow, somehow suppressing the need to click his heels. Then he looked at the flower in his buttonhole, and a look of annoyance flashed across his face. He made the most minute of adjustments to it, and then nodded as if to himself, satisfied now that everything, even at twenty minutes to midnight, was in perfect order. He gave another stiff little bow and withdrew. Proust, I thought, would most certainly have approved.

I took the smallest sip of coffee that I could manage. Even if I wasn't paying, I was going to have to make this one last. Besides, I was in the company of an unusually beautiful woman, in one of the most elegant rooms on the continent. This was almost certainly going to be one of the finest cups of coffee that someone else's money could buy, made with one of the most refined grappas in Italy, and served in exquisite china. I was going to make the most of the experience.

It tasted like coffee.

Isotta sat across the table from me. No make-up, but perfumed, even at this hour.

'I have to ask,' I said, 'but do you always come to Piazza San Marco for coffee?'

'Often. Not always. But I like to. It reminds me of what the city was like in the old days. Do you like the paintings?'

They weren't really my thing, but I thought it best to be polite. 'Very much,' I said.

'Giacomo Casa. He decorated the Apollonian rooms at La Fenice. They were all destroyed, of course. By the fire back in 1996. What remains is just a copy. Beautiful but fake.

But these are real. I like to sit here. It's another link with the past.'

I took another minuscule sip of coffee, and couldn't resist taking the briefest of glances at my watch.

'I'm sorry, am I boring you?' She didn't seem annoyed. 'Or do you have to be up early tomorrow.'

'Well I do, but, no, you're not boring me.' She smiled. 'I think you're very un-boring. But I would like to know just why you felt like inviting me for coffee just before midnight.'

'Oh, don't you know? They have a discount just before closing time.'

I laughed. 'And now you're making fun of me.'

'*Touché.*' Just two syllables, but lovely ones in her accent. 'It's simple really. I was thinking about what you said. About how I broke your heart at La Fenice. I was hoping I could make it up to you.'

'Oh, that,' I said, as if I'd forgotten all about it. 'Don't worry about it. Dinner was more than enough.'

She shook her head. 'I don't think so.' She opened her handbag. No labels, I noticed. Isotta Baldan didn't do labels. She took out three white cards, embossed with gold. 'They're for the Masked Ball at the Casino the day after tomorrow.'

'Lovely,' I said, trying to sound non-committal. Tickets were rarely available for the Casino's Grand Masquerade. They were not cheap to come by. Yet, there were grander events by far to be seen at, events that didn't need anything as vulgar as advertising. Ones that would have seemed better suited to a couple like Isotta Baldan and Thomas Joshua Lockwood.

Her eyes twinkled. 'Are you thinking, Mr Sutherland, that this is not, perhaps, my sort of thing?'

I blushed. 'I'm sorry. Was it so obvious?'

'Yes. But you're right.' Her expression changed, became serious. 'The difference is, these were a gift.'

'A generous one. Even if it isn't quite your thing.'

'They weren't for me. They were for Thomas. It seems he has a secret admirer.' She reached into her handbag, and took out an envelope. Plain, cheap-looking. She passed it to me. 'Take a look.'

I checked the postmark. Posted in Venice, the previous day. It was addressed to *Maestro* Thomas Joshua Lockwood, care of La Fenice. I could feel there was something inside, and I looked at Isotta.

'May I?' She nodded.

I opened it up, and took out a white square of card, and held it away from me as I struggled to read the words. *Chi professa Virtù non speri mai di posseder richezza, o gloria alcuna, se protetto non è dalla Fortuna.*

'You know,' I said, 'in a movie or a pulp novel, the words would have been clipped from newspapers and glued to the card.'

'And then we'd work out which newspaper, and that would give us a clue,' she smiled.

'Exactly. Tricky in this case. This is, what, seventeenth-century Italian. Maybe even older. Even the *Gazzettino* has moved on a bit since then.'

'You recognise the words?'

'They're from *Poppea*, aren't they? "He who professes virtue shall never hope to possess any wealth or glory, if he is not protected by fortune." Well now, you're a virtuous woman, aren't you, Isotta?'

She laughed, and wagged her finger at me. 'Some might not say so. My ex, for example.'

'Your ex?' I closed my eyes, trying to remember. 'A tenor, wasn't he? Came from down south. Salvatore—'

'Bonfiglio. Not an appropriate name. Not at all.'

'I remember reading—' Then I remembered exactly what I remembered reading and broke off, embarrassed.

She nodded. 'Yes. I'm sure you do.' There was an awkward silence, and then she reached across the table and rubbed my arm. 'It's okay. Everything is wonderful now.'

'I'm glad.' I went back to the words on the card, grateful to change the topic of conversation. '"Wealth or glory", then. Certainly quite a lot of glory in finding a lost Monteverdi opera. What about the wealth?'

Her expression changed, and she shook her head. 'It's not about the money for Tom. It's never, ever been about the money.'

'I understand. Really I do.' We sat in silence as I sipped at what remained of my coffee. 'So this is a challenge, then? Wealth and glory for the virtuous man, as long as he's protected by Fortune. Meaning the Casino.'

'We're going, of course.'

'Are you really sure that's a smart idea?'

Her eyes started to fill up. 'Thomas won't hear of us doing otherwise. And so I was wondering . . . would you come as well? You will come, won't you?'

I paused, but only for a moment. 'Of course I will.' As if there were any choice.

'Thank you.' I took the invitation from her, our fingers touching for just a moment. 'That's very kind. Very kind of you indeed.' I turned it over in my hand, and looked at it more closely.

'This ticket does seem to be for just one person?' I said. Isotta said nothing, but looked at me as if failing to understand. 'Federica,' I continued, 'I really can't go without her.'

Her expression, I thought, darkened for a moment, but then her hand flew to her mouth in embarrassment. 'I'm so sorry. Of course she must come.' She took another ticket from her bag, and pressed it into my hand. There had always been two spare tickets, then. It had been a test, of sorts.

I filed the tickets away inside my wallet. Giorgio, I noticed, had reappeared and was hovering by the door in his inscrutable, Proustian way. I glanced at my watch again. Five to midnight. *Caffè Florian* did not, even for Isotta Baldan, stay open after hours.

'We should go.' She nodded, and I pulled my coat on. I noticed again the thin red line above her eyebrow. 'You've cut yourself,' I said, tracing the same shape above my own eye.

'Oh this?' She brushed her fingers against it. 'Stupid of me.' She held up her left hand, and twisted the heavy silver ring on her fourth finger. 'This is too big, too clumsy. But it was a present from *Mamma*.' She waited for me to stand up so that she could take my arm again.

'Let me settle up.' I reached for my wallet in the fervent hope that she'd stop me.

'Don't be silly. This is my treat. It's already settled.'

'Really?'

'Really.'

We walked out into the cold February air, damp and foggy now. A few figures could still be seen in the half-light.

Late-night workers making their way home, perhaps catching the night boat up the Grand Canal to Piazzale Roma and then on to the mainland; and a few masked revellers in an increasingly desperate search for a late-night bar.

And someone else. Framed by one of the arches of the *Procuratie Vecchie*. I could barely make him out, but I knew exactly who, or what, he was. My old acquaintance, Doctor Beak.

I could not see him move, but knew with certainty that he was staring at me. I started, and Isotta clutched my arm more tightly.

'What is it?'

'Over there.' I gestured with my free arm, and, as I did so, the figure stepped back out of the archway and made his way with quick, deliberate steps to the monumental archway at the base of the *Torre dell'Orologio*, where he turned left in the direction of the Rialto, and was quickly lost in the darkness.

'I didn't see anything. Or maybe someone. Just a late-night tourist.' She looked around her. 'Wonderful, isn't it? When it's like this. So quiet.'

I could only agree. There were days when crossing St Mark's Square was akin to a contact sport. Many Venetians claimed that the *piazza* had become a no-go area for them. Yet, on a winter's night, the full moon shedding a gentle, blurry light behind the clouds, and the colours of the basilica looking sharper and more perfect than they ever looked in the heat of the day, it was hard to imagine a more beautiful public space in Italy.

I opened my mouth to speak but was interrupted by the mournful wail of the *acqua alta* siren, followed by a solitary *pling*. A warning that the lowest level of high water was expected. Much of the city would remain untouched at this level, but, within a few hours, St Mark's Square – the lowest point in the entire city – would be completely flooded.

'It's been a lovely evening,' I said, once the sirens had stopped, 'and thank you for these.' I patted my jacket pocket. 'We'll see you tomorrow.'

'Do you have to go just yet? We have hours before the flooding.'

'I know. But I really was serious about my cat.'

She smiled, and I was struck once more by how much lovelier she looked for the lack of make-up. 'I understand. At least I think I do. It's not really about your cat, is it?'

I blushed. 'No. Not really.'

'Well, Thomas is waiting for me at home. And I'm not going to be back until very late. But you can spare me five minutes, I think.'

She took my arm and steered me towards the *passarelle* in front of the Basilica. 'Wait here. You remember what you said to me when we first met?' She jumped up on to the *passarella* and stood, framed by the basilica, looking outwards towards the square. Then she took out her phone, tapped away at it, and laid it down. I suddenly realised what she was going to do, and my heart leapt into my mouth.

She trilled up and down a few scales, at *mezza voce*, and then nodded to herself as if satisfied. I took a quick look around the square. The few people passing through had now turned, and were looking at her. Even with an audience in single figures, it was important for Isotta Baldan to look professional.

And then she started.

In der Kindheit frühen tagen
Hört ich oft von Engeln sagen
'In childhood's early days, I often heard them speak of angels.'
Wagner.

'The Angel', from the *Wesendonck Lieder*. Something she had never sung on stage, and never would. Her accent was imperfect, and the song not quite right for her voice.

It didn't matter. I wiped away a tear as, at midnight in Piazza San Marco, Isotta Baldan sang Wagner to me.

Chapter 29

Wednesday morning stretched ahead of me, with no surgery to break it up. I could, I supposed, go to the Marciana, and have another read through Thomas Rowlanson's letters, or to see if the good Doctor Beak had left me another photograph. However, I also had some dry translation work to do for the Architecture Biennale and paid work was starting to seem important. That would keep me going for a few hours, and then I could head off to meet Fede.

There was one thing I needed to do first. I dialled the number of the *Questura*.

'*Pronto.*'

'Vanni. It's Nathan. I've got a stalker.'

There was the briefest of pauses. 'My word.'

'He followed me out to Mestre the other night, and, well, he sat near me all the way back on the tram. But in a *stalky* way, you understand?' Vanni's silence told me that he very much did not understand. I continued. 'And then there have been photographs – of me, of Federica – left for me to find. Then I saw him last night in Piazza San Marco.' My words were tumbling out now as I tried to explain my story about missing Monteverdi manuscripts, sexy sopranos – *scary* sopranos, I corrected myself – and dumpy conductors.

Vanni let me ramble on until I ran out of words.

'All right, Nathan. I understand. Can you describe him?'

'He – or she – is dressed as a plague doctor.'

There was silence on the line, and then Vanni gave a dry chuckle. 'That doesn't really narrow things down.'

'That's all I've got, Vanni.'

He paused. 'Nathan, it's going to be very hard for me to do anything with this, you understand? The best I can do is open a file recording that you've made a complaint.'

'Would that help?'

'Well, if we ever pull your lifeless body from the canal it would enable us to—'

'Okay.' I cut in. 'I understand. I just thought I'd let you know.'

'Nathan.' His voice was serious now. 'I'll put this on file if you want me to.'

'No. It sounds like a waste of time, and it's only making work for you, Vanni.'

'If you're sure?'

'I am.'

'Well, just be careful out there.'

'I will be. There are probably only about ten thousand plague doctors in the city. They should be easy enough to avoid.'

'The odds are on your side, Nathan. Most of them are perfectly nice people. Let's keep in touch, eh? *Ci sentiamo.*'

I hung up. I hadn't really expected anything more. I sighed, and went through to the kitchen to make a coffee.

Then I did my usual morning check of emails, the better to delay the moment of starting work. There was a message from Gianandrea, with his liner notes on the keyboard sonatas of Baldassare Galuppi all ready for translation. I added them to the folder that held work in progress. There were a good twenty documents for the Architecture Biennale, as well as one for flat-pack patio furniture. All of those, really, should take priority and yet *signor* Galuppi would certainly be the more interesting. I went over to the CD racks, and ran my finger along 'G'. Gluck, Glass and Gesualdo. No Galuppi. A shame, it would have put me in the mood. No matter. I opened up Gian's document and flexed my fingers, ready to set to work.

The computer plinged to announce the arrival of another email, this time from Isotta. There was no subject line. The message was brief. *Thank you, dear Nathan. I hope you enjoy this. A domani, Isotta xx.*

I clicked on the attachment. 'The Angel'. Live in Piazza San Marco. A memory of my own, private, midnight recital. I closed my eyes, and listened. Extraordinary, beautiful. I listened to it again.

My hand hovered over the mouse button, ready to start replying to Isotta. And then I thought that, just perhaps, it would be better not to.

My train of thought was interrupted by the entryphone. 'Hello?'

'Mr Sutherland. Nathan. It's Tom Lockwood. Can I come up?' I buzzed him in, and heard his feet thundering up the stairs. He looked red-faced and stressed, his white curly hair damp with rain. He shook out his coat, the droplets sending

Gramsci scurrying under the sofa, and hung it on the back of the door.

'Sit down please, Nathan.' I thought that I should be saying that to him, but said nothing.

'Sure. Coffee?'

He rubbed his forehead. 'I need a coffee. God, I need a coffee. All those stories about singers and diva-ish behaviour. There's a bit of truth in them, you know.' He gave a mirthless little laugh. 'Oh yes, there's more than a bit of truth in them.'

Not just singers, I thought. I looked over at Lockwood. With his curly white hair and big tummy, he looked like everyone's favourite uncle. Add a beard and he'd be Father Christmas. It hadn't always been so. I remembered his features, lean and gaunt, from his early record sleeves. And the stories about singers being reduced to tears. I imagined they could make quite a couple.

'Look, Thomas, a few days ago I said she broke my heart when she cancelled before *Poppea*. It was a silly joke, nothing more. And she said she wanted to make it up to me. And then she gave me two tickets for the Masquerade. That's all it was.'

He shook his head, sending more droplets flying. He'd obviously come out in a hurry, in want of hat, *tabarro* and large dog. 'I don't understand.'

'Oh, I'm sorry. I was thinking, well, coffee, Florian's and . . . you know . . .' My voice trailed off.

He looked at me in disbelief. 'Oh, ridiculous. Don't be absurd.'

'Sorry,' I repeated. 'Misunderstanding.'

'Evidently.' He looked me up and down, and for a moment I was reminded of the younger Thomas Joshua Lockwood, to whom the little people were, at best, an annoyance. 'Absurd,' he snapped, again.

I was tempted to snap back at him, and then I remembered what Maitland had said. About how this must all be a torment to him. Moreover, who did I have sitting in front of me? One of the great conductors of the world, who also happened to be a fat old man with a partner thirty, forty years his junior. Calm, Nathan, it's not all his fault.

'Look, Thomas, here's what we're going to do. I'm going to make two cups of coffee. Regular for me. I suggest decaf for you. We're going to take five minutes. And then we'll talk about things instead of shouting about them. Deal?'

His face flushed again, then he nodded his head. 'All right. I'm sorry.' He took the handkerchief from his jacket pocket and started polishing his glasses, so furiously I feared he would snap them.

I could have used the machine, but making coffee from scratch in the kitchen would, I thought, give things time to calm down a bit. I made myself a two-cup pot and drank one whilst I brewed up Lockwood's decaf.

I took them through into the office. Gramsci, having noticed the absence of Karajan, was sitting in his lap, purring.

'You don't like cats, do you?' I said.

He shook his head.

'Just push him off.'

'I can't.'

I took a closer look. Gramsci purred away as he flexed his claws, happily digging into Lockwood's leg. I hoped they weren't his best trousers.

'Here, let me.' I gently unhooked one paw from the great

conductor's trousers, and then moved on to the next one. 'Okay, I think we've got it.' I scooped him up, and plonked him on to the windowsill. 'There you go. Good cat. There are people outside. Just give them a good hard stare and be outraged, eh?' I sat back down. Lockwood brushed fur from his trousers. 'I'm sorry. He can tell, you see? If people don't like cats.'

Lockwood drained his coffee in one. 'Another?' I said.

He shook his head. 'No, no. We're wasting time. And besides he,' he nodded at Gramsci, 'might come back. Something happened this morning, Sutherland.' I'd already noticed that he reverted to using my surname when stressed. His voice trembled. 'And I'm scared. Really, truly scared.'

'Go on.'

'The Masquerade tomorrow. If you're even a little bit famous, you know, sometimes you can get rather odd things in the mail. So I kept trying to tell myself it was just a cryptic invitation.'

'And now?'

He said nothing, but picked up his briefcase, placed it on the desk, and clicked it open. He took out a small, beige envelope. 'Have you got a cloth, an old newspaper, something like that?'

'Sure.' I took a sheaf of Brexit Survival Guides and passed them to him. He took a quick glance at the text, tutted, and laid them face down on the desk.

He opened the envelope and tipped out the contents. They formed a neat little pile of fine black ash.

'Whoah.' I leapt to my feet and jumped back from the desk, accidentally banging my knee against it and sending the ash scattering to the edges of the paper. 'Tom, what the hell is this?'

'Just a pile of black ash. Burned paper. That's all it is now.'

'It could be toxic for all we know.'

'It's paper, Sutherland.' His voice was calm. 'Burned paper. And I can tell you precisely what it is. It's a threat.'

'What sort of threat? How can you be sure?'

'Because of this.' He delicately prodded a scrap of yellowed paper from the midst of the pile of ash. Then, with a look of annoyance, he took his handkerchief from his pocket, dabbed it with his tongue, and wiped the black stain from his finger.

I pulled the fragment towards me. There was some writing on it, and I turned it round, the better to read it. Again, I couldn't restrain myself from giving a little start. Only two words. A signature, but one I had seen reproduced hundreds of times.

Claudio Monteverdi.

Chapter 30

I knew what it meant. I was certain that Lockwood knew it too. I was struggling to find the words, when he saved me the trouble.

'The tickets for the Masquerade. It's not an invitation at all, is it? It's a threat. Be there, or else.' His voice started to break, and he fell silent.

'Or else we're going to send you the manuscript. Page by page. As a pile of ash.'

He nodded, and rubbed at his face.

'That figure at the opera. The night that Zambon was killed. He was waving something at you. It was the score, wasn't it?'

'I couldn't be sure. It was difficult to make out. I thought perhaps he was just waving a programme at me. *Bravo, maestro*. That sort of thing.' He blew his nose. 'That's what I told myself, anyway.'

'So what are you going to do?'

'You mean what are we going to do?'

I nodded. 'If you like.'

'There were four tickets. I assume two are for Isotta and myself. One of the other two could, I suppose, be for you. Given that Zambon wanted to contact you. The other, I suppose, could be for Maitland. He's an expert on this sort of thing.' He left the unspoken question hanging in the air.

I shook my head. 'I'm not going without Federica.'

He sighed. 'As you wish.'

'What do you think is going to happen?'

'I don't know. Perhaps some sort of demand will be made.'

'And then what?'

'I'll give them what they want, of course.'

'Seriously?'

'Whatever they want. Whatever it costs.' He dabbed at his eyes, and I could see he was on the verge of tears. 'I have money, you know,' he muttered.

'Thomas, if we're right about this, this is blackmail. I should take this straight to the police.'

'No!' His arm whipped out across the table, and he grabbed my hand with surprising strength. 'Please, Nathan, you can't, you mustn't.'

'It's blackmail, Thomas,' I repeated, my voice low. 'We could be getting involved with some very unpleasant people. You're putting your money at risk. Not to mention your safety.' And ours, I thought.

'We can't be one hundred per cent sure. Please, we must find out more. If there are police there, it could ruin everything. We could lose everything. *Proserpina Rapita*, the whole thing. You know how important this is?'

'I do know, Thomas. But—'

'But nothing.' The tears were flowing now, and his grip was becoming painful. 'I am begging you, Nathan, I will get on my knees if you wish. Please, for the love of God, don't do this.' He slumped back in his chair, and sobbed.

I let him cry for a few minutes.

'Tom. Listen to me. Have you received anything – anything at all – that could be considered to be a demand for money?' He shook his head. 'Are you absolutely sure, Tom? Because that changes everything.' Again, he shook his head.

I sighed to myself. I knew exactly what I was going to do, and wasn't happy about it. 'Okay. All we have, then, are four unsolicited invitations and an envelope full of ash. So I won't say anything. Not today, anyway.'

He blew his nose. 'Thank you, Nathan. Thank you.' He got to his feet, a trifle unsteadily. 'Look at me, I really am in a terrible old state.' He forced a watery smile on to his face.

'I know this means a lot to you,' I said.

'You're trying to be kind. Thank you. But I don't think you can possibly understand. I've had a lifetime in music. This doesn't mean a lot. It means everything. Absolutely everything.'

I nodded, and he moved around the desk and threw his arms about my neck. We hugged, awkwardly. I could feel his cheek, still damp with tears, against mine.

He stood up and took a few deep breaths. 'Thank you again.' He reached into his jacket and took out an envelope. 'This is for you. I was serious when I said I'd recompense you for your time.'

I took it from him. 'Thank you.' We stood in silence until I realised that he was waiting for me to open it. I tried to slit it elegantly with my fingernail, failed, and tore it instead. I took out the cheque within, glanced at the figure written there, and whistled. 'Very generous of you.'

'Worth every last euro, I'm sure.'

'*Grazie, maestro.*' I paused. 'This isn't why I'm doing this, you understand?'

'I do. And I thank you for it. We'll see you tomorrow night. Now, in the meantime, can you recommend a good florist near here?'

'Fantin. In Campo San Salvador. They're very good. I should go there more often myself.'

'Good. Good.' He smiled again. 'I have a very angry soprano with whom I have to build bridges.'

I smiled back at him. Then a thought struck me.

'That's a nasty cut above her eye,' I said, trying to keep my voice as light as possible.

He was struggling into his coat, and suddenly stiffened. He looked at me with suspicion in his eyes, wondering where I was going with this.

'She was telling me about it last night,' I continued, 'about scratching herself with that big ring of hers.'

'Yes, oh yes.' His posture loosened. 'Yes, I'm always telling her about that. Silly girl.' He nodded, in a half-distracted way. '*A dopo.*' We shook hands, and he left.

I moved to the window, and leaned over Gramsci. Lockwood looked up at us both, and gave a half-wave. He looked to his left and right, unsure which way to go. I pointed in the general direction of Campo San Salvador. He smiled, and set off.

'Well now, fat cat,' I murmured, scratching Gramsci behind the ears. 'What do you make of *Maestro* Thomas Joshua Lockwood, I wonder?'

He nipped at my finger, but his heart didn't really seem to be in it. Then he settled down, and went back to staring out of the window. Like me, it seemed, he had much to think about.

Chapter 31

'Thank you for meeting me,' said Fede. 'You didn't have to.'

'Oh, I think I did.'

'And for the flowers. They're lovely.' She took off her coat, and flopped down on the sofa. 'So, go on then. Tell me what you've done.'

I sighed. 'Shall I go and make us a spritz first?'

'It's a bit early, isn't it? Even for us.'

'Oh, the sun is over the yardarm somewhere in the Great British Empire.' She narrowed her eyes. 'Trust me, it's a good idea.'

As I went through to the kitchen, I saw Gramsci hop up on the arm of the chair directly behind Federica's head. He turned his head to me and I jabbed my finger as I whispered the words 'Not. A. Word.'

'Sorry. Nathan, what was that?'

'Just talking to the cat, *cara mia*.'

I had the feeling I was going to need to make the best spritz of my life.

We sat at opposite ends of the sofa, the middle section marking out a demilitarised zone. Fede nodded to herself as she thought over everything I'd had to say, took a sip from her drink and placed the glass on the table.

'So let me see if I've got this right. I've been gone for just under forty-eight hours, correct?'

'Right. Give or take an hour.'

'And in that time you've been on a date with a beautiful celebrity.'

'Well, I wouldn't call it a date, more—'

'Shut up, please. You've also managed to acquire a stalker.'

'Yes.'

'And even better than that, you've got me – lucky girl that I am – one as well.'

I said nothing.

'Is that it? Am I missing anything?'

I cleared my throat. 'Well, on the plus side, I've got us tickets for the Masquerade at the Casino. And I bought you flowers.'

'Flowers bought for the purposes of avoiding a row do not count as flowers, Nathan.'

'And I promised to cook your favourite dinner.'

'It's going to have to be the best dinner ever.'

'Oh it will be. It will be.'

She got to her feet, stretched and yawned. 'Right. I'm going to unpack.'

'Can I help?'

'No. Cook dinner. Best dinner ever.'

I felt her moving behind me, but thought it best not to turn round. Or indeed, say anything. I braced myself.

I felt her arm slip around my neck, and breathed in the smell of her hair as she rested her head on top of mine. I tried not to sigh with relief. Then she crooked her elbow, and gently but remorselessly tightened the pressure around my neck. She moved her head until her mouth was next to my ear, and whispered.

'Don't. Do. This. Again. Ever.'

Gramsci perched on the kitchen table and watched as I made up a basic béchamel, threw in a bay leaf and stuck it on a low heat. Then I cracked my way through a dozen walnuts – never the loveliest of jobs – and picked out the fragments of kernel. Then I put them in a small pan and dry-fried them for a few minutes, just to toast them ever so slightly. I usually skipped this bit but given the dish was Fede's favourite and I was desperately in need of credit, I was going to do it properly.

I took an ovenproof dish and started building layers. A sheet of pasta, a coating of béchamel and some walnuts. Then I tore a ball of mozzarella into pieces, enjoying the texture of the cheese squidging between my fingers and its fresh, milky aroma. I mixed it with some diced cubes of Asiago, and scattered them to form another layer.

The consolations of lasagne. There was something very peaceful about it. It all seemed so logical, building layers up one upon the other. I finished by topping it off with a generous dusting of parmesan. Thirty minutes in the oven and it would be golden, molten and bubbling.

Federica pushed her plate away, and refilled our glasses.

'Do you ever think you might be wasted in translation?'

'All the time. Trouble is, I don't really see an alternative.'

She nodded at her empty plate. 'You could cook.'

'I could. There are a few problems, though.'

'Such as?'

'Long hours. Hard work. Risk of developing an unhealthy relationship with alcohol and tobacco.' She raised her eyebrows. 'Okay, risk of developing an even worse relationship with alcohol. We'd hardly ever see each other—'

'But tell me the bad points, *caro.*'

'—which means that you would become Gramsci's primary care giver.'

'Ah.'

'Oh, and there's also the possibly insurmountable problem of getting Italians not to laugh when you ask if they might be interested in an English chef.'

'Hmm. Maybe you're right. It was just an idea.' She turned to look at the speakers. 'What are we listening to now?'

'I think we're on to the Third Book of Madrigals. Non-distressing, I hope.'

'Non-distressing. Are we only going to listen to Monteverdi until we find the manuscript then?'

'So I was thinking. But not if you don't like it. There's always Jethro Tull.'

'Monteverdi is fine. So tell me about last night. About Florian's. I've never been there.'

'Seriously?'

'Why would I? Other coffee is available. Uncle Giacomo went once. April the seventh, 1989.'

'You remember the date?'

'It made a big impression on him.'

'In a good way?'

She paused. 'It made a big impression on him.'

'Anyway,' I said. 'It was quite nice. Expensive, I imagine.'

'And Isotta?'

'Again, quite nice.' I paused. 'There's something about her, though. When we met for the first time the other day, something happened. A guy tried to sell us roses and she went berserk.'

'To be fair, you get angry if somebody tries to sell you roses.'

'I know, but I don't get all racist about it.'

'Hmm. So why do you think she wanted to meet?'

'Well, I assumed it was my good looks and charm.' The incoming cushion bounced off my head, but at least I'd been bracing myself for it. 'Too early to be frivolous about this?'

'Far too early. The option of sleeping on the sofa is still there. Continue.'

'Well, as I said, she just wanted to give us these tickets for the Masquerade.'

'And that had to be done at midnight in Piazza San Marco?'

'It seems so.'

'Where you saw your – or should I say *our* – stalker?'

'That's right. Well, at least I think it was.'

'Nathan.' She paused. 'Are you worried?'

I spread my hands wide, and forced as much jollity as I could into my voice. 'Oh, I don't—'

She cut me off. 'No, don't give me cheery old Nathan breezing his way through life. Because I don't trust that Nathan. Be honest.'

I sighed. 'Well, the apartment door is a *porta blindata*. Nobody is going to get through one of those in a hurry. And this is Venice, during *Carnevale*. The streets are full of people.

That all makes it very, very difficult for someone to,' I searched for the right words, '*do* . . . anything.'

We sat in silence for a few seconds. 'And so?'

'And so . . .' I looked into her eyes. There was no point in lying. 'And so, yes, I'm just a bit worried.'

She nodded. 'Thank you.'

'How about you?'

'Yes. Just a bit.' She turned her head this way and that, as if trying to come to a decision. 'Okay. Time for bed.'

I nodded towards the bedroom door and then at the sofa, making a sad little face.

'Don't push it,' she said.

'It was a pretty good dinner though, wasn't it?'

'It was, yes. But not the best dinner in the world.'

'Oh.' My face fell.

'I'll give you another chance tomorrow. Good night, *tesoro*.'

Chapter 32

'I've got nothing to wear.'

'Neither have I.'

'That's different. Things look good on you. I'll just look like a sack of spuds.'

Fede pulled her coat on, then walked over to the table and picked up the invitations to the Grand Masquerade. 'Okay, so the theme is opera. That's easy.'

'What, wear an eyepatch and carry a spear? Where am I going to get a spear from?'

'Easier than that. You have a dress shirt, don't you?'

'Yes, I needed one for a reception a few years back.'

'Is it suitably ruffled?'

'A little too ruffled.'

'There is no such thing as too ruffled. Not for tonight. How much money have you got?'

I riffled through my wallet. 'Seventy euros.'

She held out her hand. 'Give it to me please.'

'What?'

'Come on. Give it to me. I'll sort it out.'

'That's a bit steep isn't it?'

'Not for the Grand Masquerade. We'll more than make the money back on the *cicheti* and prosecco.'

I grumbled away to myself but handed the money over. She gave me a peck on the cheek. 'Don't worry, *caro*, I'll sort it out. I'll see you late afternoon.'

'But what are you going to wear—' I started, but the door slammed and she was gone.

I looked at the clothes that Federica had laid out on the bed. My old dress shirt, rumpled and in need of a good iron. I rested my hand on my stomach for a moment. How many years had it been since I last wore it? It would, probably, still fit. Perhaps a cummerbund would help? Except that I couldn't remember ever having owned one. For that matter, did people still wear them? I patted my stomach again. I was sure it would be fine.

I looked at the other items. A black felt tricorne hat adorned with a bright red feather at a rakish angle was placed on top of a thick piece of folded black cloth. I moved the hat aside and picked up the bundle, turning it over in my hands and feeling its weight.

'Is this what I think it is?'

She nodded. 'A *tabarro, sì*.'

'Wow.' I unfolded it and threw it around my shoulders. 'Cool.' I took a look at my reflection in the mirror. 'Oh, I like this. This I like.'

Federica nodded in approval. 'Good. Very good. Now you just need the hat to set it off.' I placed it on my head. She took a step back and put her head to one side. 'Not quite.' She moved it, perhaps, a centimetre to the left. 'That's better. Just a little more rakish.'

'Is rakish good?'

'Rakish is good. Absolutely.'

I admired my reflection, and put my hand on my hip. The Pose of Power. I wished, for a moment, that I had a moustache to twirl. 'Oh, that's good. That's very good. Just one thing.' I paused. 'Who am I supposed to be?'

'Don Giovanni, *tesoro*.'

'I see. Oh, that's brilliant. Quite brilliant.'

She smiled. 'I thought you'd like it.'

'Like it? I love it! I've always wanted a *tabarro*. But how on earth did you find one for seventy euros?'

'Ah. Well, that's the catch. I had to borrow it. From Uncle Giacomo.'

'Oh.' My face fell.

'Sorry, *caro*, they are rather expensive. And he will want it back, I'm afraid. He'll need it for the Gran Liston in December.' She smiled again. 'But you can keep the hat.'

I took it from my head. It was a quality hat, no doubt about that. I took a look inside. The label bore the name of an exclusive shop in San Polo. Then a suspicion formed in my mind.

'Hang on a moment. Do you mean to say you bought this?' She nodded. 'Can I ask how much it was?'

'Eighty euros. It's okay, you don't have to give me the remaining ten. It's a sort of present.'

'Eighty euros! For a tricorne hat?' She nodded. 'For a tricorne hat that I'm going to wear once?'

She nodded. 'It's the Grand Masquerade. You have to look good.'

'Couldn't you have got me one from, I don't know, a crap stall?'

'I could have. But you have to look good. Don Giovanni wouldn't wear a cheap hat from a crap stall.'

'But I'm never going to wear it again. I can't wear it around town. The Honorary Consul in Venice dressing like Adam Ant's Dandy Highwayman.'

She shrugged. 'It'll last for ever. You can always wear it for Carnival. Who knows, maybe this'll become a regular thing.'

'So I'll have to go as Don Giovanni for the rest of my life?'

'Perhaps so. Anyway, you look very dashing. Positively handsome.'

'Really?'

She smiled. 'Really.'

'Wow. But I'm not sure I'm much of a Don Giovanni.'

She raised an eyebrow. 'No?' Gramsci padded in and hopped up on the bed, gazing up at me. 'Anyway, let me show you what I've got.'

She left the room. Gramsci continued to stare at me. 'I am not a Don Giovanni, okay?' I hissed at him.

'What was that, *tesoro?*'

'Just talking to the cat again, *cara mia*.'

She came back in. It hadn't taken her long to get changed. A simple, light blue dress, faded and frayed at the edges. She hadn't worn it in years. Just a frayed and faded blue dress, and yet . . .

'What do you think?'

I broke into a broad smile. 'Mimì?'

'From *Bohème*. Of course. Do you like it?'

I shook my head. 'It shouldn't work. It really shouldn't work. But on you . . .' I couldn't keep the ridiculous smile off my face and threw an arm around her waist, bending her backwards in order to kiss her in what I hoped was a suitable Don Giovanni-esque way, an effect that was ruined by losing my balance. We tumbled on to the bed, as Gramsci yowled and leapt to the floor.

I looked up at her, still smiling. 'It really does work. You look lovely.' I put my hand on her cheek and brushed the hair back from her face. 'Really lovely,' I repeated.

She bent to kiss my forehead. 'And you look very handsome, *tesoro*.' Then she sat up, and patted my stomach, almost absent-mindedly.

'I wonder if Uncle Giacomo has a cummerbund,' she said.

Chapter 33

Nobody looks twice at a man in a *tabarro* during Carnival. Nevertheless, I took my hat off on the *vaporetto* journey to San Marcuola, afraid my rakishness would strike fear into the hearts of the other passengers. Federica draped a heavy coat around her shoulders to keep out the chill of a winter's evening.

Most of the commuter traffic had thinned out by now, as office workers made their way home. The next rush would come in the later hours of the evening, as restaurant and bar workers made their way back to Piazzale Roma and the buses to Mestre and beyond.

The cabin was nevertheless crowded with visitors. It was never anything other than crowded at this time of year. We made our way inside, pushing past Napoleon Bonaparte, who resolutely chose to remain outside, staring out at the dark waters of the Grand Canal, every inch the Man of Destiny. I wondered if it was the same Napoleon. Or perhaps all Bonapartes were starting to look the same?

'Outside?'

Fede shook her head. 'Too cold.'

'Are you sure? You're supposed to be dying of consumption,

remember? It might help you get into character. And you could snuggle under my capacious *tabarro*.'

She rolled her eyes. 'It seems you've already got into character. Oh, very well.'

Perhaps half the passengers in the cabin were masked, in various degrees of fabulousness. A family of four Japanese tourists joined us outside. Two little girls and their mum in cheap sparkly domino masks, probably bought from a kiosk, chatted excitedly away; whilst Dad, in a plastic tricorne hat, texted away on his phone. I looked down at my own hat, felt its weight and ran my thumb over the felt surface. I smiled, genuinely this time, at Fede.

'You were right. I might only wear it once, but it's a good hat.'

'Of course I was right, *tesoro*. You have to look the part.'

I turned back to the Japanese tourists. We were about to pass under the Rialto Bridge, resplendent in the moonlight, and Dad leaned over as far as he could in an attempt to film it all. Mum hoicked the two little girls on to her seat, and stood them up, the better to be able to see. They'd come halfway around the world to spend perhaps two days in Venice, and were wearing cheap carnival masks that had probably been made in China. And yet, they were undeniably having a good time. It was easy, too easy, to huff and puff about Carnival, about how it had changed from a local festival for Venetians into a grotesque money-making machine. Yet for those seeing it for the first time – for, probably, the only time – there was still a charm to it. No, more than that, there was a magic to it.

Federica noticed the expression on my face. 'Better?' she said.

I nodded. 'Easy to forget, isn't it? In a week's time they'll be back home in Tokyo, or wherever, showing their friends thousands of photographs. And they'll all be saying how beautiful it is, and how lucky people must be to live somewhere like that.' I sighed. 'Sometimes we forget that.'

They continued to snap away, this time at the house of Benedetto Marcello. I could not understand what they were saying, but they'd figured that the plaque fixed to the wall indicated it had belonged to someone of importance and was, therefore, worth recording. And so it was. The home of the man who gave his name to the *conservatorio* in Campo Santo Stefano; a man who had set the first fifty psalms to music. I quite liked what I'd heard, and thought it a shame that he'd never got around to the remaining one hundred.

More excitement, as we passed the Casino itself where, through the watergate that led into the garden, masked figures could be seen and light classical music could be heard over the sound of the engine of the *vaporetto*. This was more than enough to distract the tourists from the memorial plaque to Richard Wagner, who'd breathed his last here on 13 February 1883. I wondered what the old monster would make of it all.

The boat pulled into its stop at San Marcuola, the *campo* dominated by its eponymous church. The building had been dedicated to Saints Hermagorus and Fortunatus who, through a trick of the Venetian dialect, had become one in the non-existent personage of San Marcuola. The marble cladding on the outside had never been completed and never would be, the red-brown brick ledges and holes that would have served to support the marble now providing homes and resting places for pigeons. It looked shabby and unloved, although its local congregation strived to keep it open, visitors being attracted by a Tintoretto *Last Supper*.

I gave a smile and a nod to the Japanese tourists as we got off. We made our way along the *calle* to the right of the church, where *passarelle* had been laid out in readiness for high water. Federica took the coat from around her shoulders and draped it over her right arm. She shivered.

'Aren't you cold?'

'Of course. But I think we should arrive in character, don't you? Go on, put your hat on.'

'Are you sure?'

'Of course. Without the hat you're just a man in a cloak, and there are hundreds of those. With the hat, you are the notorious Don Giovanni.'

I did as she said. And I have to confess that I did, perhaps, swagger just that little bit more.

We made our way to the gates of the Casino, where large men with guns waited for us. Fede never so much as batted an eyelid at this sort of thing, but I thought I would never become used to the sight of armed private security guards. Immediately, I wanted them to think well of me. I smiled as ingratiatingly as I could, as I reached – slowly – under my *tabarro* and produced our tickets. One of the guards gave a barely perceptible nod to his colleague, and they moved aside to let us through, stony-faced. I smiled and nodded, again. I was, I knew, being a very uncool Don Giovanni.

We walked through the courtyard and up to the main entrance where an impossibly thin young woman with cropped black hair stopped us.

'We're here for the Masquerade,' I said, and flashed my

brightest smile; a smile so Don Giovanni-esque it would have melted the hearts of any Donna Anna, Donna Elvira or Zerlina.

If I'd been expecting a response, I was to be disappointed. 'The upstairs reception is open now, sir. Or, if you prefer, you'd be welcome to take a glass of prosecco in the garden.'

'Oh.' I placed a hand on Federica's bare shoulder which, like her tiny hand, was frozen. 'It is rather cold. And my companion is dying of consumption,' I added, with what I hoped was an even more winning smile.

I'd hoped for a smile in return, but her heart remained resolutely unmelted. 'There are space heaters outside, sir.'

'Nevertheless, I think we'd prefer to go up, dear lady.' I gave a low, sweeping bow. Her eyes narrowed, ever so slightly. Too much Don Giovanni, perhaps?

Fede took my arm and gently pulled me away. 'Well done, *caro*. That was just a little bit gallant. Almost.'

'Was it? Oh good.'

'Of course. It's not your fault she's immune to the charms of Don Giovanni.' Then her grip on my arm tightened, just ever so slightly. 'Although I think I see someone who may not be.' There, framed in the archway at the top of the stairs leading to the *piano nobile*, was Isotta. Her hair had been backcombed to within an inch of its life, whilst bright red lipstick and thick black mascara made her skin look paler than ever. She was wearing a simple, low-cut black velvet dress that was probably not so simple at all, and an intricately patterned fine gold headband that just about concealed the cut above her eye. Her character was not immediately identifiable from her clothes, but I could guess.

'Isotta,' I smiled. 'Or, tonight, should we call you . . . ?'

'The Queen of the Night?' said Federica.

She beamed. 'You guessed?'

'Of course.'

'And you make a fine Don Giovanni, Nathan.'

'You guessed?'

She giggled. 'Of course.' She turned to Fede. '*Cara* Federica . . . or, what should we call you tonight?' Her expression changed, and she looked puzzled. Deliberately, I thought.

Fede smiled back at her. '*Mi chiamano Mimì, il perchè non so.*'

'Of course. Of course.' She reached out to touch her shoulder. 'You're freezing. Come inside to get warm.'

She led us into the *Sala Palma,* one of the three rooms that made up the dining area, named after the paintings by Palma il Giovane that decorated the walls. They were, as ever, brown. Tables and chairs had been cleared away, and a string quartet played at the far end of the room. Vivaldi, The Four Seasons. Of course.

I looked at the open space, where guests and waiters were circulating, and a terrible thought struck me.

'I see they've cleared the tables away. That doesn't mean there's going to be dancing, does it?'

'Oh, but of course,' said Isotta.

I shook my head. 'Nathan Sutherland does not dance.'

She smiled. 'But I'm sure Don Giovanni does.'

A white-suited waiter appeared from out of nowhere at my shoulder, holding a silver tray with three champagne flutes filled with a light pink liquid. Bellinis. My heart sank further. Prosecco was probably considered too prosaic for an occasion like this, and the humble spritz far too earthy. The Bellini, crushed white peaches and prosecco, would have been seen as that little bit more elegant. Even if it had almost certainly come out of a bottle. I'd always found them far too sweet.

No matter. We clinked glasses, and I took a closer look around. I was by no means the only Don Giovanni, but we were easily outnumbered by Wotans. A number of men were in simple fur jerkins with swords at their side. Siegfrieds, probably. Or could they even be Parsifals? It was difficult to be sure. No matter; Wagner, I was sure, would have been proud.

There were other Queens of the Night, but nobody was looking at them. They, by contrast, were staring at Isotta with barely concealed jealousy.

'Where's Thomas?' I asked.

'Come with me.' She took us both by the arm and guided us into the adjacent room, the *Sala Rossa,* so called because of the yards of red plush drapery that hung everywhere, and then into the *Sala Gialla*, so called because it wasn't very yellow.

Isotta waved her hand in the direction of the balcony. It was difficult to make him out under the lights, but I could see his stout little shadow silhouetted in front of the window, and the drift of smoke from a cigarette in his hand.

'I didn't know he smoked,' I said.

Isotta shook her head. 'He doesn't,' she replied. 'He's unhappy. Stressed.'

'I know.'

Lockwood turned, as if he had heard us. I could see him more clearly now. A white smock with black buttons, and billowing sleeves. His face, chalk-white with a painted red smile.

'*Vesti la giubba e la faccia infarina*,' I murmured. On with the motley, and powder your face.

Isotta nodded. 'Canio. The sad clown. From Leoncavallo's *I Pagliacci*.'

The demon conductor. The man who'd reduced hardened professional musicians to tears. Now appearing as Leoncavallo's ill-fated jester. The cuckolded little clown.

Isotta looked sad, and shook her head. 'Go and talk to him, Nathan. Please.' I looked at Fede. 'The *dottoressa* and I can chat for a while.' She took her by the arm. 'Let's get another Bellini, *cara* Federica.' She turned back to me. 'He won't talk to me at the moment. Please, Nathan. Go and talk to my sad clown.' I nodded.

I walked over to Lockwood. He nodded as I approached him, and attempted to toss his cigarette into the canal. It fell short, and I could see the butt glowing on the dock below. Like Isotta's outbreak of swearing a few days past, it seemed so incredibly out of character that I could hardly reconcile it with the dapper figure on the insert of so many record sleeves. He reached for another, his hands shaking. He clicked away at a cheap lighter that refused to keep its flame in the breeze off the canal.

'Allow me,' I said. 'Here, take this.' I lit a cigarette and passed it to him to light his own. I held his hand steady, and he shrank, just a little, from the unexpected intimacy. He inhaled, and then coughed a little. In spite of the cool air, the make-up on his forehead was starting to run.

'Tom, you don't smoke.'

'Not any more. Started when I married my first wife. Gave up when the second one left me. I don't miss it.'

'Except?'

'Except I bloody well need one tonight.'

'I understand.'

'Do you, Mr Sutherland? Do you really?'

'Tom, I may not ever have found a missing Monteverdi manuscript, but I know about loss. I know about being unhappy. Most people do.'

I worried that I might have angered him, but he smiled, which gave a faintly grotesque effect through his make-up and the painted red grin. He patted my arm.

'I never saw you as Canio, Tom. I always imagined you as a Wotan figure.'

He smiled again. 'In my younger days, perhaps. The King of the Gods. Looking down from Valhalla, out across the Rainbow Bridge, lord of all he surveys. Except, of course, that he's not. He says it himself. He's the most wretched of them all. I didn't realise that as a young man.' He swept his arm in a semi-circle, his fingers splayed, as if he could contain the whole of the room and the people within it in the palm of his hand. 'Look at them all – four, five, six Wotans? I can't count them all. They're all young men still. They don't realise yet. He has all the trappings of power, but none in reality. They just see the superficialities. It's an ego thing. At least, it was for me.'

I whistled. 'You're a bit deeper than me, Tom. I just assumed it was an easy costume. Cloak, eyepatch, spear. Job done.'

He chuckled. 'That might very well be true, Nathan. Perhaps I'm over-analysing. So, tell me then, why are you Don Giovanni?'

'My girlfriend has an uncle with a cloak.'

'Marvellous.' He peered a little closer at me. 'Is that all?'

'That's all.'

He paused for a moment. 'Isotta finds you very charming, you know.'

'I'm flattered. But I can't think why.'

'Your partner—'

'Federica.'

'How did you meet?'

'Over a Titian. And then over a Bellini.'

'Lovely. She seems charming, too. How long—' He left the question dangling.

'Three years now.' He nodded as if satisfied. The conversation was making me feel awkward, and so I tried to move on. 'So, why Canio?'

'Well now. I suppose I could say that after the hubris of Wotan, a little humility is needed. And what could be more humble than a sad clown. A poor little cuckold.' Had he paused for just a moment there? 'But that would be over-analysing. The truth is more prosaic.' He patted his stomach, and grinned broadly. 'It's much easier for me to find a flattering costume as Canio.'

I laughed. 'There's always Falstaff?'

'Oh, there is. But I don't really feel a connection with Falstaff. That great roistering, rollicking old braggart. No, I don't think I take quite as much of a bite out of life as good Sir John. Canio, in his own little way, is a man of the theatre. And that's much more me.'

'That's a good answer.'

'It's an honest one.'

'Okay.' I paused for a moment. 'Here's another one for you. Which Monteverdi character are you?'

'Well now. What would you expect me to say?'

'Seneca. Mainly on account of being very wise.'

'Well, I thank you for that. But that's not true at all. It's Orpheus, of course.'

I raised an eyebrow. 'I hadn't expected that.'

'No? Why not?'

'Well, descending to the underworld to rescue his one true love. He's a romantic figure.'

'And I'm not?' I bit my tongue. I'd been thinking out loud about his relationship with his two ex-wives. He saw my embarrassment, and moved swiftly on. 'Anyway, you'd be right. I'm not at all. But you're wrong as well. Orpheus isn't a romantic figure. Not at all. He's not going to the underworld to rescue Eurydice. He's there to rescue music.'

I nodded. 'I understand. And that's what you're doing.'

'Exactly.' There was no qualification, no 'in my own modest way' to be added. Thomas Joshua Lockwood had no doubts that he was rescuing music.

'Is that what we're doing here tonight?' A waiter passed by the window and Lockwood hushed me with a motion of his hand. He reached inside, took a Bellini from the tray, and swirled the bright pink contents in the glass. The waiter inclined his head in my direction.

I shook my head. 'Not just now.' My glass was still half full, the contents, sweet and sticky, slowly warming up. A martini would be nice. A Negroni, even better. I'd settle for a prosecco. I would, it seemed, have to wait.

'We're rescuing music?' I repeated, after the waiter had gone upon his way.

'Oh that's exactly what we're doing, Mr Sutherland. That's

exactly what we're doing.' His voice was hushed. I looked over at him. He'd changed again. If our conversation of a few minutes previously hadn't exactly been easy, there'd been a certain lightness to it. Now, I could almost see him changing physically before my eyes, the obsessiveness returning. He placed his hand on my arm, and nodded towards the crowd in the *Sala Gialla*. 'Look at them, Mr Sutherland. One of them has it. One of them is a cheap crook.'

'Thomas, I told you I should have gone to the police.'

'You will not,' he hissed. It wasn't a request this time. His grip tightened on my arm.

'So what do you suggest we do, *maestro*?'

'We wait. We just wait and see what happens.'

I nodded. 'Okay. I understand. Shall we join the others?'

'I think we should. They seem to be calling us in, anyway.'

There did indeed seem to be a movement into the *sala* itself. We made our way over to Federica and Isotta.

'You have a most charming partner, Nathan.'

'I know. I'm a lucky man. She tells me so every day.'

We laughed and clinked glasses, as the waiting staff gently moved us to the sides of the room. There were well over one hundred of us. And one of us, as Lockwood had said, was a cheap crook.

A cheap crook who could quote from a seventeenth-century opera libretto. There was something about that which bothered me.

Chapter 34

'*Care signore, Cari signori.* Welcome to the *Casinò di Venezia.*'
The speaker was the crop-haired young woman from down-stairs, now smiling broadly. Like everyone else, she, of course, was also expected to get into character. 'If your glasses are charged, let us raise a toast to the spirit of *Carnevale.*'

'The spirit of *Carnevale,*' we repeated, and clinked glasses.

'And with that, ladies and gentlemen, the comedy will begin.' She gave a little bow, and moved to one side as a fanfare rang out from a group of four musicians.

A figure bustled into the room. Dressed entirely in black, his face was partially obscured by a one-third mask that cover-ed his forehead and nose. He wore a black felt hat and long, trailing academic robes.

I recognised him at once, and a chill ran through me.

Il Dottore.

'My God,' I whispered under my breath.

'What's the matter?' said Federica.

I had no time to speak before another brass fanfare rang out, and two other figures entered. A pretty young woman, dressed in a faded and slightly ragged white dress, carrying a tambourine, who pirouetted around the four corners of the room before coming to rest in front of Federica. She put her head to one side, and then a finger to her lips, as if surprised to see someone dressed so plainly in the company of so many fine gentlemen and ladies. Then she smiled, shrugged and rattled her tambourine before dancing away. Colombina.

'*Commedia dell'arte,*' I whispered.

'And?'

'That means only one thing. Audience Participation.'

'Don't be silly. Just don't make eye contact. It'll be fine.'

'It's no good. These people are like sharks. They can smell fear.'

As if provoked by my words, Colombine danced her way over to me, and delicately whisked my hat from my head. I made a grab for it, but she danced away with it in her hands. Then she sat cross-legged on the floor, turning it over in her hands and nodding in appreciation.

The audience looked as one in my direction and laughed. I forced a smile on to my face, and wondered what Don Giovanni would do. Should I try and retrieve it in the most dashing way possible? The choice was taken out of my hands when Arlecchino, dressed in his classic multi-coloured che-quered clothing, tumbled into the room. Colombine made great play of trying to conceal the hat from him, deftly passing it behind her back and to another member of the audience. It passed from Wotan to Brunnhilde to Falstaff, who roared with laughter and tossed it back to her.

Some of them were getting far too much into character, I thought.

Harlequin seemed distracted by something on the other side of the room, and Colombine made use of this to dance over to me and place the hat back on top of my head. Then she grabbed my head with both hands, pulled me towards her with surprising strength, and kissed me full on the lips.

There was a sharp intake of breath from the audience, and she put her hands to her cheeks in mock horror.

Harlequin had turned and was now staring directly at me.

Colombine danced away from me.

We continued to stare at each other. I gave a little shrug, and held my hands apart in a gesture of peace. Sorry, Mr Harlequin. Bit of a misunderstanding. No offence meant.

He took his slap-stick, or *bataccio*, in one hand, and rhythmically slapped it against his open palm, as he started to walk, slowly but ever so deliberately, towards me.

I forced myself to keep my eyes open. 'Please, make it stop,' I muttered through my fixed grin. Fede rubbed the small of my back, but she was laughing now along with the rest of the audience. Then she, treacherous little seamstress that she was, moved away from me. I looked to my right. Isotta and Lockwood had done the same.

Harlequin continued to approach me, rapping his slap-stick all the while, as the musicians played a delicate little minuet. I thought an Ennio Morricone soundtrack from a spaghetti western would be more appropriate.

He stood perhaps a foot away from me, and nodded his head as if sizing me up. Then he turned back to Colombine, whilst pointing at me. She shook her head. He looked back at me. Then he stuck his slap-stick into his waist band, put his hands on his hips and laughed uproariously. He grabbed me by my shoulders and gave me what I thought was a friendly shake. He continued to laugh. I joined in.

It must be nearly over, I thought. Please let it be nearly over.

We continued laughing. I put my hands on my hips as well. Perhaps getting into character would help a bit?

He suddenly stopped laughing, and gave me a hard stare of which Gramsci would have been proud. He pointed at my hat. I pointed to it as well. I took it off and held it out to him. This? He nodded again. I placed it in his hands.

Silence for a few seconds, and then he laughed again. He placed the hat on his head, and turned to face Colombine. Do you like me like this, my sweetheart? She smiled and clapped her hands together.

His expression changed, became serious. He took the hat off – my hat, I reminded myself, although by now I was past caring and was losing the will to live – and shook his head. Then he smiled again, twirled around a few times, and placed it on Lockwood's head. He stood back to admire his work, and looked from one to the other of us in turn. Then he laughed in my face, and threw his arms in Lockwood's direction. See, he seemed to be saying, it looks better on the sad clown than on you. He ran, lightly, to Colombine, embraced her and twirled her around in his arms.

Lockwood looked just a little embarrassed. The rest of the audience, including my perfidious Mimi, exploded in laughter. I stood there, hatless, and prayed for a quick death.

The laughter was interrupted by the entrance of Pierrot. Harlequin and Colombine broke their embrace and danced away in opposite directions. Pierrot looked at the two of them, and shook his head, sadly. He walked over to Lockwood and stared at him, face to face. He moved his head from side to side, as though he was expecting Lockwood's face to move as if in a mirror. He removed the hat from Lockwood's head, and gently shook his head, before returning it to me. This is a hat for fine gentlemen, he seemed to be saying, not for sad clowns. And then, with a final despondent look at Harlequin and Colombine, he was gone.

I closed my eyes and breathed deeply. It was over. And one day, perhaps, I would be able to forget.

I felt a gentle tap on my shoulder. Colombine was there, smiling sweetly and offering me a glass of Bellini. I took it from her, my hand trembling. She pirouetted away from me, and over to Harlequin and the two of them stood and applauded me, encouraging the audience to join in. I smiled, feebly, and raised my glass.

The Bellini didn't even touch the sides.

Fede gave me a hug. 'You were brilliant, *caro*.'

'You were, Nathan. You should be on the stage too,' said Isotta.

Lockwood clapped me on the shoulder. 'Thank you, Nathan. There's always someone who gets roped into this. I'm just very grateful it wasn't me.' He paused for a moment. 'Although I have to say, that really wasn't very authentic as *commedia dell'arte*.'

'No, perhaps not. I must say it wasn't the authenticity of the piece that was bothering me.' I shuddered, and my hands trembled as I swirled the dregs of my Bellini in the hope that it would magically refill my glass.

Fede hugged me again. 'You were brilliant, anyway.'

'Perhaps more of a Leporello than a Don Giovanni?' said Lockwood.

I felt myself starting to relax. Okay, Sutherland, you stepped up to the crease. And people did, genuinely, seem to be having a good time. Even Lockwood seemed to have loosened up. My personal humiliation seemed to have taken his mind off the manuscript, if only for a moment.

'I think you need a martini,' said Federica.

'I do.' Then I did a double-take. 'How did you know that?'

'I know you don't really like Bellinis. It's not really an evening for a spritz or a prosecco. And Nathan Sutherland might like a Negroni, but Don Giovanni would definitely have a martini. Anyway, we're in a casino. A martini is far more James Bond.'

I hugged her. 'You are brilliant, you know that?'

'I know. Okay, now none of these waiters are going to have a martini so I'll go and get you one. Get me some *cicheti* if anything nice goes past.' She made her way through the crowds now thronging the dance floor, the string and brass quartets having been replaced with a DJ and a mixture of unfamiliar Europop that meant nothing to me.

'Would you like to dance?' asked Isotta.

'Seriously?'

'I never joke about dancing.'

'You haven't seen me dancing.'

'No matter. Come on, let's go.' She kissed her fingers and touched Lockwood's cheek, her fingertips coming away ever so slightly stained with white. 'I won't be long, darling. As lovely Federica said, just get me some *cicheti* if any go by.' Then she took my arm and gently, but insistently, led me on to what passed for the dance floor.

I vaguely recognised the music. I'd heard it blaring out of

every sound system on the Lido often enough, during the summer months. It wasn't really my thing. Taking a look around my companions on the dance floor, I couldn't believe it was theirs either. Nevertheless, everyone seemed to be having a good time. The Wotans had abandoned their spears, regardless of the possible consequences, and the Falstaffs seemed as one in their earthy good humour.

Isotta smiled, and giggled.

'What's so funny?'

'Nothing. It's just—'

'Just what?'

'It's just that you dance like an Englishman.'

'And you – well – you don't,' I said. 'But you should be dancing with Tom.'

'Thomas doesn't really dance.'

'And I certainly don't.' I paused. 'Won't he be jealous?'

She put her hand to her mouth and giggled. 'Oh my goodness, no. He really won't.' Then it was her turn to pause, and she looked straight into my eyes. 'He doesn't *expect* anything, you know. You understand?'

I really, really hadn't needed to know that.

'Anyway,' she continued. 'What about your lovely Federica? Won't she be jealous when she comes back and sees us dancing?'

'Oh no. Of course not. We're just dancing, aren't we?' I knew I was lying. I really wished Fede would hurry up and get back from the bar. I looked over Isotta's shoulder in the direction of the staircase, in the hope that I'd catch sight of her.

And there he was.

The familiar masked figure of the plague doctor making

his way, not upstairs to the gaming rooms and bar areas, but downstairs.

Isotta saw the expression in my eyes. 'What's wrong?'

I didn't want to point, or shout, so I grabbed her and spun her round so that she was facing in the same direction I had been. I pulled her closer so that I didn't have to raise my voice. 'There!' I whispered. 'Do you see him?'

'See who, Nathan?' She took a step back and pulled away from me, making the minutest adjustment to her dress. She looked at me with a mixture of flirtatiousness and slight annoyance.

I leaned in towards her. 'The plague doctor. That's not an opera costume. That must be him. The one we're supposed to meet.'

She looked alarmed for a moment, then recovered herself and placed her hand on my chest. She breathed deeply. 'Okay. Where's Thomas?'

I turned around and scanned the room. There was no sign of him. 'Hell, where's he gone?'

'He must have seen him before you did.'

'Stupid bastard, he'll get himself killed. Come on.' I grabbed her arm and pulled her after me, through the crowd of opera characters. A Siegfried raised his voice in protest but I paid him no heed.

'Nathan? What's going on?' Federica was speaking from the top of the stairs, carrying two martinis.

'I don't know. I'm trying to stop Lockwood doing something stupid. Just ditch the glasses and follow us.' I didn't wait to see what she did, and Isotta, in her heels, was holding me back so I released my arm and started running.

A security man was stationed at the bottom of the stairs, speaking occasionally into a radio mic.

'Did you see him?'

'What? Who?'

'Someone came down here, maybe just a minute ago. The plague doctor.'

He shook his head.

That could only mean one thing. He'd gone to the mezzanine level. The Wagner Rooms. I turned to my left. The entrance was cordoned off with a velvet rope, and an extremely visible 'No Entry' sign in a dozen languages.

Hell.

I hurdled the rope and ran into the corridor beyond. There were no lights on and my eyes strained against the darkness. Which way? From behind me I could hear the guard shouting for backup. I suddenly became very, very aware that I was running into a room full of irreplaceable musical artefacts whilst being pursued by men with guns. There was, I thought, the potential for a very messy misunderstanding.

I heard the sound of glass breaking, nearby. I could see a faint glow from the room to my left, and ran towards it.

I recognised it, even in the half-light. Wagner's music room, lined with display cases of memorabilia from his time in Venice and then, at the end of the room, a piano. The Master's piano, placed next to a window overlooking a small garden and the Grand Canal.

There was another crash of glass as the window broke. The light from outside illuminated two figures, both immediately identifiable. The short, stocky silhouette of Lockwood, struggling with the taller, masked figure of Doctor Beak.

'Bastard. Give me it, you bastard. Give it to me.' Despite the swearing, Lockwood was on the verge of tears. His adversary was clutching a rolled-up sheaf of papers. Lockwood threw himself at him, but Doctor Beak taunted him, holding the papers just out of reach, and outside of the window as if he was prepared to let them fall.

There was something tragic, something pathetic in the sight of the old man, in his clown's costume, throwing himself again and again against his bigger, stronger foe. There was also something ineffably cruel about it. The casual sadism of the school bully.

Doctor Beak grabbed Lockwood by the front of his smock, dragged him towards him and then, just as suddenly, pushed him back, sending him stumbling into Wagner's piano and falling to the ground.

I rushed to help him but he pushed me off as he struggled to get to his feet, constrained by his ungainly costume. The plague doctor nodded, as if realising that he had a few seconds' grace, and then reached into his greatcoat. He took a step towards us brandishing the papers in one hand, and, in the other . . . My eyes strained to make it out, and then I realised what it was.

A cigarette lighter.

He clicked it, just once or twice, and waved it in the direction of the papers. Then he stopped, waiting for our reaction.

'Dear God, no!'

He clicked the lighter again, keeping the flame alight and bringing it closer, ever closer, to the papers.

'Listen to me.' Lockwood was struggling to keep his voice calm. 'Please listen. What you're about to do is irreversible.

If you do it, something precious will be lost to the world for ever. For ever. Do you understand that?'

The figure paused. The flame kept burning, yet he brought it no closer to the paper.

'Please. Just put everything down. If it's money you want, I have money. Whatever you want. I promise you.' He reached inside his smock, and drew out a padded envelope. He held it out, his hand shaking. 'It's all there. Every last penny. As I promised. Now give me the manuscript.'

Doctor Beak reached out and took the envelope, weighing it in his hands, before tucking it away inside his coat. He put his head to one side, as if considering the offer. Then he shook his head, and slowly and deliberately put the flame of the lighter to the paper.

'No!'

I tried to get past Lockwood, but, again, he pushed me back. There was a tearing of cloth as his costume ripped while he pulled himself to his feet with all his strength and flung himself at his tormentor. The remaining panes of glass fell from the frame. I could hear cries and screams from outside.

Doctor Beak did his best to fight him off, but was constrained by having to use one hand to hang on to the burning sheaf of papers, whilst Lockwood's horror and fury gave him strength. Somehow, the old man was pushing the plague doctor further and further through the window.

Another moment, and he'd fall. Maybe both of them, through the window and into the garden. I grabbed Lockwood around the waist, and pulled him backwards with all my strength. All of a sudden, he lost his grip on the Doctor, sending us sprawling backwards.

He brushed some fragments of broken glass from his greatcoat, and looked down at us. I could move just one arm, pinned down as I was by Lockwood's weight. Doctor Beak looked at the sheaf of papers burning away. I could not see anything behind the mask and those impenetrable black lenses, but I imagined him smiling.

He dropped the burning sheaf on top of us, just catching the edge of my *tabarro*. I flapped at it with my hand, desperately trying to extinguish the flames.

A posse of security guards entered the room, closely followed by Federica and Isotta. The first paused for a moment, but it was enough. Before he could reach for his gun, the masked figure was running at him, barging into him and sending him flying into those behind him. By the time they got to their feet, he was gone.

I managed to roll myself out from under Lockwood, and got to my feet, brushing fragments of charred paper from my *tabarro*. I held out my hand to him, but he swatted it away. He raised himself up, and kneeled in front of the pile of crumpled, charred papers. He smoothed out what fragments remained, blackened now by the flames, and shook his head, his fingers tracing patterns in the ash.

I hunched down beside him. 'Tom,' I whispered, 'Tom, I am so sorry.' He looked at me, his face now grotesquely streaked where his make-up had run with sweat and tears. 'Tom, I had to do it. You could have killed him. You could both have been killed.'

He said nothing, but reached into his smock, from which he took a white handkerchief with which he started to wipe his face clean of powder, sweat and black ash. Then, finally, he spoke, his voice calm.

'Please go away, Sutherland. I have nothing to say to you. Not now. Not ever again.'

I was about to protest, but I felt a hand on my shoulder. I turned to see Federica looking down at me. She shook her head. She looked over at Isotta. 'I think we should go.'

Isotta nodded, but I couldn't read her expression. 'I think perhaps it would be better if you did. Go and speak to the guards. There will be trouble about this but nobody has been hurt, nothing valuable has been damaged. I will deal with that. But it would be best if you were to go.'

Lockwood was still tracing patterns in the ash, finding tiny little charred scraps and turning them over in his hands in the hope – or fear – of finding something. Then he found a more substantial piece, a corner, not completely burned. No music, just a few scribbled words. A signature.

I let Federica help me to my feet. I didn't need to see any more. I knew whose it would be.

Chapter 35

'So you're saying, Nathan,' said Vanni, 'that things could have gone better?'

I rubbed the back of my neck. 'Yes. Pretty much. All things being considered.' I started ticking things off on my fingers. 'Fragments of a lost Monteverdi opera burned to cinders. A fight and criminal damage at a high-profile private event. Little, if any chance, of Lockwood or Baldan ever speaking to me again. And I have to explain to Uncle Giacomo that I managed to set his *tabarro* on fire. Yes, I think you could say things could have gone better. We didn't quite manage to destroy Richard Wagner's piano, but it wasn't through want of trying.'

Vanni chuckled. He still looked tired, but my discomfort seemed to be cheering him up. 'Ah, Nathan, you worry too much. I'm sure *zio* Giacomo will understand.' I shook my head. 'No? Still, try not to worry.' He looked at his notes. 'A lot of this is actually very useful, you know?'

'Oh good. Well that's something, I suppose.'

'It is. Everything seems that little bit clearer. Straightforward blackmail. Send us some money, or we set fire to your precious manuscript, one page at a time. Except—'

'Except?'

'No ransom note. Well I don't know if you can ransom a musical score or not, but let's call it a ransom note. We don't have one. And that complicates things.'

'Why so?'

'If we did, we could take action. We could freeze *signora* Baldan's bank account, for one thing?'

I gave a little start. 'You can do that?'

He nodded. 'Of course. First thing we do in a case like this. Prevent the blackmailer from actually being paid. As soon as people realise there's no money to be made, they'll stop committing crimes of this nature. So the theory goes.'

'Wow. And does it work?'

He laughed. 'Of course not. It stops people from contacting the police, though.'

'It wouldn't work in this case, anyway. I suspect the money is coming from Lockwood.'

'Why so?'

'He's a wealthy man, and this is his obsession.'

'I see. Of course, Mr Lockwood is a British citizen and, as such, we'd be in no position to freeze his account, even if we had a ransom note to work with. And there's one other thing—' he paused.

'Which is?'

'This manuscript. Have you actually seen it?'

I nodded. 'A couple of pages, anyway.'

'And what did you think?'

I shrugged. 'I wouldn't know. A couple of pages of the libretto. A fragment of music. They looked convincing to me, but I'm no expert.'

'And Mr Lockwood, what does he think?'

'Oh, he's convinced. He has no doubt about it at all.'

'Hmpph.' He tapped a pencil on the table. 'You mentioned there was someone else at dinner with you. On Torcello.'

'Maitland?'

'And he's another expert on this sort of thing?'

'As I understand. I don't know much about him. He's not a VIP like Lockwood, just a music teacher at a public school.'

'Hmm. Okay. Nathan, can you do me another favour?'

'Sure.'

'Have another chat with Mr Maitland for me. It might be good to get another expert opinion on this. Because, as it stands, we've got a case of blackmail with no demand being made, and no evidence that the thing being ransomed even exists.'

'There were the papers last night. I saw Monteverdi's signature myself.'

'I know. That was the only thing which survived. Convenient, isn't it?' He looked at his watch. 'Well now. I'm due to be shouted at by my superiors in thirty minutes' time. That should give us time for a spritz and *panino* at Bar Filovia. And then, perhaps, you could think about doing me that favour?'

'Are you buying lunch?' He smiled and nodded. 'Then I'll think about it.' And afterwards, I thought, there would be other people I needed to speak to.

The Giudecca canal was choppy in the February wind, and I huddled in the cabin until the last possible moment before getting off at Spirito Santo. I put another five-euro umbrella up against the rain. It lasted all of five seconds before the wind blew it inside out. I cursed, and tried to bend it back into shape, but the ribs were bent and twisted beyond repair. I dropped it into a bin, and ducked into the shelter of the portico of the eponymous church as I took out Lockwood's business card to double-check the address. Corte Tramezina, just a few minutes' walk. I turned my collar up against the rain, and strode it out.

There was no name-plate fixed to the door, Lockwood and Baldan seeing it only as a temporary address until the house on Torcello was properly fixed up. I raised my thumb to the bell, and then paused, letting it rest there. I could hear voices inside. Angry voices, a man and a woman.

I sighed. This was obviously not the best time to call, but I didn't feel like coming back again, especially if the weather were to continue like this. I pressed the buzzer and waited.

The voices stopped, but only for a second. I pressed the buzzer once more. Then, when there was no answer, I leaned on it until I could hear someone coming to the door.

Baldan yanked it open and stared expressionlessly at me.

'Isotta.'

She said nothing.

'Isotta. I need to speak to Tom. It's important.'

She shook her head. 'He's not here.'

'Are you sure, I thought I heard—'

'I said he's not here. What do you want, Nathan?'

I sighed, and tried to pull my coat further around me. 'Look, I'm getting wet out here. Is there any chance I could come in?'

She did nothing but stare at me, her eyes cold. Then she spoke. 'What do you want?'

'Okay, so we're not going to be friends. Fine, if that's the way it has to be. I want to ask Tom why he lied to me.'

'What do you mean?'

'I did Tom a favour, and he lied to me. I should have gone to the police when I realised he was being blackmailed. But he promised me there'd been no demand for money.'

'There hadn't been. Not when you spoke. It was on the morning of the Masquerade. A phone call.'

'Oh, a phone call. That's convenient. And you just forgot to tell me. I don't believe you.'

'I don't give a damn if you believe me or not.' She made to slam the door, but I was too quick and stuck my foot in the gap.

'How much, Isotta?'

'I'll give you five seconds before I start screaming.'

'How much?' She said nothing. From inside, I could hear the indistinguishable muttering of a male voice. I dropped my voice. 'Listen. Is there anyone with you? Please, just tell me. I can help you.'

She drew in a deep breath, ready to unleash what would have been the mother of screams, and I hastily pulled my foot from the door, which slammed shut a millimetre from my nose. As I stood there, my ears ringing with the violence of the sound, I was sure of one thing. The voice inside had not been that of Tom Lockwood.

I looked around. There was nowhere nearby where I could just sit, get a drink and keep an eye on Isotta's door. It was still raining, steadily rather than hammering down, but without my disposable umbrella I was going to get properly wet.

To hell with it. If this was what it took, I would wait all afternoon if necessary. I took shelter under a nearby *sotoportego*, and lit a cigarette. Then I lit another. And then the third, as if trying to send me a message, failed to light in the damp air.

A wooden shrine in the shape of an altar had been fixed to the wall at the end of the *sotoportego*. The Madonna, holding the infant Christ. Both crowned, and dressed in eighteenth-century clothing. I smiled, despite the cold and the rain. You could miss so much in this city, simply by failing to look upwards.

I had plenty of time to study it over the following thirty minutes. Thirty minutes in which I smiled and nodded at the occasional passer-by, and pretended to be photographing and making notes on the *capitello*. Than, at last, I heard the door opening. I grabbed my phone, zoomed in as much as possible, and snapped off a photo. I didn't even wait to see if he'd noticed me, but turned and half ran, half squelched my way back to the *vaporetto* stop.

'So you've been out stalking Isotta Baldan?' said Fede.

'Not Isotta. Just whoever was in the house with her. And whoever he was, it sure as hell wasn't Lockwood.'

'She is allowed to have other friends, you know.'

'I know. But there was something different about her today. She just seemed so *different*. Very cold, very distant.'

'Not responding to your manly charms?'

'Yes. Hard as that may be to believe.' My socks steamed

away on the radiator, as I padded barefoot into the office. 'Now, let's take a proper look at this.' I brought the photograph up on the monitor. 'Come on, tell me what you think.'

Fede bent over behind me and put her arms around my neck, then jerked back. 'My God, you're freezing. You're absolutely soaked. You need to get changed.'

'In a moment.' I expanded the image as much as I could. 'Now, what have we got here?'

I'd caught him side on, at the moment of pulling the door closed. He was, perhaps, in his early fifties, with greying hair tied back in a ponytail. His cheekbones were prominent, as were all the bones of his face. Not conventionally handsome, not by any means, but there was something compelling about his features.

'What do you think?' I said.

'Well, firstly, no man of that age should ever have a ponytail.'

'On that we agree.'

'Secondly, good bone structure. He's got a face that seems to be composed entirely of angles.'

'But do you recognise him?'

'No. How about you?'

'No.' I paused. 'No, that's not true. There's something about him that I recognise. Don't ask me where. But I've seen him before.'

Chapter 36

June 29ᵗʰ 1632. It is with a heavy heart that I record these words, for news has reached me from Paris that good Sir Isaac is dead. A most excellent servant to his God and to his King, and a better, wiser master no man could wish for. It may be by now that his body rests in English soil, God rest his soul.

I held the book as flat as I could, and ran my finger down the centre, feeling a roughness from where the pages had been cut.

September 25ᵗʰ 1632. It was both a joy and a sadness to me to be once more in the company of Sig. Monteverdi. We wept together as I told him the news of Sir Isaac. He has recently been ordained a deacon of the church, and, he confesses, finds it increasingly difficult to compose in his old age. I wished him well, and trusted it would not be too long until our next meeting.

I read onwards until I came to the end of Thomas Rowlanson's memoirs. He remained in Venice following the death of Wake, but was officially recalled to England in 1634. In 1636, he left the city for the last time, and disappeared from history. For over a decade he'd stood, Zelig-like, at the shoulders of the most eminent members of Venetian society and then, one day, a letter arrived from Turin informing him

that his time was now done. It put me in a melancholy mood.
I patted Maitland on the shoulder, and inclined my head
towards the exit.

'Something happens in that three-month period. There's
something in those missing pages which could tell us what
happened to the manuscript.'

'Narrows it down, doesn't it?'

'So, what do you think?' I said. 'Is there any chance there
might be somewhere else with a copy of Rowlanson's journal?'

He sighed. 'Who knows? The trouble is that Rowlanson
was just a humble little bureaucrat. No offence.'

'None taken.'

'And as such, it's unlikely that someone would have thought
it worthwhile making a copy. What about the state archives
here?'

I shook my head. 'Unlikely. I mean, I can check, but
everything they have is from the Venetian point of view. If
they have any documentation on the British ambassador it's
more likely to be about spying on him than anything actually
written by him.'

'I understand. Still, perhaps they might repay checking.'

I nodded.

Maitland continued, 'The other thing we can do is check
the Isaac Wake archive.'

'I thought you said that would take for ever?'

'It would. But we've narrowed it down. Now the entries
immediately before and after the missing pages relate to Wake,
yes? So – and this is a bit of a leap in the dark, I admit – we
might assume the lost pages also relate to him. Yes?'

I smiled. 'So we check whatever correspondence Wake wrote in, say, the last month of his life; and specifically anything that relates to Rowlanson.'

'Exactly.'

'Can you do that?'

'I can. I know a few people at the National Archives. Old student friends, you know. They should be able to speed things up nicely. And I've logged a request with the Monteverdi Institute in Cremona to see if they know anything about an attributed extract from *Proserpina*.'

'I'm sorry. You do seem to be doing rather a lot of the work.'

'It's quite all right. It takes my mind off the schoolchildren. Buy me one of those drinks with olives in and I'll forgive you.'

We made our way through Piazza San Marco, in search of lunch. 'There's a little place over towards San Moisè which is delightful. *Signora* Baldan took me there last night.'

I stopped in my tracks. 'You went for dinner with Isotta?'

'Yes. I think it was a sort of peace offering on her part. She'd been rather brusque on Torcello, as you know, and I think she wanted to make things right. She's actually quite charming when you get to know her.'

I bit my lip. 'So. What did she want to talk about?'

'I think partly she needed a shoulder to cry on after the scene at the Casino. Thomas not taking it terribly well, as you might expect.'

'A shoulder to cry on, eh?' I tried to keep my voice light.

'Yes. And we talked about *Proserpina*, of course. And of what we might do next.'

'Lovely. Well I'm glad you've managed to set things straight.'

We walked off in the direction of San Moisè. I was not, I told myself, feeling jealous.

The State Archives were held in the ex-convent of the church of the Frari. They were rarely open to the casual visitor, and gaining access to their records involved a depressing amount of form-filling. I emerged two hours later having done nothing more than confirm what I expected; namely, that they held no papers belonging to Thomas Rowlanson, one time secretary general to the English ambassador.

No matter. My hopes hadn't been high. I'd just go home and start thinking about what to cook for dinner. And then, tomorrow, I could meet up again with Maitland and we could continue with whatever research was still open to us. I did wonder why I was bothering. Lockwood was not speaking to me. Baldan was refusing even to be civil. I should just leave them to deal with whatever trouble they'd managed to get into by themselves. But there was, of course, the money that Lockwood had paid me. I felt duty-bound to continue doing what I could. And there was still the possibility – no matter how slim – that somewhere there might just be a missing score by Monteverdi waiting to be discovered. That by itself was enough reason to keep going.

I made my way back through the Campo dei Frari, and towards San Pantalon. I paused to look in through the window of Tonolo. It was busy, yes, but at least the queue was not stretching out of the door. I could pick up some *frittelle* for us both. Why not? It would be a nice thing to do.

I went inside. As always, it felt like being wrapped up in a great, fluffy cloud of good things. Getting served in Tonolo was a matter of projecting the right air of confidence. Tall men with hats always seemed to have an advantage. Being an Englishman was a positive disadvantage. It took me about fifteen minutes to battle my way to the front. Fifteen minutes of 'no, please, after you' and 'yes, I'm quite sure you were first'.

Frittelle alla Veneziana were, quite clearly, the best. I left with two of them. And two with *crema,* and two with *zabaione.* And two *cioccolato.* And two with apple. It was, I thought, best to cover all bases.

I walked back through Dorsoduro, and across the Accademia Bridge. I stood for a moment to look out to the church of the *Salute* and over to the *bacino* of San Marco, only half visible in the drizzle and the twilight. I found Carnival hard work. But it was still Venice.

I could feel the rain starting to patter harder. A crap vendor looked at me inquisitively, smiling as he proffered his disposable, one-journey-only umbrellas. I shook my head. I'd be home in five minutes. I made my way down the bridge, past the church of San Vidal, and across Campo Santo Stefano and through into Campo Sant'Angelo. The rain was driving people into shops, bars and restaurants and the *campo* itself was quiet.

At first I thought the figure by the newsstand was just another masked tourist, taking advantage of the little shelter it afforded from the rain. Then, as I approached, I recognised him.

Doctor Beak.

I broke my stride for an instant, and then carried on, walking as close to him as felt comfortable. It was impossible to tell if he was looking at me through those dark lenses. I walked past, and then stopped, waiting for him to react.

I heard nothing except the patter of rain on stone. I turned around. He hadn't moved.

'Can I help you?' I said. 'It's just that you seem to be lost?'

He didn't answer. Could he not hear anything under the mask, or was it another attempt to play head games with me? Or, more likely, was he just another plague doctor in a city full of plague doctors?

I stared at him and shook my head. I'd see if I could put him to the test. Instead of carrying straight on down Calle della Mandola, I took a left and headed off down the Calle dei Avvocati. I paused at Campiello Michiel and turned around. He was there, keeping a steady distance behind me.

I turned right into Calle Pesaro. The street was quiet, but reassuring voices could be heard nearby. Then I turned left into Calle Benzon, walked halfway along, and realised I'd made a mistake. There was no exit from the *calle*, which led directly on to the Grand Canal.

I heard footsteps behind me, and spun round. Doctor Beak was there, just a few metres away from me. He did nothing but stare at me. To be fair, it would be hard to tell if he was doing anything else.

I sighed, and ran a hand through my wet hair.

'You know, I'm getting tired of this.'

Silence.

'I said I'm getting tired of this. I'm getting sick and tired of you following me. If you've got something to say, say it.'

He took a step towards me, and I tried to stop myself from flinching. He could, I reminded myself, have a knife.

'It's five o'clock, on a Saturday evening, during Carnival. How long do you think before a horde of tourists walk past?

So if you've got something to say, say it now. And make it good. Or I'm going to tear that damn mask from your face right now. Understand?'

I was expecting him to move, possibly take a step back even. Instead he just balled his fist and punched me in the mouth.

The force of the blow took me by surprise, and sent me sprawling as my box of *frittelle* went spiralling through the air. He was wearing soft leather gloves, but there'd been a heft to the punch which made me think there must have been a metal weight or similar concealed within it. Absurdly, as my head spun, it made me think of Charlie Chaplin concealing a horseshoe within a boxing glove.

I tried to raise my hands to defend myself, but he gave me no time, grabbing me by the lapels of my coat and slamming me into the wall. The beak of the mask prevented him from pushing his face too close to mine, but he spoke clearly and distinctly in Italian-accented English. 'Now you listen to me, you piece of shit. Next time there'll be a knife in this hand.'

My head was still spinning from the blow.

'Nod if you understand.'

I nodded.

'Good.' He relaxed his grip, and then appeared to change his mind, pulling me towards him and then pushing me back against the wall. My head spun again as it cracked against the brickwork. 'One more thing.' He continued to slam me into the wall, knocking the breath out of me. 'You. Stay. Away. From. Isotta. Baldan. Understand?'

He released me, and I dropped to the ground, gasping for air and trying to shake the stars out of my head.

'Understand?' He cupped his hand to his ear. 'I'm sorry, Mr Sutherland, but I'm not hearing anything.' He drew his foot back, and for a moment I feared he was going to kick me in the face.

'Understood.' I coughed the word out.

'Well done. Now go home to your nice girlfriend and make sure you take good care of her.'

His foot was still half raised, and I made a grab for it, hoping I could tip him off balance. Wrong decision. He kicked me in the chest, knocking the air out of my lungs once more. 'Bad move, Englishman. Bad move.'

I could hear voices from the end of the *calle*. People would be here, in just a matter of seconds. Evidently he realised the same. 'Think about what I said, Mr Sutherland,' he said, then turned and walked away as casually as if he was a regular masked tourist taking an evening *passeggiata*.

The voices were clearer now, and I could hear feet breaking into a run.

'Hey, are you okay?' I had never been so grateful in my life to hear an American accent. I looked up to see two young faces staring down at me, full of concern. 'Can you move?' I nodded. 'Here, let me help you up.' One of them slipped his arms under my shoulders and helped me to my feet.

'Thank you. You're very kind.'

'Did you fall? You're bleeding.'

I raised my hand to my face and touched my lip. Bruised, a little bloody, but nothing too serious. I rubbed the back of my head. I could feel a bruise coming up, but there was no blood.

'I'm okay. Just a bit shaken.'

'Did you fall?' one of them repeated.

I shook my head, and wished I hadn't. 'No. Someone tried to rob me. Did you see them? A man, about my height, dressed as a plague doctor.'

'A big guy? Wearing one of those weird beak masks? He just walked past us. I'm sorry, we didn't know.'

'Come on.' Without waiting for their reply, I shuffled to the end of the *calle* and looked both left and right. The street was empty. I shook my head and wished I hadn't. I winced, and bent over, placing my hands on my knees for support.

'Have you got all your stuff? Do you want us to call an ambulance, or whatever they have here? The police?'

'No, it's okay. He didn't get away with anything. Just need to catch my breath, that's all.'

'There's a bar just round the corner. Come with us, we'll get you a coffee.'

'That's kind. Thank you. But I'm all right. Really. And I live very near here.'

One of them looked a little dubious, but the other smiled. 'You live here? That's so cool.' Then he looked a little embarrassed. 'I mean—'

I smiled. 'I know what you mean. Yes, it is cool. Most of the time, anyway. I'll be on my way home. And thank you, once again.'

'Are you sure?'

'Sure I'm sure.' I patted him on the back. 'Have a great evening, okay?' I made my way along the *calle*, back to the *campo*, and in the direction of the Street of the Assassins.

God Bless America, I thought.

Chapter 37

Federica was perched on a bar stool, and spun round when she saw the expression on Eduardo's face.

'Nathan. My God, what happened to you? Are you all right?'

'Ciao, *cara*. Evening, Ed. I'm fine, thanks.'

'You don't look it.' She raised a hand to my lip. 'You're bleeding.'

'Only a little. It's nothing serious.'

'And your coat!' She brushed some brick dust from my back. '*Che casino!*'

'I'm okay. Really. I've just been in a fight with a plague doctor, that's all.'

'We should go to *Pronto Soccorso*.'

'No. We should stay here and have a Negroni.'

Ed looked dubious. Federica looked at me, then sighed and nodded. 'At least put a lot of ice in it. It'll help the swelling go down. Go on then, tell us all about it.'

'I don't suppose there's any chance of you just going to the police and making a *denuncia,* is there?' said Fede, after I'd finished.

'No point in queuing up to make a complaint against an anonymous man in a mask, in a city full of anonymous men in masks.' Then I saw the expression on her face. She was serious this time. 'Look, I'll give Vanni another call. There won't be anything he can do, but at least it'll be something to add to his in-tray.' I sipped at my Negroni, wincing a little as the alcohol stung my cut lip.

'Promise?'

'I promise.'

I could see her shoulders relax. 'Thank you. He knows your name, he knows where you live, and I'm not thrilled that he knows who I am. And now it's got violent.'

I gave her a hug. 'It'll be okay.'

'Oh, I'm sure. Still not thrilled about it, though. I suppose you don't feel like cooking tonight?'

'We were going to have *frittelle*. They're lying in Calle Benzon being eaten by pigeons at the moment. They were from Tonolo, as well.'

Fede touched my cheek. 'That was sweet of you. Never mind.'

'Well, I think I've learned something. Mainly, never threaten a man whilst carrying a box of cakes.'

'You'll know next time. Anyway, I'll cook tonight. My treat.'

'Really? Should we have another drink then?'

'I don't think so, *caro*. Drunk cooking is more your thing.' She reached into her handbag, and drew out her purse. 'I'll settle this.'

I finished my Negroni, and slid the glass across the bar. 'See you tomorrow then, Ed.'

He grinned. 'Are you sure?'

'Not helping!'

I had my key in the lock of the main door, when Fede put her hand on my arm. 'A cigarette would be nice.'

'I thought you'd given up?'

'I have. I'm taking a night off.'

I took the packet from my jacket, and passed her one. I lit hers, and then one for myself. 'You really are worried about this, aren't you?'

She shrugged. 'Yes. Just a bit. Aren't you?'

'More than a bit.'

We smoked in silence, watching the masked revellers come and go. Then she ground the stub under her heel. 'Okay. You get to choose the music tonight. Pour some wine out, I'll be back in about fifteen minutes.'

'I thought you said you were cooking?'

'I'm getting pizza. For me, that's cooking.'

'You star.'

'I do my best. It's not always easy having an accident-prone boyfriend.'

'I know. Right, these drinks aren't going to pour themselves. I'll see you in a bit.' I kissed her on the cheek, and made my way upstairs.

Gramsci came to meet me, and prowled around my feet. It is not an easy thing for a purr to be imbued with a subtle menace, but it was a technique he'd refined over the years.

'Food is it, Grams?' I asked, and made my way through to the kitchen. No, there was plenty of food in his bowl, as there usually was at this time. There was no point in him finishing anything until at least an hour before I was due to get up. 'So what is it then?'

He hopped up on to the living-room table, and swatted at a foam ball that was lying there, sending it bouncing across the room.

'Oh Christ, you want to play, don't you?' He yowled. 'Look, I've had a hard day.' I pointed to my lip. 'I've been beaten up. I could really do with a lie-down.' He fixed me with a hard stare, and yowled again, an octave lower this time.

I sighed. 'Look. If I let you choose the music, would that be okay?' This time, the yowl was a barely perceptible *basso profondo* rumble, but I decided to take that as a yes.

I went to the CD racks. Hawkwind, *Choose your Masques*. It seemed appropriate. Jethro Tull, *A Passion Play*. Suitably theatrical. Goblin, *Suspiria*. Suitably nasty.

I turned the cases over in my hands. Fede, bless her, was not going to like any of this stuff. She'd offered to cook, in her own particular way. And yet, she had said I could choose the music.

I rubbed the back of my head, and winced. No, it wouldn't be fair. I'd give her a chance, at least, to listen to something she might consider non-horrible. I looked through my opera recordings and decided I really wanted a break from Monteverdi. Mozart, then? *The Magic Flute*? Again, it seemed to fit the *Carnevale* theme. Which recording? I smiled to myself. Lockwood and Baldan, of course. I took it down off the shelf, and sat down on the sofa.

'Okay, fat cat, it's like this,' I said. 'You get to choose. You know what to do.'

I laid the CDs out on the table, left to right.

Gramsci stared at me, and then down at the discs. He prodded at *The Magic Flute*, pushing it towards the edge of the table. Then he moved on to *A Passion Play*, looked down at it, and swiped it off the table in one clean move.

I picked it up off the floor. It was not to be a Tull night then.

He moved on to *Suspiria*, and swatted it away without a second glance. It was probably for the best. I'd made Fede sit through the film once, shortly after we'd met, and had been forced to conclude that, for all his manifest gifts as a director, Dario Argento did not make date movies.

Hawkwind or Mozart. Hawkwind or Mozart. How many times had I struggled with a choice like that? Gramsci pushed *The Magic Flute* closer and closer to the edge of the table. One more little jab, and it would fall. Then he lost interest, and moved back to *Choose your Masques*, and pushed it with his nose. The Mozart was a double-disc set and would make a more satisfying crash as it fell to the ground. The Hawkwind had a better cover, but surely that wouldn't be enough in itself? There was no real choice to be made, was there?

He turned away, as if bored with the game, but not before his tail scythed the Hawks' 1982 masterwork to the floor.

Mozart it was to be, then. I slid the disc into the player.

Chapter 38

'Oh, that's nice,' said Fede. 'I was expecting something horrible.' I hurried to replace the *Suspiria* CD on the shelves. Not quickly enough. 'Oh. It was going to be something horrible.'

'Gramsci's choice,' I said.

She didn't even bat an eyelid. She knew how things worked by now. She picked up the jewel case of *The Magic Flute*, and teased out the libretto with her fingernails. 'With Mr Lockwood and *signora* Baldan, no less.'

'Yes. It's my only recording of *The Magic Flute*. Can't remember the last time I played it. It's never been my favourite work, to be honest.'

She rubbed the top of my head, taking care to avoid the bruise. 'Look. You can play that horrible Italian prog if you want.'

'No, really. I don't mind. It'd be good to listen to this again.' The smell of warm pizza was percolating through the flat, and my stomach growled. 'What did you get?'

'Pizza Margherita and Pizza Margherita.'

'Two Margheritas?'

She shrugged. 'The simplest ones are the best.'

'Quite so. Plates or boxes?'

'Boxes. Save on washing-up. There's some beer in the fridge, isn't there?'

'Beer for you. Some rough red wine for me.'

'I'll never understand you, you know. All this time in Italy and you still don't understand about *pizza e birra.*'

'I don't think I ever will. It's a British thing. Pizza to us is still just a little bit foreign. So it demands red wine. And not even a good one. Something from a plastic bottle or a jug is just fine.'

'British people.' She tutted, and went through to the kitchen where I could hear the top being cracked on a bottle of Peroni. She came through with the bottle, a half-empty bottle of red for me, and a single glass. 'You see, if you joined me in a beer we'd have no washing-up at all. Now we'll have a single annoying glass to wash.'

'I'm sorry. I'll do it. Promise.'

We sat and munched away in silence, and listened to the overture, as I regularly swatted Gramsci away from my box.

'Why do you think he shows so much interest in pizza?' said Fede.

'He's an Italian cat. It's his birthright. But I think mainly he sees it as something else that can be pushed off a table.'

'So what's she singing on this? Your friend Isotta, I mean.'

'The Queen of the Night.'

'Appropriate. Is there anyone else we should know on this?'

'Her ex, Salvatore Bonfiglio. I'd kind of forgotten about him until she mentioned him the other night.'

'Oh. Did she need a shoulder to cry on?'

'Not like *that*. She just mentioned him as her ex. There were stories about him when they were married. Not a nice man, it seems. Unreconstructed views on domestic violence.'

'Bastard. What's he singing on this?'

'Monostatos. It's not much of a role, really, but his voice was shot by this stage. Quite a lot of it is spoken.'

We finished the pizzas, and I went to the kitchen to fetch Fede another beer. Then we lay on the sofa and listened. It was a good recording, Lockwood evidently as confident with Mozart as he was with Monteverdi. Fede yawned, and I ruffled her hair.

'Tired?'

'Yes. Do you mind if I don't listen to the rest of it? I think I'll have an early night.'

'Just give it five minutes. The best bit is coming up.' She nodded.

Monostatos began his aria 'Everyone feels the joys of love'. Perfectly well sung, and yet you could tell this wasn't a singer in his prime. No matter, the highlight was about to start.

The Queen of the Night, and the aria *Der Hoelle Rache*. 'Hell's Revenge burns in my heart.' Diabolically difficult. There have never been that many singers capable of doing it justice.

Fede sat up, and leaned towards the speakers.

I smiled. 'This is a bit special, yes?' She waved at me to be silent, in irritation. The aria came to an end, and she reached for the remote control to replay it. We listened again, this time in complete silence.

She paused the recording, and nodded. 'Yes. You can see what all the fuss was about, can't you?' She flicked through the CD insert until she came to Isotta's face. She smiled. 'And you have to say, she looked the part. Just like last night.' She yawned. 'Do I need to listen to any more, or should I go to bed?'

'Oh, there's another bit with Monostatos coming up. Just spoken dialogue in this section. I wonder how the two of them felt, making this recording?'

'How do you mean?'

'Isotta's at the height of her powers, singing one of the most difficult arias in the repertoire. And almost directly afterwards, up comes Bonfiglio, and his part isn't much more than a spit and a cough. They must both have known their careers were on different tracks by then.' I reached over to the remote control, and pressed play.

It's a nasty scene by any reckoning, as Monostatos tries – not for the first time – to force himself on the heroine, Pamina. It's never an easy listen, made more uncomfortable by the fact that Monostatos is undeniably identified as a black man. Much of the time, I could happily skip it. But there was a certain curiosity as to what Bonfiglio would do with it. He started to speak, in his low tenor voice . . .

'Bloody hell!' I dropped the remote control, and scrabbled around for it in order to pause it.

'What's the matter?'

'That voice.' I stabbed at the controls. 'Let me listen again.'

'I don't understand . . .' And this time it was my turn to wave for silence.

'Listen. Just listen.' That voice. Slightly rough, as if the speaker smoked too much.

I listened to the whole of the scene, then replayed it again. Then once more. It had to be him. It simply had to be him.

'That voice,' I said. 'It's him. It's the man who attacked me earlier today.'

'Are you serious?'

'Absolutely.' She cast her eyes over the amount of remaining red wine in the bottle, and raised an eyebrow. 'I'm absolutely serious, okay?'

'How can you be sure? You heard him for, what, thirty seconds? He said perhaps twenty words to you. He was wearing a mask.'

'I heard him close up, I heard every single word, and there was something about that voice. He sounded like he should have been a singer, you know?'

She shook her head. '*Tesoro*, you're tired. You should go to bed.' There was concern in her voice.

'I am tired, yes.' I rubbed my head, and winced as I accidentally touched the bruise. 'But come on, let's just think about this. It makes perfect sense. Whoever has the manuscript is someone who knows its worth. Not just a cheap crook or blackmailer, this is someone who can quote from *L'incoronazione di Poppea*. Someone with a grudge against both Lockwood and Baldan. And someone with a history of violent and abusive behaviour.'

Fede sat in silence for a moment, and then nodded, slowly. 'Okay. There's some sense in that. It could be. But there's no proof at all.'

'I know. Wait a minute, give me that.' I snatched the booklet from her, and flicked through it. 'Salvatore Bonfiglio. Look.' I held the photograph up to her. The same gaunt features, albeit without the unflattering ponytail. 'It's him, isn't it? The man I saw at Isotta's yesterday.'

She nodded. 'So he's stalking us and threatening her. Lovely man. But is this really enough to go to Vanni with?'

'No. I've got a better idea.'

'Which is?'

'We need to find a link between Bonfiglio and Zambon. Then we might be getting somewhere.' I looked at my watch. It was still early. 'So I'm going to go to bed. I'm going to get a proper night's sleep. And then tomorrow I think I need to have a chat with Dario.'

Chapter 39

Federica wasn't convinced the following morning. If truth be told, neither was I. She kissed me goodbye on her way to work, and left me replaying the recording again and again and again. What had seemed crystal clear the previous evening seemed less convincing in the cold light of day. Still, there was no doubt that the man I'd seen outside Isotta's house had been her unpleasant ex-husband.

And so I stood in the Coffee Shop of Death, a converted mortuary in Campo Santa Maria Formosa, nursing a *macchiatone* and waiting for Dario. He arrived just as I was stirring around the foam at the bottom of the cup, and wondering if it would be possible to drink it without the undignified position of leaning so far back you ended up staring at the ceiling as the last remains trickled into your mouth and deposited a blob of foam on your nose.

'Nathan. Sorry, man, I came as quick as I could.' He stared at my face. 'You've been in a fight.'

'I'm not sure it was anything so dignified as a fight. More some pushing and shoving. And a single punch.' I filled him in on the events of the previous evening. It took him a while to stop laughing.

'You got beaten up by a retired opera singer?'

'I didn't get beaten up. I've got a cut lip, that's all.'

'Yeah, but still. An old guy.'

'He's not old. He retired because of ill health.'

'Okay, you got beaten up by a sick guy.'

I rubbed my lip. 'You're making it sound worse than it is. Now are you going to help me or not?'

'Sure *vecio*, anything at all. You want me to help you across the bridge?' I glared at him. 'Sorry, sorry. Come on, tell me.'

'I looked him up in the White Pages. He lives near here. Corte dei Orbi.'

He shook his head. 'I don't know it.'

'It's kind of on the way to Acqua Alta. You know, the mad bookshop.'

'Oh yeah. I know it. Nice guy, stores books in gondolas. Keeps too many cats.'

I nodded. 'That's the one.'

'Valentina bought a cookbook there once and he asked her to marry him.'

'I didn't know that. She must have made a big impression. Come on, let's go.' I put a couple of euros on the counter, and we made our way outside.

'So. What are we going to do?'

'We're just going to have a little chat.'

'That's it?'

I shrugged and lit a cigarette. 'All I could think of.'

'Are you sure it's him? Really sure?'

'As certain as I can be.'

'It's just that when this guy spoke to you he was wearing a

mask. And you recognised his voice from, what, a recording of an opera?'

'Yep. That's pretty much it. And I'm almost certain he's the guy I saw leaving Isotta's house the other day.'

'Okay, but you'd better be right. It's going to be kind of embarrassing otherwise.'

'Dario, we're just going to have a chat. We're not going to trash the place. I've got a cut lip, that's all, we don't need to turn it over.'

'Just talk, then?'

'Just talk.'

'Okay. So why did you ask me to come along?'

'In case he wants to do more than just talk.'

We walked across Campo Santa Maria Formosa, and turned right just before Acqua Alta. A narrow *calle*, too narrow for us to walk abreast. We took another right and entered a small courtyard.

A *vera da pozzo* sat in the middle of the square, heavily weathered and stained green with moss. There was a feeling of damp about the entire space. The plaster on the lower floors of the buildings had long since crumbled away, whilst the bricks of the pavement were thick and slippery with moss. The height of the buildings would ensure that the yard only saw light for a few hours each day. The one exception to the surrounding grey and green was a bright red mat outside the door of a cheap bed and breakfast.

I found the building we were looking for, and checked the names on the buzzer. S Bonfiglio. Top floor. I looked upwards. Many of the windows on the second and third floors were bricked up, but the ones on the top floor were smaller, and modern, and without the usual heavy green shutters. I could see an *altana* on top of the building, surrounded by a balustrade painted in white. Despite the shabby exterior this was a desirable place to live.

My hand reached for the buzzer, but I pulled it back when an elderly woman opened the main door and came out wheeling a shopping trolley. She tutted audibly when I ground my cigarette underfoot. I held the door open, and nodded Dario through. She looked at us suspiciously, but I gave her a cheery smile, went in, and let the door close behind us. Not ringing the bell would give us a little extra element of surprise.

We made our way up to the top floor, and rapped on the door.

'*Chi è?*' came from inside.

'ENI,' I lied. The gas company. Dario stood to the side.

'Just a moment.' We heard a key turning in the lock, and the door opened, just a few inches. Bonfiglio, dressed in just a T-shirt and pyjama trousers, did a double-take when he saw me. He tried to slam the door, but Dario was too quick for him and leaned his weight against it.

'*Signor* Bonfiglio,' I said. 'We'd like to talk.'

He continued pushing against the door; then realised it was hopeless and stood back. 'You'd better come in,' he said.

We made our way into the living room as we sized each other up. The photo of him in the CD booklet, I thought, had not been taken yesterday. Nevertheless, I was sure it was the figure I had seen in the flesh two days previously. Dario looked at the gaunt figure of Bonfiglio, and then caught my eye. 'Not a word,' I mouthed at him, and he did his best not to grin.

An inexpensive electronic keyboard was perched on a metal frame in front of a music stand, whilst a shabby two-seater sofa bed was pushed against the opposite wall. The remaining wall space was lined with shelving, holding what must have been hundreds, if not thousands, of vinyl records. Indeed, the one concession to luxury in the whole room was an expensive-looking record deck hooked up to two monolithic black speakers, spiked for optimum performance.

'What do you want Mr . . . ?'

'Sutherland. I think you already know. We just want to talk.' I rubbed my lip. 'About this. And other things. But first, coffee would be nice.'

'You what?'

'Coffee,' repeated Dario, 'would be nice.'

He looked the two of us up and down, then nodded and went into the kitchen.

Dario looked over at the record deck. 'Fantastic,' he said.

'Is it?'

'Serious piece of kit. You ever thought about going back to vinyl?'

'Sometimes. I don't have the space, though.' I took a look at his record collection. Mainly classical with some rather difficult modern jazz thrown in. One record was placed on a small wooden stand on top of a writing desk. I took a closer look. *Vespro della Beata Vergine*, written in thick gothic script. I recognised the cover. The Virgin enthroned in heaven between Christ and God the Father. Beautiful, attenuated figures. El Greco, possibly? I had a copy at home, in between the operas and the books of madrigals. The Monteverdi Vespers. The sleeve had been signed, underneath the title. *To Salvatore, with love and all good wishes. Nikolaus Harnoncourt.* Harnoncourt, the grand old *maestro*, dead now almost a year to the day. I traced my thumb over the contours of his signature.

'Be careful with that!' Bonfiglio's voice rang out. He was standing in the doorway that led from the kitchen, a tray in his hand with a *Moka* pot and three cups. He put the tray down on the coffee table with haste, rattling the cups, and then scurried over to me holding out his hands. I passed it back to him, and he almost snatched it from me. He wiped his sleeve over the cover, as if to remove any trace of my sacrilegious hand, and replaced it on the stand. He flapped his hand towards the sofa. 'I suppose you'd better sit down.'

'You met Harnoncourt?' I said. He looked at me as if I were stupid. 'I wish I'd met him. Although, I have to say, that recording isn't my favourite.'

'You needed to have been there,' he said, drily.

'Maybe so. I don't think the chorus comes over at all well in the recording.'

'I'm sorry you feel that way.' He paused, just for a moment. 'I sang in the chorus. I was twenty-five years old and it was my first job.'

'Oh.' I poured out three cups of coffee, and spooned some sugar into mine. We sat in silence for a moment.

'So what's this all about?' said Bonfiglio.

'I think you know what it's about, *signor* Bonfiglio. I'd like to know why you attacked me last night.'

'I don't know what you're talking about.'

'I think you do. You've been following me for days. Following me out to Mestre, for example. Spying on me at the Caffè Florian. And then you decided to swing a punch at me in Calle Benzon.'

'You're deranged.' His hands were shaking now, ever so slightly.

'I don't think so. You recognised me when you opened the door.'

'I thought you were from ENI.'

'No you didn't. Now I want to know what this is about. Why do you want me to stay away from Isotta Baldan?'

He got to his feet. 'I don't know who you are. Just a crazy man. You and your friend. Now you get out of my house before I call the police.'

'Call the police. I'll tell them you attacked me.'

'You got any proof of that?' This was a tricky one. I had to admit that recognising his voice from an opera recording was evidence that was unlikely to stand up in court. 'You have any proof? Eh?' he continued. 'No?' He was smiling now. 'Then you get the hell out of my house. And take Mister Strong and Silent with you.'

Dario got to his feet. 'He's right, Nat. I think maybe this has been a big mistake.'

'What?'

He shushed me. 'Come on. Look at this place.' He spread his arms wide. 'All this stuff. *Signor* Bonfiglio's a cultured man. Not some crazy guy who attacks people in alleyways. You've made a mistake.' I knew what was coming next and tried not to smile.

Bonfiglio nodded and pointed at him. 'You should listen to your friend, I think.'

I stood up, and put my hands to my face. 'Okay, I

think you're right. This has been a terrible mistake. I'm so sorry.'

'Okay. We say no more about it then?' He offered me his hand and I shook it.

Dario, in the meantime, had slid one of Bonfiglio's records from a shelf. I recognised the cover. Glenn Gould. *The Goldberg Variations*. 'Hey Nat, you've got this one, right?' I nodded and tried not to wince. I knew what was coming next. 'I love vinyl,' he continued. He held the album in one hand, and gestured with the other. 'You get that warm sound, don't you? Not like CDs. And you got proper album covers in those days.' He held the record at arm's length, the better to appreciate the sleeve. Gould, resting his forehead against his right hand, his left draped languidly over the back of a chair. Then Dario, in a movement almost too fast to see, flexed his wrists and a muffled crack came from inside the sleeve.

Bonfiglio shot to his feet. 'You idiot!'

'Oh Christ, I'm sorry, I'm so sorry.' Dario put the record down, and slid out another. 'That's the problem with vinyl, you know? It's so fragile. I don't know how many I've broken over the years.' He moved to the next shelf and slid an album out, halfway. Berlioz. *Symphonie Fantastique*. Colin Davis.

'Put that back. Don't touch it.'

Dario looked back over his shoulder at him. He looked a little hurt. 'Sure,' he said. He slid it back in, but not before he'd given it a quick but violent twist. The pressure of the records to each side held it like a vice and, again, a dull crack came from inside the sleeve. He pushed it back in as if nothing had happened, and moved over to the writing desk.

Silence hung in the air, as Dario ran his fingers caressingly along the top of the Harnoncourt sleeve.

'You wouldn't,' Bonfiglio stammered. He summoned up all his courage and jabbed his finger at me. 'He's a diplomat, eh? Mister English Consul. You know what'll happen to him if I make a complaint? What'll happen to him when I call the cops? He'll lose his job, eh?'

I threw up my hands and hurried over to Dario. I gently removed his fingers from the record, and patted him on the shoulder. 'He's right, buddy, you know that. I'm the honorary consul. I can't be part of anything like this.' He looked at me, the corners of his eyes crinkling ever so slightly.

I checked my watch. 'And I've got a surgery in thirty minutes. I've got to go. I'll see you later, okay, maybe we'll grab a beer?'

'Sure, Nathan. I'll see you later.'

I buttoned up my coat and made my way to the door. I'd pulled it open and was halfway through before Bonfiglio realised what was happening. 'No, stop, stop!' he cried.

I closed the door. 'Sorry, have I forgotten something?'

'Look. Just sit down, please. Perhaps we should talk.'

I smiled. 'Perhaps we should.'

Chapter 40

'So, *signor* Bonfiglio, why have you been following me around the city for the past few days?'

'I want you to stay away from my wife.'

'Your wife?'

He nodded. 'We're still married.'

'Right.'

'Divorce in this country, you know? It takes time, gets messy. It seemed easier just to stay married. And I always thought, if we're still married then maybe . . .' he let the sentence trail off.

'That's it. That's it? You stalked me and attacked me because you were jealous?'

'It's very operatic, Nat,' muttered Dario.

'I still love her, you know.' Bonfiglio was hunched over in his chair, staring at his shoes.

'I'm sorry but this makes no sense. You followed me out to Torcello, you lurked around Piazza San Marco at midnight, you attacked me just five minutes from my house because you were jealous.' He nodded. 'This is crazy. Isotta's just a friend. Not even that really, she's just someone I know. Because someone working for her wanted to use me as a translator.'

'I'm sorry. Can't stand the thought of her being with someone else.'

'If she's with someone else, she sure as hell isn't with me. She's "with" Lockwood now. But, of course, you know that. Given that you were at his house on Friday afternoon. So perhaps you'd like to tell me why *signora* Baldan was so upset when she answered the door to me? You wouldn't happen to know the reason why, would you?'

'What kind of a person do you think I am?'

'I think you're the kind of person who enjoys hurting women,' said Dario.

'She told you that?'

'That you used to beat her up?' I said. 'Isn't it common knowledge?'

'Bitch!'

'That's not helping, Salvatore.'

'Liar. Whore. *Porca troia.*'

'Not getting any better.' He reached for the coffee pot, but Dario reached out and gently but firmly stopped him.

'I think you'd better stick to decaf for the time being, Salvatore,' I said. 'So when did it start going wrong?'

He shrugged. 'About ten years ago. She started to become famous. Really famous, I mean. And me,' he patted his chest, 'things started to become, well, not so great. Smoking, you know. My voice isn't what it was. Our careers were going in different directions and one day she decides that poor old Toto is maybe starting to hold her back.'

'That's when she took up with Lockwood?' He nodded. 'So why come after me?'

'I keep seeing you together. And I know she doesn't love the old man. She just wants his money.'

'Again, that makes no sense. She must be wealthy.'

'Not wealthy enough. Can you imagine her living here?'

I took another look around. The apartment was smallish, and the exterior of the building was shabby, but that was by no means unusual in Venice. 'Why not? It seems like a nice apartment to me.'

He gave a hollow laugh. 'Isotta Baldan doesn't do "nice". "Nice" is never quite enough.'

'What about her career then? She's barely forty. She has years ahead of her.'

'"At the height of her powers", you mean?' He laughed and shook his head.

I was puzzled. 'Yes, I suppose I do.'

'You know she had surgery five years ago? For a vocal chord haemorrhage?' I vaguely remembered reading something about it and nodded. He continued, 'You hear about the operation she had last year? For the same problem. No?'

'No.'

He smiled. 'Same problem. Fixed again, but for how long? Twelve months. Two years?'

I sipped at my coffee, to buy myself time to think. 'How many people know this, Salvatore?'

'Including you and Mister Big here?' I nodded. 'Four of us. People will still pay to listen to Isotta Baldan. But it won't be long now. Why do you think she cancels so much? She's preserving what's left of that voice for as long as she can.'

One day, then – maybe not tomorrow, maybe not even next month, but one day – she'd reach for that high C in *Der Hoelle Rache*, and the note would not come. I tried to imagine what that could possibly feel like.

'I'm sorry.'

He gave a mirthless grin. 'So, maybe one day, we'll both end up back here. And our neighbours will talk about the couple upstairs who used to be singers.'

'Why would she come back?' said Dario. 'Or are you going to promise – I mean, really promise this time – not to bounce her off the walls again?'

He was, I knew, trying to needle Bonfiglio. Enough to make him angry. Possibly enough to give him an excuse to hit him. But Bonfiglio just shook his head, sadly. 'Maybe because I'm the one who understands her.'

I got to my feet, and nodded at Dario. There was little more to be said. 'Okay. Do I take it I'm free to walk around Venice without being followed now?' He stared at us, trying to face us down, then dropped his gaze and gave the briefest of nods. 'I'll take that as a yes. Come on, Dario.'

We made our way to the door. I made to open it, then paused and turned around. 'For what it's worth, Salvatore, I think you're wrong.'

'Wrong?'

'I think she's going to marry Lockwood.'

'Really? You think so?' He laughed, and then started to cough a long, rumbling smoker's cough. Dario shook his head at me, and we left.

Chapter 41

We went back to the Coffee Shop of Death, this time for a spritz.

'What do you think?' said Dario.

'I think he's lying.'

'I think he's lying too. But why?'

'Because he's got hold of the copy of *Proserpina* that Zambon found and he's using it to hurt Lockwood and Baldan as much as he can.'

'And to extort money.'

'That too. But I don't think that's the most important thing. I think it's mainly to hurt them. Lockwood will be destroyed if anything happens to the manuscript. It'd probably be enough to break them up.'

Dario tapped his fingers against his glass. 'But do you think he'd kill, Nat? Seriously?'

'I don't know. He's a spiteful little bastard. We know he can be violent. Killing someone, though . . . ?'

'So what are we going to do?'

'Zambon initially contacted Isotta. Not Lockwood. Bonfiglio is her almost-ex. And I know he was round at her apartment two days ago. So there's a connection there. But I wonder if there's a direct connection between Bonfiglio and Zambon. That's the next thing to find out.'

Dario nodded, and finished his drink. 'Can I ask you a question?'

'Sure.'

'Imagine someone finds an unreleased Hawkwind album. Imagine it's got both Robert Calvert and Huw Lloyd-Langton on it.'

'Okay. I'm imagining. But the two of them weren't in the band at the same time.'

'That's what makes it special. What would you pay for it?'

'I don't know. It's sort of beyond price, isn't it?'

He smiled. 'But would you kill or blackmail anyone to get hold of it?'

'No point. Sooner or later it would turn up on the bootleg site anyway.'

'That's what I thought you'd say. It's a different world, this classical music, isn't it?'

'It certainly is.' I took my wallet out. 'I'll get these. I owe you one.'

'No problem.' He checked his watch. 'Right, I've got to go. I'll give you a call, eh?'

'Sure. You should all come around some time. As I keep saying.'

'What are you going to do now?'

I smiled. 'Now, Dario, I am going to talk to the communists about grand opera.'

If nothing else, I needed to go over to Giudecca to speak to Sergio. I didn't know if Vanni had already sent anyone round to have a word with him, but there was an awkward conversation that needed to be had. I walked down to the vaporetto terminal at San Zaccaria, the Riva degli Schiavoni already choked with visitors making their way over the Ponte della Paglia for a selfie in front of the Bridge of Sighs.

I took the next boat out to the Palanca stop on Giudecca, and wandered down to the communist bar. I was starting to think of it as a left-wing version of Conan Doyle's Diogenes Club. The two of them, of course, were there.

Lorenzo smiled. '*Ciao, compagno!*'

Sergio grunted.

'Erm, could I sit down perhaps?' I said.

They both nodded.

'Red wine?'

They nodded again.

I gave a nod to the barman.

Silence.

'I think perhaps there's something we need to talk about?'

Sergio grunted, again.

'I'm sorry,' I said. 'It was an accident. I was just speaking to Vanni and . . . well . . . I didn't think.'

The barman arrived with a jug of red, and Sergio poured out three glasses. 'Yeah. You speak to cops and this is what happens, you understand?'

'Vanni's not like that. He's kind of a friend.'

'Yeah. You make friends with cops and this is what happens.'

'Are you okay?'

'Sure I'm okay. Couple of *sbirri* came around. We had a talk, they went away again. Nothing for them to find. Not that that ever stops them.'

Lorenzo coughed. 'To be fair, Sergio, one might say that one can never be a proper member of The Struggle until one's actually been in trouble with the police.'

Sergio raised his eyes from his glass and stared at us both. A half-smile flickered across his face. 'Okay. You let me kick your arse at *scopa* again and we'll forget about it, eh?'

I nodded, and smiled.

Three hours passed during which I had need to visit the nearest *bancomat* twice.

Sergio smiled, and folded my money away within his wallet. 'Okay, *compagno*. Let's talk.'

I took a look inside my own wallet, and was both pleased and surprised not to see moths fluttering out. I shook my head, and tucked it away inside my jacket.

'You know, Sergio, for a communist you're very good at the accumulation of capital.'

'I'm bringing the system down from within, *investigatore*.' He grinned and waved at the barman. 'More drinks. On me this time. Or on you I should say.' They both laughed.

'So. I know you were paying Matteo Zambon's rent.' Sergio gave Lorenzo a hard stare. Lorenzo gave an apologetic shrug. I held up my hands. 'We don't have to play *scopa* again, do we?' I pleaded.

Sergio shook his head. 'Okay, *pentito*, maybe not this time. What do you want to know?'

'How did you pay his rent? Bank transfer or cash?'

'I couldn't trust him with cash. And I don't trust the internet. The government uses it to keep track of you. So I gave a cheque straight to his landlord. He's got an apartment in the same building.'

'What did you do? Send it in the mail?'

Sergio gave a hollow laugh.

'Let me guess, you don't trust the post office either?' He shook his head. 'So you went round to his building?'

'Yes. But I never spoke to the son of a bitch.'

'I get that. But did you ever see people, you know, coming and going?'

He shrugged. 'Sure. Lots of people.'

'Anyone you recognised?'

'A few. I think he still had some friends from the *conservatorio*. And there were others—' He paused.

'Others?'

'Gambling men. Petty crooks. You get to recognise people after a while.'

'Okay.' I took the libretto from *The Magic Flute* out of my pocket, and flicked through it until I reached the photographs of the cast. I spread it open on the table. 'Do you recognise any of these people?'

He looked at the first photograph, a black and white photograph of Lockwood, taken many years previously, hands folded across his chest with his baton held in his right hand.

'No.' He licked his finger, and flicked to the next page, shook his head and moved further on. He came to the image of Isotta, all black hair and eyeliner. He smiled, and shook his head. 'No,' he said, 'her I'd remember.' He passed the little booklet over to Lorenzo who smiled in recognition.

'Isotta Baldan,' he said. 'I saw her once. Very fine singer. And very pretty, so I'm told.'

Sergio grunted, and turned to the next page. Then he

tapped his finger up and down on the photograph of Salvatore Bonfiglio. 'This guy I recognise.'

'You're sure?'

'Sure I'm sure. A number of times.'

'Do you remember when?'

'Over the last six months. Whenever I went round he seemed to be there. Coming or going.'

'Did you ever hear them talking?'

'I never used to hang around. Much of the time they seemed to be listening to music.' He saw the expression on my face. 'Don't ask me what it was, I'm no expert. Classical music, you know. Lorenzo would have known.'

'You could always try humming it, Sergio,' said Lorenzo with a little chuckle. Sergio gave him a withering look. 'But seriously, Nathan,' Lorenzo continued, '*Signor* Zambon worked at the *conservatorio*. It wouldn't be unusual if someone came round and they just listened to music together.'

'You're right. You're right. And yet there's something not right.' I drained my glass and got to my feet. 'Thanks, Sergio. That was very helpful.'

'No problem, *compagno*. Are you sure that was worth three hours of *scopa*?'

'Oh, I think it was. And, well, I just want to say I'm sorry again.'

Sergio grinned, reached into his pocket, took out his bulging wallet and riffled through the contents. 'And, as I said, no problem.'

The phone rang post-washing-up, as Fede and I lay on the sofa together.

'Nathan? It's Christopher. Can you talk? It's rather important.'

'Go ahead.'

'What do you know about the Teatro San Moisè?'

'Closed nearly two hundred years ago. I think it was demolished. At any rate, there's nothing left of it that you could go around.'

'That doesn't matter. What I need is some kind of record of performances. As much detail as you can find. *Proserpina* was performed there in the 1640s. Anything you can find that might help us track the path of the score over the years.' His words were starting to trip over each other with excitement, his voice just a little higher-pitched than normal. I moved the phone further away from my ear.

'Okay. Looks like I'll be going back to the Marciana again. It sounds like you've found something?'

'I think I have. Oh, I think I have!'

'Care to tell me what it is?'

'You'll find out. Get there first thing tomorrow. Find whatever you can on San Moisè. And then we'll talk.'

He hung up.

Fede looked over at me. 'Mr Maitland?'

'The very same.'

'He sounded very excited. Even from here. He thinks he's solved it then?'

'Yes. Whatever "it" is. I'm not sure I've ever heard anyone preening on the telephone before.'

She sighed. 'So he couldn't just have told you all about it?'

'I think he needs to play his little games. He's a bit insecure.

Lockwood is the big, famous conductor. Isotta's been nasty to him. He needs people to tell him how clever he is.'

'So you're going back to work on this in the morning?'

'It looks like it. Anyway, this is just going to the library and I think *signor* Bonfiglio is off our backs now.' She nodded, but looked unconvinced. 'Look, if you like, I'll call Maitland back and tell him I won't do it.'

'Really?'

'Of course.'

'That's sweet of you. But no. This is a missing Monteverdi opera we're talking about. The Ravagnan–Sutherland edition, remember?'

'How could I forget?'

'So let's just give it a few more days.'

'Thanks.' I yawned. 'Time for bed. I'll be glad when this is all over you know. I miss my old non-operatic life.'

Chapter 42

I was at the Marciana for opening time at eight o'clock, waiting impatiently as staff unlocked. I locked my coat and scarf away, and sat myself down at a computer terminal, away from Petrarch's disapproving gaze. I tapped away at the keyboard, searching the archive for anything held on the Teatro San Moisè.

As I thought, the building had long since been demolished and was now a shop. A few black and white illustrations and watercolours gave little idea as to what it might have looked like. It had served as one of Venice's many *opera lirica* theatres for almost two hundred years. And then, after a production of Rossini's *Cenerentola* in 1818, its doors had closed for the last time. It reopened for a while as the Teatro Minerva, a puppet theatre. A plaque on the wall in the Corte del Teatro San Moisè recorded that the first cinema projection in Venice, under the direction of the Lumière brothers, had taken place there in 1896.

Its years as a lyric theatre had been well documented. Obsessively so. One hundred and seventy-nine volumes recorded every production from 1640 to 1818. Each year had a volume detailing productions, cast and crew, and the associated expenses. The very first opera staged at the theatre had been Monteverdi's *Arianna*, conducted by the composer himself during the Carnival of 1640. A revival of one of his earliest works, that also turned out to be the last. The score disappeared, presumed lost for ever. The Teatro San Moisè had not been a lucky theatre for Claudio Monteverdi. He had been in his grave for a year by the time *Proserpina rapita* was revived there in 1644.

I scrawled down the details on a yellow sheet, passed them to the librarian, and went into the reading room to wait.

I yawned and wished I'd made time to have breakfast at home, or, at least, to have a coffee. Why couldn't they at least have a coffee machine in the vestibule? I was still stretching, my eyes closed, when the archivist gave a discreet little cough and placed the volume in front of me. I gave an apologetic smile and thanked him, as I got to work.

The book was not indexed, and so I started on the very first page. January first, 1644. A revival of Francesco Cavalli's *L'amore innamorato*. Another lost work? I couldn't remember. I made my way through the book, encountering half-familiar names and ones unknown to me, composers forgotten to all but the most dedicated musicologists. Lists of singers whose voices we would never hear, and whose fame had long since passed. Expenses incurred, and ticket receipts.

It didn't take long to find what I was looking for. A revival of *Proserpina rapita*, performed for the first time in fourteen years. I looked at the date and smiled. February eighteenth. My birthday, and Yoko Ono's.

I read on. The condition of the book – heavily foxed and water-stained – made it difficult to read. Nevertheless, I could tell that there was a page dedicated to the performing edition of the score and libretto. Try as I might, I could not make it out. I rubbed my eyes and looked again, but the text swam and blurred in front of my eyes.

The time had come. I was now forced to admit I needed glasses.

I took a look around the reading room. I was still the only one there. The archivist was seated behind a desk at the far end of the room. I beckoned him over with a sheepish little wave.

'Are you finished with the book, *signore*?'

'No. It's just that I don't have my glasses. I wonder, could you just read that page out for me?' I added the words 'if it's not too much trouble,' just to sound extra-British.

He took a look at the page, and adjusted his own glasses. 'It's difficult to read.'

'I know. But can you do it?'

'It's in *Veneziano*, *signore*. Seventeenth-century *Veneziano*.'

'Hell. I'm sorry, I'd be completely lost with that. Can you translate it?'

'English or Italian?'

'Italian is fine.'

'Very well.' He adjusted his glasses again. '*Proserpina rapita*, work of *signor* Claudio Monteverdi, is presented in the original edition of 1630. The libretto is by Giulio Strozzi, here writing under the name of Luigi Zorzisto. The score is that presented by the composer to the English ambassador Sir Isaac Wake, and returned to him as part of Sir Isaac's bequest in 1632.' He removed his glasses, 'I'm translating as best I can, but that's roughly what it would be in modern Italian.'

'That's brilliant. Perfect.' I got to my feet, my chair scraping and echoing in the empty room. I scribbled my signature on the yellow chit. 'I'm finished with this now. Thank you so much.'

I pulled on my coat, retrieved my ID card and half walked, half ran outside into the chilly morning air. Too early for lunch, almost too late for breakfast. Coffee would be good, but a café would be too public for a call like this. I sat on a *passerella* and lit a cigarette, as I dialled Maitland's number.

'Good morning, Nathan.' His voice was bright and full of good humour. Even in those three words he managed to sound excessively pleased with himself.

'I've just come from the library,' I said.

'I'm very glad to hear it. A productive morning's work, I hope?'

'Absolutely. Lockwood's edition of the libretto. It's signed by Zorzisto, not Strozzi. Which means it's almost certainly the one that was used at San Moisè in 1644.'

'Yes. I rather thought it might be. Anything else?'

'The edition of the score was the one that Monteverdi gave to Isaac Wake. It seems Wake returned it to him as part of his bequest.'

'I thought that might be the case as well. But thank you for checking. It's all coming together nicely.'

'Look, I'm freezing my arse off on a *passarella* and haven't had breakfast yet. So can you please just tell me what's going on and I can finish my cigarette and get out of the cold. And then I'll tell you how clever you've been.'

'Let's meet for breakfast, Nathan. My treat. Church Pub seemed rather jolly, didn't it? I'll see you there.'

He hung up, and I stared at the screen, shaking the phone in anger and disbelief.

I hopped on the next *vaporetto* from San Zaccaria, cursing the boat for its slowness and Maitland for his clever-cleverness.

Church Pub was empty, except for Alessandro, who smiled and waved from behind the bar. I gave a little wave in return. '*Salve*. I was here the other day, I don't know if you remember?'

'*Sì*, I remember. You are friends with the *padre*.'

'That's right.' I looked around, but I was the only customer.

'Coffee? Cappuccino? Something to eat?'

'Er, yes. That'd be nice, thanks. *Macchiato* and a brioche.'

'*Subito*.' He waved at the cabinet. 'Help yourself.'

I munched away at a pretty good *brioche integrale* thinking that it was perhaps the healthiest option, as the coffee machine hissed and steamed away. Alessandro smiled as he passed my coffee across the bar. I tipped in a sachet of brown sugar, stirred it my regulation ten times clockwise, and licked the spoon. I sipped at it, savouring the rush of warmth into my body.

I felt a chill draught of air as the door opened, and I turned around expecting Maitland.

It was Lockwood. The two of us stared at each other like Gramsci and Karajan.

'Good morning, *maestro*,' I said, assuming that by now we were no longer on first-name terms.

'Sutherland. Good morning.' He looked around.

'Are you expecting someone?'

'Maitland. We're meeting for breakfast.'

'Oh. Me too.' Lockwood said nothing, but continued to stare at me. 'I think he's got something he wants to tell us, don't you? That's why he called you this morning?'

He nodded.

'Can I get you a coffee?' I said. 'Come on. I'm sorry about what happened the other night. Let's have breakfast, and wait for Maitland, and then we can all have a talk.'

He sighed. 'All right. Thank you, Sutherland.' He nodded at Alessandro. '*Cappuccino, per favore.*'

Alessandro nodded, and went to the machine. 'Mr Maitland is the man who was with you and the *padre* the other day, right?' he called over his shoulder.

'That's right.'

'Okay, he came in for a coffee. Then he said he was going to your church. Said he needed to print things.' He took a look at his watch. 'Fifteen minutes ago.'

'Print things?' said Lockwood.

'He was trying that the other day,' I said. 'He needed to print some music off. Maybe this is something to do with what he's found?'

We finished our coffee in silence. I checked my watch again. Twenty minutes now. Then I took five euros from my wallet and slid them across the bar. 'I'll pay,' I said to Lockwood. 'Come on, let's go.'

'Go? Go where?'

'The church. The *padre* told me that nothing works properly. He could be there for hours trying to get the printer sorted out.'

We went back down the *calle* until we reached the side door of the church. There was nothing as useful as a door knocker, let alone a doorbell, so I rapped on the letter box as hard as I could.

There was no answer. I took out my phone, and dialled

Maitland's number. It rang four, five times before it was cut off. I dialled again, and this time it rang out.

'Something's not right.'

I rapped on the letterbox again. And again. And then I started hammering and kicking at the door. Lockwood pulled me back.

'What in God's name are you doing?'

'Have you got a key?'

'What?'

'A key to the bloody church. Have you got a key?'

'Of course I haven't got a key. Why would I?'

I started kicking at the door again, and shouting Maitland's name. People were stopping and staring at us. Again, Lockwood pulled me back.

'Call the priest, Sutherland. He doesn't live far away, does he? Ask him to come out.'

I breathed deeply. 'Okay. That makes sense. You try Maitland again.' I searched through my phone for Michael Rayner's number, and called.

'Chaplaincy?'

'*Padre*, it's Nathan. Nathan Sutherland.'

'Nathan. To what do I owe the honour? Bible Study doesn't start until three this afternoon, if you're interested.'

'*Padre*, I'm serious. I'm at the church. I need to get in. I need you to come out right now.'

'Don't tell me you've had an *experience*.' Rayner's voice was still jokey.

'I'm serious. Right now. Please.'

'Okay, Nathan. I'll be right there.'

I turned back to Lockwood. 'Any luck?'

He shook his head. 'Not answering.'

'Hell.' I barged the door with my shoulder but, despite its weatherbeaten look, it showed no signs of moving. I tried a second time, and then a third. Then I gave up and rubbed my shoulder, wishing that Dario was with us.

Too many people were staring at us for my liking, and the narrowness of the *calle* was making it difficult for people to get past.

'Come on, Tom, let's check the front doors just in case.' I walked back to Campo San Vio, not waiting to see if he was following me. I rested my hands against the great bronze doors and pushed, in the hope that they'd only been pushed shut from inside and not locked. Not a chance. Nothing moved, and nothing was likely to move them.

I took out a packet of cigarettes and offered one to Lockwood, who shook his head. He didn't seem to be in a conversational mood, but I thought the wait would seem even longer in awkward silence.

'Did he tell you what this was about, Tom?' I asked.

'Not really. Just that he'd found something, and was asking you to check at the Marciana. Nothing more.' He shook his head. 'Bloody Maitland. He's always like this, you know. Never misses an opportunity to show off how clever he is.' He took a deep breath, and then hammered on the bronze doors with his fists.

'Leave it, Tom. If he can't hear us from the side door he's not going to hear us through those.'

We stood in silence, as I smoked and Lockwood shuffled his feet and wrung his hands. The awkwardness was broken by the arrival of Father Rayner, who smiled at us before plucking the cigarette from my mouth and grinding it underfoot.

'Terrible habit, Nathan. Good morning, gentlemen, what can I do for you?'

'*Padre*, just let us in please. Right now.'

He shrugged his shoulders, and took a bunch of keys from his pocket. 'Okay, follow me.' He led us back into the *calle* and to the side door. 'Takes a bit of time, I'm afraid. Five turns in the top lock, five turns in the bottom one.' No wonder I hadn't managed to make any sort of impression on the door. He pushed it open, the door juddering and scraping against the floor. He bent his head, and squeezed his way through.

'Damn!'

'What is it?'

'Bloody lights are on. I hope that wasn't Mr Maitland and company. And I hope they haven't been on overnight, that all costs us money. Anyway, come in, come in.'

The tiny vestry area was crammed with the three of us in it, but I forced my way past, through the swing doors, and into the church itself. Immediately, I could tell that something was wrong.

The floor was strewn with papers, so widely scattered that I could only assume they had all fluttered down from the organ loft. I dropped to my haunches to take a closer look. Music scores. Charles Villiers Stanford. The parts for the concert tomorrow. There was more. They were all spattered with blood, a trail of which led up the aisle to where Christopher Maitland lay sprawled at the foot of the steps to the sanctuary; his arms flung wide, and one leg bent underneath him.

'God,' breathed Lockwood. Rayner rushed over to him, and knelt down to him. 'Don't touch him, for God's sake don't touch him.'

'I've seen dead people before, Mr Lockwood,' murmured Rayner. He touched two fingers to Maitland's neck, then crossed himself. He laid his hand on his forehead, and closed his eyes, silently praying. Then he got to his feet, and placed his hand on Lockwood's shoulder. 'I'm so sorry.'

'Ah, Christopher.' Lockwood's voice was low, controlled. He pushed Rayner aside, and then knelt on the ground next to his friend's body. 'You silly man. Always had to try to be one up, didn't you?'

'Mr Lockwood, please.' Rayner gently but firmly pulled him to his feet. 'There's nothing to be done now.' He turned to me. 'Nathan, you know how this works?'

I nodded, and took my mobile out. 'I'll call the police.'

'No!' It was Lockwood, again. 'Not the police. Not yet. Whatever he found, it might still be here, somewhere.' He pulled away from Rayner, ran to the back of the church and dropped to the floor, rummaging through the papers, and scrunching them up and hurling them away when they proved to be of no interest. 'Somewhere, here.'

I ran over to him. 'Tom, this is a crime scene now. Stop it.' He paid me no heed and continued working his way through the scattered sheets. I put my hand on his shoulder. 'Tom,' I repeated. He shook off my hand, but got to his feet. He looked me up and down, the ghost of a smile upon his lips. The same expression of contempt that I'd seen in Cardiff twenty years ago. Little people were getting in his way. He turned and made his way back up the aisle, where he bent over Maitland's body and started to go through his pockets.

Rayner caught my eye, shook his head, and tried to pull him back. Lockwood pushed him off, not so much in anger but more in annoyance that somebody should be interrupting his work. I ran back towards them and grabbed one arm as Rayner took the other. Together we managed to pull him back, and forced him into a pew.

I bent over, resting my hands on my knees. 'Tom. You're interfering with evidence. I'll have to tell the police that, you understand?'

He continued to stare at me with the same withering look. Then it changed to one of absolute hatred. His hand cracked out, slapping me across the face. Not a powerful blow, but the shock of it sent me staggering back.

I raised my hand to my cheek. I was sick of this now. Sick of him.

'Treat Isotta like that, do you?' I said.

'You what?'

'You contemptible, arrogant little shit. Maitland was right. You've got nothing apart from music. Take that away and you're just a boring, obsessive little man.'

'Bastard.' Lockwood hurled himself from his seat, and locked his hands around my throat. Rayner threw himself in between us, and prised him off me. I glared at Lockwood, as I gasped for breath.

I was about to speak, but Rayner raised his hand. 'Shut up, please, Nathan.'

'I—'

'Shut up, please. He's in shock, can't you see?' Lockwood stumbled as he tried to sit down, but Rayner was there to catch him and lower him into his seat. 'Call the police, eh? And why don't you make us all a cup of coffee?'

I was about to protest, but the expression on his face

suggested that might be a bad idea. I turned and stalked back down the aisle and into the vestry.

I dialled 113, explained the situation and left my details. I suggested the cops might want to come to the side door. I could feel myself shaking. A cigarette would be good, but I couldn't bring myself to smoke in the vestry. Neither did I want to open the door and stand in the *calle*, attracting attention. I found three non-matching cups, and put a spoonful of instant coffee in each. Then I filled the kettle and plugged it in.

Immediately all the lights went out. A stream of creative swearing came from inside the church.

I opened the door from the vestry and poked my head inside. Lockwood was still immobile. Rayner turned to me.

'Kettle?'

'Sorry.'

'Bloody thing. The fusebox is in the cupboard next to the side door.'

'Okay.' There were about twenty different switches in there, but the important one, I guessed, was the one with the big red light. I flipped it upwards. The lights came back on and I could hear the sound of the fridge humming back into life.

Not just the fridge. There came a *kerchunk* from alongside it. The printer was warming up. Rayner had indeed put it on top of the electric hob. Next to it, the lights on the wifi router were flashing green. The printer slowly clunked into life.

I watched the first page feed through, and drop into my hand. Then a second. I laid them out on the work surface, and ran my eyes over them, as quickly as I could. The first was an email from the National Archive in London. The second from the Monteverdi Foundation in Cremona.

Maitland had been right. He'd found the answer.

I made three cups of nasty coffee, and took two back into the church, setting them down for Rayner and Lockwood. I bent down over Maitland's body, and then stopped myself. What I had told Lockwood also held true for me.

'Tom,' I said.

He didn't even raise his head.

'Tom,' I repeated. 'This is important. Does Maitland have anything on him. Keys, wallet?'

He shook his head.

'What about his phone?'

Again, he shook his head.

'Okay. I understand. Thank you. Michael, the police will be here in just a couple of minutes.'

Rayner nodded, his eyes closed and lips moving in silent prayer. I forced myself to look down at Maitland. His shirt was soaked crimson, and his mouth was bloodied. Again, I forced myself to look closer. Then I recoiled, my hand flying to my mouth. His front teeth had been knocked out.

I heard the sound of a siren from outside, and, shortly, a hammering at the side door. The police had arrived. I made my way back into the vestry to let them in, closing my eyes momentarily as I tried to shake the image of Maitland's face from my mind.

Chapter 43

'First time I'd ever been inside that church, you know?' said Vanni. 'I've spent my whole life in Venice and never seen it before.'

'Shame it had to be like this,' I said. 'So. Are you going to tell me what happened to him?'

'I'm not allowed to.' He paused, and smiled ever so slightly. 'He'd been stabbed – you probably worked that out for yourself. Most likely with the same weapon as they used on *signor* Zambon. Not a knife. Could be a sharpened screwdriver, something like that.'

I shuddered. 'Christ.'

'We found bloodstains on the balustrade in the organ gallery.' He winced. 'And worse.'

I flinched. 'Teeth?'

'Yes. Whoever it was had banged Maitland's face repeatedly against the rail. Then pushed him down the stairs. And then finished him off in front of the sanctuary.'

I shook my head. 'I don't get it. From the base of the stairs he could have got to the vestry and the side door. Why did he run to the sanctuary? He must have known there was no way out in that direction.'

'I doubt he knew where he was. Or who he was. Not after the job that'd been done on him upstairs.' He lit up a small cigar. 'He was an old man.' He shook his head and cursed, under his breath. Then he tapped the two sheets on his desk. 'You've read these, of course?'

'Of course.'

'Interfering with evidence?' He kept his voice light.

'I wasn't going to let them drop to the floor and have your people trample all over them when they arrived, Vanni.'

'Quite right too, Nathan.' He nodded approvingly. 'Now why don't you tell me why Mr Maitland was killed?'

'I think you know why.'

He spread his hands wide. 'Indulge me. It'll help me to think.'

'Maitland was being too clever for his own good. He wanted to show off, show us all how clever he was. He might only be a music teacher but he was smarter than the great Thomas Joshua Lockwood. He'd found something out about the Monteverdi score. And he wanted to gather us all together to share it with us. To tell us all that the score doesn't exist any more.'

'And someone found out about it, and killed him beforehand?'

'That must be it. Maitland went to the church to use the printer. He'd tried to print off those two emails but the damn thing wasn't working. Until I accidentally switched it off and on again. That's why the murderer took everything off his body. To remove everything that could be a clue. He couldn't have known those two documents were in the print queue.'

Vanni puffed away on his cigar. 'I think that you think you know who it is, Nathan.'

'Salvatore Bonfiglio. Almost ex-husband of Isotta Baldan.'

'Okay. Tell me why.'

'He's got a history of violence. He's got a grudge against both Lockwood and Baldan. His career is finished and he needs the money. He knew and met with Zambon a number of times. And I believe he met with Baldan the other day in order to put the frighteners on her again.'

Vanni scribbled away, then leaned back in his chair and drew on his cigar, exhaling great plumes of toxic smoke into the smoke-free environment of the *Questura*. 'It makes sense.'

'You know it does.'

'I think we'll have a word. Thanks, Nathan, I appreciate it.'

'Is that it?'

He sighed, and shook his head. 'Not quite. Mr Lockwood came in for a little chat.'

'A chat?'

'I say "a chat". What I mean is he came round here to shout at me. I don't need that. I've got plenty of other people who like to do that sort of thing.'

'What did he want?'

'To be kept informed of any information we come across which might lead to the discovery of this wretched opera he's obsessed with. Of course, Mr Lockwood, I said. Should the Italian police uncover such information in the course of their murder investigation, you shall be the first to know.'

'How did he take it?'

'Not well.' Again, he indicated the two sheets spread on the table in front of him. 'I didn't tell him about any of this. I didn't think it was my business. But I wondered—'

'If I'd do it?'

'Oh, Nathan.' He chuckled. 'You took the words right out of my mouth. And I suppose it is consular business.'

'I think that's stretching the definition to its utmost, Vanni.' I sighed. 'But okay. I'll do it.'

'Good man.'

'It's going to break his heart.'

'All the better coming from you, then. You have a copy of all this, of course?'

I gave him a weak smile. 'I photographed them. Just in case you didn't want to let me see them.'

'Disgraceful.' He riffled through his papers. 'I think that's it. I'll be in touch.' He got to his feet, and reached across the desk to shake my hand. 'Thank you, Nathan. *Ci sentiamo.*'

Federica found me at home, slumped against the wall of the living room, and throwing balls for a fractious Gramsci as if we were recreating Steve McQueen's role as the Cooler King in *The Great Escape*.

She said nothing, but went through to the kitchen, and came back with two beers. She sat down next to me, passed me one, and we clinked bottles.

'Everything okay?'

I took a draught and shook my head. 'Not really.'

'Want to tell me about it?'

'I think you know it all by now.'

'I'm sorry about Mr Maitland.'

'Me too. A nice man. Too clever for his own good, though. Not a pleasant way to go.'

'So tell me, then. What does this all mean? Those emails?'

I picked up the first sheet. 'This is from the National Archive in London. It's a detail from Wake's bequest. Pass me your glasses, would you?' She twitched them from her nose and slid them on to mine.

I started to read. '*It is my wish, therefore, that the music and text of* Proserpina *be returned to my beloved Serenissima and my dear friend Sig. Claudio Monteverdi. I ask that copies be made of* Come dolce hoggi *and* Quanto nel chiaro mondo *for my faithful secretary, good Thomas Rowlanson, in the hope they will bring him delight in years to come.*

'Copies, note. That's why they're not in Monteverdi's hand.'

'And the missing pages in Rowlanson's book?'

I shrugged. 'We'll probably never know. Looking at the dates, I think it might have been an acknowledgement of receiving Sir Isaac's gift. Something that would have made it obvious that he never had a complete score.'

'But we know Zambon had a libretto, and two extracts. How did he get them?'

I waved the other sheet. 'This is from the Monteverdi Foundation in Cremona. Two lots were sold at auction in London, ten years ago, by a private collector. A copy of the libretto of *Proserpina*, signed by Monteverdi. No further details. A copy of the aria *Come dolce hoggi l'auretta*, dating from the seventeenth century. And "miscellaneous fragments". Fragments. Nothing more.' I passed her glasses back to her. 'They were bought by a *signor* Zambon of Venice.'

'So *Quanto nel chiaro mondo* just got, what, misfiled?'

'It could be. Remember, it's not signed and it's not in Monteverdi's hand. It gets passed down from Rowlanson, generation after generation. And then sold on and sold on again, until no one quite knows what it is any more. Then Zambon buys it for,' – I checked the details again – 'a very modest sum of money. He realises what he's got. And they become the last things he has left to sell.

'He shoots his mouth off to Bonfiglio, who tells him he can make some serious money by selling them to Lockwood. So Zambon sells the libretto, the aria and – the real kicker – the final dance. It's a gateway drug. For more money, he tells Isotta, I can get you the complete score.'

'But how could they do that, knowing it doesn't exist?'

'It doesn't have to. They just have to make Lockwood and Baldan believe that it does, and that it's in the hands of some seriously dangerous people. And after they've screwed as much as possible out of them, they just turn around and say sorry, you've lost your money, we can't risk getting involved in this.

'The trouble is, Zambon has been researching the history of these particular manuscripts trying to give them provenance. He's traced them back to Thomas Rowlanson. He needs a translator, and Sergio and Lorenzo give him my card. And then he tells Bonfiglio what he's done.

'Now Bonfiglio knows that if this English guy discovers that the score doesn't exist any more, *signora* Isotta and Mr Lockwood are going to turn off the money tap. But this has given him an opportunity as well. He tells Zambon they need to make this story look convincing. They'll get a box at the opera, wave something that could be a score at Lockwood before the interval. It won't mean anything to him at the time, but it will in the future. When he starts receiving demands for money.

'And that's what they do. But only one person leaves the box. Zambon never realised he was going to play such a big part in making the story look convincing.

'Bonfiglio uses Zambon's library card to access the Marciana. It's a hell of a risk, but there's big money involved now. His English is good, but it's still going to be difficult. It takes him some time, but eventually he finds the pages in Rowlanson's journal that reveal he never had the score. When he's sure it's safe to do so he removes them. He inserts that page of photographs for me to find, and begins stalking me around the town. So now the two of us start to think that the score exists and people are prepared to kill for it.'

Fede nodded. 'Then he sends a pile of ash to Lockwood, and invites him to a Masked Ball where he burns – what?'

'Anything. Could be the *Corriere dello Sport*. All it needs is something that looks just enough like old Claudio's signature in the bottom right-hand corner. And by now, Lockwood has been wound up so tightly that he'll pay almost anything to have it.

'Then somehow Bonfiglio found out that Maitland had discovered the truth. Perhaps he found out he'd been for dinner with Isotta and that's what took him to her apartment the other day. Whatever it was, Maitland had become a threat. And so he killed him.' I shook my head.

Gramsci, irritated by the lack of attention, swatted a ball in our direction. Fede picked it up and passed it to me. 'So what now?'

'Nothing. Nothing left to solve. I'm sick of grumpy

conductors, scary sopranos and homicidal tenors. Let the cops sort it out.'

'Good.' She paused, and leaned her head on my shoulder. 'It was a lovely dream, though. Even we thought so.'

I stroked her hair. '*Proserpina rapita,* by Claudio Monteverdi. The Ravagnan–Sutherland edition.'

'Or Sutherland–Ravagnan.'

'No, you'd have to go first. Alphabetically, if nothing else.'

She laughed, and got to her feet. 'Okay, what's for dinner? Do you feel like cooking or shall I go out for pizza again?'

I shook my head. 'No, I think cooking will do me good. Besides, there's something about having pizza more than once a week that makes me feel as if my life is coming apart at the seams.' I squeezed her hand. 'Reminds me of the single years, you know?'

She smiled. 'Okay. What are we having?'

'I've still got half a pumpkin. And there's some fresh pasta in the fridge. Veggie lasagne? It'll take a while but it's worth it.'

'That's great. I can do some work in the meantime.'

'There is just one thing . . .'

She frowned over the top of her glasses. 'Which is?'

'Someone is going to have to tell Lockwood – sooner rather than later – that his precious manuscript does not exist.' I took a breath. 'I told Vanni I'd do it.'

'Isn't that going to be difficult, given that he's not speaking to you?'

'He won't, but I wonder if Isotta might. At any rate, it seems I have to go over there tomorrow and break his heart.'

Chapter 44

I stood outside Lockwood's apartment, running through the words in my head again. *Sorry, Mr Lockwood, but the thing you've set your heart on doesn't exist. If you're lucky, the police might just be able to get your money back.*

It needed to be a little better than that, I thought. I could, I supposed, just have telephoned. I could even just have left a message, but that seemed like the coward's way out. He had been a hero of mine, once. I wanted one more chance to try and straighten things out with him.

I pressed the bell.

The door opened, just a couple of inches. Isotta's face, pale, and red-eyed, was framed in the gap. She said nothing, not even acknowledging my existence.

'Isotta. Can I come in? It's about Thomas,' I said.

She said nothing, and we stood in silence. Then she gave a brief nod and stepped back from the door to let me in.

'Isotta. We need to talk. About what happened yesterday. About the Monteverdi manuscript. Has Thomas been asked for any more money?'

She looked behind me to the open door, and motioned with her hand. I reached behind me and pushed it shut.

'You shouldn't have come,' she said, and her voice was little more than a whisper.

I ignored her. 'You have to make him listen. The next time he's asked for money you must go to the police. If you're scared, then you can call me. But you must make him understand. There is no *Proserpina rapita*. There is—'

'There is no missing score. I think we all understand that by now. Except for poor Mr Lockwood.' Bonfiglio stepped out of the shadows at the end of the corridor, a gun in his hand. I gave a half-glance behind me. Just too far from the door to be able to reach. Bonfiglio shook his head. 'Come in. Please.' He stepped to the side and waved the two of us into the living room.

'Are you okay?' I asked. 'Has he hurt you?'

Isotta said nothing. I looked around the room. A garish candy-coloured Murano glass chandelier stood out in stark contrast to the sober dark wood panelling on the walls, and the *terrazzo* floor. French windows led on to a small *cortile*. The room was dominated by a grand piano. I took a closer look. Fazioli.

'Lovely,' I said, indicating the piano.

'It belongs to Thomas,' said Isotta, her voice little more than a whisper.

'A man of good taste. I'd love an instrument like that. I'd need a bigger apartment, of course. And to be able to play the piano.'

'Shut up,' said Bonfiglio.

'Sorry. Just trying to lighten the mood.'

He said nothing, but just smiled. And then punched me in the face. I rode the punch but lost my footing, and fell to the floor, desperately trying to avoid the piano. I got to my feet. Bonfiglio was still covering me with the gun.

Isotta hadn't moved. I turned to her, rubbing my jaw. 'You could call the police, you know? Or start screaming. If you wanted to be useful.'

Her lips moved. 'I'm sorry,' was all I could hear.

'Are you waiting for Lockwood, Salvatore?'

'Something like that.'

'Nowhere else to go, I suppose? The police will have already been round to your place. How long do you think it will be before they try here?'

'Long enough.'

'And you need Isotta here, the better to threaten the old man?'

He shook his head. 'Is that what you really think?'

I looked over at Isotta. 'Do you think Tom would mind if I smoked?' She didn't reply, so I reached – slowly – into my jacket. Bonfiglio waved the gun at me. 'I'm getting my fags out, Salvatore. I'm an honorary consul. We don't carry weapons.'

I lit up. 'How old are you, Salvatore? Fifty-something, I guess. Am I right?'

He said nothing.

'Am I right?'

He nodded.

'It must be difficult, mustn't it? Ex-opera singer. Soon going to be an ex-husband. Soon going to be an ex-free citizen.' I dragged on the cigarette. I couldn't think of anything else to do other than keep talking. To try and buy as much time as possible. 'Tell me, Salvatore, what did she,' I nodded over at Isotta, 'ever see in you?

'The good looks and charm?' I shook my head. 'I don't think so. Money? Maybe. I think you were right when we spoke the other day. I think *signora* Baldan loves money more than people. I don't think she ever loved you. She just squeezed you dry. And then moved on to someone else.'

Salvatore showed no sign of engaging with me, so I pressed on. 'Now, I thought you were a simple misogynist pig, but maybe there's more to it than that. I think you're just someone too stupid to see any solution to a problem other than violence.'

'Shut up!' He punched me again, and, again, I managed to ride the blow and stagger back.

'Kind of proving my point, Salvatore. A man who's failed at everything and no longer knows what to do in the world other than punch it, kick it, stab it . . .

'And I know there were those stories about how you used to treat Isotta. So let's not talk about how she got that scratch above her eye. I really don't want to know. You know what I think? I think that in the end, she was the one who used you. She was the one in control. You were her useful idiot, and then one day she woke up and decided you were simply an idiot.'

I stopped. I looked over at Isotta, who stood motionless, simply shaking her head. Then I looked back at Salvatore. I was ready for him to punch me again, but he didn't move.

'Now, I don't know if Isotta and Tom are going to make old bones together. Given they've racked up three failed marriages between them – no offence Isotta – the odds are kind of against it. But I know this: she is never, ever coming back to you. You can blackmail and bully and murder but sooner rather than later you're going to find yourself in a prison cell.

At the same time that your brilliant and beautiful *ex*-wife is on stage at La Fenice.'

He said nothing, but he was staring at Isotta now and not at me. For a moment I thought I might be able to make a grab for the gun, but decided against it. Even if it worked, that would just switch him back into thug mode. I needed to keep him thinking.

'I'm right, aren't I, Salvatore? She is never, ever coming back to you. Sharing a bed with a man old enough to be your father is better. You know that. Don't you?'

'Yes.' The word was a long, drawn-out sigh.

I could feel my shoulders starting to relax, when he raised the gun, moved towards me, and pressed it directly against my forehead. He held it there for seconds, staring into my eyes as I did all I could not to blink.

'Turn around. Slowly.' His voice was thicker now, his accent stronger.

I turned, and could hear him stepping backwards.

'No, Toto, please don't do this.' Isotta's voice now, on the edge of hysteria.

I heard him place something on the piano, but dared not move. And then the music started.

In der Kindheit frühen Tagen.

'The Angel'. From the *Wesendonck Lieder*.

Hört ich oft von Engeln sagen.

Die das Himmels hehre Wonne

Tauschen mit der Erdensonne.

Isotta Baldan, singing Wagner.

I heard the sound of the gun being cocked. And then, the final verse.

Ja, es stieg auch mir ein Engel nieder,
Und auf leuchtendem Gefieder
'Toto, please,' begged Isotta.

I clamped my eyes shut, trying to control my breathing.

Führt er, ferne jedem Schmerz,

One line left. One final line. Do it now, Nathan, before the moment passes. Something. Anything.

Meinen Geist nun himmelwärts!

I heard movement behind me and a jarring, discordant sound from the piano. Salvatore spat the word *puttana*. Whore. The sound of struggling, a punch, and Isotta screaming over and over and over. Then a shot rang out, deafening in the confined space. I could hear her howling, as if in pain, above the roaring in my ears.

I whipped around. She was slumped on the floor, her arms wrapped tight around herself, and her face and hair soaked in blood. Salvatore's blood. His body lay slumped at the base of Lockwood's precious Fazioli, the keyboard now spattered with red.

She gazed at me, wild-eyed. 'I couldn't stop him,' she whispered. Then she threw herself on top of his corpse, and began to sob uncontrollably.

Chapter 45

'*Salute*, Nathan,' said Vanni, and we clinked glasses. He looked tired, but happy. We stood on the corner of fondamenta Santa Chiara, at Bar Filovia. A bar that, being open to the elements on two sides, could in some ways be said to have neither an inside nor an outside. Vanni smoked away happily, conscious that the strange construction of the bar meant that everything was, most probably, in accordance with Article 51 smoking regulations.

'You've done well,' he said.

'I don't feel like it,' I replied. 'I really don't.'

'I'm serious. You've wrapped this up most satisfactorily. We had a crime, then a suspect, and then a culprit. A dead culprit as well. No need for a trial.'

I shook my head. 'It's a horrible business, Vanni. A nasty, grubby business.'

'Oh, I agree. Greed. Blackmail. They're never nice, you know.'

'He was a bastard. But I feel like I talked him into it. He knew the game was up. That the police would find him sooner or later. And he wanted to leave with one grand, theatrical gesture. Not just to frighten me. I wasn't important. It was to leave Isotta with one final, horrible image. Killing himself in front of her.'

'His greatest performance, perhaps? Do you think *signor* Monteverdi would have approved?'

'No. Not Monteverdi. There's a bit more of Puccini in this, I think. The way she threw herself on his body at the end.' I shook my head, trying to push the images from my mind. How I'd tried to pull Isotta from Salvatore, how she'd screamed and pushed me away with her bloodied hands. 'There were all those stories, you know? About how he used to treat her. But there was a small part of her that still cared for him. I don't think I'll ever understand that.' I paused. 'How is she?'

'Still in shock. And the bastard punched her straight in the face when she tried to grab the gun. But she'll be okay.'

'She's got a concert scheduled at Fenice next week. I guess she'll cancel again. The difference is that everybody will understand this time.'

'You won't be queuing up for returns, Nathan? Just in case?'

I grimaced. 'Not this time. There's still work to be done on repatriating Maitland. No direct family in the UK from what I can make out. He really did seem to be married to his public school. That makes things a bit easier, for me at least. But there's a stack of things to be sorted out with the Embassy. Press releases and the like. That's never nice.'

Vanni dropped his cigar, and ground it underfoot. I finished my spritz. 'Okay, Vanni, I'm done. I'm going to go home and sleep for about a day.'

He chuckled. 'Me too.'

We placed our glasses on the bar. I reached for my wallet but he waved me away. 'No, no, Nathan. My treat.'

'Are you walking?'

'I think so. It'll do me good. I've been chained to that damned desk for the last week. A chance to stretch my legs will be most welcome.'

I looked at the queue for the number 2 line. It was late in the day now, but the queue of visitors snaked back on to the *fondamenta*. I sighed. I didn't feel like walking home, but the *vaporetto* didn't promise to be a particularly pleasant journey either. At least, I consoled myself, there were no plague doctors to be seen.

'I'll see you whenever, Vanni. Take care.'

'You too, Nathan. Thanks again.' He paused. 'You know, perhaps I should have given you a badge after all.'

I gave a weak laugh, and made my way to the back of the queue. He tipped his hat, turned, and made his way off to Piazzale Roma from where he would cross the bridge that would take him down into Dorsoduro.

Fede was fast asleep on the sofa by the time I got home. Gramsci was lying across her feet. He looked up as I came in.

I scratched him behind the ears. 'You've never done this before, Fat Cat. Are you trying to make me jealous?' He miaowed. 'I see. Nathan's not the only game in town any more, is that it?'

I went into the kitchen and fixed a pair of spritz Nathan. I took them back through to the living room, and set them down on the coffee table. I sat on the arm of the sofa, leaned over and kissed Fede's forehead. She opened one eye, sleepily.

'How are you?' I said.

'Fine.' She yawned and stretched, the sudden movement causing Gramsci to leap off her and onto the back of the sofa.

'At least I was until you woke me up.' Then she smiled. 'How are you?'

'I'm okay. There's stuff to do. To sort out poor Maitland, I mean. But that'll wait until tomorrow. Spritz?'

She craned her head to look past me, and then stretched out her hand. She couldn't quite reach so I passed the glass to her. 'Thank you, *caro*.'

'Dinner?'

'Nothing planned.' I looked around the room. 'I've got to be honest, my heart isn't really in cooking tonight. How about we just go downstairs and see what Ed's got?'

'Negroni, *panino* and bed?'

'In that order?'

'I think so.'

'I think so too.'

I was woken up by the sound of my phone ringing. I checked the time – gone midnight – and then the number. Isotta. I got out of bed, as quietly as I could, and padded through to the living room.

I answered, but said nothing, waiting for her to speak.

'Nathan?'

'Hi there.' Again, I waited for her to speak. 'It's very late. Are you okay?'

'I can't sleep.'

'I understand. About everything.'

'I don't think you do. But thank you for saying so.' Again, she paused. 'He wasn't a good man. I know that. But he was my husband.' There was another long pause. 'I wanted to say thank you.'

'Isotta, is there anything I can do?'

'You're right, of course. There is no manuscript, is there? There is no *Proserpina rapita*.'

I sighed. 'All I know is that Zambon only had those two fragments. He never had the complete work. Nothing's been heard of it since 1644. It may be that it's out there somewhere. In Cremona, or Mantua or Venice. Perhaps it's in an oligarch's vault. Or it really has gone for ever.'

'I don't think Thomas will let it go,' her voice cracked.

'I'm sorry.'

'He thinks the police will find it now. Maybe at Salvatore's, maybe somewhere else.'

'But you know that's not going to happen.'

'I know. But he doesn't. So let me tell him. Please.'

'I understand. Really, I do. What will you do now?'

'Thomas and I have a concert next week at La Fenice. Favourite arias.' She sounded so tired. 'That sort of thing. As you say in English, the show must go on.'

'*Vesti la giubba . . .*'

'*E la faccia infarina.*' She paused. 'We won't see each other again, Nathan.'

'No. I don't think we will. Goodnight, Isotta.'

'Goodnight, Nathan.'

She hung up. I stared at the blank screen for a few minutes, and then went back to bed.

Chapter 46

I sat at the back at St George's, and felt awkward.

I felt I needed to be there. To pay my last respects to Christopher Maitland. A week had passed, and his body now lay back in the UK in a small parish church near Shrewsbury. Rayner had thought it appropriate to have a memorial service for him.

I sang along with hymns I hadn't sung in over thirty years, and did my best to remember when to stand, kneel or sit. I clamped my eyes shut during prayers, and hoped that Maitland was now in a better place, swapping stories with Monteverdi. Perhaps the two of them were poring over the *Proserpina* score together, old Claudio smiling as Maitland's eyes widened in delight. Perhaps. Who knew?

I hung around the *campo* afterwards, waiting for the Tall Priest to finish meeting and greeting, and then made my way back inside, just as he was on the verge of bolting the great bronze doors.

'Nathan.'

'Father Michael.' I'd never used his honorific before, and he smiled, with a mischievous look in his eyes.

'Thank you for coming.'

'Least I could do, I think.' I paused. 'Listen, do you fancy a drink?'

'Church Pub?'

'Indeed.'

'Marvellous. If that's what it took to bring you back into the fold. Mysterious ways indeed.'

'I'm not back in any sort of fold.'

He just smiled, and patted me on the back. 'Come on, let's go.'

He squeezed himself through the side door, locked up, and we made our way to the end of the *calle*. Alessandro smiled as we entered.

'*Il solito?*'

Rayner held up two fingers. '*Il solito.*' He elbowed his way through the crowd at the bar, and took a quick look into the back room. He shook his head. 'Too many of the flock back there. I think perhaps it's best if we don't join them. I have the feeling that you want to talk, is that right?'

'Yes.'

Alessandro reached over the heads of the customers at the bar to pass two spritzes to the Tall Priest. We clinked glasses, and stood in awkward silence for a moment.

'So I was wondering,' I said, 'if there are things you needed to do. After what happened the other day.'

'Things?' He arched an eyebrow.

'Well. Somebody was murdered. In a holy place. Those sorts of things.'

'Oh. Those sorts of things.' He took a drink. 'Yes, there are things you need to do. But I don't think that's why you're here.'

'You're right. It's not.'

'And I don't think you came this morning because you wanted to pray for Mr Maitland.' I opened my mouth to speak, but he shook his head. 'No, no. I'm very grateful, whatever the reason was.'

'You're right. Again. It's just . . . something isn't right.'

'Hmm. Tell me more.'

'It just seems like, well, like Bonfiglio got away with murder. Two people are dead. And in a way he got away with it. He didn't have to face justice. His last memories would have been of listening to that recording of Isotta singing the *Wesendonck Lieder*. Of her standing in front of him, crying with pain and fear. And then, just one final flash and oblivion. It's just—'

'Not fair?'

'Not fair.' I took a taste of my spritz, the ice cubes clinking against my teeth, enjoying the icy bitterness in my mouth.

A low, rumbling sound came from his chest, something that might have been a chuckle. 'You know, Nathan, when you've spent as long in this job as I have, you start to realise that "fair" doesn't really come into it.'

'No?'

'No. I'm sorry, were you hoping for something more?'

'I was hoping you might be able to give me the answer.'

'Oh, everybody wants me to give them the answer. Trouble is, if I gave them it there'd be no bloody point in any of us being there every Sunday morning. And if you want me to say that he's facing eternal justice for his crimes, well I can't tell you that either. And I could tell you that *signor* Bonfiglio was a sad and lonely man who'd made his own hell here on earth, if that would make you feel better, but—'

'But you can't.'

Rayner smiled. 'No. I don't really know. The terrible thing, Nathan, is that being a nasty, violent and brutish man might actually have made him happy. I hope that's not so, but I don't know.'

'What kind of priest are you?'

'A painfully honest one. I think He appreciates that.' He rolled his eyes heavenwards. 'Bloody hope so. I'm in a bit of trouble otherwise. Anyway, have you seen the *Gazzettino* this morning?'

I shook my head.

'Your friends are front page news. Tonight's concert at La Fenice, and it seems no one can beg, borrow or steal a ticket. *Courage as Isotta returns to the stage.* Quite a lot of that sort of thing.'

I shrugged. 'I thought she'd cancel again. I wouldn't have blamed her.' I finished my spritz. 'Okay. Now, I think I'm going to have one of those Negronis made with a pipette.'

Rayner shook his head. 'No, you're not.'

'No?'

'No. Firstly, I've got work to do this afternoon, and I'm not leaving you here to drink alone. Secondly, I was joking the other day when I told you about giving in to temptation.'

'We're only talking about a bar, here.'

'Oh, Nathan. Don't ever say that it's just a bar.' He slid off his stool, and put his hat on, barking his knuckles on the beam as he did so. 'Bloody thing. I'll never get used to it.' He smiled. 'See you next week.'

'Don't count on it.'

'I'll see you next week. For a drink. That's all.' He grinned.

'Plenty of time to get round to the other stuff.' He looked down at his bruised knuckles. 'The *Wesendonck Lieder*, eh? Not a bad choice. I'd probably choose some Tallis or Vaughan Williams myself, but not a bad choice all in all. You know, I didn't even know she'd recorded them.' He patted me on the back. 'See you around, Nathan.'

I waited until I was sure he was gone. Then I turned to Alessandro. 'I don't suppose you'd care to make me one of your Negronis?' I said, as casually as I could.

He gave me a conspiratorial wink, and went to the window just to be quite sure that the Tall Priest was safely out of sight before setting to work. He dropped a few ice cubes in a tumbler, and swirled them around to chill the glass. Then, with his arm at head-height, he poured in a shot of gin, whilst unscrewing the cap of the Campari bottle with his free hand. He put down the gin and repeated the procedure with the Campari, before moving on to the vermouth. No measures needed. Not a drop spilled. He swept the bottles to one side, moving like a dancer, and then took out a pipette and a tiny flask of Angostura bitters. Crouching down so as to be at eye-level with the drink, he squeezed five drops into the tumbler. He put his head to one side, with a quizzical look in his eyes, as if to assure himself that all was well. Then he nodded, gave it a stir, and passed it across the counter to me.

I raised the glass and made a 'cheers' sign. Then I held it up, enjoying the play of colours made by the light.

Eduardo need never know.

I raised it to my lips.

Then I stopped. 'My God,' I whispered.

I didn't even know she'd recorded them.

'Is there something wrong, *signore?*' Alessandro looked worried, as well as a bit hurt.

'I don't know. Possibly everything.' I slid ten euros across the counter. 'I'm sorry, but I've got to go. Next time, okay?'

I turned and ran from the bar, Alessandro's cry of 'Your change, *signore*' following me down the street.

Chapter 47

The sheer number of tourists on the Accademia Bridge held me back and I fought against them like Omar Sharif trying to reach Julie Christie in *Doctor Zhivago*. At least it gave me time to catch my breath and organise my thoughts.

Why had Maitland let Bonfiglio into the church? Why hadn't he tried to get out when he could? And how did Bonfiglio have that extract from the *Wesendonck Lieder*, a work that Isotta Baldan had never recorded?

Lockwood. Maitland. Bonfiglio. And myself.

I leaned on the railing at the top of the bridge, and closed my eyes, gathering my thoughts.

Bonfiglio, raising the gun, as the final notes of 'The Angel' died away . . .

His finger tightening on the trigger . . .

And then Isotta – bigger than him, younger than him, stronger than him – grabbing for the gun. But not to stop him from killing himself. The gun had never been pointing at his own head.

Useful idiots. All of us.

I opened my eyes and pushed my way through the crowd as best I could.

When I reached the other side of the bridge I was able to run, through Campo Santo Stefano and into Campo Sant'Angelo and the Calle Caortorta where, again, the crowds held me back. Then, after much cursing and swearing, I was over the bridge and in the Calle de la Fenice, and then the great opera house lay to my right.

I checked the time. If I was correct, they'd still be rehearsing. I looked up at the entrance, and tried to run through the distances in my mind. How many people would be on the door at this time of day? I could just take a run for it. Yes, and what if there's a cop there? A cop with a gun? A cop with a gun seeing a crazy guy trying to force his way into the auditorium? I shook my head. I'd have to bluff it as best I could.

I took a few more deep breaths and tried to steady myself. Then I made my way up the steps, and into the foyer. A young man came to meet me, but I was too quick for him and was on my way to the auditorium before he could block my path.

'Sir. Sir! A moment, please.'

I turned and smiled. 'I'm with the chorus,' I said, and gestured with my thumb towards the auditorium. From within, I could hear the sound of Baldan warming up. 'You hear that?' I said. 'We're on in a minute.'

He looked suspicious. 'Sir, the musicians' entrance is around the side.'

'Is it? I do apologise, it's my first day here.'

'I'm sorry, sir,' he was frowning now, yet looked embarrassed at the same time, 'but can I just ask to see your pass?'

'Of course. Of course.' I took out my wallet, and flicked through it. 'You won't believe this, but it seems I've left it in my hotel. Tell you what, I'll rush back there after rehearsals and bring it back here, okay? Just so you can check everything off. And well done for being so vigilant.'

He laid his hand on my arm, gently but firmly. 'I'm very sorry, sir. But I do need to see your pass.'

'Oh, you don't, do you? Look, I can't be late, it's my first day. I really am in the chorus.' I burst into the opening phrase of *La donna è mobile*.

There was an awkward silence.

'That bad?'

He nodded.

'Okay. I know you're just doing your job. So I'm very sorry about this.' I didn't want to hit him, so I planted my hands in the centre of his chest, hooked my foot around the back of his right leg and pushed as hard as I could, sending him sprawling to the ground. Then I turned and ran, straight through the foyer, up the stairs and into the stalls.

Baldan and Lockwood didn't even notice me as I ran up the central aisle. She was on stage, dressed in blue jeans and white blouse, kneeling as she sang the dying notes of *non piu s'interporrà noia o dimora* as Lockwood accompanied her with Nerone's vocal line on the piano.

I stopped, and clapped slowly. Baldan stared down at me from the stage, as Lockwood got to his feet.

'Nathan, *caro*,' Baldan smiled at me but, even at this distance, I could tell it was forced.

'Sutherland, what are you doing here?' Lockwood's tone was unfriendly.

I continued to make my way down the aisle, until I reached the edge of the stage. 'I'm sorry, Thomas. But we need to talk.'

Chapter 48

'I've got nothing to say to you, Sutherland.'

'I'm sorry, Tom. If there was any other way, I'd take it.'

The attendant burst in through the rear doors. He opened his mouth to speak, but Lockwood waved away his apologies. 'Call the police, please,' he said.

'Oh, please do,' I said. 'Lots of them. The more the merrier.' He looked confused, and paused for a second. 'Go on, call them.' He ran from the room, phone in hand.

I hauled myself up on to the stage. Lockwood and Baldan moved away from me, in opposite directions.

I spoke to Lockwood but kept my eyes on Baldan. 'Maitland is dead, Thomas.'

He shook his head. 'I know that.'

'Maitland is dead. And Zambon. And Bonfiglio too.' I paused, waiting for my words to sink in. 'Isotta killed them. All of them.'

'Nathan, *caro*, I don't understand.' That lovely, lovely voice, but with an edge to it this time.

'Oh, but you do, Isotta, you do,' I said, wearily. 'I thought I'd actually managed to talk Salvatore into killing himself. I hadn't, of course. He really was going to shoot me in the back of the head. But then you realised that if you got rid of him there'd be nothing left to incriminate you. Even better, you'd get all the money. Salvatore Bonfiglio, murderer and blackmailer, kills himself in front of his estranged wife. How wonderfully operatic.

'You grabbed the gun from him. He'd never have expected that. Then after you'd shot him you flung yourself on his body. Not because there was still some little spark of love remaining in you. No. You needed to get rid of the gun, to leave it near him.'

'But there was something you forgot. That recording he played on his mobile phone. The one you made that night when you sang the *Wesendonck Lieder* to me. You don't send recordings of yourself to someone you despise. Both of you were involved with this. What did you say to him? *Darling Toto, just do this one thing for me and then we can be together again?*'

'Sutherland, I said I never wanted to see you again and I meant it. Now get the hell off this stage and out of here and maybe I'll pretend this never happened, and perhaps I won't even make a formal complaint to the ambassador.'

'Tom. Just tell me this. Maitland telephoned you, the day he was killed. Did you tell anyone?'

'Of course I didn't.'

'No one?' I paused. 'Not even Isotta?'

'Of course I told Isotta. I . . .' He fell silent.

'Maitland wouldn't have let Bonfiglio into the church, would he? He didn't know him from Adam. But Isotta – lovely, charming Isotta who'd been so nice to him over dinner two nights before – he'd let her in.'

'Liar,' she hissed.

'He let you in, didn't he, Isotta? And then you let Salvatore in after you. Maitland walked with a stick, he couldn't have run very fast. What did he do, chase him upstairs? Just to frighten him even more? And then he beat him up and tortured him. I wondered why Maitland hadn't tried to get out through the vestry after being thrown down the stairs. It's because there were two of you. You were there to stop him getting out. And then what happened? Did Salvatore hold him down whilst you stabbed him?'

'Liar,' she repeated, shaking her head, her voice barely audible now.

'Am I?' I turned to Lockwood. 'Did Isotta tell you that *Proserpina* is lost?'

'What do you mean?'

'It's just that she telephoned me a week ago. She thought the news might be best if it came from her. She hasn't got round to it yet, then?'

He shook his head. Then he turned to look at Isotta.

'It's gone, Tom. It disappeared nearly four hundred years ago. All that remains are those two fragments.' I turned to Isotta. 'But what if you had those two fragments? What if you could persuade the great Thomas Joshua Lockwood that some big-time crooks now had the whole thing, and were prepared to ransom it. A man who wanted to find *Proserpina rapita* so much, that it was almost as if he could will it into existence. How much would he pay?'

He shook his head, but his face was ashen now. 'We had pages from the score. You saw them as well.'

'An aria that was already known to exist, and a copy of the

final dance. That's wonderful, surely? You've found a long-lost piece by Monteverdi – congratulations. Just not the whole thing. Why can't that be enough? The complete score is gone for ever, Tom. You have to let it go.'

'That man. That man at the Casino. The one who burnt those pages. You saw him as well.' He was half shouting now, but his voice was breaking at the same time.

'A burnt page with Monteverdi's signature conveniently at the bottom. We don't even know if it was genuine or not. There was no reason for it to be. And that man was Bonfiglio of course, wearing a plague doctor costume.'

'Thomas, my love, don't listen to him.'

'Oh, and I'd almost forgotten about Matteo Zambon.' I turned to face Isotta. 'It wasn't Bonfiglio who killed him, it was you. After all, you know La Fenice, you knew when that corridor would be clear. All you had to do was pretend to be ill. Who would think it strange? You do, after all, carry something of a – reputation, shall we say?'

'Thomas, darling, he's lying.'

'Is he?' Lockwood's voice was raw. He turned to her, and, for the first time, he looked his age. Not the demon conductor of his youth, not the avuncular figure of late middle-age. Just a sad old man, going through his own, personal *Gotterdammerung*.

'You know he is, my love. You know he is.' Isotta turned to him, that lovely voice imploring, beseeching. She had always been as good an actress as she was a singer.

'Her voice is going, Thomas. Her best years are behind her. The Met stopped calling long ago. So did La Scala. And one day, not long now, even the *sovrintendente* at La Fenice will decide that Isotta Baldan is no longer up to it. But you know that, don't you? Like you know that *Proserpina* is lost for ever.' I knew I was hurting him, but could see no other way, and so I pushed on, hating myself for it. 'Like you know, in your heart of hearts, that Isotta never loved you. You're not Tristan to her. You're not Siegfried. You're Canio. You're *Il Pagliaccio*. You're the sad clown.'

I don't know what I expected. That'd he'd scream, perhaps. That he'd rage at me or at Isotta. But he just looked at her, as if seeing her properly for the first time, and shook his head. 'No,' he said, as the tears fell. He dropped to his knees. 'Oh my love, what have you done?'

I crouched beside him, and put my hand on his shoulder. 'Thomas, I am so sorry.'

Pain shot through my head, and I sprawled backwards. I struggled to get to my feet, but, before I could do so, Isotta had kicked me in the face again. 'English bastard, I'll kill you for this.' She pulled her silver comb from within her blouse. I raised my hands to protect myself as best I could, and felt my palms burn with pain, as she slashed the handle against them. Sharpened. She kicked me once more and, try as I might to raise myself, none of my limbs would do as they were told.

Then Lockwood was on her, grabbing her and pulling her back. She turned on him, and elbowed him in the face. She was stronger than him, and, as he staggered backwards, she punched him again.

'Poor Thomas.' She slashed at him with the comb. 'Poor Canio.' Another slash, and blood sprayed across the stage. 'Poor little clown.' She raised her hand to strike one final time.

'No.' I could barely hear Lockwood speak, his voice sounding as if he was speaking from the bottom of a pit as my head spun. 'No, Isotta. No, my love.' He caught her arm at the moment of descent and, from somewhere, found the strength to force it back, as he pulled her to him with his free hand. The two figures locked together for a moment, as if they were two lovers dancing, and then broke apart.

Isotta raised her hands to her face, which was deathly pale. She stared at them, covered in blood, and then clutched at her chest from where blood was now spreading across her white blouse. She looked at Lockwood, with disbelief in her blue eyes. In his right hand, Lockwood held Isotta's bloodied comb. She toppled to the stage floor, and spoke no more.

My vision was clearing now, and I could make out two police officers at the back of the theatre.

Lockwood said nothing, but moved to stand over the body of Isotta. One of the cops drew his gun, but Lockwood waved his hand and shook his head. He dropped the comb to the stage.

'*La commedia è finita*' was all he said.

Chapter 49

'So what happens now?' Eduardo asked.

I swirled the ice cubes at the bottom of my glass. 'I don't know. Vanni is being cagey about it.'

'But Lockwood – he was acting in self-defence, wasn't he?'

I sighed. 'Probably. Almost certainly.'

'You're not sure?'

'No. Not one hundred per cent.' I drained the icy water, flavoured with just a hint of Campari, from the bottom of my glass, and looked over at Federica and Dario. 'Same again, is it?'

Fede smiled and slid her glass across the bar to Ed. Dario shook his head. 'I'm cooking tonight.'

'You're cooking? Dario, you never cook.'

'I know. Valentina thinks it's about time I started.'

'You're kidding. Why?'

'Spending too much time in Venice. Either I'm working or I'm trying to stop you getting into trouble. If I have to cook, it means I have to get back home earlier.'

'Ah, so it's my fault is it?'

'Yep.' He looped his scarf around his neck and pulled on his coat. 'But she told me to tell you she's very grateful you didn't need to be rescued this time.'

I laughed.

'Come on, Dario, at least stay for a small one,' said Fede.

He checked his watch. 'I would do. Really. But I want to do something nice if it's my first time.'

'Then Valentina's a lucky woman. What are you cooking?'

'Stuffed pasta.'

'Impressive. Stuffed with what?'

'I don't know. I didn't really check the packet.' We fell silent for a moment. 'Look, I need to do this in easy stages, all right?'

Fede laughed. 'You know, Dario, have you ever thought about moving back to Venice?'

He looked puzzled. 'Why would I do that?'

'Less time travelling. More time at home.'

'And besides,' I added, 'Venice needs more people. We were talking about it the other day. Just before we saw the population rise by one.'

'Yes, and it's just gone back down by three.'

'Exactly. So if you, Valentina and Emily move back it will even itself out, even if Lockwood goes to prison.'

'And besides,' said Fede, 'if you ever wanted a night off, Nathan could come round and do the cooking.'

'It's a thought, isn't it?' He nodded and smiled. 'Yes, definitely a thought. I'll think about it.' He leaned over and gave Federica a peck on the cheek, and gave me a quick hug. 'I'll see you soon, eh? *Ciao, vecio.*'

Eduardo slid two Negronis across the bar. Fede waved to Dario as he made his way past the window. 'Do you really think he might?'

'He might do, you know. It'd be cool. Easier for us to hang

out together. Hell, we could even go and babysit Emily from time to time.'

She punched my arm. 'Not Dario. Lockwood. Do you really think he might go to prison?'

I sipped at my drink. 'I don't know. If I was a gambling man, I'd say not. Well, probably not.'

'We know it was self-defence. She hurt you, she stabbed him.'

'I know. But Vanni says he's not helping himself. All he's saying is that he loved her and he killed her.'

'Very operatic.'

'Too operatic. He could be in big trouble. And I'm a witness, of course.'

'Exactly. You saw everything that happened.'

I shook my head. 'Not everything. She'd kicked me in the head, everything was spinning around. I couldn't see anything clearly. And at the end, when the two of them were locked together – maybe it was an accident. Or maybe he deliberately turned the blade on her. I can't be sure.'

We drank in silence for a minute. Then Ed spoke up, hesitatingly. 'Does it matter?'

I sighed, and drank a little more. 'You know, Ed, I've been asking myself that.'

'And?'

'I don't know. Not for sure. But I think perhaps it does. I could tell Vanni that I saw everything, that Isotta was trying to kill us both—'

'Which she was.'

'Which she was. And I could tell him that she slipped when she was grappling with him, and stabbed herself leaving the comb in his hands. But—'

'But?'

'It wouldn't be the truth, would it? I don't know. Not for sure.'

Fede rested her head on my shoulder and squeezed my arm. 'Proud of you, *caro*.'

I sighed. 'And, you know, I ruined his life. If it hadn't been for me, Isotta would still be alive, they'd be living together and they'd still be hot on the trail of *Proserpina rapita*.'

'But it'd all be a lie. She never loved him and the opera doesn't exist.'

'I know. And I think he knows, deep down, that it was all a lie. But there's a little part of him that still thinks, "*What if*?"'

'Basically,' said Fede, 'you broke his heart.'

'That's about it.'

'But you had to, didn't you? It's not just about Thomas Joshua Lockwood. People died. And maybe more would have in the future.'

'Exactly.' I finished my Negroni. 'You know, I don't feel like cooking tonight.'

'And I never feel like cooking tonight. So what are we going to do? Pizza?'

I shook my head. 'Pizza's fine but I've got to say – it's never quite the same without Dario.'

'You know, maybe I shouldn't have suggested he move back to Venice. I worry you'll leave me for him.'

'Don't be silly, *cara*. You know there's only ever been you. I'd no more leave you for Dario than I would for a beautiful international soprano.'

She grinned, and I realised that if Isotta Baldan had been possessed of a million-euro smile, well, Federica Ravagnan's was worth at least a few euros more. 'I think you mean a *murderous* international soprano.'

'Isn't that what I said?' I asked, innocently. 'So what are we doing then? I think it's *Il Barbiere di Siviglia* tonight. We could try and get returns, maybe eat at Al Teatro first?'

She made a wry face. 'Do you know, I'm not really in the mood for the opera.'

'Me neither.' We laughed. 'Paradiso Perduto?'

'What's on tonight?'

'Can't quite remember. I think it's a blues covers band.'

'Perfect.'

'Seriously?'

'Seriously. Fried fish and a blues covers band. And one beer too many. Perfect.' She stood up and put her coat on. 'Goodnight, Ed.' She made her way to the door.

Ed grinned at me. 'You're a lucky man, Nathan.'

'I know.' I buttoned my coat and followed her out of the door. 'Luckiest man in the world.'

Later that same evening, my ears still ringing from the band, after far too much fried fish and beer, and with Federica gently snoring next to me, I took out my mobile phone and checked for updates.

There was an email from Ambassador Maxwell, suggesting I call him as soon as possible. I sighed. I'd been expecting that. Oh well. There'd be a difficult conversation to be had, but that would be it. Ambassadors were here today and gone tomorrow. Honorary consuls always outlasted them.

Isotta and Lockwood were still front page news. The discovery of a missing work by Monteverdi hadn't gone unnoticed either. *Diapason, Gramophone* and the *Neue Musikzeitung* were all speculating on who'd be the first to record it. Poor Lockwood. If only he'd been able to leave it at that.

There was just one thing left to do.

I opened the music folder. There it was, from the previous Monday. From when Isotta Baldan had sung Wagner to me, at midnight in Piazza San Marco.

'The Angel', from the *Wesendonck Lieder*.

The only known recording in the world of Isotta Baldan singing Wagner.

Fede muttered something unintelligible in her sleep, as she turned on to her side. I smiled, and stroked her hair. Then I looked back at my phone.

The only known recording in the world of Isotta Baldan singing Wagner.

My thumb hesitated above the keypad, but only for an instant. 'Are you sure?' the screen flashed up at me. I nodded. Of course I'm sure.

I deleted it.

Chapter 50

Federica and I stood at the top of the stairs that led up to the ancient and rare manuscripts section of the Marciana Library, and looked down upon the reading room. Petrarch stared back at us with mournful, sightless eyes.

'It could actually be here, you know?' I said.

'Or in Mantua. Or Cremona. Or perhaps in Rome. Or maybe there's a family of crooks who pass it down from generation to generation.'

'Do you think so?'

She shook her head. 'No.'

'Gone for ever then?'

'I didn't say that. It might exist. But how would we ever find it? Somebody made a filing mistake four hundred years ago and now it's as if it's disappeared from every library, every archive in the world.' She gestured with both hands, pointing left and right to the rows of shelves that lay behind glass doors on either side. 'Look at this. When was it last catalogued? I mean properly, seriously catalogued? A needle in a haystack doesn't even begin to cover it.'

We stood in silence, staring out upon the lines of stacks. Somewhere in the middle of them, just possibly, Monteverdi's lost opera was waiting for someone to open its pages, waiting to sing out at the world again.

Fede broke the silence. 'Almost impossible,' she said.

I nodded. 'Almost impossible.'

'Except, of course—?"

I smiled at her. 'That there are two of us?'

She smiled back at me. A million-and-a-bit-euro smile. 'Exactly.' She checked her watch. 'It's four o'clock. Let's meet in two hours. It'll be the Negroni hour, and then time to find somewhere to eat.'

'I'll take the left.'

'And I'll take the right.' She kissed my cheek. 'See you later.'

We entered the archive through separate doors, and made our respective ways to the bookshelves.

Glossary

a dopo	see you later
al banco	to take a drink *al banco* is to stand at the bar, without the surcharge for sitting down or waiter service
al bitter	with Campari, as in *spritz al bitter*
acqua alta	the phenomenon of seasonal high tides in the Adriatic sea and Venetian lagoon, leading to periodic flooding of areas of the city
bacino	the San Marco basin, typically used to refer to that area in front of Piazza San Marco, where the Grand Canal and Giudecca Canal merge
beh (or *be*)	well, so. The equivalent of giving a shrug
Borsalino	the classic Italian fedora, immortalised by Humphrey Bogart, Jean Paul Belmondo and Marcello Mastroianni
borghese	bourgeois, middle-class
caffè corretto	coffee with a shot of alcohol
calle	a narrow street, alley
cappellano	chaplain

casino	a brothel or place of ill repute, a complete mess
casinò	a casino. As you can see, the accent is important
centro storico	historic centre. In Venice this is typically used to refer to the main area of the city, and not the outlying islands
che carino	how lovely, how charming
che gelida manina	from Puccini's *La Boheme*, typically translated as 'your tiny hand is frozen'
cicheti	small snacks available in bars from which a splendid and economical lunch can be constructed
Ci sentiamo/ vediamo	talk later / see you later
compagno	comrade
coperto	cover charge, commonly applied in restaurants
cronaca nera	the crime section of a newspaper
Cynar	artichoke-based alcoholic drink
denuncia	a complaint or report of a crime
esatto!	exactly!
Frecciarossa	the 'red arrow', the fastest Italian train service
frittelle / fritole	Venetian-style doughnuts, a description that does not perhaps do them justice. Typically, and mercifully, only available during *Carnevale*
giallo	A genre of Italian dark crime fiction, so

	called because of the yellow (*giallo*) covers or page edging on the cheap paperbacks associated with the genre
Gran Liston	The *Gran Liston in tabarro* is an annual winter event involving a stroll through the streets of Venice, usually from Piazza San Marco to the house of Carlo Goldoni, with the promenaders wearing *tabarri* and singing traditional songs along the way
Magari!	as if!
il miglior fabbro	'the greater craftsman'. T S Eliot's dedication (taken from Dante) to Ezra Pound in *The Waste Land*
il solito	the usual
ombra	literally, a shadow. However, in this case *un'ombra* is a glass of wine, taken from the days when wine sellers in Piazza San Marco would keep moving with the sun, in order to keep their wines constantly in shadow
passerelle	raised platforms around the city that allow pedestrians to move around in the case of *acqua alta*
passeggiata	a stroll
pentito	an informer or 'supergrass'
piacere	pleased to meet you
pronto	a typical greeting upon answering the phone, roughly equivalent to 'Hello, I'm ready to speak'
Pronto Soccorso	the A&E department of a hospital

Questura	central police station
salve!	hi!
scopa	A card game (do be careful if using this as it can also mean something very rude!)
scuola superiore	Secondary school, high school
sestiere	a district of the city. There are six districts in Venice: Cannaregio, Castello, Dorsoduro, San Marco, San Polo and Santa Croce
sotoportego	an alley that passes through the ground floor of a building
straniero	a stranger or foreigner
subito!	right away!
tabarro	the classic Venetian cloak, made from a single piece of material
traghetto	the gondola ferry service for transporting pedestrians from one side of the Grand Canal to the other
tramezzino	A triangular sandwich. But so much more than that
vaffa	'Please go away.' But much stronger than that, and not to be used in polite conversation
vera da pozzo	the wellhead around a well, frequently beautifully decorated, and a common feature of streets and *campi* in Venice
vino sfuso	wine from the cask, typically available to take away in plastic bottles, or as the cheapest option in a restaurant

Historical notes

The poet Giulio Strozzi first collaborated with Claudio Monteverdi in 1627 on the opera *La finta pazza Licori*, a work that is now lost. Although Strozzi occasionally used the pseudonym Luigi Zorzisto, his libretto for *Proserpina rapita* – which can be found at the Marciana library – was written under his own name.

We know that Sir Isaac Wake was one of Monteverdi's private patrons in Venice, and we may speculate that the composer might also have encountered Thomas Rowlanson. There is, however, no evidence of a score being gifted to either of them.

Proserpina was first performed on the 16th April 1630, at the palazzo Mocenigo. It may also have been performed at the Teatro San Moisè in 1644, but conflicting accounts suggest that the theatre was closed during that period. What we can say with certainty is that only the aria *Come dolce hoggi l'auretta* is still known to exist. The final dance *Quanto nel chiaro mondo* is missing, as is the rest of the opera. How I wish that were not so!

Finally, there are many fascinating items of memorabilia in the Richard Wagner rooms at the Casino, but the piano – sadly – is not one that ever belonged to him.

Acknowledgments

I am immensely grateful to the staff of the Marciana library in Piazza San Marco for their assistance, and to the Fondazione Querini Stampalia for providing such a lovely space in which to write.

I would like to thank the ministry team and congregation of St George's Anglican Church, Venice for their friendship over the years, and Father Malcolm Bradshaw who seemed remarkably unperturbed when I asked him what the correct procedures would be following a violent death in an Anglican church. Do come and visit us if you're in Venice. To the best of my knowledge nobody has ever been horribly murdered there.

Many thanks to Alessandro, Virginia and everyone else at the Corner Pub for some excellent lunches, and possibly the best spritzes in Venice.

Thank you to my brilliant students Elena, Sebastiano and Vera of the Liceo Benedetti who came up with an imaginary encounter between Nathan and a time-travelling Giovanni Bellini in Piazza San Marco, an idea so lovely I really should steal it! One day, perhaps . . .

I finish, as always, with thanks to my agent John Beaton, my editor Colin Murray, Krystyna, Rebecca, Jess, Andy and everyone at Little, Brown and, of course, to my wonderful wife, Caroline, for nothing in particular but everything in general.